Iris Murdoch was born in Dublin of Anglo-Irish parents. She attended Badminton School, Bristol, and read classics at Somerville College, Oxford. During the war she was an Assistant Principal at the Treasury, and then worked with U.N.R.R.A. in Belgium and Austria.

She held a studentship in philosophy at Newnham College, Cambridge, for a year, then in 1948 returned to Oxford where she was for many years a Fellow and Tutor in philosophy at St Anne's College. In 1956 she married John Bayley, professor and critic in the field of literature.

A Word Child
'Funny, unbearably sad, enigmatic and beautifully harmonized'
The Times

Also by Iris Murdoch

Iris Murdoch

A Word Child

TRIAD PANTHER

Published in 1976 by Triad/Panther Books
Frogmore, St Albans, Herts AL2 2NF
Reprinted 1977

ISBN 0 586 04430 2

Triad Paperbacks Ltd is an imprint of
Chatto, Bodley Head & Jonathan Cape Ltd and
Granada Publishing Ltd

First published by Chatto and Windus Ltd 1975
Copyright © Iris Murdoch 1975

Made and printed in Great Britain by
Richard Clay (The Chaucer Press) Ltd
Bungay, Suffolk
Set in Monotype Times

To
PETER ADY

THURSDAY

'I SAY, an absolutely stunning coloured girl was here looking for you.'

'She was looking for you.'

'No. I offered myself. She was uninterested. She said she wanted to see Mr Hilary Burde.'

That was me. 'Oh.' It was all very improbable however. 'Did she say what she wanted?'

'No. By the way, the rubbish chute is jammed again.'

The first speaker was my lodger Christopher Cather. We had met accidentally in the street, I on my return from the office, he on his return from whatever he did during the day. We were in the lift. The lift held two people and rose slowly, groaning with diffidence. To intensify mutual inspection it contained a long mirror. Christopher was easy to look at.

We emerged on our floor, the fourth, where a smell confirmed the jamming of the rubbish chute. Mr Pellow, a suspended schoolmaster, standing half inside the doorway of the next door flat, retired slowly. He wanted a drinking companion. Christopher and I shunned him.

We entered our own flat. I picked up two letters which were lying on the floor. We parted company, I to my bedroom, he to his. I turned on the light, revealing my unmade bed, a pile of underwear, dust upon the discarded debris of my struggle with the world. I stuffed the underwear inside the bed and dragged up the blankets, inhaling without displeasure the familiar badger smell. The curtains had remained pulled across the windows since my hurried early morning departure into the dark. It was winter: November, with late gloomy dawns and a cold wind smacking the leaves about on sticky pavements. The season suited me. Even at forty-one it dawns on one that one will not live forever. *Adieu jeunesse.*

My 'home' was a small mean nasty flatlet in Bayswater, in a big square red-brick block in a cul-de-sac. Outside the cul-de-sac was a busy noisy street, beyond that street were some modest dingy shops, beyond the shops was Bayswater tube station (District Line and Inner Circle), beyond that was Queensway tube station (Central Line), beyond that was Bayswater Road, and beyond that was, thank God, the park. I instinctively denigrate my flat: it was doubtless my own life which was small and nasty. The flat was certainly cramped and dark, looking out onto a maze of fire escapes in a sunless well. There were three little rooms, my bedroom, Christopher's bedroom, and the so-called sitting-room into which Christopher, who preferred life at floor level, had lately moved most of the furniture, including the bed, out of his own room. Thus rendered uninhabitable, the sitting-room was never used in any case. The flat was simply a *machine à dormir* as far as I was concerned. I never spent my evenings there as the place swarmed with demons. The week-ends posed problems. I cursed the five-day week. I had never attempted decoration, having no taste. I desired no personal objects, no 'elegance', nothing that could remind me of the past. There was nothing here to love.

I will briefly explain Christopher. Christopher, whose estranged father was a solicitor in Essex, was, at the time of this story, twenty-three, but already had a glorious past. He was rather beautiful and turned many heads, including some in the pages which follow. He was tall and extremely thin with a lot of tangled fairish hair hanging to his shoulders and a narrow face of clear-complexioned pallor. In summer he had freckles. His eyes were of a blue so pale as to have given him an appearance of weakness had not his large straight nose manifested a countervailing strength. He was graceful, it was like having a lynx or a leopard around the place. He always wore what I would describe as 'fancy dress'. As a lodger he was less than satisfactory, being an out-of-work genius. At least he did occasionally work, cleaning people's flats. I do not know who the lunatics were who allowed Christopher to clean their flats. The glorious past amounted to this, that at the age of eighteen Christopher created and led a pop group called the Treason of the Clerks which had a brief but considerable success. The success took place mainly on a tour of Australia, but one of the Treason's songs made the 'top ten' in this country. It was called *Waterbird* and may still be remembered by connoisseurs. It was a song about somebody leaving somebody and the chorus ran *Think again, waterbird, do do do, waterbird, waterbird, boo boo boo*, or something of the sort. The group made a lot of money (which vanished leaving only debts to the Income Tax) and then broke up. One stayed in Sydney, one went to Mexico, another (the composer of *Waterbird*) took to heroin and died. Christopher returned to London and for a while earned a precarious living as an organizer of 'happenings'. (His father

2

paid the Income Tax.) Then he underwent a conversion to Buddhism and dedicated himself to overcoming duality and passing beyond the bounds of conceptual thought. He was wished on me as a lodger by a friend who said, as you need money and are never in why not let a room? Christopher now owed six weeks' rent. At least he obeyed the rules I made: no hi fi, no girls, not more than three visitors at a time, no eating of chocolate in the house, no discussions of sex in my presence (etcetera, etcetera). Girls in the flat would have disturbed me. Boys came and went, especially two, Mick Ladderslow and Jimbo Davis. Mick was a layabout from a rich family who wanted Christopher to start a new group to be called The Waterbirds (only Christopher was now given to God). Jimbo was a ballet dancer and even more graceful than Christopher, a laconic Welsh boy whom I liked and who could at least dance. (I saw him do so once in a theatre.) Mick had no talents except for trouble. I thought of them as 'students' though they studied nothing but pleasure. They were beautiful mindless creatures who padded in and out like animals; I did not have the unnerving feeling of being surrounded by rational beings. They (and sometimes others) would sit in Christopher's room and partake of various drugs, a remarkably quiet occupation of which I took care to know nothing. Christopher was learning to play the 'tabla', a dreary little oriental drum, but at least it was not a noisy instrument and would always stop abruptly at my command. In general they were, for young people, all remarkably silent, sitting together I presumed in a kind of daze, in intervals of drawing mandalas and consulting the *I Ching*. I did not know whether these boys were 'queer' (in the slang sense). Quite possibly not. Christopher said he had had a surfeit of girls in the old Treason days when they were 'all over him'. I felt sorry for him. There is nothing like early promiscuous sex for dispelling life's bright mysterious expectations.

The wind was moodily rattling the windows, producing that odd not unpleasant sense of solitude which winter winds evoke. After a long day in the office and undergoing my fellow men in the tube rush hour I felt tired and crumpled and begrimed with weariness. A hard monotonous life favours salvation, so the sages say. There must have been some other element, absent in my case. Oh the piercing sadness of life in the midst of its ordinariness! I looked at the two letters. One was from Tommy, and I set that aside unopened. The other was the telephone account. I opened this and studied it. Then I went out and kicked Christopher's door and entered. Christopher was sitting cross-legged on the floor examining some stuff in a box. He looked up guiltily and when he saw the telephone account in my hand he blushed. He had a remarkable gift for blushing.

'Christopher,' I said, 'you promised you would not make any more long-distance calls.'

Christopher stood up. 'I'm very sorry, Hilary, I ought to have told you at the time, only I was too scared to, please don't be cross! I promise it won't happen again.'

'You promised last time. Or was that a Buddhist promise, remote from the world of mere appearance where one pays telephone bills?'

'I really promise this time. And I'll pay you back.'

'What with? You already owe me six weeks' rent.'

'I *will* pay. Please forgive me, Hilary, and don't be cross. I can't bear it when you're cross. I really truly promise not to do it again.'

'You promise. You really promise. You really truly promise. Where in the series does genuine promising begin?'

'I really and truly and honestly promise—'

'Oh cut it out,' I said. 'I told you if you did it again I'd get rid of the 'phone.'

'You can't mean it, Hilary, we must have the telephone, you'll think better of it—'

'I won't have time to,' I said.

I went into the hall. The offending instrument stood on a small bamboo table beside the front door. I took hold of the wire low down and pulled hard. There was a rending pattering sound and the box came away from the wall together with some of the skirting board and a shower of plaster. The wire would not break. I put one foot on it and pulled hard until it snapped, precipitating me back onto the table. I crushed the table against the wall, smashing one of its legs. The telephone crashed onto the floor and broke open disgorging multi-coloured wirey entrails. The dial came off and rolled away into a corner. Silence.

'Oh—Hilary—' Christopher, pale under his pallor, stared down at the wreckage. He was shaken.

I went into my bedroom and shut the door. I would have liked to leave the flat immediately after this episode, but it was my night for dining with the Impiatts (Thursday) and I usually changed for them (not into 'evening dress', just my shirt and tie). I shaved for them too. I always needed a five o'clock shave, only had one on Thursdays. Having dealt with that matter at the wash basin in my bedroom, I took off my dirty office shirt and greasy tie and put on a white shirt and a decent foulard. I combed my hair and resumed coat and over-coat. I already regretted my destruction of the telephone. I had only had two drinks at the Sloane Square station bar on the way home. Suppose Crystal were to need me urgently? I emerged.

Christopher, still agitated, was waiting for me. 'Hilary, I'm frightfully sorry, please don't be angry with me, I'll mend the table—' He spoke as if he had done the damage.

'I'm not angry,' I said. He was between me and the door. I took him by the shoulders and set him gently aside. I felt him wince (with alarm, with distaste?) as I touched him. I got out of the door. Mr Pellow watched me with glazed eyes from the darkness of his hallway. He was sitting down now. He had been suspended for hitting a troublesome pupil. How I sympathized with him. I went down in the lift, alone this time. Outside, the breath of autumn's being was chasing round in circles after leaves and newspapers and old cigarette packets. By the time I reached the park I felt a little better. London is unreal north of the park and south of the river. Unreality reaches its peak on the horrible hills of Hampstead. For me the park was the great divide between myself and a happier land into which I once thought that I was destined to enter. It was not to be. It turned out that I was unfit for ordinary life. I was always sorry that I had been too young to be in the war. I would have enjoyed the war.

'Hilary *dear*,' said Laura Impiatt, opening the door and kissing me.

The Impiatts, a childless couple full of good works and enterprises, lived in Queen's Gate Terrace, occupying the lower part of one of those rather overwhelming houses. I hung up my clothes in the hall in the way in which Laura had long ago taught me to do, and followed her into the drawing-room.

'Hello, Hilary,' said Freddie, who was opening a bottle.

THURSDAY

Clifford Larr, who sometimes came on Thursdays, bowed aloofly.

Freddie Impiatt and Clifford Larr both worked at my office. I call it my office, but it was more like their office as they were both considerably senior to me. It would have been difficult not to be. I worked in Whitehall, in a government department, it boots not which. I worked in the section called 'establishments' which deals with the administration of the office itself. I dealt with pay, not with the metaphysics of pay but with its mechanics. It was a dullish unexacting job, but I did not dislike it. I occupied a humble obscure position and when promotion time came was regularly 'passed over'. (Expressive phrase: a beat of triumphant wings, then silence.) In the office hierarchy I was, if one omits typists and clerks, near to the bottom. I worked to a man called Duncan, now briefly seconded to the Home Office, who worked to a Mrs Frederickson, now on maternity leave, who worked to Freddie Impiatt, who worked to Clifford Larr, who worked to someone too exalted to be in question here, who worked to someone more exalted still, who worked to the head of the department Sir Brian Templar-Spence, who was now about to retire. Arthur Fisch worked to me. Nobody worked to Arthur.

Freddie then was much my senior, and Clifford Larr almost at vanishing point. It was therefore notably kind of Freddie and Laura to invite me regularly to their house, since I was so particularly nobody. It was the more notably kind since both Freddie and Laura were snobs: not gross snobs of course, but quiet intelligent surreptitious beavering-away snobs, as most cultured middle-class people are, unless there is some positive quality of character or education to stop them. They pursued and cultivated all sorts of 'grandees' and had them to dinner, but of course not on the days when I was there. When they gave cocktail parties I was not asked. Important office men such as Clifford Larr rarely appeared on my days, and titled people and famous writers never. Laura imagined that she concealed this discrimination by remarks such as 'It'll be just us, we're going to be selfish and keep you to ourselves!' However these aspirations made their unrewarded kindness to me the more touching. It took them a little while to understand the peculiar rigidity with which my life was arranged but they did understand it and they respected it. I had dinner with the Impiatts every Thursday. Sometimes, though not too often, they cancelled me in favour of something more amusing. But they never asked me to change the day.

As I may sometimes seem in what follows to mock the Impiatts let me here make it clear once and for all that I thoroughly liked them both, as we often do those whom we mock. I thought they were decent people and I admired them because they were happily married, quite a feat in my estimation. Of course this latter achievement is not always totally endearing. The assertion made by a happy marriage often alienates, and often is at least half consciously intended to alienate, the excluded spectator. The brightness of the Impiatt hearth made me feel sometimes like a slinking sniffing wolf. And they, the happy ones, like to have a wolf about, like to glimpse him now and then from the window and hear his hungry howling. How rarely can happiness be really innocent and not triumphant, not an insult to the deprived. How offensive it can be, the natural instinctive showing off of decent happy people.

'Have some more sherry, Hilary, just a smidgin?' A new fashionable word of Laura's. Diminutive of 'smudge'?

'Thanks.'

'You're wearing odd socks again. Look, Freddie, Hilary's wearing odd socks again!' This was a regular joke which I was tired of. I would have checked my socks but for the telephone episode.

'I've been admiring your luscious stockings, I can't take my eyes off your ankles.' I talked this sort of vulgar nonsense to Laura. I always acted the goat with the Impiatts, they seemed to expect it. Sometimes there was not a pin to choose between me and Reggie Farbottom, the office comic.

Laura, no longer either young or slim, was a good-looking woman. She came of a Quaker family and had given up her education to marry Freddie, a fact to which she often alluded. She was, like her husband, extremely energetic. There was something of the games-mistress. Will and energy poured from her, often in the form of a sort of anxiety, possibly an anxiety always to be doing something worth-while. She had a sweet radiant intense face and those very wide-apart eyes which give a slightly dazed and dazing mesmeric effect to the glance. She grinned rather than smiled and had a deep resonant emphatic incisive cultured voice which could be tiring to listen to. Some word in each sentence had to be rather comically emphasized: a sign more of shyness than of the bossiness which it often seemed to express. She was always quipping. Her eyes were a fine chestnut brown and her hair, once a dark brown and now rather grey, had until lately been bound about her head in two severe plaits. Now however she had taken to wearing it loose, streaming down her back nearly to her waist. This was disconcerting: a woman with long streaming grey hair cannot but look a little strange, especially if her eyes glitter with some exalted yearning. Now that her hair was down Laura's energy, quite undiminished, seemed to have become more diffused, less directed and prosaic, as if she were recovering some of the misty electrical indeterminateness of youth. She had also lately developed a taste for flowing robes. Tonight she was wearing an ankle-length tent of green shot silk, split up the side to reveal blue stockings. She always dressed up for our Thursdays, even if it was only me. I did not fail to note this, and she knew I noted it. No wonder I shaved.

'How is Christopher?' said Laura. She took a maternal interest in my young people.

'Much the same. Harmless. Picturesque. Useless.'

'Have you given Christopher a day?' The reference was to my having regular days of the week for seeing my friends.

'No one under thirty is allowed to have a day.'

'Is that a rule? I think you've just invented it!'

'Hilary lives by rules,' said Freddie. 'He separates everything from everything.'

'And everyone from everyone!' said Laura.

'Separation is the essence of a bachelor's existence,' I said.

'He likes to live in other people's worlds and have none of his own.'

'Hilary is all things to all men.'

'Who do you think will succeed Templar-Spence?' said Clifford Larr.

They went off into office gossip. Laura disappeared to the kitchen. She was a good cook if you liked that sort of cooking. I contemplated the drawing-room and marvelled at the expensive knick-knacks and the absence of dust. Freddie and my fellow guest had got on to the economy. 'The Sibyl's leaves, what an image of inflation!' said Clifford Larr.

I never minded being left out of serious conversations. Ignorance should prompt modesty. And it suited me to be the one left to amuse the girls. Women are rarely pompous. I had no instinct to play the man as layer down of law. Freddie Impiatt did so with a touching unawareness. Freddie was stout, a waistcoat wearer, not tall, a little bald, monumental and greying, a kind conceited man with a big honest head and a pleasant horsy smile. He could not pronounce his r's. Clifford Larr was thin and tall, a bit dandified, not an easy man, nervous, sarcastic, armed with conscious superiority, no sufferer of fools, one of those prickly unwelcoming reserved eccentrics in whom the Civil Service abounds.

'*A table, à table!*'

Talking of the pound, they followed me down the stairs in answer to Laura's shout.

'Fancy French muck again, Hilary!'

'I sympathize with Wittgenstein who said he didn't mind what he ate so long as it was always the same.'

'Hilary lives on baked beans when he isn't here. What did you have for lunch today, Hilary?'

'Baked beans, of course.'

'Have some white wine, Hilary.'

'Just a smidget.'

'Are those boys at your place still smoking pot?'

'I don't know what they do.'

'Another case of separation!'

'I must come and see them again,' said Laura. 'I'm writing another article. And I feel I might be able to help them somehow. All right, Hilary, no need to sneer!'

Laura, as part of the latest exaltation, was attending lectures on sociology and writing intellectual women's page journalism about 'the young'.

'The young are so selfless and brave compared with us.'

'Yah.'

'I mean it, Hilary. They *are* brave. They take such big decisions and they don't worry about money and status and they aren't afraid to live in the present. They put their whole lives at risk for the sake of ideas and experience.'

'More fools they.'

'I'm sure you were fearfully anxious and careful when you were young, Hilary.'

'I thought about nothing but my exams.'

'There you are. When are you going to tell me about your childhood, Hilary?'

'Never.'

'Hilary is pathologically discreet.'

'In my view, the pound should not have been allowed to float,' said Clifford Larr.

'With this crisis on we've decided to stay at home for Christmas.'

'You know so many languages, Hilary, but you never travel.'

'I think Hilary never leaves London.'

'I think he never leaves the perimeter of the royal parks.'

'Do you still run round Hyde Park every morning, Hilary?'

'What's your view of the pound, Hilary?'

'That it should bash every other currency to pieces.'

'Hilary is so competitive and chauvinistic.'

'I love my country.'

'So old-fashioned.'

'If you sing *Land of Hope and Glory*, Freddie will sing *Soviet Fatherland*.'

'Patriotism used to be taught in schools,' said Clifford Larr.

'My school regarded patriotism as bad form,' said Freddie.

'Eton is so bolshy,' said Laura.

'The government will fall on price increases,' said Clifford Larr.

'I'm fed up with hearing the proles binding about the price of meat,' said Freddie.

'Why don't they eat caviare.'

'Hilary has missed the point as usual.'

'They don't have to eat beef all the time, we don't.'

'They could live on beans, Hilary does.'

'Or pilchards. Or brown rice. Much healthier.'

'All right. I just don't like Freddie's vocabulary.'

'Hilary is so combative.'

'Talking of proles, Hilary, I wish you'd tell Arthur Fisch not to let those drunks visit him at the office.'

'They aren't drunks, they're drug addicts.'

'But do you agree, Hilary?'

'I agree.'

'I mean, it won't do.'

'Hilary, has Freddie told you about the office pantomime?'

'No, I haven't told him. It's to be *Peter Pan*.'

'Oh no!'

'Don't you like *Peter Pan*, Hilary?'

'It's my favourite play.'

'Hilary thinks Freddie will desecrate it.'

'No need to ask who will play Hook and Mr Darling.'

'The director always bags the star part.'

'Freddie is an actor *manqué*.'

'A great ambiguous work of art,' said Clifford Larr. 'Will you favour a Freudian interpretation?'

'No, I think a Marxist one.'

'Ugh.'

'Don't be so negative, Hilary.'

'Why not a Christian interpretation, Peter as the Christ Child?'

'Hilary says why not a Christian interpretation!'

'Reggie Farbottom will play Smee.'

'Aaargh.'

'Hilary is envious.'

'I must be going now,' said Clifford Larr. He always left early. We all trooped upstairs.

After he had gone and we were sitting in the drawing-room drinking coffee he was of course discussed.

'Such an unhappy man,' said Laura. 'I'm so sorry for him.'

'I don't know anything about him,' I said, 'but I don't know why you assume he's unhappy. You two are always assuming people are unhappy so that you can pity them. I suspect you think he's unhappy just because he isn't married. You probably think I'm unhappy. As soon as I've gone you'll say, "Poor Hilary, I'm so sorry for him, he's so unhappy".'

'Don't bite us, Hilary,' said Freddie. 'Some whisky?'

'A smudgeling.'

'A what?'

'A smudgeling.'

'Well, I persist in thinking he's unhappy,' said Laura, pouring the whisky. 'He looks like an interesting man but he's so stiff and solemn and he only wants to talk about the pound. He never talks about anything personal. I think he's got a secret sorrow.'

'Women always think men have secret sorrows. It's a way of separating them from other women.'

'And men like you, Hilary, always think women are against other women.'

'That's right, darling, hit him back.'

'And he wears a cross round his neck.'

'Clifford? *Does* he?'

'Something on a chain anyway, I think it's a cross, I saw it through his nylon shirt last summer.'

'You aren't angry with me, are you, Laura?'

'Of course not, silly! Hilary talks big but it's quite easy to put him down.'

'Clifford can't be *religious*, can he?'

'I don't know,' said Freddie, 'he's so remote and clammed up, I doubt if he has any real friends at all. He might be a Roman Catholic. I certainly daren't ask.'

'Laura thinks he needs a woman.'

'Hilary's crest soon rises again!'

'I want to play Smee.'

'Hilary just wants to spite Reggie.'

'Are you serious, Hilary? If you would like to you can be a pirate—'

'Of course I'm not serious. You know what I think about the office pantomime.'

'Hilary is anti-life.'

'Yes, thank God.'

'I'm just going to find that brandy,' said Freddie. He went off.

I was never sure whether Freddie's departures on my Thursdays were purely accidental or whether they were concerted with Laura so that she could interrogate me in a more intimate way. She certainly always set about probing at once and made the most of her time.

'I think you've got a secret sorrow, Hilary.'

'I've got about two hundred.'

'Tell me one.'

'I'm getting old.'

'Nonsense. How is Crystal?'

'All right.'

'How is Tommy?'

'All right.'

'Hilary, you are a chatterbox!'

When I left the Impiatts the evening was not yet over for me. I did not stay late since I was expected elsewhere well before midnight. Of course I did not tell my hosts this, they would have thought it 'bad form'. On Thursdays I always went to fetch Arthur Fisch away from Crystal. (Crystal is my sister.) This 'fetching away' was an old tradition. The idea was that Crystal sometimes found Arthur hard to get rid of and so I was to come and remove him. Or was it that I had decided to control, in both the French and English senses, my sister's relations with this young fellow? The origin of the arrangement was lost in history. And indeed Arthur was no longer all that young, none of us was.

Crystal lived in a bed-sitter flat in one of the shabby little streets beyond the North End Road, and at a brisk pace I could do the walk from Queen's Gate Terrace in about twenty minutes. I always walked in London if I could. Crystal was over five years my junior and, like myself, unmarried. She had had various jobs. She had been a waitress, a clerk, she had worked in a chocolate factory. She was now modestly set up as a dress-maker, but seemed to spend most of her time altering her neighbours' skirts for a few pence. I subsidized her a bit. No one could have lived more cheaply than Crystal. Her biggest weekly expenses were entertaining Arthur and me. The Impiatts never invited Crystal to dinner as she was too ignorant to be presentable. Laura used to invite her to tea occasionally.

Crystal lived alone in a small shabby terrace house. Her bed-sitter, with tiny kitchen annexe, occupied the upper floor. There was a bath in the kitchen. The lavatory was on the ground floor, where there was also a dentist's surgery and waiting-room. The basement was intermittently occupied by a motor cycle repairer and (we thought) receiver of stolen goods in a small way. The whole area was, or was then, very decrepit and poor. The stucco of the fronts, once painted different colours, had faded into a uniform grime and fallen off in patches to reveal ochre-coloured brick beneath. Here and there a gaping or boarded window or a doorless doorway proclaimed the abandonment of hope. The inhabitants were mostly 'protected tenants' at low rents (Crystal was such a one) for whom the landlords found it not worth their while to do repairs.

I let myself in with my key and made my way upstairs. Crystal and Arthur were sitting at the table. They both rose when I entered, behaving as usual as if they were slightly afraid of me. They always acted a little guiltily on these occasions. Not because they had been making love, because they had not. Crystal, at thirty-five, was still a virgin. Arthur was in love with her, but nothing happened, that I certainly knew. This evening I thought the atmosphere was rather more charged than usual, as if I had interrupted some particularly intense discussion. This annoyed me. Arthur was rather red in the face, and Crystal made little awkward darting movements to simulate some neutral and innocent activity. Perhaps they had just been holding hands. A bottle of cheap wine, brought by Arthur, stood on the table. Crystal hardly drank. There was always plenty left for me.

13

I sat down at the table in the third chair. They sat down. The table was an ancient kitchen table of straw-coloured deal with a pleasant ridgy grainy surface out of which Crystal vigorously scrubbed the bread crumbs. It never wore a cloth, except when I came to supper with Crystal on Saturday evenings. We sat there under the naked central light like three conspirators. Crystal had cleared the dishes. Arthur poured me out a glass of wine.

'What did you have for supper?'

'Shepherd's pie and beans and apricot tart and custard,' said Crystal. She shared my taste in food. She still had her northern accent. I had got rid of mine.

'What did you have at the Impiatts?' Arthur asked. We always asked each other this.

'*Quenelles de brochet. Caneton à l'orange. Profiteroles.*'

'Oh.'

'You did better,' I said.

'I'm sure we did!' said Crystal, smiling her utterly innocent uncomplicit smile at Arthur, who grinned.

Let me try to describe Crystal. She cannot be said to be beautiful. She was short and dumpy, she had no perceptible waist. She had pretty small well-worn capable hands which moved a lot, like a pair of little birds. She was round-faced and rather pallid or even pasty. She rarely took any exercise. Her hair was orange-brown and fuzzy and fell in a thick heavy mat almost to her shoulders. She had a large mouth with a prominent moist lower lip, very mobile. Rather bad teeth. A wide and distinctly upturned nose. Her eyes were hazel, of the kind which are pure golden without a hint of green, but they were usually hidden behind thick round spectacles which made them look like gleaming stones. None of this really describes Crystal however. How is it possible to describe someone to whom you are oned in love? Crystal often appeared stupid. She was like a sweet gentle patient good animal.

Arthur was a little taller than Crystal, considerably shorter than me. He had a tentative humorous face of a rather dated sort. (Not that he was ever witty, he was far too timid.) He had soupy brown eyes and an apologetic much-chewed mouth and a well-grown but not quite drooping brown moustache. His hair was rather greasy, not long, hanging in lank brown waves. He looked like some unidentified person in a nineteenth-century photograph. He wore oval steel-rimmed glasses. This sounds like a prejudiced description. Let me try to amend it. He was an honest man devoid of malice. His

14

soupy eyes could express feeling. (I do not wear glasses. My eyes are hazel like Crystal's. Crystal and I had different fathers.)

I never lingered long on Thursday evenings. I liked to condition those about me, and Arthur was conditioned to reach for his coat as soon as I arrived. He had in fact already reached for it. I took Crystal's little busy hand. I did not mind Arthur's presence any more than that of a dog. 'All right, my darling?'

'All right, dear. Are you all right?' We always asked each other this.

'Yes, yes. But are you really all right?'

'Of course. I've got a new lady. She wants a cocktail costume. Such lovely stuff. Shall I show you?'

'No. Show me on Saturday.' I kissed her wrist. Arthur rose. A minute later we were outside in the wind.

I felt that emotion again, the emotion in Arthur from whatever had happened during the evening, something more than usual. I wondered if I should question him, decided not to. We walked up the North End Road. Arthur lived in Blythe Road. The wind was suddenly very cold, a winter wind. I felt something out of darkness grab at me, an old old thing.

'Freddie was on about your junkies again,' I said.

'I can't stop them from coming to the office.'

'You could stop collecting them.'

Arthur was silent. The wind blew bitterly. Arthur was wearing a sensible absurd woollen cap. My head was uncovered. I usually wore a flat cloth cap when it got really cold. Time to dig it out. I had forgotten to tell Crystal about the telephone. I must remember to do so on Saturday.

'Has Freddie decided about the panto?' Arthur asked.

'Yes. *Peter Pan.*'

'Oh goodie!'

We reached the corner of Hammersmith Road, where we parted.

'Good night.'

'Good night.'

'Hilary—'

'Good night.'

I walked abruptly away. It was after midnight when I got to Bayswater. There was silence in the flat. I glanced quickly through Tommy's letter. The usual rigmarole! I went to bed in my underclothes. (This shocked Christopher.) I had never had any sleep problems since the orphanage. A talent for oblivion is a talent for survival. I laid my head down and merciful pain-killing sleep covered me fathoms deep. Not to have been born is undoubtedly best, but sound sleep is second best.

BEFORE describing the events of Friday I must (while, as it were, I am asleep) talk at more length about myself. I have mentioned my work, my age (forty-one), my sister, the colour of my eyes. I was born in a town in the north of England which I will not name since for me its memory is accursed. Let it for whom it may be holy ground. I do not know who my father was, nor who Crystal's father was. Presumably, indeed certainly, they were different men. I was informed, before I knew what the word meant, that my mother was a 'tart'. It is strange to think that my father probably never knew I existed. My mother died when I was nearly seven and Crystal was an infant. I have no memory of my mother, except as a sort of state, a kind of Platonic remembrance. I think it is a memory of a state of being loved, a sense certainly of some lost brightness, an era of light before the darkness started. Immense tracts of my childhood are inaccessible to memory, and I cannot remember any incident from those first years. Crystal used to possess a photograph allegedly of our mother, but I tore it up, not of course out of resentment.

After our mother's death we were taken over by Aunt Bill, my mother's sister. I suppose her name was Wilhelmina. (I never knew my mother's first name, and later it was impossible to ask. Aunt Bill always referred to her, in an indescribably offensive tone, as 'your ma'.) Aunt Bill lived in the same town, in a caravan. I cannot to this day see a caravan without shuddering. Aunt Bill kept Crystal with her in the caravan, but me she fairly soon (I do not know exactly how soon) despatched to an orphanage. I had, with my first self-consciousness, an awareness of myself as 'bad', a bad boy, one who had to be sent away.

It is impossible for me to 'try to be fair' to Aunt Bill. There are some things which are so difficult that one does not even know how to try to do them. Because of an incident concerning a pet mouse, which I can scarcely bring myself to think of let alone to relate, I detested Aunt Bill forever with a hatred which can still make me tremble. The particular way Aunt Bill had of stepping on insects provided my earliest picture of

17

human wickedness. I am not sure that I have ever bettered it. In any case, Aunt Bill and I were instant enemies, not least because she deliberately separated me from Crystal. Aunt Bill was an uneducated ill-tempered spiteful woman full of malice and resentment. I will not use the word 'sadistic' of her; this suggests a classification and thereby a sort of extenuation. When, many years later, I heard of her death, I intended to go out and celebrate but found myself simply sitting at home shedding tears of joy. Aunt Bill was, of course, a tough egg. ('Brave' carries the wrong implications.) She carried on her war against the world in her own personal way exerting her own personal power, and in this she might even be said to have had some kind of distinction. She was my first conception of a human individual. (Crystal was part of me.) Let what can be said for her. She got rid of me. She might have got rid of Crystal too. Crystal was small enough to be adopted. (I was of course too old for adoption, even apart from my precocious reputation for being thoroughly disturbed and 'bad'.) But she kept Crystal and looked after her; and though she got an allowance for doing so I doubt if she did it for the money. Aunt Bill never worked that I can remember. She and Crystal lived on National Assistance in the caravan.

I shall not talk about the orphanage: again, fairness is probably impossible. It was not that I was beaten (though I was) or starved (though I was always hungry); it was just that nobody loved me. In fact I early took in that I was unlovable. Nobody singled me out, nobody gave me their *attention*. I have no doubt that some of the people there were good well-intentioned folk who tried to approach me, and that I rejected them. I have a shadowy idea that this may have been so. I can hardly remember the early years at the orphanage. When the light of memory falls I was already as it were old, old and scarred and settled in a posture of anger and resentment, a sense of having been incurably maimed by injustice.

The most profound and maiming piece of injustice was the separation from Crystal. I cannot remember anything about the event of Crystal's birth, but I can recall her in infancy and trying to carry her in my arms. I felt none of the jealousy the earlier child is supposed to experience. I loved Crystal at once in a sort of prophetic way, as if I were God and already knew all about her. Or as if she were God. Or as if I knew that she was my only hope. My younger sister had to be my mother, and I had to be her father. No wonder we both became a little odd. The orphanage was not too far away from the caravan site, and I must have seen quite a lot of Crystal in the earlier time after my mother's death. I have memory pictures of Crystal aged two, three, four, and the sense that we played together. But as I developed more and more into a 'bad' boy I was allowed to see less and less of my sister. It was supposed that I would be 'bad for her'. And by the time I was eleven we were almost completely separated. I saw her on occasional holiday outings and at Christmas. The anguish of these occasions did nothing to lighten my reputation for being 'disturbed'. One Christmas time I arrived at the caravan to find Aunt Bill slapping Crystal's face. I attacked Aunt Bill's legs, which was all I could get at. She kicked me and I spent Christmas Day in hospital.

My reputation for 'badness' was not unmerited. I was a strong child and soon given to violence. I was not bullied by other children. I did the bullying. (These are disagreeable memories. Am I still a monster in the dreams of those I injured then?) I was good at games and excelled at wrestling. These activities gave me my first conception of 'excellence', inextricably mixed up with the idea of defeating someone, preferably by physical force. Many years later a social worker (little knowing that I was myself something of an expert on the matter) told me that criminals who not only rob but quite gratuitously injure their victims as well, do so out of *anger*. This seems to me very plausible. I was brimming with anger and hatred. I hated, not society, puny sociologists' abstraction, I hated the universe. I wanted to cause it pain in return for the pain it caused me. I hated it on my behalf, on Crystal's, on my mother's. I hated the men who had exploited my mother and ill-treated her and despised her. I had a cosmic furious permanent sense of myself as victimized. It is particularly hard to overcome resentment caused by injustice. And I was so lonely. The bottomless bitter misery of childhood: how little even now it is understood. Probably no adult misery can be compared with a child's despair. However I was better off than some. I had Crystal, and I lived in and for the hope of Crystal as men live in and for the hope of God. When we parted from each other, mingling our tears, she used always to say to me, 'Oh be *good*!' This adjuration doubtless resulted from her having so often heard what a rascal I was. Not that her love wavered. Perhaps she felt that somehow if I became better we would meet more often. But for me Crystal's little cry was and is the apotheosis of that word.

Religion, of a low evangelical variety, was everywhere at the orphanage. I detested that too. Crystal's 'Be good' (which had little or no effect on my conduct) meant more to me than Jesus Christ. Christ was always purveyed to me by people who clearly regarded me not only as a delinquent but as an object of pity. There is an attitude of complacent do-gooding condescension which even decent people cannot conceal and even a small child can recognize. Their religion seemed to me overlit, over-simple, covertly threatening. There was nowhere in it to hide. We roared out 'choruses' about sin and redemption which reduced the hugest theological dogmas to the size of a parlour trick. I rejected the theology but was defenceless against the guilt which was so fruitlessly beaten into me. The mood was brisk and impatient. Either you were saved by the blood of the Lamb or else you were for it, a black and white matter of breath-taking rewards or whipping. The efficacious Saviour almost figured to me as a sort of *agent provocateur*. Again and again the trick failed to work, the briskness turned to severity and the jollity ended in tears. In so far as there were mysteries and depths in my life I kept them secret from Christ and his soldiery. I was more moved by animals than I was by Jesus. One of the porters had a dog, and this dog once, as I sat beside him on the ground, touched my arm with his paw. This gentle gesture has stayed with me forever. And I remember stroking a guinea pig at school and feeling such a piercing strange pain, the realization that happiness existed, but was denied to me. I hardly ever visited 'the country'. I pictured it as a paradise where 'the animals' lived.

Those who regarded me as a thoroughly bad lot were in no way unreasonable. One of my earliest memories is of kicking the tulips to pieces in the public park. I progressed to grander acts of destruction. I liked hitting people, I liked breaking things. Once I tried to set fire to the orphanage. I was in a juvenile court before I was twelve. After that I was regularly in trouble with the police. I was sent to a psychiatrist. A Christmas came when I was not allowed to see Crystal. I was just coming to full awareness of myself as an outcast, a person totally and absolutely done for, when I began very gradually to discover a quite novel source of hope, to grow the hope in myself like a growing seed. I was saved by two people, neither of whom could have done it alone. One of course was Crystal. The other was a wonderful schoolmaster. His name was Mr Osmand. I did not discover his first name.

Mr Osmand taught French and very occasionally Latin at the modest unambitious filthy little school which I attended.

He had been at the school for many years but I did not become his pupil until I was about fourteen, with my loutish reputation well developed. I had, until then, learnt practically nothing. I could (just) read, but although I had attended classes in history and French and mathematics I had imbibed extremely little of these subjects. The realization that people had simply given up trying to teach me anything enlightened me at last, more than the lectures from magistrates, about how utterly ship-wrecked I was; and increased my anger and my sense of injustice. For with the dawning despair came also the tormenting idea that in spite of everything I was clever, I had a mind though I had never wanted to use it. I *could* learn things, only now it was too late and nobody would let me. Mr Osmand looked at me quietly. He had grey eyes. He gave me his full *attention*.

I suspect that many children are saved by saints and geniuses of this kind. Why are such people not made rich by a grateful society? How exactly the miracle happened is another thing which I cannot very clearly recall. Suddenly my mind woke up. Floods of light came in. I began to learn. I began to want to excel in new ways. I learnt French. I started on Latin. Mr Osmand promised me Greek. An ability to write fluent correct Latin prose began to offer me an escape from (perhaps literally) the prison house, began in time to show me vistas headier and more glorious than any I had ever before known how to dream of. In the beginning was the word. *Amo, amas, amat* was my open sesame, 'Learn these verbs by Friday' the essence of my education; perhaps it is *mutatis mutandis* the essence of any education. I also learnt, of course, my own language, hitherto something of a foreign tongue. I learnt from Mr Osmand how to write the best language in the world accurately and clearly and, ultimately, with a hard careful elegance. I discovered words and words were my salvation. I was not, except in some very broken-down sense of that ambiguous term, a love child. I was a word child.

Probably Mr Osmand was not a genius at anything except teaching. He encouraged me to read the classics of English literature; but his own preferences were more narrowly patriotic. I buried Sir John Moore at Corunna, I threw my empty revolver down the slope, I shouldered white men's burdens east of Suez, I played up and played the game. My father, from the terrace below, called me down to ride. My head was stored with images of the East, Newbolt's East, Conrad's East, Kipling's East. What I read in these books thrilled me with a deep mysterious significance which brought tears to my eyes. I who had no mother could claim at least a mother land, and these exotic tales were about England too and, after it all, hearts at peace under an English heaven. There was a sense of family. But most haunting of them all to my young mind was the story of Toomai of the elephants. 'Kala Nag, Kala Nag, wait for me.' Perhaps this beautiful picture of the elephant turning round to pick up the child symbolized for me my own escape. The elephant would turn and would carry me away, would carry me to goodness and salvation, to the open space at the centre of things, to the dance.

Mr Osmand was a member of the Church of England, but I think that his religion too was largely patriotic, concerned less with God than with the Queen. (Queen Victoria, of course.) I do not recall that we ever talked about God. But I did imbibe from my wonderful teacher a sort of religion or ideology which certainly influenced my life. Mr Osmand believed in competition. It was necessary to excel. He loved and cherished the examination system. (And rightly. It was my road out of the pit.) *Parvenir à tout prix*, was my own conception of the matter. We were both very ambitious for me. But Mr Osmand did not simply want me to win prizes. He wanted me, in his own old-fashioned and austere conception of it, to be good. His message to me was the same as Crystal's. Of course he chided my violence, but more profoundly, and through his very teaching, he inculcated in me a respect for accuracy, a respect, to put it more nobly, for truth. 'Never leave a passage until you thoroughly understand every word, every case, every detail of the grammar.' A fluffy vague understanding was not good enough for Mr Osmand. Grammar books were my books of prayer. Looking up words in the dictionary was for me an image of goodness. The endless endless task of learning new words was for me an image of life.

Violence is a kind of magic, the sense that the world will always yield. When I understood grammatical structure I understood something which I respected and which did not yield. The exhilaration of this discovery, though it did not 'cure' me, informed my studies and cast on them a light which was not purely academic. I learnt French and Latin and Greek at school. Mr Osmand taught me German in his spare time. I taught myself Italian. I was not a philological prodigy. I lacked that uncanny gift which some people have for language structure which seems akin to a gift for music or calculation.

I never became concerned with the metaphysical aspects of language. (I am not interested in Chomsky. That places me.) And I never thought of myself as a 'writer' or tried to become one. I was just a brilliant plodder with an aptitude for grammar and an adoration for words. Of course I was a favourite and favoured pupil. I suspect that Mr Osmand regarded me at first simply as a professional challenge, after I had been generally 'given up'. Later he certainly came to love me. Mr Osmand was unmarried. His shabby sleeve often caressed my wrist, and he liked to lean his arm against mine as we looked at the same text. Nothing else ever happened. But through the glowing electrical pressure of that arm I learnt another lesson about the world.

I went to Oxford. No child from the school had ever been farther afield than a northern polytechnic. In the milieu in which Crystal and Aunt Bill had their being Oxford was a complete mystery: 'Oxford college', somewhere in the south, like a teacher's training college only somehow 'posh'. I told Crystal about Oxford when I knew scarcely more about it myself. This was to be the escape route. For of course, as I worked away at irregular verbs and gerundives and sequence of tenses I was working not only for myself but for Crystal. I would rescue her and take her with me. And when I had learnt everything, I would teach her. At fourteen I had been a small though muscular imp. At sixteen I was a six-foot adolescent. With Mr Osmand and my new talents and my new ambition I feared no one. I visited Crystal whenever I pleased, I intimidated Aunt Bill, and Crystal and I made plans to become rich and live together.

At Oxford I studied French and Italian. Mr Osmand wanted me to read 'Greats' but I preferred a more linguistic course; the idea of philosophy frightened me and I wanted to be sure of excelling. I was extremely diligent but also played games. Intoxicatingly soon after playing cricket for the first time I was grinding my teeth over missing my blue. I learnt Spanish and modern Greek and started Russian. I got rid of my northern vowels. Crystal, at school, then working in the chocolate factory, came down occasionally to marvel at my new Jerusalem. We went into the country on bicycles. Mr Osmand visited me once during my first year. Somehow the visit depressed us both. He reminded me of too many things. And doubtless he felt that he had lost me. I wrote to him for a while, then stopped writing. I soon gave up returning to the north. I spent my vacations in college or on occasional grant-aided trips to France or Italy. I travelled alone; these journeys were not a success. I was an anxious and incurious tourist and my linguistic abilities never made me feel at home. I scarcely even tried to speak the languages I could read so easily. I was always relieved to be back in England. Oxford changed me, but also taught me how hard to change I was. My ignorance was deeply engrained, the grimy misery of my childhood had entered my mode of being. 'Catching up' was going to be a longer job than I had anticipated when I wrote out my versions for Mr Osmand. I made no real friends. I was touchy and solitary and afraid of making mistakes and well aware that I was a big tough healthy chap devoid of ease and physical charm. I could not get on with girls and scarcely attempted to. I did not mind. *Parvenir à tout prix*. I was working for me and Crystal. Other things could wait. I won every prize I went in for: the Hertford, the Heath-Harrison, the Gaisford Greek Prose, the Chancellor's Latin prose. I did not attempt the Ireland (for which Gladstone and Asquith strove in vain). I got one of the top firsts of my year and was almost immediately elected to a fellowship at another college. I made plans for Crystal to come and live with me in Oxford. I gave a party in my college rooms, and Crystal came down, wearing a flowery dress and a floppy white hat. She was seventeen. She said to me with tears in her eyes, 'This is the happiest day of my life!' A year afterwards, as a result of a catastrophe which will be mentioned later in these pages, I resigned my post and left Oxford for ever.

FRIDAY

IT WAS Friday morning and I was just leaving for the office. Darkness had not yet really given way to day. There might have been some sort of yellow murk outside, but I did not pull back the curtains to look at it. I had swallowed two cups of tea and was my usual hateful early morning self. I emerged from the flat onto the bright electrically lit landing and closed the door behind me. The curious smell was still there. Then I stopped dead.

On the opposite side of the landing, not far from the lift, a girl was standing. I saw at once that she was, wholly or partly, Indian. She had a thin light-brown transparent spiritual face, a long thin fastidious mouth, an aquiline nose: surely the most beautiful race in the world, blending delicate frailty and power into human animal grace. She was not wearing a sari, but an indefinably oriental get-up consisting of a high-necked many-buttoned padded cotton jacket over multi-coloured cotton trousers. She was not tall, but in her gracefulness did not look short. Her black hair in a very long very thick plait was drawn forward over one shoulder. She stood perfectly still, her thin hands hanging down, and her large almost black eyes regarding me intently.

I felt shock, pleasure, surprise, alarm. Then I recalled Christopher's words, completely forgotten since, about a coloured girl looking for me. Fear. For *me* surely no one could search with an amiable motive. I was about to speak to her when the fact of the silence having lasted, as it seemed, so long made speech impossible. How after all could this girl, such a girl, concern me? There were other flats on the corridor behind her, containing shifting populations of which I took care to know nothing. She was doubtless somebody's girl friend going home. Lucky somebody. I unfixed myself from the door handle and walked to the lift and pressed the button, turning my back upon the apparition. As the lift arrived and the automatic doors opened I heard a soft footstep. The Indian girl entered the lift after me. She stood beside me, staring up at me with an unsmiling expression of dazed puzzled interest. I could see and hear and only not quite feel her breathing. She was wearing a black woollen sweater, visible at neck and sleeves, underneath the jacket. I looked at the reflection of her back in the mirror. The long thick unsilky plait, which she had evidently tossed back over her shoulder as she entered, fell straight to the buttocks where it arched out and ended in a fanlike brush like a lion's tail. The slightly frayed sleeve of the jacket moved and came into contact with the sleeve of my mackintosh. I felt my features stiffen as a current of electricity, generated by the contact, passed on into my flesh. The lift had creaked its way to the ground floor and the doors opened. She stepped out first. I went past her to the street door and out into the street. It was a dark morning, a little rain riding upon the wind, the street lamps still on. I reached the corner resolving not to turn round. The electrical connection still held. I turned round. She was standing upon the steps of the flats and staring after me.

I really did once upon a time run round the park every morning. The goal of keeping perfectly fit was *a* goal, the gift of a strong and healthy body was *a* gift. Running was a method of death, of life in death, not the saint's marvel of living in the present, but a desperate man's little version. There was a kind of sleeping or half-sleeping which I sometimes tried to achieve (especially at weekends) when I lay like a floating turtle, just breaking the surface of consciousness, aware and yet not self-aware, not yet tormented by being a particular person. So too with the running. I ran, and was cleansed of myself. I was a heart pumping, a body moving. I had cleaned a piece of the world of the filth of my consciousness. I was not even capable of dreaming. If I could always so have slept and so have waked I would have achieved my own modest beatification. I stopped running not (I think) because of a warning tap from the finger of age, but just out of sinful degenerate laziness of soul: the same laziness and failure of hope which still prevented me from starting to learn Chinese. I would, however, on a good morning when time allowed, walk briskly across the park to Gloucester Road station and proceed to Westminster from there. On bad mornings when I was late I took the Inner Circle from Bayswater. This morning (Friday) was a bad morning.

As I now cram myself into the rush hour train at Bayswater station perhaps I should pause again to describe myself a little more. I have spoken of the cult of my body. I still was very much that body. It had defended me in childhood and I had always identified myself with it as with one of my chief assets. I was (am) just over six feet tall, sturdy, dark, clean-shaven against a fierce beard, with a head of thick greasy crinkly dark hair descending to my collar. A similar mat of thick hair furs my body to the navel. I have hazel eyes not unlike Crystal's, only not so golden and not so big. (Aunt Bill also, I regret to say, had hazel eyes only hers were very small and distinctly greenish.) It is difficult to describe my face. It satisfies no canon of beauty, not even that of a gangster. My wide nose, like Crystal's, turns up a little at the end. If I valued my physique it was certainly not for its charm. Because of my hair I was called 'Nigger' at school and for a time I did in some curious way think of myself as being black. A boy once told me that I had a black penis, and convinced me of it in spite of the visual evidence. Intended to wound, these taunts did not altogether displease me. I liked (though I expected no one else to) my copious fur, my blackness, my secret being as a black animal. Of other uses of my body, in acts of love, I knew nothing, even when I became a student. I knew that I was unattractive and that I radiated a paralysing awkwardness; moreover a ferocious puritanism, doubtless purveyed to me by my Christian mentors, made me feel that sex was unclean.

I relied upon routine, had done so perhaps ever since I realized that grammatical rules were to be my salvation; and since I had despaired of salvation, even more so. Routine, in my case at least, discouraged thought. Your exercise of free choice is a prodigious stirrer up of your reflection. The patterned sameness of the days of the week gave a comforting sense of absolute subjection to history and time, perhaps a comforting sense of mortality. I could not consider suicide because of Crystal, but I wanted to have my death always beside me. My 'days' were a routine, and in the office I conceived of myself as far as possible as a man on an assembly line. Week-ends and holidays were hells of freedom. I took my leave for fear of comment and simply hid (if possible slept). I used once to attempt holidays with Crystal, but it was too much. She cried all the time. It was true that, as Freddie Impiatt had said to me, I liked to live in other people's worlds and have none of my own.

None of this entirely describes what I 'lived by'. By what after all does a man live? Art meant little to me, I carried a few odd pieces of literature like lucky charms. Someone once said of me, and it was not entirely unjust, that I read poetry for the grammar. As I have said, I never wanted to be a writer. I loved words, but I was not a word-user, rather a word-watcher, in the way that some people are bird-watchers. I loved languages but I knew by now that I would never speak the languages that I read. I was one for whom the spoken and the written word are themselves different languages. I had no religion and no substitute for it. My 'days' gave me identity, a sort of ecto-skeleton. Beyond my routine chaos began and without routine my life (perhaps any life?) was a phantasmagoria. Religion, and indeed art too, I conceived of as human activities, but not for me. Art must invent new beauty, not play with what has already been made, religion must invent God and never rest. Only I was not inventive. I did not want to play this play or dance this dance, and apart from the activity of playing or dancing there was nothing at all. I early saw that the nature of words and their relationship to reality made metaphysical systems impossible. History was a slaughterhouse, human life was a slaughterhouse. Mortality itself was my philosophical robe. Even the stars are not ageless and our breaths are numbered.

Let us now get on to the office. Very little of my story actually takes place in the office, but as the office was so much a part of my mind it is necessary to describe it. I existed, as I have explained, near to the bottom of the power structure which rose above the clerical and stenographical level. I dealt with 'cases' concerning pay, little individual problems, not always unamusing. (Should this man's 'danger money' affect his pension? Should that man's paid sick-leave be extended in these circumstances? Should another man's pay-rise be back-dated in those?) I did not invent rules, I merely applied rules made by others. Sometimes the rules did not quite fit the cases, and there was a tiny occasion for thought. Usually no thought was necessary. I wrote out my view in the form of a 'minute', which I sent to Duncan, who sent it to Mrs Frederickson, who sent it to Freddie Impiatt, who sent it to Clifford Larr, and after that, or even before that, I did not really know or care what happened to it or whether it survived. Arthur Fisch, who devilled for me, wrote no minutes so there was someone to be superior to.

I worked in a room with two other people. This Room and

these people have a certain tiny importance because, as so often, the physical world figured the mental world. The two people who shared my room were Mrs Witcher (Edith) and Reggie Farbottom. Arthur worked in a cupboard (almost literally), a little room partitioned off from the corridor, with a corridor window as its only source of light. I regretted that I had not installed Arthur long ago in the Room, but it was too late now, and Arthur liked his cupboard. Mrs Witcher, it was said, had once been a shorthand typist who had risen to power through being someone's Personal Assistant. When I first knew her she was a self-styled 'head' of the Registry, the vast complex where the files were stored. This might have been an important job but in her case it was certainly a standing up job and not a sitting down job; and could one actually say that such a one as Mrs Witcher was 'head' of the Registry? There was in fact another head, a man, who sat down, called Middledale, who really ran the Registry, while Mrs Witcher was just one of the more important of the filing clerks. There was some uncertainty about this even at the time. Later Mrs Witcher received a promotion and a desk, first in the Registry itself, and then in an adjoining room (not Middledale's room, which had by then been converted to another purpose). During a period of office redecoration she moved into my room (the Room) which I then shared with a man called Perry (who afterwards emigrated to Canada). Mrs Witcher came in as a temporary and junior third, but somehow managed to stay, partly because Perry and I were too polite to turn her out, later because it had become a custom. What Mrs Witcher's work was at first supposed to be I never understood, or tried to understand, as I regarded her presence as ephemeral. She had some task concerned with the checking of classifications, doubtless a routine matter of seeing that papers were being filed correctly. Later on however Mrs Witcher set herself up (or was set up by some superior authority) as a sort of watchdog over the classifications themselves, not only checking the files but controlling the divisions and sub-divisions into which they were separated: a task which raised very fundamental questions with which Mrs Witcher was patently not qualified to deal.

That Reggie Farbottom had (as some people said) originally been a messenger was very unlikely. He had probably started life as some sort of trotting boy clerk. How he ceased being a standing man and became a sitting man I do not know. This was perhaps Mrs Witcher's doing: he had long been her

creature. The relation between them was mysterious. Mrs
Witcher was immemorially divorced. (Of old Witcher nothing
was known.) Reggie Farbottom was considerably younger, unmarried, much given to boasting of 'conquests'. He was foul-
mouthed into the bargain. Perhaps Mrs Witcher liked that.
At any rate Reggie was soon to be found occupying the desk
which Mrs Witcher had invented for herself in the Registry,
and later, on Perry's departure occupying Mrs Witcher's desk
in the Room, while Mrs Witcher occupied that of Perry. My
conception of the matter was that Reggie did what Mrs
Witcher ought to have been doing (whatever that was), while
Mrs Witcher pretended to do a job which she had invented for
herself and in reality did nothing. On Perry's departure, as I
realized later, I ought instantly to have installed Arthur in
Perry's desk. Only Arthur was sentimental about his cupboard, and the true significance of Farbottom only dawned on
me when it was too late.

As office rooms go, the Room was not unattractive, though
it was lit by the sort of neon lighting which recreates a lurid
winter afternoon. It was quite large and had a sort of bay
window from which, through a cleft in an inner courtyard, one
could see Big Ben, and above him a slice of sky which could be
felt to be hanging over the river. In this bay window, on the
far side of the room, I sat. My desk, moreover, rested upon a
strip of brown carpet which reached from the door to the
window and made my side of the room, which also boasted a
print of Whitehall in 1780, quite elegant. The desks of Reggie
and Mrs Witcher were both nearer to the door, facing the wall
in the uncarpeted half of the room. So certain fundamental
distinctions were at least preserved.

I always attempted to arrive at the office before nine. This
was not required, but there were advantages in being first. I
could get quite a lot of work done in the blessed interval
before the others arrived. The old joke about civil servants
being like the fountains in Trafalgar Square because they
played from ten to five had no application as far as I was concerned, or indeed in the department generally, except for a
few freaks such as Edith Witcher. There was always far more
to do than I had time for, though on the other hand nothing
was urgent. This suited me. If I had ever *finished* I would have
felt in danger of going mad. I sometimes had nightmares in
which I had no more 'cases', my in-tray was empty, and as I
had no more work to do I was there under false pretences. On
this particular day (we are still on Friday morning) a hold-up

in the tube made me later than usual. The irritation of this hold-up (jammed breast to breast and back to back in ominous silence) drove from my mind any further speculation concerning the Indian girl. She probably had nothing whatever to do with me. As I entered the building I met Clifford Larr. I was making for the lift, he for the stairs. He worked on the first floor, what one might call the *piano nobile*. I worked a good deal nearer to the attics. We said good morning. He paused. 'A pleasant gathering last night, was it not?' 'Very pleasant,' I replied. He passed on.

When I reached our corridor I saw at once that the light was on in Arthur's cupboard. I did not stop, though I saw that the door was ajar. Arthur, shy of the Room, perhaps wished to trap me. He was easy to elude however, as I had trained him never to talk to me in the office except about work. I did not want any sort of *tête-à-tête* with Arthur just now. I went on into the Room. Reggie and Mrs Witcher were both there. They had already set up an 'atmosphere'. This was another reason why I usually came in early.

'Good afternoon, Hilary!'

'Good morning.'

'I said, good afternoon!'

'He was beating it up last night with the Impiatts,' said Reggie.

'It's not Impiatts on Thursday, it's his girl friend.'

'No, it isn't, it's his girl friend tonight.'

'It's his girl friend on Thursday!'

'Hilary—*Hilary*—listen—isn't it your girl friend tonight?'

'I have no girl friend,' I said, settling down with my back to them and spreading out a case.

'Oh fib, fib, coy, coy!'

'Hilary's a mystery man, aren't you, Hilary?'

'He means it's his *lady* friend,' said Reggie. ' "Hello, hello, who's your lady friend" '—

'That's no lady, that's my—'

'Do shut up, there's good darlings,' I said.

'Oh good, it's one of Hilary's soft soap days.'

'No flying ink pots today.'

'Hilary, *Hilaree*, did Freddikins tell you about the panto?'

'Yes. You are to be Smee.'

'Hilary is to be the crocodile, only they haven't told him!'

'Hilary should just play himself, it would bring the house down!'

'I gather Edith is to be Wendy,' I said.

31

'Oh witty, witty, clever, clever!'

'No call to be sarky, Hilary, making inferred allusions to a lady's age!'

'Jenny Searle in Registry is to be Wendy, one of Reggie's numerous ex's.'

'No wonder they call me Divan the Terrible.'

'Reggie is feeling bronzed and fit after a plunge into the typing pool!'

'They haven't chosen Peter yet.'

'Fischy would make a good Peter, he hasn't reached puberty.'

'Isn't Peter usually played by a girl?' I said.

'Exactly! Fischy for Peter!'

'Shall we go and examine his organs?'

'Edith, you are *awful*!'

'We mustn't be nasty, after all Hilary and Fisch are sort of—aren't they?'

'That's no lady, that's my Fisch.'

'That's no lady, that's my Burde!' (Screams)

'Hilary is so mysterious.'

'Hilary never tells the truth.'

'Is that Directory enquiries? What number do I ring so as to have my telephone removed?'

'Why do you want your telephone removed, Hilo?'

'The girls won't leave him alone.'

'So as to have my telephone *removed*—'

'Fisch keeps ringing him and making improper suggestions.'

'Thank you.'

'Hilary, Hilar*ee*, why do you want—?'

'I want to have my telephone removed—'

'Hilary, why—'

'A post office engineer will call tomorrow?'

Skinker, the messenger, came in with the tea. Reggie Farbottom used to make the tea once, now of course no more. I could not prevent Arthur from making it sometimes, thereby bringing comfort to the Witcher interest. Arthur had no sense of status. Skinker was a gentle elongated creature who had been some sort of hero in a German prison camp and had later, or perhaps then, given himself to Christ. He was a lay preacher in an evangelical mission. He was the only person in the office who called me 'Mr Burde'. The downstairs porters despised me and called me nothing. I was 'Burde' (or sometimes 'Hilary') for ordinary purposes. Skinker's 'Mr' was a tender attention which I appreciated.

Perhaps I ought to describe the appearance of Edith Witcher and Reggie Farbottom; not that they are important, but they were at that time my daily bread. In our daily bondage what can be more preoccupying and ultimately influential than the voices of our fellow captives? How they go on and on: nothing perhaps, in sheer quantity, so fills up the head. I suppose there are situations where idle chatter adds to the good stuff of the world. It may be so in happy families. I knew nothing of that. My daily chatter-ration was a daily sin, and I knew it well. That which religious orders are so right to forbid. I lived in the Room in a kind of moral sludge into which I could not prevent myself from sinking. Given the possibilities of rage, silence, or repartee I usually chose the latter. Edith was a stoutish smartish lady of about fifty with hair dyed brown and cunningly waved to look wind-blown. She had a slightly hooked nose which gave her an air of distinction, and may indeed have been the secret of her success. She had little education and spoke in a loud would-be grand voice. As far as manner went, she might just have been a would-be fashionable head mistress. I suppose there was no harm in her if one could pardon her mind. Reggie sometimes called her Dame Edith. I sometimes called her that myself. I had descended a long way in the Room and was still going down. Reggie spoke in a, possibly put on, slightly Cockney voice. He was slight and fair and quite good-looking in a perky way, with a self-consciously funny expression, as if he were always about to tip his hat on one side and strike up a comic song. He and Mrs Witcher used to make endless jokes about sex. Practically any observation about sex could send them into fits. They giggled at life like a music hall audience who will laugh at anything. About myself of course I misled them steadfastly, offering false incompatible accounts of my past. And Crystal's existence I kept a dark secret from those gross intelligences. The fact that I had a sister would probably have seemed to them irresistibly amusing. At the idea that Arthur loved her they would never have stopped laughing. Another cue for dread.

I was able to continue my daily work perfectly well amid the almost endless stream of Reggie and Edith's 'wit'. My tasks, as I have explained, were not exacting. I got through three cases before lunch. I had never made any attempt to redeem the lunch hour. It remained a period of unmitigated gloom. I ate late so as to have at least the interest of hunger, and took a ham roll and half a pint of beer in a Whitehall pub. Round about three o'clock in the office was the worst time. At four Skinker brought in tea. Today (Friday, now in the afternoon), while Reggie and Mrs Witcher were discussing whether or not Clifford Larr wore a wig, I was writing a minute about a complex back-dated pay award and thinking about Tommy. In fact I had been thinking about Tommy ever since lunch. Friday was Tommy's day.

Tommy, as I should have perhaps explained earlier, was my mistress; though this awkward word scarcely conveys the odd relation in which she stood to me. 'Ex-mistress' would be more accurate in some ways, less truly descriptive in others. Tommy was a major phenomenon in my life. Tommy was, now, a crisis. Her name was of course Thomasina, and her whole name, which had struck me very much when I had first seen it on a theatre programme, was Thomasina Uhlmeister. Indeed I first became interested simply in the name. Uhlmeister was however an interloper who had married Tommy (*née* Forbes) when she was eighteen and abandoned her when she was twenty. (Uhlmeister is not part of this story. Only his name got left behind.) Tommy was now thirty-four. She was Scottish. She spoke Scottish, she even contrived some-how to look Scottish. Her father, never visible, was a dispensing chemist in Fife. Tommy, in referring to him, always mentioned that he was a 'gentleman': presumably a Scotticism. Tommy's mother was dead and her elder brother had been killed in the war. Tommy herself was one of those casualties of a stage-struck childhood. (Ex-husband Uhlmeister had been an actor, I bet a rotten one.) She had originally, in a small provincial way, been trained as a dancer, but nothing came of that. She was a failed dancer, failed minor actress, failed deputy stage-manager, failed assistant scene-painter, failed unpaid typist, failed extra and Green Room dogsbody. She had been the sort of young person who would do anything at all for no money so as to go on living in that tawdry magic cave and breathing that stuffy perfumed air and racketing along with all that brittle gaudy caravanserai. Now no longer young, she earned a pittance by teaching 'drama' two days a week at a teachers' training college somewhere near King's Lynn.

Thomasina Uhlmeister was on the programme as assistant stage-manager. I met her at a party after the play. The play was a piece of Soviet Russian nonsense which had been translated into a piece of English nonsense and put on at a tiny Stalinist theatre, and I came into the picture because I had been asked to help with difficult points of the translation. So I appeared at the party garbed in a tiny bit of prestige, and there was long-legged Tommy. She had grey eyes. I have always attributed a great importance to eyes. How mysteriously expressive those damp orbs can be; the eyeball does not change and yet it is the window of the soul. And colour in eyes is, in its nature and inherence, quite unlike colour in any other substance. Mr Osmand had grey eyes, but his eyes were hard and speckled like Aberdeen granite, while Tommy's were clear and empty like light smoke. Their hue was transparent, as the hue of a clear sky. The purity of the pigment, a washed apotheosis of grey, was most unusual, a colour sample straight from God.

I cannot exactly say that I fell in love with Tommy immediately or indeed that I ever really fell in love with her at all. This was a subject for argument later. I noticed her eyes, her legs. My heart, in so far as, for these purposes, I had one, was in strict seclusion with another lady. And my more recent experiences of 'girls' had been mucky and brief and had persuaded me that I was indeed, as I had been early taught, unlovable. That Crystal loved me must be enough for my life, I often thought. It was not that I was in any way homosexual, though I sometimes attracted men. I liked girls all right, there were reactions. But as soon as I got anywhere near I began to feel nausea and they began to feel fright. It is only in books that a violent nature is attractive. (Not that I often behaved violently, but they could smell it.) I could never develop a language of tenderness. It was a matter of organs, and I wanted to get into bed and get it over with; and as I had not the temperament for this either I disgusted myself. So in practice there was not much of that, and for a while pre-Tommy, none.

Tommy, darling girl, was not only remarkable for her name and her legs and her lucid Cairngorms misty eyes. (Mist is perhaps a better image than smoke. Smoke suggests coils and movement, and although mist too can move it is more blandly uniform in colour; and there was not even the ghost of blue in Tommy's grey.) She was also exceptional in her heroic determination to love me. I suggested in the last paragraph that it was my rude and rugged nature that put women off, but there is more than a hint of self-protective romance in this explanation. Probably it was my face rather than my soul which repelled them. Alas how important this salient surface is, this notice board which the world looks at, and usually does not penetrate beyond. I had a charmless face. Nothing could redeem that nose (except I suppose plastic surgery). This is a singularly depressing fact to have to admit, and I would not have admitted it except out of justice to Tommy and to what I have called her heroism. I shall try to be just in telling the story, however unjust I am in the story told.

I put out a few mechanical lures to Mrs Uhlmeister, not meaning very much by them, and to my great surprise she began to love me and continued to do so. We became lovers. This was quite good. She made me trust her, and this trust set loose a lion of desire. There was a short time when I felt that I was, not cured, that could never be, but somehow soothed, somehow housed. Tenderness and gentleness and a loyal woman in one's bed. Tommy became a part of my life. She visited Crystal, she met Arthur; the Impiatts (until I put a stop to it) occasionally invited her out of curiosity. Then it all began, for me, to blow over, not for any particular reason. Perhaps I was just too puritanical to put up with an extra-marital relationship for long. She had proposed marriage. I just laughed. I could not marry anyone because of Crystal.

This too was complicated and had become hideously more complicated since two things had happened, Crystal had passed her thirtieth year, and Arthur Fisch had come to love her. Crystal wanted a child. (So did Tommy. I shall come to that.) When she told me this or when (she never exactly told me) I realized it by means of the kind of telepathy which we used for communication, I was appalled. Of course the idea had been around that Crystal might marry. Why not? At Oxford I had even looked about a little for suitable paragons. But later, when it came to it, although I kept telling her she should marry, she could read my eyes, she could read those thought waves. This did not matter so much when we were still young and life was provisional. The notion that there was, for her, a time limit, filled me with anguish and with a kind of irritated disgust, and produced a quite different kind of problem. And then, so unfortunately, there was Arthur. In fact Crystal had hardly ever had any serious beaux and was still a virgin. She was sweet, she was pure-hearted, but she was not in the least pretty. And she had always, all of her life, waited and waited and waited upon me.

'You've got a cold.'

'I haven't.'

'You have. You've got a cold and you're concealing it.'

'What makes you think I've got a cold?'

'It's obvious. Your cheek is hot. Your nose is red. Your lip is inflamed. You keep surreptitiously dabbing with that filthy handkerchief.'

'It isn't filthy!'

'Don't wave it at me. You know the rule about colds. I never see people with colds.'

'You and your stupid rules!'

'You've got a streaming cold. I'm going home.'

'Go then, go!'

Tommy lived in a lost region on the confines of Fulham and Chelsea, with distant hints of Putney, not far from the New King's Road, uncheered by the proximity of any tube station, in a little neat flat in a little neat house in a terrace of little neat houses, each with its tiny ornate portico and its tiny cracking flight of steps and its smelly basement full of dustbin litter. I usually reached her by walking from Parson's Green. I got to her place after seven, sometimes well after seven, as I had something to do before. This was another part of my routine. After leaving the office I would travel either to Sloane Square or to Liverpool Street to have a drink in the station buffet. In the whole extension of the Underground system those two stations are, as far as I've been able to discover, the only ones which have bars actually upon the platform. The concept of the tube station platform bar excited me. In fact the whole Underground region moved me, I felt as if it were in some sense my natural home. These two bars were not just a cosy after-the-office treat, they were the source of a dark excitement, places of profound communication with London, with the sources of life, with the caverns of resignation to grief and to mortality. Drinking there between six and seven in the shifting crowd of rush-hour travellers, one could feel on one's shoulders as a curiously soothing yoke the weariness of toiling London, that blank released tiredness after work which can somehow console even the bored, even the frenzied. The coming and departing rattle of the trains, the drifting movement of the travellers, their arrival, their waiting, their vanishing for-ever presented a mesmeric and indeed symbolic fresco: so many little moments of decision, so many little finalities, the constant wrenching of texture, the constant destruction of cells which shifts and ages the lives of men and of universes. The uncertainty of the order of the trains. The dangerousness of the platforms. (Trains as lethal weapons.) The resolution of a given moment (but which?) to lay down your glass and mount the next train. (But why? There will be another in two minutes.) *Ah qu'ils sont beaux les trains manqués!* as I especially had cause to know. Then once upon the train that sense of its thrusting life, its intent and purposive turning which conveys itself so subtly to the traveller's body, its leanings and veerings to points of irrevocable change and partings of the ways. The train of consciousness, the present moment, the little lighted tube moving in the long dark tunnel. The inevitability of it all and yet its endless variety: the awful daylight glimpses, the blessed plunges back into the dark; the stations, each unique, the sinister brightness of Charing Cross, the mysterious gloom of Regent's Park, the dereliction of Mornington Crescent, the futuristic melancholy of Moorgate, the monumental ironwork of Liverpool Street, the twining *art nouveau* of Gloucester Road, the Barbican sunk in a baroque hole, fit subject for Piranesi. And in summer, like an excursion into the country, the flowering banks of the Westbound District Line. I preferred the dark however. Emergence was like a worm pulled from its hole. I loved the Inner Circle best. Twenty-seven stations for fivepence. Indeed, for fivepence as many stations as you cared to achieve. Sometimes I rode the whole Circle (just under an hour) before deciding whether to have my evening drink at Liverpool Street or at Sloane Square. I was not the only Circle rider. There were others, especially in winter. Homeless people, lonely people, alcoholics, people on drugs, people in despair. We recognized each other. It was a fit place for me, I was indeed an Undergrounder. (I thought of calling this story *The Memoirs of an Underground Man* or just simply *The Inner Circle*.)

Today, Friday, I had been at Sloane Square. The two stations are dissimilar, indeed in a sense opposites. Sloane Square has a simple bright modest up-to-date air which can cheer in a homely way, whereas Liverpool Street is menacing and metaphysical and vast. The bars differ too, in that at Liverpool Street you can actually stand on the platform with your drink, whereas at Sloane Square you watch the trains through a window. I had had the needful refreshment in the cosy bright retreat, and had arrived chez Tommy at half past seven. Tommy had a bit more sense of style than Crystal and her flat was comfortable and pretty in a muddled sort of way. She had a television set but covered it with a Cashmere shawl when I came. (I detest television. I am told that the average person now spends twelve years of his life watching it. No wonder the planet is done for.) Tommy childishly collected 'pretty things', cheap stuff from Japan and Hong Kong, Victoriana, junk shop sub-antiques, vases, plates, scrolls, fans, figurines, model animals, quaint unclassifiable entities which no one else wanted. Anything cheap and gaudy attracted her. (Hence the passion for the theatre.) The flat was crammed. (It was also speckless, spotless.) Perhaps, as for many unhappy women, simply shopping had become an addiction. She continually bought cheap jewellery, cheap clothes, never a serious garment which looked like anything, just a mish-mash of togs which she put on in random variations. Her hands were always covered in rings. I do not think that she possessed a dress. This evening she was wearing a garish yellow kilt and green tights and a long dark blue sweater with a leather belt and a necklace of black glass beads with a jet locket. She was slim and graceful but not especially good looking apart from her eyes and her legs. Her eyes were long and faintly almondesque, unlike Crystal's which were large and round like a cat's. Her legs were long and shapely. A woman's legs can be perfect: Tommy's were. I never told her so. I had to keep any advantage I could. Her face had lost the freshness of youth and the cheeks were slightly pockmarked. I found this quite attractive, though again I never told her so. Her hair was a mousy brown and hung about her in limp unravelling natural ringlets. She spoke with a mincing precision in a lightweight slightly Scottish voice. She had a fastidious little nose and a fastidious little mouth, features which could express a remarkable amount of sulky stubbornness and become thoroughly repulsive when they did so.

'Well, why aren't you going then? Why are you sitting there drinking when you've had enough to drink already judging by the smell of you? You do plague me, but you don't mean anything by it, do you? We're still us, aren't we, darling? Aren't we?'

'No,' I said. 'I don't think we are.'

'Wouldn't you rather be in here with a woman that loves you than out there in the rain and the storm? Wouldn't you, wouldn't you? Oh you do hurt me so with your vague threatening talk, you're as bad as a gangster, you deliberately spoil our days, you sit here and drink and sulk and spoil, and you won't give me another day, why can't we meet on Wednesdays?'

'You know we can't meet on Wednesdays.'

'Why not? Just because you decree it? I'm sick and tired of living by your decrees. Wednesday isn't a day. Why can't I have Wednesday too?'

'Wednesday is a day.'

'How is Wednesday a day?'

'Wednesday is my day for myself.'

'You're miserable by yourself, you just mope. Don't you, don't you?'

'I enjoy misery and moping.'

'Anyway I don't believe you. You're a proven liar. I don't believe you see Mr Duncan on Mondays. And I don't believe you're alone on Wednesdays. There's some other woman.'

'Oh Thomas darling, don't make things worse by being silly and vulgar and please please take that horrible aggressive look off your face. I'm so tired.'

'Tired! Tired! I'm tired too.'

'You've been doing nothing all day except trailing round the shops buying rubbish.'

'I've been writing my lecture for Monday.'

'Ha ha.'

'And I've been making glove puppets.'

'Glove puppets, God! We're glove puppets.'

'All right. You scorn what I do. I scorn what you do.'

'You don't know anything about it.'

'And there is another woman. It's Laura Impiatt. You see her on Wednesdays. I know her style, she collects men, she's after you.'

'Don't be boringly catty about other women. It makes me feel your sex really is inferior.'

'I'm not catty, and I'm not talking in general, I'm saying about an individual person!'

'That's not an argument, neither is shouting.'

'You make me cross on purpose so as to muddle me.'

'It's not my fault if you think intuitively rather than logically. Women are supposed to be proud of that.'

'If we met more we'd quarrel less. I must see more of you. I'll come to the office.'

'If you do it'll be the last time you see me.'

'When are we going to paint the flat like you said? You said a man was never more innocently engaged than in painting his flat.'

'Tommy, we can't go on like this.'

'I don't want to go on like this. I want to marry you. I want a baby. I'm thirty-four.'

'I know you're thirty-four! You mention it often enough!'

'You've taken years of my life.'

'Only three, dear.'

'You owe it to me.'

'No one owes anybody anything for that sort of reason.'

'You came after me—'

'Be accurate. You came after me.'

'I want a baby.'

'Well, go and get yourself stuffed somewhere else.'

'You talk in a coarse common way, you use hateful rude language, and you do it to hurt me. Don't you? Don't you? *Don't you?*'

'Oh stop asking these maddening pointless questions!'

'Who's shouting now?'

'You just keep evading my arguments, you won't listen to anything you don't like.'

'I haven't noticed any arguments. I love you. I don't want just any baby. I want your baby.'

'Well, I don't want a bloody baby and I don't want to get married and as you want both it follows that we must part.'

'We can't part.'

'If I could make you believe that we *could* the thing would be as good as done.'

'That is why I shall never believe it. We're each other's last chance.'

'I may be yours. You're certainly not mine, thank God! Look, Tommy, let me go. Let's have a clean slice not a bloody massacre.'

'You're never nice to me now—'

'How can I be nice when I'm trapped?'

'You aren't trapped or else everyone is. We could have freedom together if—'

'Who said anything about freedom?'

'You did, you said you were trapped.'

'I don't care a fuck about freedom, I don't think there is such a thing, I just don't like the sensation of being trussed.'

'After all, most marriages are second best, and—'

'When I don't want a marriage at all you hardly recommend this one by admitting it would be lousy!'

'I didn't say that, and it wouldn't be second best for me because I love you—'

'I don't want your love, Tomkins, so it gratifies not. I'm afraid this is not one of your clear-headed days.'

'But what's your reason for spoiling things?'

'There isn't a reason! Love can end. That's just one of the horrors of human life. My interest in you was purely physical anyway.'

'Oh you wicked liar! And there is a reason. It's Crystal.'

'It isn't Crystal. Just be careful, Tommy.'

'Is she going to marry Arthur Fisch?'

'No.'

'You won't let her.'

'Be careful. Do you want me to break something?'

'You think you can always defeat me by violence, don't you! Oh you should be so ashamed! I mended that little vase you broke. Look. Things can be mended.'

'Don't try and touch my heart, it isn't within your reach. You talk as if there were just one or two difficulties and if they were fixed we could live happily ever after, but everything's wrong here, everything! God, can't you see the difference between big things and little things? Perhaps no woman can.'

'Who's generalizing now?'

'Don't madden me. I just don't want to marry you, I don't even want to go to bed with you any more, very few human arrangements can last long and this one has run its course. There's nothing more to it, no secret motives, not even anything to argue about.'

'Why are we arguing then?'

'Because you won't face facts.'

'I'll tell you why we're arguing. Because we're bound together. You can't leave me. All you can do is talk about it. If you could go, you'd go. The arguing is instead, so that you can pretend to go and not go. Why don't you face a fact or two?'

'If you want to be shown what going is like—'

'All right. Do you mean that you won't come next Friday?'

After that there was silence, except for the wild west wind rather gently shaking the windows, as if afraid of its own strength, and pattering the panes with little ripples of rain. We had had, before dispute made eating impossible, the beginning of a supper (lamb cutlets and broccoli) and a good deal of wine. We were still drinking the wine. I had taught Tommy to drink. We were sitting at a round table covered by a pretty French table cloth, a brilliant red cloth thickly covered with tiny green leaves. The lamps glowed, perched among the bric-à-brac, it was like sitting in a shop. Tommy's small hand, the fingers covered with little enamel and silver rings, began to crawl across the table towards me. Tommy's question was a jerk of the noose. The situation had its own characteristic hopeless mechanical structure. A lot of what Tommy said was true. She had been a surprise package. After I had despaired of communication this soft-voiced clever little Scot had managed to get through. For she was clever. She argued quite well, she remembered things, one had to keep one's wits sharp, there was even a pleasure in arguing with her about leaving her. There was even a sense in which the argument was, as she said, a surrogate for the parting, at least tonight. With her grammar school education and her extensive vocabulary and her sharp little mind she might have been somebody if the theatre had not done for her. She was gallant and intelligent, she tried to coerce me with her words, not with her tears. We did indeed understand each other and this was rare and now that we had given up the sex act I still enjoyed the word act with her, simply the unusual experience of communicating. Only nothing further followed from this. With relentless authority my own special personal aloneness was calling me away, my own pain was calling me into its privacy, out of this irrelevant scene of minor gratifications. I wanted now to clean the whole business off myself and be done with it. It had become an idle nonsense. And yet : just tonight and because I was so tired I could not say that I was not coming next Friday. The achievement was beyond me.

'I'll come.'

'There you are! You see! You just like a skirmish!' She pronounced it 'skairmish'.

'No I don't. *Think* about what I said, will you. We've got to end this, Tommy. And it's no good talking about just being friends either. So long as we meet you'll go on loving me, and that's what's so hopeless, especially if you want a child. It's unfair to you.'

'You say that to pretend it's altruism!'

'What the hell does it matter what it is. We're finished. Now I'm going home.'

'You can't go, it's not ten yet.'

'If I stay I'll get angry and smash things. And you've got a cold.'

'I haven't. Go then. I'll see you tomorrow . . . at Crystal's . . . won't I?'

Once a month Crystal invited Tommy to a brief drink at six o'clock on a Saturday.

'Maybe. Don't you give that bloody cold to Crystal. If you find tomorrow morning—'

'Oh you do nothing but give orders and lay down rules!'

'Good night!'

I careered away down the stairs, pulling my mackintosh on as I went. Outside it was raining a small cold rain and the street lamps were spilling big blurry reflections onto the wet pavement. I set off walking north. I felt upset and alarmed. And tomorrow was Saturday. I was more connected with young Thomas than I had realized when I had decided, for such excellent reasons, to leave her. Had I ever considered marrying Tommy, stowing myself away as Tommy's husband, an equivalent of the suicide which I could not commit because of Crystal? No. Life does not end even with the most desperate of marriages, it prolongs itself drearily: new occasions for cruelty, a life of crime. I was not as bad as that. Besides, my bonds with Crystal made death by marriage equally unthinkable. Of course I had lied to Tommy at the start. I had implied too many encouraging half-truths, to pave the way to bed. I had got myself into a false position and, I suspected, would not be able to get out until I felt so frenzied by the pain of it that I would be prepared to use an axe. I knew soberly that I had not yet reached the axe-using stage. Meanwhile I could not afford to sympathize with Tommy: that awful withdrawal of sympathy, like our refusal to sympathize with the dying. But I would have to wait a little while yet before I could finally dispose of Thomasina Uhlmeister. There was moreover another factor. For reasons which I shall explain shortly I did not want to break with Tommy until I could see more clearly what Crystal felt about Arthur Fisch.

SATURDAY

'I SAY, Hilary, that Indian girl was here again last night.'
'What was she wearing?'

'A sort of long blue jacket and trousers with peacocks on.'

I had not noticed the peacocks, but it was clearly the same girl.

'Did she ring the bell?'

'No, she didn't. She didn't the other time either. She was just hanging about.'

'But she said she wanted me?'

'She did the other time, because I asked her if I could do anything.'

'And this time?'

'I said hello and she just smiled.'

'Mysterious. Did you remember to buy those candles?'

'Hell, no, I forgot again. I'm sorry.'

It was Saturday morning. I was in the kitchen ironing handkerchiefs. To avoid the torment of social life at the launderette I had bought a washing machine. I would not let Christopher use it. Of course Crystal would gladly have come over and washed and cleaned, and of course I would not let her. The flat was my private hell. It was only moderately filthy. Handkerchiefs were the only things which I ironed. Unironed handkerchiefs could lead to madness. Before that I had been browsing in a Danish dictionary over my toast and tea. (On week-days I breakfasted on two cups of tea. Toast was a week-end treat.) Before that I had attempted to shave, after having absently, while thinking about the past, squeezed all the shaving cream out into the basin and screwed the tube up into a twisted ball. It was now only nine-thirty. Sweet Christ help me until opening time.

Christopher had paid me some rent, not much, but it had improved our relations. He was sitting on the kitchen table swinging his legs and brushing his long golden hair, pausing every now and then to extract balls of glittering fuzz from the brush and drop them with care upon the floor. Brushing of hair always set my teeth on edge since experience at the orphanage but I said nothing because of the rent. We now, after the interlude recorded above, reverted to the sort of

45

conversation we usually had on Saturdays. I had admired
one of his mandalas and said he ought to have been a painter.
He had idiotically taken this seriously and said yes perhaps he
ought. I had told him he had not enough industry and self-
discipline to make himself anything. He said with revolting
humility that indeed he would never be a saint. I said hang
saint, he would never do anything properly. He said how true,
except live, which he implied I could not do. He said I was a
typical anxiety-ridden product of a competitive society and
ought to practise meditation to calm my nerves. I said I
would rather be anxious than drug myself with a lot of false
lying oriental mumbo-jumbo. He denied it was mumbo-
jumbo. I said if it were not mumbo-jumbo how was it he had
never been able to explain it to me in ordinary words.

'It's beyond words.'

'Pshaw!'

'I mean, it's like an experience, not a sort of belief.'

'What's it an experience of?'

'It's like mind is everything.'

'Is this electric iron mind and this handkerchief and this
gas stove?'

'Yes.'

'All part of the same mind?'

'Well, ultimately—'

'So the mental and the physical are really one?'

'Yes, you see—'

'And the difference between one mind and another is
merely apparent?'

'Well, yes, and—'

'So really nothing exists at all except one big mind?'

'Yes, but it's—'

'And you tell me that's not mumbo-jumbo?'

'But it's not like ordinary abstract thought—'

'I'll say. A man on the wireless last week was saying everything in the universe was determined in the first hundred
seconds after the Big Bang. He was lucid by comparison.'

'I know you dig concepts—'

'There's nothing else to dig.'

'But you see, the basis of all being is mental, I mean it's
got to be, so you are sort of in all things right from the start.
You see, I make that iron exist, I mean it looks different to a
spider, doesn't it?'

'But a spider is part of your mind too.'

'Yes, of course, and what the spider sees is part of my mind and then I realize that I don't really exist at all as me, I'm really everything and I have to try to experience everything as me —'

'I don't see why. Is this supposed to be moral? Why is it moral not to believe in a lot of separate things? Why is it moral only to believe in oneself? I thought morality was forgetting yourself and making careful distinctions and respecting the existence of other people.'

'But this is forgetting yourself and when you realize you are everything then you love everything and you're good automatically —'

'And even if we are all thoughts in the mind of God or whatever why should you be able to become God?'

'What's stopping me? You see God isn't a big person, you see it isn't personal at all, that's the point.'

'But we are persons.'

'No, we're not, that's just the old Christian nonsense, personality is an illusion.'

'Unless other people have definite structures they can't have definite rights. No wonder you don't want to vote. If nobody exists why bother.'

'You see, Christianity gets it wrong because of a personal God, it's the most anti-religious idea ever. The idea of God looking at you makes you feel you're a little real thing, a nitty gritty, whereas you must think that you are God, that you're universal mind, you see it's just the other way round, it's the female principle, you see Christianity is such a male-oriented religion, it's all about father, that's why unisex is so important, you see we in the West with our Jewish father figure civilization, I mean — How did you get on with your father, Hilary?'

'Fine.' Full fathom five my father lies, of his bones are coral made.

'What did he do?'

'He was a diver.'

'A *diver*?'

The front door bell rang. I went to the door, stepping over the wreckage of the telephone. I wondered if it was the Indian girl.

It was Mick Ladderslow and Jimbo Davis, both carrying cushions. Mick was a burly chap with reddish hair and huge glowing drugged eyes. He had great prestige because he had once got as far as Afghanistan where he contracted jaundice and was returned to England at Her Majesty's expense.

47

He marched into the flat without the ceremony of words. Possibly he grunted. Jimbo was slim and wriggly and apologetic with a long-lashed gentle expression. He rarely spoke beyond murmurs of 'yes . . . yes . . .', and confronted with human beings would drop in a bow, sagging a little at the knees, expressive of a sort of surprised respect. He now, whispering to me 'Yes, yes, Hilary, hello, yes', took hold of my hand (he always did this) and drew it downwards in an intimate sort of way as if he were about to press it against his thigh, more like a holding of hands than a shaking of hands. I suspected him of being sorry for me. I did not mind this in Jimbo. The two boys and their cushions (I suppose they were making some kind of nest in there) disappeared with Christopher into Christopher's room, and I returned to my ironing.

The front door bell rang. I went to the door. I wondered if it was the Indian girl. It was the porter, who said that the rubbish chute had been cleared at considerable expense to the management and that I would not be able to imagine the filth some people thought fit to pour down it and did I know that plastic bags had been invented just for this purpose to prevent rubbish chutes from becoming jammed and stinking because people with no more sense and manners than pigs threw their potato peelings down them without even the benefit of a bit of newspaper? I replied with suitable spirit to this rhetorical question. The Saturday wrangle with the porter was mechanical and regular and today neither of us had our heart in it. I went back to my ironing, completed it, and began rather feebly to sweep the kitchen floor. The floor was coated with grease and needed washing, indeed scraping. I propelled a cluster of bread crumbs over the greasy surface. When opening time came I would be off to the pub, possibly to the bar at Sloane Square (the Liverpool Street one was closed at weekends), if I felt like riding the trains for a while, or else to one of the locals, where I would spin out my drinking time, have a late sandwich and face the horrors of the afternoon. I could do my weekly shopping, buy a few tins and some sliced bread. Then in summer I often dozed in the park. In winter I might return to the Inner Circle, or else go home and to bed and to sleep until the pubs opened again, a device which appalled Christopher who felt a genuine moral horror at this wilful waste of consciousness.

The front door bell rang. I went to the door. I wondered if it was the Indian girl. It was a strange thin young man with long straggly hair and an orange moustache, wearing faded jeans. I said, 'You want Christopher?'

'What?'

'You want Christopher?'

'Do I?' A comic.

'Well make up your mind.'

'What do you mean, make up your mind? Who is Christopher anyway?'

'My lodger.'

'What are we talking about?'

'Goodbye,' I said, beginning to close the door, only the young man had put his foot in it.

'Wait a mo, wait a mo. Are you Mr Burde?'

'Yes.' Another mysterious person looking for me.

'Well, just think. I'll let you guess who I am. Just guess.'

'Look,' I said, 'I don't like guessing games and I don't like people who put their foot in my door, it's a nasty habit. Either explain yourself or fuck off.'

'Dear me, what naughty language! Now just think. Did you or did you not ring up yesterday to ask if somebody could come round to remove your telephone?'

'Oh—why didn't you say so?'

'I didn't have a chance, did I? You were on about Christopher as soon as you opened the door. Hello. Are you Christopher?'

The telephone engineer greeted Christopher who had just emerged, opening a vista of Mick and Jimbo reclining.

'My name's Len.'

'He's the telephone engineer,' I explained.

'Now, what's your problem. Bless me, look at that, it looks as if you've had the IRA in here, what a shambolic scene, whatever occurred?'

'I pulled it out,' I said.

'Pulled it out! I'll say you did. An unprovoked attack on a poor little defenceless telephone that was minding its own business and not harming anybody. The junction box busted, the handset smashed into little pieces. You realize you'll have to pay for all this, don't you? It's not your property you know. Kind old Mother Post Office only lends you these gadgets, my, my! And think of all the poor people wanting telephones. Wilful damage to a perfectly good up-to-the-minute handset, why it's a crime, makes me feel quite faint. Do you think I could have a cup of tea?'

I retired into my bedroom. By this time Mick and Jimbo had emerged from the nest. All four boys went into the kitchen and I heard animated voices and the clatter of crockery. They were at once a fraternity. Here at any rate class no longer existed. The Beatles, like Empedocles, had thrown all things about. At their age I was a fierce tormented solipsist. I lay down on my bed and wondered if I should try to sleep until they were open. By some miraculous retardation of the pace of the expanding universe it was not yet ten o'clock. So far so good, however. I had not yet pulled the curtains back and the bedside light was still on. I switched it off. I closed my eyes and an awful cinematograph show of events out of the past started up automatically. I tried as usual to preserve myself by thinking about Crystal the way some people with such problems think about the Virgin Mary. Only now the saving image did not rise alone, another rose with it. Arthur.

The front door bell rang. I got up and went to the door. I wondered if it was the Indian girl. It was Laura Impiatt.

This was unusual but not totally unprecedented. 'Come in, Laura. The place is almost full but there's room for you.'

Laura was looking her most energetic and eccentric, her greyish hair streaming back and front onto her shoulders from under a beret which had been pulled down well over her ears. Beneath a voluminous grey cloak a tweed skirt reached her ankles. 'I *say*, Hilary, it's *cold* out, *winter* has come. Oh it's *warm* in here, oh how *nice*!'

'Come in. Unfortunately the only place where I can entertain you is my bedroom. The boys have jammed the sitting-room with furniture, there is no room for human beings.'

Laura followed me into my darkened bedroom. I switched on the light and kicked a lot of clothing under the bed and drew the crumpled coverlet up over the crumpled sheets and blankets. I felt no embarrassment. Why? Because I was depraved, saintly? Or because of some sort of merit, decency, calm, warmth of heart in Laura? I recalled Tommy's idea that Laura was 'after me'. Nonsense.

'Hilary, could we have some daylight? There is some you know.'

'Not much here.' I pulled back the curtains and the grey light of the dark inner well sheeted the windows like gauze but did not enter. 'Is it raining?'

'No, rainy and cold but quite bright. Do turn off that lamp, it looks awful. May I put my cloak here? Who's chattermagging in the kitchen?'

'Christopher, Mick, Jimbo and one Len, a telephone engineer.'

'How *young* they are. It makes one feel ancient.'

'Golden lads and lasses must like electricians come to dust. You however are eternally young. I love that swirling skirt. You look like Natasha Rostova just in from a brisk walk along the Nevsky Prospect.'

'Silly *dear* Hilary.'

'What a nice party on Thursday.'

'Did you think so? I find Clifford Larr a bit depressing. We'd have had more fun by ourselves.'

'Fun? What's that?'

'Hilary, you're not to go off into one of your *things*. I know you want me to mother you, but I won't.'

'Aaargh.'

'Yes, you do. I understand you better than you imagine. I can read you like a book. You lead a selfish shut-in life. You're afraid of anything new. You ought to try and do things for others now and then instead of just expecting people to look after you.'

'You'll always look after me though, won't you? Take me out of myself. Just grab and pull.'

I was sitting on the bed. Laura, dressed in a high-necked white blouse and the ankle-length brown skirt (she was too plump for this gear) was sitting in an upright chair, her tweedy knees about nine inches from my knees. Her face was rather indistinct in the murky gauzy light, but I could see her brown eyes glowing, even moist perhaps, with fearful sympathy. Why did I automatically, by stupid flippant badinage, evoke these feelings in Laura? I did it every time. That fearful sympathy, that frightful energy. Yet I felt at home with her, that was the trouble. She calmed me.

'I wish you'd really tell me about yourself sometime, Hilary.' Laura often expressed this wish.

'I thought you could read me like a book.'

'I can't see your past. How did you get that scar on your chin, for instance? I feel sure there's something which it would do you good to tell me.'

'My past is boring. No sins or crimes. Only the selfishness upon which you kindly animadverted.'

'And I'd like to talk to you about Tommy. Oh if I could only get you *talking*!'

'I chatter artlessly in your presence.'

'You do nothing artlessly. You use words as a hiding place. You're always *hiding*. But what from? Anyway I didn't really come to see you at all. I came about the panto. I want to talk to Christopher. I wonder if we could persuade him to write us a song? And Freddie thought he might invent a sort of happening for the finale.'

'Like setting fire to the theatre. Excellent.'

(Example of one of Christopher's happenings designed for a garden party. Each guest was enclosed in a huge brown paper bag and told to stay quiet until a trumpet blew and then tear his way out. The point was that there was no trumpet and after a long and agonizing silence the guests began to react in a variety of ways. There was a lot of embarrassment and annoyance and impromptu play-acting. The event ended in a most appropriate manner when the paper bags blew away across the main road and stopped the traffic and the police arrived.)

'I want to talk to the boys anyway about the drug scene. I'm writing another article. I feel like a probation officer to these kids.'

The front door bell rang. Closing Laura in, I went to the door. I wondered if it was the Indian girl. It was Tommy.

Tommy in a red mackintosh and matching hat, her dark ringlets unravelled into rats' tails by the wind, opened her little mouth in a beseeching prayerful O. 'Hilary, I know I'm not supposed to—'

There was an absolute rule about no visits at the flat. And Tommy would arrive when Laura was in my bedroom. I felt blind exasperated head-mislaying rage. I pulled her inside and we both stumbled over the trailing telephone wires. I pushed her in through the door of the sitting-room and squeezed in after her and closed the door. There was just space enough for us to stand hemmed in by the furniture. My shoulder grazed a table which was standing on another table and there was a small crash. I pinned Tommy against the door, gripping her by both arms and pressing her violently back, squeezing the flesh as hard as I could and I *whispered*, 'I told you—never to come—never to come like this—I told you—'

Tommy's small mouth remained open and her long innocent grey eyes filled instantly with tears. Her hat was tilted awry by the pressure of her head against the door. I thrust her back, pressing upon her arms, as if I wanted to drive her body back through the wood or flatten her like an insect. She uttered a little whining gasp of pain. I went on whispering, 'I told you never to come here, I told you—'

The front door bell rang. I released Tommy and sidled out

of the room and closed her in. I went to the front door. I wondered if it was the Indian girl. It was the Indian girl.

I did not hesitate for a second. One hand reached for my overcoat, the other drew the front door to behind me. I did not even look at my visitor, nor did I wait for the lift. I passed her, crossing the landing to the stairs, and as I did so I plucked peremptorily at the sleeve of her blue jacket. I began to run down the stairs, hearing the light patter of her feet running behind me. In less than a minute after the sound of the front door bell we were outside in the street, where by some miracle a great bright blue rainy light was shining.

We were walking along the northern walk of Kensington Gardens in the direction of the Serpentine. I wondered briefly how long the two women, like the people in Christopher's paper bags, would stay quietly in their rooms, unaware of each other's presence. I had still not looked at my mysterious pursuer. Crossing the main road I had held her sleeve, not her arm. Not a word had been said, we walked onward in silence.

No sun was shining but there was a great diffused brightness over the park. The asphalt paths, wet from earlier rain, shone with a blue glow, full of shadowy reflections. The damp light bestowed a faintly lurid clarity. To our right the russet vistas disclosed Watts's Bronze Horseman, Speke's obelisk. A chill wind moved the brown leaves in steady droves, then plastered them flat upon the asphalt. Most of the trees were bare now, only a few oaks retained their withered foliage. Looking like huge vines, the plane trees held up their bobbled fruit against the radiant clouded sky. Excited by the damp electrical atmosphere, distant dogs ecstatically raced.

I felt detached, extraordinary, as if a calm doom had come. I now looked at the Indian girl and she looked at me and smiled. Today she was wearing a black mackintosh and black trousers. A sodden blue scarf (she must have been walking in the rain) which had covered her head, had been pushed back onto her shoulders. Her long plait was inside her mac. Her

53

face and hair were damp. Her features, though more irregular, less spiritual, than they had seemed in my first vision, had the bony refinement of her race. Her eyes were very dark and luminous and expressed some emotion. (Surely not pity? Simply a desire to please?) Her mouth, rather thin, rather long, was almost abstract in its delicacy, and hardly more highly pigmented than its surroundings. The whole face was pale, pale, the palest creamy brown, with that uniform pallor which far outpales the banal pink and white of coarser races.

As we neared the Serpentine I said, 'Well?'

She simply smiled again.

I said, 'Look here, you started this. Hadn't you better explain yourself, Miss Mukerji, or whatever your name is? You came to me, not I to you. You were looking for me, weren't you? Hilary Burde is my name.'

'Oh yes—I know.' Her voice was something of a surprise. I had expected the chi-chi accent, so unmistakable, so indelible, so charming. But this was an English voice, even, as I later discovered, with traces of London vowels.

'Well, what do you want?'

She smiled, flashing excellent teeth, and made a sort of helpless gesture, raising her eyebrows, as if my question were unexpected, complex, difficult.

'I mean,' I said, 'I don't want to be tiresome, but if, out of all the men in London, you sought for me there must have been some reason, maybe something which I can do for you. But if you won't tell me what it is I can do I can't do it, can I?' I wondered if she was a little deranged, a mad girl. The speculation was uncanny.

'I just wanted to know you.'

'But why? Why me? How did you even know my name?'

'I knew it. I wanted to see you. To talk to you. That's all.'

I said, 'Are you a tart?' This was a little abrupt, but her vague smiling replies were unnerving me.

She seemed upset at this suggestion. 'No, of course not.'

'Well I can't make you out. Do you want money?'

'No, no.'

'What *do* you want then?'

'To know you,' she said again.

We had now passed the little fountain of two bears embracing (which Crystal so much liked when I brought her there once) and reached the mysterious stone garden at the end of the lake which always seemed to me to be part of some other city (Leningrad?) or else a camouflaged entrance to some strange region (Acheron?). Urns enclose five octagonal pools and a little stone pavilion faces between more distant nymphs the tree-fringed curve of the lake. In summer fountains play. In winter the place is pleasantly derelict. We crossed the slippery pavement and sat down on a rather damp seat. Some pigeons and sparrows approached with desultory hope.

'What's your name, Miss Mukerji?' I did not expect her to tell me.

She replied at once, 'Alexandra Bissett.'

'Alexandra Bissett? No, no, there are limits, you can't look like that and be called Alexandra Bissett!'

'My father was an English officer. My mother was a Brahmin.'

'I see. That makes you some sort of princess, I think. Where were you born?'

'In Benares.'

'Well, Miss Bissett—'

'Please call me—'

'Alexandra?'

'No, no one calls me that. They call me Biscuit.'

'Biscuit?'

'Yes. I was called Bissett. Then Chocolate Biscuit. Then just Biscuit.'

'Who are "they"?'

'Who—they—?'

'You say they call you Biscuit. Who are they?'

'My—friends—'

The voice, the manner, eluded classification. She did not seem quite like an educated person, there was a certain awkward simplicity. Yet she had a confident dignified directness which was itself a sign of culture, and there was none of the giggling forwardness of an amateur whore. She smiled, obviously amused at my puzzlement.

'But Biscuit,' I said. 'Why me? *Why me?*'

'I saw you on the tube train. Perhaps.'

'Yes, perhaps. And perhaps I was wearing a placard round my neck with my name on it. And perhaps you decided at once that I was the most attractive man in London. I know I'm a big handsome chap—well big anyway. But no, that won't do. Try again.'

'I saw you in the bar at Sloane Square.'

'Maybe you did. But why did you follow me home and how did you know my name? Biscuit—look—may I hold your hand?' I took a cautious firm hold of her long delicate hand, so frail that it felt as if it might break in my grasp. And as I took her hand I felt a stirring of the old crude male desire which had been present before but diffused in wonderment.

She laughed awkwardly. If I had still thought her a designing tart that laugh alone would have proved me wrong. She turned her head away, pressed my hand back with surprisingly strong fingers, and then withdrew her hand, moving a little away from me and standing up. 'I must go now.'

'Biscuit! You can't go! You haven't even called me Hilary!'

'Should I?'

'Yes, of course. If I call you Biscuit you must call me Hilary. That's a rule.'

'Hilary—'

'Good. And now you're going to come along with me and have a drink and then some lunch and tell me what this mystery is all about.'

'No, I must go. I have to be back.'

'Back where? Why? Have you got to go to *them*?'

'I don't understand. I must go. Forgive me. Oh, yes, forgive me.' She sounded a little foreign at last.

'I won't forgive you if you just go away. Where do you live? Where can I find you? When shall I see you again? I *will* see you again, won't I? Biscuit, please—'

'Yes. Again. Yes.'

'Promise me. Swear to me. Swear by—by Big Ben.'

She laughed. 'I swear by Big Ben that I will see you again.'

'Give me your address.'

'No.'

'Let me give you something. Something to prove later that it wasn't all a dream. Oh God—what—' Standing now, I leaned down and picked a stone off the wet pavement. It was a blackish smooth elliptical stone. I gave it to her.

She displayed more emotion than at any previous moment. 'Oh thank you, thank you, so much—'

'Actually I need the proof, not you. Let me see you to where you're going.'

'No. You must stay here. I shall go away.'

'But how shall I ever find you? Will you come to me again, will you come to my flat?'

'Yes, I will come.'

'Because of Big Ben.'

'Yes, yes.'

'When?'

'I must go. You stay here.' She began to walk away from me, backwards at first, then looking back over her shoulder, as if riveting me to the spot with her glance. She walked away, holding the stone in her hand, holding it clear of the swinging skirt of her black mackintosh. She disappeared from view at last behind the stone pavilion at the head of the courtyard, vanishing in the direction of the Bayswater Road. As soon as she was gone I began to run. I darted round the corner, to the park gate. She must have started to run at the same moment. There was no sign of her among the people moving in both directions along the wet crowded pavements. I hurried up and down and searched and looked for some minutes, but there was no sign of her. She was gone.

Saturday was my day for Crystal. I usually went there fairly early, about six-thirty. Once a month, Tommy, arriving separately (she was not allowed to arrive with me) came in for a brief drink, disappearing at my nod about ten past seven. So as not to miss any minutes of my valuable presence she invariably arrived first. She and Crystal were not designed by nature to understand or like each other, but they were good girls and they loved me so they had to get on. They were both possessive about me of course, but with deep tact they had sorted out their spheres of influence so that there was almost no conflict. The tact was mostly on Tommy's part in fact. She occupied the junior position and she had the intelligence to appreciate the absolute nature of my relation to Crystal. Tommy knew that a foot wrong in that respect and she would be finished. She never put a foot wrong. I should say that I had told Tommy a little about my childhood but only in vague general terms and, so far as it was possible, without emotional colour. Of course Crystal and Tommy never had confidential chats. They would both have been far too frightened to do so. But as I say, they were good girls and they were kind to each other.

I was in a strange mood. The baffling events of the morning had filled me with a kind of nervous exhilaration. Laura had

57

said that I hated new things. This was not entirely true. I did not initiate change but I could still be refreshed by it. What a beautiful and strange visitation and what could it mean? Very occasionally in my life something, it might be almost anything, it could be something much more trivial than this, disturbed me with some sense of a possible salvation. Must every sign be sinister, every unexpected visitor be from the secret police? Were there no more bright innocent surprises to prick the weary and depraved hide? But perhaps, indeed it was most likely, the whole business would prove to be neither delightful nor menacing but just senseless. Perhaps I had already had the best of Biscuit. Perhaps I had already had all of her. And now, as I approached the North End Road that evening, a deep apprehension about Crystal began to absorb my mind and the strange image of the Indian girl faded away.

Crystal's room was quite big and could have been pleasant if she had had the faintest idea how to embellish it. There was a bright centre light and also a dim lamp with a parchment shade, portraying a scorched galleon, which was turned on for guests. There was the wooden table, which only had a cloth on on Saturdays, and a sideboard of shiny veneered wood with a row of ebony elephants upon it. There was Crystal's little narrow bed with a green satin bedspread. There were two junk shop armchairs and three upright chairs and a thin dark trampled carpet which seemed to be growing upon the floor. The faded wallpaper had a design which it was hard to believe that any sentient, let alone rational, being could have invented. There was a wireless set but no television. I would not let Crystal have television. She might have picked up a few facts from it, but better decent ignorance than such a teacher. Also I connected television with the orphanage where I had become an addict, and deprivation of it had been a regular punishment far more effective than thrashing.

As I came in the two women rose. Tommy looked very nervous and anxious until reassured by some ineffable feature of my manner. They could both read me as dogs read their master, probably noticing tiny traits of behaviour of which I was myself unconscious.

'I told you not to come,' I said to Tommy. 'You've got a cold.'

'I haven't got a cold,' said Tommy bravely. 'You've just got a silly phobia about colds, hasn't he?' She was perky and
58

timidly uppish because she saw that I was sorry I had hurt her in the morning.

'If Crystal gets that cold there'll be trouble.'

'I don't think Tommy's got a cold,' said Crystal.

They both smiled at me. I threw off my coat and sat down at the table which had been covered with a white lace cloth in my honour. I felt a bit better. Every occasion of entering Crystal's presence was an access of brightness, a lightening of the load. They sat down too and Crystal poured out a third glass of sherry for me.

'Is it still raining?'

'Yes.'

I knew that Tommy would have said nothing to Crystal about what had happened that morning at my flat, nothing about the way I had received her, nothing about my sudden departure, nothing about whatever had happened (whatever that had been, another subject for anxiety) after I had gone. I had trained Tommy well. Equally of course she would make no reference to such matters now. There were in fact so many subjects which the three of us could not discuss, and *a fortiori* which Tommy and Crystal could not discuss, that it might have seemed that conversation would languish. However we always chattered easily enough about trivialities, and I imagine Crystal and Tommy did the same when I was not there.

'What's the weather forecast?'

'Rain, and colder.'

'The shops are getting ready for Christmas already.'

'They are beginning to put up the decorations in Regent Street.'

I detested the subject of Christmas and steered off it. 'Show me the stuff your new lady brought.'

'Oh yes! I was just showing it to Tommy.'

Crystal took the stuff from a box on the bed and spread it on the table. The design was a close relation of the wallpaper. 'Isn't it lovely?'

'Lovely.'

Crystal folded the stuff into the box and took it away into the little kitchen where she kept her materials in a trunk.

Tommy was sitting next to me with her skirt hitched up displaying those long perfect legs. (Quite unconsciously. She was, apart from Crystal, the most uncoquettish woman I had ever met.) (Crystal's legs were like tree stumps.) She now began to roll up the sleeve of her jersey, and looking at me meaningfully, displayed two large dark spotty bruises just above the elbow. I looked at the bruises and then at her face. She knew at once she had done wrong. Any surreptitious behaviour or hint of secrets was absolutely taboo. Also I was prepared to be sorry, but not to be grossly reminded of my fault. I frowned. Tommy hastily pulled down her sleeve. Crystal returned.

'Well—' I said, and almost imperceptibly nodded, the sign for Tommy to go.

She got up hastily, her face stiffened, on the verge of tears. 'I must go now. Thank you so much, Crystal.'

I watched Tommy put on her raincoat. She was struggling hard to repress the tears and succeeding. They would have constituted yet another serious crime.

'Good-bye—' in a trembling voice.

I let her make for the door. 'Good night, Tommy dear.'

Relief. Mercy had prevailed. 'Good night—Hilary—see you next week—and I'll write Monday as usual. Good night then.'

Of course Crystal made no comment on the fact that I had sent Tommy away half an hour early.

Crystal and I now faced each other.

I should make it clear that there was nothing physical in my relation with Crystal. (Except in the sense, which I must leave to the reader to determine, that anything mental is physical.) I did not want to go to bed with her or kiss her or caress her or even touch her more than minimally. (Though if I had been told that I could never touch her I should have gone mad.) I did not 'find her attractive'. I simply was her. I had to have her there, like God. And by 'there' I mean again, not necessarily in my presence. I needed to see her regularly but not very often. She just had to be always available in a place fixed and controlled by me. I had to know, at any moment, where she was. I needed her sequestered innocence, as a man might want his better self to be stored away separately in a pure deity. Did I want her to remain a virgin? Yes.

None of all this however decided anything about Arthur. I wanted Crystal to go on forever being whatever it was she was to me, but I also wanted her to be happy, and had perhaps too long been content with the formula that her happiness was to make me happy, or as near to it as I could ever be, which was certainly not very near, since the Oxford smash up. Of course Crystal had not married because of me, though this too could be a little hazed over by the thought that she was the old maid type anyway and being no beauty would never have been likely to have suitors. There had been in fact one or two, a chap in the north and a Canadian in London, but I thought poorly of them and Crystal never really took them seriously at all. A few years ago I had actually been settling down to the comfortable feeling that the dangerous time was over and Crystal had passed the marrying age. Then somehow, as I explained earlier, I had begun to see a new picture. Two things had come up to change the world. One was that Crystal wanted a child. This surprised me, and how she had put it into my head I do not know. She never said so in plain words, but I was by now thoroughly aware of it. The other thing of course was Arthur.

If Arthur had been either wonderful or impossible the situation would have been a good deal easier. As it was Arthur was not at all what I would have chosen (but then what would I have chosen, would I ever have chosen?), yet he was a possibility. He was not clever or impressive or rich (but then someone clever or impressive or rich would not have loved Crystal). Arthur was indeed something of a 'wet'. He was not notably vertebrate and could hardly look after himself, so how could he look after Crystal? I was not so sunk in egoism that I could not see that Crystal's life was dreary. In an abstract way I wanted her to go away and be saved and not to be damned with me, and yet of course I did not and could not want her to go away. If she could have been metamorphosed into a happy well-off wife and mother living in a big country house with a huge garden and six dogs (she wanted a dog, I never let her have one) I should have been, not pleased, but satisfied that this had to be and also somehow glad of a new happiness for her; at least, this was what I sometimes imagined when no such thing was in prospect. I had intended to transform her life, I had intended to transform her mind, but I had failed, and this was the fundamental and awful failure for which I should be damned. I had, I suppose, pulled her up a little way out of the Aunt Bill caravan world, but only a little way. I had never, as I once meant to, educated her. Crystal knew her Bible, but she did not know who Tolstoy was or whether Cromwell lived before or after Queen Elizabeth. In this respect Arthur was not exactly a foothold. Arthur's rag-tag of junkies and criminals whom he 'helped' (or was victimized by) led straight back into the world I myself was about to enter when I was rescued by Mr Osmand. I felt a horror of that world and I did not want the smell of it to come near Crystal ever again. What was Arthur himself anyway? A poor clerk with no talents and no prospects. Would Arthur be strong enough to protect Crystal? Arthur was a muddler. He might even become some sort of drop-out. Would not a marriage with him mean some ultimate subsidence into confusion and poverty and thereby misery? Married life if not organized is hell. Neither of these two could organize themselves out of a wet paper bag. Although it might not be so thrilling, there was a kind of purity and cleanness about Crystal's present position which I knew was a support to her; and protected by me she felt perfectly secure. Would she be strong enough to exist as Arthur's wife, to become the (oh God) quite different person Arthur's wife would be? On the other (to all this) hand, Arthur was thoroughly decent and he loved her and it had begun to look as if perhaps she could love him; only of course everything ultimately depended on me.

My relations with Tommy had begun before Arthur became important on Crystal's scene, and it was a cause of bitter pain to me to think that that entanglement had possibly in some way encouraged the other. Unfortunately these dramas had proceeded at a different pace. I never deliberately isolated my sister, I introduced her to some few of my few friends, but it had never hitherto happened that any friend of mine had really become a friend of hers. Arthur, however, with some diffidence and caution I must admit (for he feared me) did begin to move in, and this was made easier by the fact that I was then so involved with Tommy and was seeing less of Crystal. Something which I could never measure was the *fright* which I had then perhaps given to Crystal by some seeming desertion of her. Had this fright created a space, a need? This question, from which my mind recoiled in horror, was by now perhaps of historical interest only. What was more crucial was this. I had been watching Crystal anxiously to see if she ever showed signs of getting married, and of course (though naturally she never breathed a word about it) Crystal was watching me anxiously to see if I ever showed signs of getting married. I had earlier on told Crystal in the most forthright terms that I would never marry. (I did not notice then, but did later, that she did not offer me a similar resolution.) And for a long time it seemed to me as if I was perfectly right about myself, and my bachelor existence had become a steady and established fact. Then I fell in love with Tommy. I was not of course 'really' (totally) in love, but I was physically in love in a way which I had not imagined ever again to be possible. And although this love had ceased its consequences remained. Crystal knew that I *could* love, and so could conceivably want to marry. She even now perhaps thought that I wanted to marry Tommy. She knew that Tommy and I had our difficulties and she had seen them on display before tonight. But I had never told her that I did *not* want to marry Tommy, and I had refrained from telling her for a good reason. Crystal was quite capable of sacrificing Arthur, even if she wanted desperately to become his wife, if she felt that I was opposed to the marriage. To say she was quite capable understates the matter. She would have no hesitation, it would be at the drop of a hat, the hat need not even begin to fall. And so of course I had done my best to conceal my thoughts, even if possible not to formulate them. Equally this state of mind in Crystal presupposed her knowledge of a similar state of mind in me where a possible marriage with Tommy was concerned. Crystal knew that her marriage with Arthur would facilitate my marriage with Tommy, assuming that I wanted to marry Tommy, just as my marriage with Tommy would facilitate hers with Arthur, assuming she wanted to marry Arthur. Now I had no intention of marrying Tommy, only I was not going to tell Crystal this, because I wanted Crystal to be able to make up her mind about Arthur without being crippled by anxieties about leaving me abandoned. The danger of the whole situation was of course this, that there was the possibility of a catastrophic altruistic error *à deux*! That is, we might each of us do what we did not want to do so as to help the other to do what he (she) did not want to do either.

None of all this needless to say was coming to utterance as we sat at the table after Tommy's almost tearful departure. I poured the remainder of Tommy's sherry into my glass. I opened the bottle of wine which I had brought along as usual and placed it in front of the electric fire. Then after a little while Crystal got up and began to warm our supper and put it on the table (scrambled eggs and baked beans, followed by stewed apples and cream) and we were talking.

'Are you all right, darling?'

'Yes, I'm fine. Are you all right?'

'Yes, fine. I'm so glad about Christmas.'

'I'm not! And I don't think it should begin in November.'

'Well, everything's nicer when you can think about Christmas. I so much want to see the Christ Child in Regent Street.'

'The Christ Child in Regent Street?'

'Yes, the decorations. They've got such a lovely thing of the Christ Child in lights. I thought perhaps you might take me, like we did once?'

'And we had dinner in that grand restaurant after, do you remember?'

'Oh, I did love that. And they had black bread.'

'I don't remember the bread.'

'Well, it was almost black. Oh, I meant to tell you, there's this new health food shop—'

'*Health food?*'

'But it's nice, it has nice things, I got some special brown sugar and a special loaf which they said—'

'Crystal, for God's sake don't start buying fancy foods. Ordinary food is good enough for us.'

'All right, dearest—'

'These places just exist to sell expensive rubbish to silly women.'

'I'm sorry, I won't—'

'Come now, dear, I'm not really vexed. Tell me about your new lady. Do you think she'll ask you to do other things?'

We talked about Crystal's lady. This lady knew another lady and if the cocktail costume was a success there might be quite a stream of ladies. Crystal told me about bargains she had found when shopping for 'linings', then about something she had heard on the wireless about dogs. I told her about the office pantomime. We talked about what we would do when we went to Regent Street. I reminded her of the little fountain of the embracing bears and said we would go there again one day. I did not tell her about Biscuit. Told as a story this would sound rather weird and might frighten her. It would have spoilt the cheerful silliness of the chatter in which Crystal and I expressed our love. Tonight however this was spoilt in any case, since I increasingly knew that I would have at last to raise the question of Arthur. It was not clear why this was *now* necessary, but, as a result of secret silent movements in both our minds, it was so, and we both knew it as we smiled at each other and reminisced about the horrid old days in the caravan. About Oxford of course we never spoke.

Crystal was wearing a shapeless dove-grey woollen dress with a green scarf tied round the collar. This suited her more than most of her clothes. Her thick fuzzy orangy hair, more like a kind of solid stuff than anything composed of strands, was pushed well back behind her ears, and her big much-chewed lower lip was prominent and moist. Her big golden eyes, appearing even larger behind the thick spectacles, were troubled with emotion but maddeningly obscured. Her small plump hands danced on the tablecloth, collecting crumbs and fingering them to pieces. The traffic gurgled jerkily in the North End Road. She was staring at me and wondering whether to touch my hand which was lying near to hers on the table. I felt in an anguish of irritation.

'Crystal—'

'Yes, Hilary—'

We always called each other by endearments or else by our names, never by nicknames. I think Crystal's name meant a lot to her. Crystal Burde. It had been a talisman, a sort of strange consoling thing of beauty in her life: a significant fragment of a splendour past or to come. My name, I felt, derived from hers by some sort of linguistic law, and it was she alone who beautified it.

'Crystal, I—I saw Arthur in the office yesterday.' This was fairly obvious, since I saw Arthur in the office every week-day.

'Oh yes.'

'You are rather fond of Arthur, aren't you?'

'Yes—yes—'

'Crystal, you would like to marry Arthur, wouldn't you?'

I had not, a second beforehand, intended to ask this terrifying question, or to ask it in this form.

The round spectacles regarded me, then turned away. 'You put it—as if—'

'As if I expected the answer yes?'

She said nothing, and after a pause, trying to keep calm, I said, 'Well, I do expect it. Am I right?'

Crystal's hand was now touching mine, her knuckles brushing the back of my hand making trails in the long black hair. I made no responsive movement. Crystal said, 'You know that all I care about is you and your happiness.'

'OK, and all I care about is you and your happiness. Crystal, we mustn't just mesmerize each other here. Things do happen, times do change, and even we two have our separate histories. You could be happy with Arthur, you could have a real house and children. It's no fun for you living like this.'

'Fun?' said Crystal, withdrawing her caressing hand. 'Fun? Do you think I care about that? My life here—' She could not find the words. 'Oh, you know—'

I knew. 'I want you to marry and be happy,' I said. Was there a shade too much pressure in this? Would she think I was saying it because of Tommy? Oh *God*.

'I am happy.'

I'll leave it here, I thought. I have said enough to open the door for her if she wants to go through it. Oh let her not want to. Better not let the talk come round to Tommy. Get away now.

'You want to get married too, after all,' said Crystal.

'So you *do* want to get married?' I said.

'I didn't say so—'

'You said "too".'

Crystal, gathered away into herself, staring now at the tablecloth, gave out a sort of shuddering sigh.

'All right. Yes. I do want to get married, I think perhaps I do—want to get married to Arthur—I suppose—'

I had tried to imagine that she might conceivably say this, or I had thought that I had tried, but the shock was very violent and I had to concern myself at once with concealing it. 'I see,' I said quickly, 'good, good—'

'But I don't really want it,' said Crystal, who was now watching me carefully, 'I don't want it *at all* if you would anyhow, for a second, prefer us to go on like this. You talked of changes and I thought perhaps—you see—well, I care for Arthur, but compared with you Arthur is nothing. I thought you might prefer—'

'Never mind about me.'

'Oh don't be—silly—how could I ever possibly be happy if I had not been and done whatever you wanted?'

'Whatever you do,' I said, 'you will be and do that. I'm so glad—I really am glad—that you've decided—about Arthur—at last.'

We stared at each other, both appalled.

'I haven't decided,' said Crystal in a whisper.

'Yes, you have. Be brave, Crystal,' I said. 'Write to him if you want to, tell him!'

After a silence she said, 'So you will marry Tommy.' She uttered this flatly, not as a question.

This was the corner into which I had prayed not to be

driven. I replied with a light briskness. 'I expect so. Maybe, maybe not. Like you I'm not much of a decider.'

Crystal sighed again, her lower lip trembling.

'Oh God,' I said at last, 'oh God, if I could only see inside your mind!'

'If I could only see inside yours!'

Crystal took her glasses off. Huge glittering tears were filling her eyes and leaping off her plump cheeks onto the tablecloth. I watched her for a moment. I imagined myself kneeling on the floor, as I had so often done when we were children, and grimacing like a devil into the folds of her skirt. I kept calm.

'Oh, Crystal, cut it out, cut it out, dear, cut it out.'

MONDAY

ON MONDAY winter had really come. Monday was one of those yellow days which are so very Londonish, not exactly foggy, but pervaded from late dawn to early dusk by a uniform fuzzy damp cold dirty yellowish haze. Sunday was windy, the last fling of the wild west wind before he had business elsewhere. Monday was still.

Sunday produced no noteworthy events. I stunned Christopher by spending the whole day at home. I did this because I thought it possible that Biscuit might call. But she did not. (Had *they* locked her up?) She would have been a distraction and I needed one. I lay on my bed hour after hour waiting for her (waiting for what?) and reflecting about Crystal. The terrible thing had happened, it seemed. It had at last become *fairly* clear (or had it?) that Crystal really did in some sense want to marry Arthur; and if this was so the insane-making possibility that I would be sacrificing my own interests for nothing would at least be excluded. Had I been keeping Crystal all these years in a cage from which she would be glad to escape? No, it was not like that. She had been sincere when she had described herself as 'happy'. But with an impressive and surprising resolution she had been capable too of conjuring up other possibilities. I may have seemed in these pages (so far: and there will be no improvement) to be a monster of egoism, but I was just capable of willing Crystal's happiness as something separate from my own. The idea of her marriage sliced into me like a knife. It was not exactly jealousy. Crystal had said 'compared with you, Arthur is nothing' and that I knew was the truth. It was just a sense of utter dereliction, the end of the world, the vanishing forever of some absolute security, some indefeasible right to be protected and cherished. So many things would change, I dared not list them, and would these changes not rip me and leave me in tatters? Did Crystal herself realize what her marriage would involve? Possibly not. Against these desperate thoughts I kept thrusting forward the idea of Crystal's happiness. When we had talked after her weeping I had seen (or imagined?) some shadow of pleasure in her, as if she were suddenly amazed at herself for conceiving of another

68

mode of being, and not just the endless round of Thursdays and Saturdays. I hated the sight of that shadow; and yet if I were to press her to this action, it was as well to know that I was not doing so under a misconception, but had rightly guessed that this was what she wanted. Unless perhaps what I had seen was not an anticipation of her happiness, but an anticipation of *mine* (with Tommy)! Of course I had deliberately misled her about Tommy. We had not spoken of that again. How much was she being influenced by this fake idea, and how much did it matter if she was? Some of the time, as I lay there in tormented thought, it seemed to me that Crystal really did want this marriage with Arthur, however readily she might have sacrificed it under slightly different circumstances. And if so, did this mean that Crystal could be saved and become an ordinary person after all? If only, if only I could be certain that she was not simply doing it for my sake. The best and final consolation was that nothing yet had actually happened. I managed to sleep in the afternoon. In the evening I saw no one. Not that I preferred it so, I was just short of people.

Monday, as I have said, dawned cold and yellow. I did the walk to Gloucester Road and arrived fairly early at the office. I was surprised on emerging from the lift to see that Mrs Witcher and Reggie Farbottom were there before me. They were standing at the door of the Registry. As soon as they saw me they gave a little scream and started to giggle and ran back inside. A few steps further on I met Arthur. He was very red in the face and began to say something. Feeling exceptionally bad tempered I walked past him without a word and entered the Room. I saw at once what had happened. I also saw that I must make an instant and not unimportant decision.

The Room had been rearranged. My desk had been moved out of the bay window and put facing the wall on the near side where Reggie Farbottom's desk used to be. Edith Witcher's desk had moved onto the carpet and into the bay in place of mine, and Reggie's desk was now just behind hers, also on the carpet and facing out of the window.

There was a lot of loud ostentatious giggling going on behind me. I turned round. Arthur, red and agitated, was standing at the door of his cupboard. Mrs Witcher and Reggie were having a little struggle in the corridor which ended with his pushing her in front of him into the Room. They were both now pretending to be helpless with laughter.

'Hilary, we thought—be *quiet*, Reggie!—we thought it would be much easier for you to be nearer Arthur—Oh, Reggie, do stop making me laugh so—do be serious—'

'I am serious,' said Reggie. 'What could be more serious than nearer Arthur?'

'Reggie, please—!'

'But really seriously, Hilary,' said Reggie, holding up the wilting form of Mrs Witcher, who was squeaking with nervous mirth, 'it's turn and turn about now. We reckoned it was fair. We was feeling frustrated! You've had that place for years and we reckoned it was Edith's turn. And anyway she's a lady. Or something.'

'Reggie!'

'We reckoned it was fair do's. Democracy and all that. No need to take on.'

'He isn't taking on!' said Edith with an affected scream.

Skinker the messenger arrived. 'You've moved Mr Burde's desk.'

'How true,' said Reggie.

'But Mr Burde's always sat there in that window place.'

'All the more reason for this,' said Reggie. 'The old order changeth, giving place to new. That's all right, isn't it, Hilary? You don't mind, do you, dear?'

'I don't see that it's right,' said Skinker. 'A man's place is his place. It's Mr Burde's room, in' it?'

'It's our room too,' said Reggie, 'and there are two of us and only one of him, two against one, and his Arthur has got a room to himself, it's logical. Come on, Edith, stop suffocating, assert your rights, get your behind onto that chair, he won't have the face to pull it off it.' He pushed Mrs Witcher on into the window and sat himself behind her, swivelling round to see what I was going to do. Arthur and Skinker also stared at me, waiting for the explosion.

I walked out and went into Arthur's cupboard and sat down at Arthur's desk. Arthur followed me in. Skinker stood sympathetically at the door, clucking with concern. Triumphant though still nervous laughter echoed in the Room, voices intended to be heard followed after me.

'Talk about paper tigers!'

'You could knock me over wiv a fevver!'

'You were quite right, Reggie. Stand up to a bully and he just collapses!'

'Get us some tea, would you, please?' said Arthur to Skinker.

'Mr Burde's a deep one, in' he,' said Skinker and disappeared.

Arthur closed the door. 'Hilary, aren't you going to—?'

I shook my head.

'Well,' said Arthur doubtfully, trying hard to read me and to find the proper thing to say. 'I agree it's not worth fighting people like that. And I suppose there is something to turn and turn about—I mean I suppose it's not—or perhaps you think—or something—I mean.'

I did not help him out.

Arthur climbed onto the desk and sat there, his knees close to my shoulder. He was probably relieved at not having to second me in some scrimmage. He made as if to pat me, then fluttered his hand back to his lapel. 'You certainly flummoxed them, Hilary. That was the last thing they expected.'

I had flummoxed myself. Had Crystal's decision just deprived me of will-power or was this simply the inevitable beginning of some end which I had not foreseen as starting now? Officewise, lifewise, the beginning of the end? Why was I totally unable to react? Was I afraid I might kill them? No. I had behaved quietly not out of any decent or even intelligible motive but out of an absence of any motive at all. Perhaps this was the collapse of a bully, perhaps this was what collapsing bullies were like. For a desperate man, any setback can tap a deep base of nightmare, every sin represents the original one, indeed is part of it, every crime is The Crime. A sort of quiet ecstasy of pure hate possessed me. I hated Arthur. I hated his stupid knees and shabby shiny shapeless blue trousers which were pushed up so near to my face that I could positively smell them. I abhorred his capture of Crystal about which, I now saw as in a vision, I would have to behave perfectly. What had just happened in the Room was nothing, was a symbol merely, a blank occasion of some older larger state of the universe. A vista, a view of the light, a gateway to salvation was closed, the immuring process one stage further on towards the final pit and pendulum. It was as if an abstract form of some past *or perhaps future* suffering had coldly come upon me. Misery and sin are inextricably mixed in the human lot. I experienced the inextricability.

'Are you all right, Hilary?'

Arthur's cupboard was tiny, constructed of slatted wood like a shed, unpainted on the inside. A high window gave upon the corridor. There was an electric light, only Arthur had not switched it on, perhaps because he did not dare to expose my

71

face. I looked up into Arthur's mild anxious eyes. My future brother-in-law already looked a different man. Would he and Crystal discuss me with sympathy and concern?

Skinker arrived with the tea. He was a kind man, and had been trying to think of something suitable to say. 'Our Lord said we was to turn the other cheek.'

The matter was thus summed up as a slap in the face, meekly received. 'Thanks,' I said to Skinker. I took the tea. 'Thanks,' I said to Arthur, and patted his shoulder. I went with the teacup back into the Room and sat down at my desk.

Edith and Reggie, who had been anxiously waiting for me, began giggling again. There was a charged silence while I drank my tea and fiddled my papers into shape.

Reggie said at last, 'Say something, Hilary.'

'What do you want me to say?'

'Say you're not cross.'

'I'm not cross,' I said. I was not.

It was Monday evening. I let myself in with my key to the flat in Lexham Gardens. 'Hello.'

'Hello, darling,' said Clifford Larr from the kitchen.

'It's so bloody hot in here.' I dropped my coat in the hall on a lemon and white striped settee thing, and went on into the kitchen where Clifford (a serious cook), dressed in a long blue apron, was pouring some oil into a bowl.

'How was your day?'

'Something terrible happened.'

'Oh?' He looked up, interested.

'Mrs Witcher and her minion moved my desk out of the window and puts hers there instead.'

'Was that all? Then you moved yours back again?'

'No.'

'Why not?'

'You know why not. What's the point?'

Clifford, the oil bottle still poised in one hand, looked at me coolly. 'You want me to sympathize with you. You want me to appreciate some interesting suffering. No. I just think you were a fool. You have lost another trick in the game of life. You will never be able to get your place back now, never. It's gone for good.'

'I know, why rub it in? I don't want you to cry over me.'

'I can't be bothered with the metaphysics of your self-pity.'

'Who's asking you to bother, fuck you?'

'I think less of you, that's all. And there is less of you. Because of this defeat there is that much less of you. Someone has taken a slice off you, Mrs Witcher has, she has drawn your blood. And since you let her do so she will do it again. You will become a dull man whose sufferings will interest nobody.'

'I am that already, according to you.'

'And your clothes smell. I wish you'd do something about it.'

'Do you want me to smash something before the evening has even started?'

'You get excited so easily.'

'You are deliberately hurting me.'

'Oh don't be so boring. I can see that you are going to bore me tonight.' He was now stirring his horrible blackish oily mixture.

'Am I? Crystal is going to marry Arthur Fisch.' I had not told Clifford anything about this romance.

Clifford went on stirring. His face changed, contracting, then slowly relaxing into an almost angelic calm. 'You needn't go as far as that to amuse me.'

'It isn't a joke.'

After a pause, Clifford said, 'It couldn't happen.'

'What couldn't?'

'That marriage. It couldn't happen.'

'Why not? Would you prevent it?'

'No. But confess. You're not serious.'

It rarely happens that one can construct a friendship with someone which is as complex as one's thoughts about that person. Clifford Larr interested me very much. I felt admiration, affection. But our relations, though close, remained curiously abstract. This was partly of course because he ran the whole thing, decreeing himself mysterious, a sort of elusive prince. We were not lovers, of course. I was irredeemably heterosexual. That he was homosexual, invisible to me at first (because I tended not to notice such things) was later the essence, the cornerstone, the key: yet a key that could not be used, or which only opened doors to reveal other ones. This was the quality of his unhappiness, which hung like a canopy over our, so oddly as I said abstract, even formal relations. That he had hoped to find a partner in me, had with the most exquisite tact and discretion tried me for this role, now seemed to belong to the remote past, a kind of legend of a time which may not even have existed in reality, but which pervaded and determined the present, coloured it certainly. Nothing was said of course, and I received no confidences about Clifford's life. The only link with his other existence was Christopher Cather, who figured here as a portent rather than as a source of information. I had met Christopher through Clifford. It was conceivable that Clifford and Christopher had been lovers, though they apparently never saw each other now. I preferred not to think about it. This was not because of any dislike or disapproval of homosexual practices. I harboured no prejudice of this sort. If I shuddered at all it was at what was sexual rather than at what was homosexual. It was that my friendship with Clifford Larr took place under the sign of a vast reticence. It depended on a kind of vow of silence. At any rate it depended on my being passive, incurious, even seemingly insensitive. Second fiddle, of course. But also in a way set up as unsatisfactory, something of a brute, as if unconcerned, and *ipso facto* perfectly discreet. How was it that I understood all that, the essential structure of the thing, without any explanation, and that I also knew that Clifford knew I understood? It was part of this vast understanding that I never felt that Christopher had been planted on me as a spy, and that Clifford was well aware that Christopher and I never discussed him. Discretion was doubtless something which Clifford imposed on anyone who came near him. If there were to be revelations, and he sometimes teased me with the possibility of one, these would be a grace decreed by him. They could never be extracted by questioning, indeed questioning was made almost impossible by the rigidly impersonal-personal tone of my communication with Clifford. He wore always round his neck upon a chain the talisman which Laura Impiatt had imagined to be a cross. In fact it was a man's signet ring. Sometimes when I was with him, Clifford, undoing the front of his shirt in the disgustingly hot centrally-heated atmosphere of his flat, would let the dangling ring be visible, would almost seem to display it. I looked at it, I once even touched it, but I had never so far asked him about it. This was in accordance with the myth of our relations. There was an inhibition of tenderness, a check of curiosity, a sheer silence which, by making me play, under his direction, a slightly unnatural role, provided him perhaps with a weird substitute for the sexual connection which we did not have. Another aspect of this silence was the total secrecy which, again at his wish, covered our Mondays. Perhaps the secrecy mimed a state of affairs which might have existed but did not. I myself would have been glad to let it be known that Clifford and I were friends. I was proud of this friendship which would certainly have improved my standing at the office. There Clifford was an important man, a dark horse, admired, yet also feared because of his sharp tongue; and it is always flattering to be petted by someone who is generally feared. I sometimes wondered if Clifford simply felt ashamed of me, ashamed of liking me, and so did not want our names linked. Even this possibility contributed to the odd tension between us which clearly gave him some satisfaction or he would have dropped me without a pang and forgotten me instantly. That one might at any moment be thus dropped and forgotten was of course itself part of the tension.

No one knew of our meetings except Crystal. This was another complication, perhaps another bond. I should explain that I had known Clifford, who was exactly my age, very slightly at Oxford. He knew a good deal about the Oxford débâcle. He had told nobody at the office. (I successfully mystified my colleagues about my past.) This fact indeed first suggested that he felt some sort of interest in me. When I first joined the department I had discerned him with dismay and waited fearfully for rumours. There were none. Clifford had said nothing. Then one day he invited me for a drink. It shows how little I understood him that I went to this assignation half fearing that I was to be faced with some sort of blackmail. As it was, it was a little while before my slow mind perceived what it was that he was, so delicately, after, and by then he had already found out the answer to his question. But that, it turned out, was just the beginning of our strange friendship which by now probably meant more to me than it did to him. He was without doubt the most intelligent person that I knew well, and was in this respect a considerable blessing. He animated what was left of my intellectual life. The thing about Crystal was quite unexpected.

Clifford Larr had evidently noticed me at Oxford more than

I had noticed him. This was not only because of the disaster which ended my life there (and in many ways ended my life) but because he was, as he told me later, a connoisseur of oddities, and I was an oddity. Perhaps I was discussed more than I realized. He knew that I had a sister to whom I was devoted. Clifford also had a sister. She was very unlike Crystal. She was a distinguished mathematician and died of cancer in her twenties. After it had become clear between Clifford and me that we were to see each other regularly (the Mondays arrangement was the only part of my mode of life which I managed to impose on him) he expressed a desire to meet Crystal, and I brought her along once or twice to his flat. He also visited her occasionally at her place with me. Crystal fell in love with him. I was very upset and totally amazed. I should not have been. Who after all did poor Crystal ever meet? She might as well have been Miranda on the island for all she really saw of men. Clifford was a glittering object, good-looking, clever, charming when he wanted to be so, and surrounded with the sort of melancholy and the sort of mystery which make women feel for men pity, then quickly love. Moreover he behaved to Crystal in a wonderful way, with a gentleness and a tact which I never otherwise saw in him. He even looked different, his face was different, when he was with her. And when he was with her he also enacted, or perhaps this was instinctive, a sort of respectful affection for me which helped to win her heart. He treated her, not quite as an equal, that would have been impossible, but more nearly so than did any other of my friends (except Arthur of course). He *explained* things to her. The Impiatts patronized Crystal. They were kind to her but they never saw her quite as an individual person. She did not interest them. She did interest Clifford. Under his interest she flowered, and she loved him.

Of course Crystal never told me in so many words that she had fallen in love, but it was sufficiently evident and she knew that it was. It was also evident that this was a hopeless love. Clifford was totally homosexual and in any case could have no deep relationship with an uneducated person. Crystal had clearly inspired some sort of warmth in him, perhaps simply pity. It may even have been that he liked the *idea* of Crystal. It amused him to inform me that I was fixated on my sister. (A harmless rival?) And he took a curious and lively pleasure in the fact that she was a virgin. 'And is she really a virgin?' he would say to me with satisfaction, wanting to have this information repeated again and again, like a child who wants the repetition of a story. 'It's so nice to think of *anybody* being a virgin in these days.' When it became clear what had happened, Clifford did what I suppose was the only thing he could do, and doubtless also the right thing, he withdrew completely. 'He won't come again, will he,' Crystal said to me in the monotonous tone which she used for grief. 'No,' I said. He did not, nor did she ever go again to his flat which had seemed to her like a magic palace. Silence fell again, falling like snow upon this so unlikely moment of communication. She never spoke of him. He rarely spoke of her, though he sometimes asked me, formally and without curiosity, how she was. At the severance of relations between them I felt profound relief.

When my friendship, if that was what it was, with Clifford Larr began, I imagined it would, even if not very dramatic, be a moderately dynamic business with a beginning, a middle and an end. Basically I suppose I had no confidence in my ability not to bore a man as cultivated as Larr. He was an *âme damnée*. Of course I was one myself. Only I was a coarse stupid accidental semi-conscious *âme damnée* and he was a refined and highly self-wrought one. I could not believe that, given I manifestly did not share his preferences, he would go on wanting to see me. He did, however, and that without seeming to want things to develop beyond a certain point which he fixed. (And we reached this point relatively early.) There was no dynamism, yet at the same time there was no stability. Knowing Clifford was a pleasure, but it was also a pain. He saw to that. I naturally felt envious and inferior, and Clifford knew exactly how to make me feel more so. Clifford was rich. His father had been a successful barrister, later a judge. Clifford had grown up in a wealthy bookish home. He was educated and cultured in a way in which I would never be, and probably could never have been even if I had stayed at Oxford. Clifford's flat was like a museum, a temple, a House of Mysteries. At night it was, though full of lamps, curiously dark. When Clifford was depressed, which was often, he went out and bought an *objet d'art*. The place was crammed with tiny fancy bookcases and little rugs and Chinese vases and bronzes and things. He had a collection of Italian drawings, a collection of Indian miniatures (I liked these) representing princesses in palaces, in gardens, on boats, conversing with animals, awaiting lovers. It was an education to visit him, or would have been if I had been willing to be taught anything. He soon gave up trying to make me listen to music or to let him teach me to play chess. However, I knew more languages than he did and I never let him forget it.

Clifford went on wanting to see me, but he made me pay. He was often out of spirits and talked regularly about committing suicide. When he was in black moods he needled me mercilessly. At first I gratified him by becoming frantic. One day in a rage I broke a valuable bowl of red Bohemian glass. He was amazingly upset and practically cried over the thing. (Possessiveness is fed, I suppose, by multitude of possessions.) His anger came later. After that I became more restrained, though there were still occasional rows when I had to rush blindly away out of a sheer inability to answer him back. His malice was universal and, when not directed at me, amusing. He enjoyed inciting people to be complacent so that he could despise them. (The Impiatts were especially easy game in this respect.) I felt privileged when he was contemptuous of the world but exempted me. Perhaps that was my form of complacency. He was, as I have said, dry and thin and tall. He had slightly waving pallid hair, the kind that goes grey without anyone noticing. He had narrow close blue eyes and a straight pointed nose and a thin mouth which usually looked sarcastic, but which, when he was listening to music or looking at a picture or looking at Crystal or (very occasionally) looking at me, became relaxed and pouting and conveyed a look of serene sweetness to his whole face. He dressed in soft expensive velvety corduroys and soft expensive vividly coloured shirts.

We were sitting at dinner eating some sort of veal stew and a salad covered with oily dressing. (I had given up asking him not to put oil on my salad.)

'So why couldn't it take place?' I said. (Crystal's marriage to Arthur.) 'Because of me, I suppose.'

'Why do you imagine you are the centre of everything?'

'I don't. I just imagine I am the centre of this.'

'He is such a nothing. Credit her with some taste.'

'You underestimate Arthur. He has many good points.'

'Mention one.'

'He is good-natured.'

'He is weak. Come, come, my dear, it is too late to start building Arthur up for my benefit.'

'Marriage may transform him.'

'Transformation belongs to passionate pursuit, Apollo seizing Daphne. There is none of that here.'

'I don't see why you should assume so.'

'Arthur deified by love?'

'Anyone can be.'

'You must admit you have never hitherto had a good word to say for him.'

'You mock him. You mock everybody. I just went along. I shouldn't have. I respect Arthur.'

'Nothing is more important than that everybody mocks everybody.'

'I don't think Arthur does.'

'Then that's because he's too timid. He lacks the energy to perceive the absurd.'

'She wants a baby.'

Clifford said nothing to this, but fastidiously registered the enormity of the remark. He removed the plates. He brought in the cheese soufflé. I had been trained to sit still.

'I suppose if Crystal marries her dull swain you will marry yours?'

'No.' Clifford was hateful on the subject of Tommy. I now refused to be drawn. Marriage with Tommy would mean the end of Mondays. 'That's another thing.'

'Everything is what it is and not another thing.'

'So you have observed before.'

'Why not a double wedding!'

'There won't be any weddings.'

'So you agree with me about Crystal and Arthur?'

'Yes. It won't happen.'

'Why did you bring it up then? Just to annoy me?'

'Yes.'

'Why?'

'You said I was going to bore you, you said—'

'Oh how tedious you are,' said Clifford. 'You are nothing but a lout who has been taught a few tricks. You are the sort of lower class product who never grows out of his grammar school. Always the little prize boy who was top in the exam. Always envious, always anxious. You exist by excelling, by knowing just that little more than the others and understanding nothing. You haven't even got a sense of humour. When there are no more exams and you can't excel you cease to exist.'

'Shall I go home and relieve you of my non-existence?'

'Do as you please. If only you knew chess we could concentrate on that and not talk. But of course you will only do what you can win at.'

'Of course!'

'You conceal your inferiority from yourself, though not from anyone else, by cramming your head with foreign words which you can't pronounce and will never use—'

'You wish you knew Russian, you said so—'

'This conversation is worthy of the nursery. Go home if you want to. I must make my will tonight.' This was a routine remark, a sort of familiar turning post in our exchanges.

'Don't forget to leave me the Indian miniatures.'

'You only like pictures that tell stories. You only like music with tunes. What did you say the Czech word for music was?'

'Hutba.'

'Hutba. That's what you like. I must make my will, or else my piggish cousin will inherit. *Non amo, ergo non ero.* Is life a thorn? Then count it not a whit, man is well done with it. Soon as he's born he should all means essay to put the plague away. As flies to wanton boys are we to the gods. Even Wittgenstein did not think that we would ever reach the moon. So am I a happy fly, if I live or if I die, only dying is very much to be preferred.'

'Good. Just let me know when you're going so that I can find someone else for Mondays.'

'The Messiah will change only one thing in the world. If I remove myself the world will be saved. Hey presto. Yes, I must make a will. So Crystal is going to make a present of her virginity to that little worm. But it won't happen. You won't let it happen, will you?'

'I won't let it happen. Give me some more wine will you? Must you hog the bottle?'

He poured the wine. 'Your hand, please.' This too was routine. At a certain moment during the evening he held my hand across the table. Nothing else. Sometimes this firm clasp comforted me. Sometimes it annoyed me. It annoyed me tonight. I gave him my hand.

'So,' said Clifford, in a different tone, his lips beginning to take on the pouting look, 'they moved your desk out of the window, and you let them.'

'Yes.'

'Poor little prize boy. Has anything else . . . odd . . . happened to you lately . . . darling?'

I looked into the narrow clever blue eyes, a light but cold blue, like Scandinavian seas in the sunshine. I saw behind the fair pale head an Indian girl in a diaphanous sari standing on a terrace and watching a flight of birds. Some instinct had warned me earlier not to mention Biscuit. I decided again for concealment. What a strangely apt question, however. 'No. Nothing.'

'And you have not . . . heard anything?'

'Heard anything? What should I hear? About what?'

Clifford's fingers closed very hard upon my hand. 'You haven't heard—?'

'No. What? You're frightening me. What am I supposed to have heard?' I pulled my hand away.

He pushed his chair back. 'Oh, nothing—nothing. I'm feeling rotten. I can't sleep. The pills don't work any more. I'm just saving them up now. It's no good imagining gardens and garden gates, that used to help. Now I lie for hours just staring at the ceiling. Human life is a scene of horror. I hope you enjoyed the cheese soufflé. Nothing could be more important than that Mozart died a pauper, except that Shakespeare stopped writing. A scene of horror. You'd better go home.'

'But what were you saying?'

'Nothing. What you can't say you can't say and you can't whistle it either, as my old philosophy tutor used to observe. Bugger off, will you.'

'OK,' I said. 'Good-bye, in case you should decide to kill yourself tonight.'

'Good-bye.'

TUESDAY

I WAS in an examination hall which was also a tube station. I had finished some time ago turning a piece of Carlyle into faultless fruity Tacitean Latin. Complacently I watched the other examinees who were desperately writing. Idly I turned the examination paper over. There were a whole lot of questions on the back which I had failed to notice, and there were only twenty minutes left in which to answer them all. I began frenziedly to write, but now my pen was refusing to function, no ink was coming out of it, it was simply making holes in the paper which was moving steadily towards me over the desk off a big paper roller. With a terrible feeling of helplessness, I began to crumple up the paper. 'You mustn't do that,' said the invigilator who was Tommy dressed in a black gown and mortarboard, standing on the desk in front. I was in a court room throwing balls of screwed up paper at the judge who was Laura Impiatt in a white wig. 'He has failed,' she said, 'he did not answer the questions. Take him away.' I was in a motor car driving faster and faster. A man beside me with blue eyes began to take me by the throat. I screamed. Crystal was lying dead on the grass beside the road.

I awoke from this typical nightmare into relief that it was a dream and sadness that I was no longer a young man with an unspoilt life. I got up and began to make some tea. Then I remembered that it was Tuesday and went to see if Tommy's usual letter had arrived. It had. Tommy spent Monday and Tuesday at King's Lynn where she earned her pittance teaching would-be teachers to be autumn leaves or how to make horses' heads out of papier-mâché or puppet theatres out of tea chests. She always wrote me a letter on the Monday which I received on the Tuesday. Lately she had taken to writing on other days too. That must stop. These letters gave no pleasure. At best they could be quickly glanced through and declared harmless.

My darling one, I am so miserable. I am so terribly sorry I came on Saturday. I felt desperate and I just wanted to see your face. My cold has come out, I do hope I didn't give it to you or Crystal, I don't think I can have done. It will be over by Friday. I love you so much. I waited for ages in that room as quiet as a mouse, only you didn't come back, and then I heard Laura Impiatt talking to the boys in the kitchen. I tried to get out without her seeing me but she did. She said, 'Where did you spring from? What have you done with Hilary?' She always seems aggressive to me now. I didn't know what to say. I didn't stay as I knew you wouldn't want me to and I was starting to cry anyway. You don't realize how I do everything you want as if I were your slave. I live a stupid life because of you, a life not worthy of a human being, and we might be so happy if only you would. It isn't as if you were happy either, you're wretched, I think you're the most unhappy person I've ever met. Why can't you just decide to be happy for a change? It's that you won't love for some reason, you hold back. You are your own worst enemy. There's a rage in you against all ordinary joys. We could be so happy you and me and if we had a little child, living together, and you would have somebody to work for and your life would be full of meaning if you would. You can't be waiting for somebody else. You do love me and we do understand each other and it's rare, you said so yourself. Oh darling, don't cast me away, don't waste me, you can't, you know I'm your little Thomas forever . . .

And so on for several pages more. I classified it as harmless and tore it up. I dressed and drank my tea and set off for the office. The lift was out of order, so I walked down.

Raw rainy air was waiting for me outside the swing doors, it rushed into my throat and made me feel that I had got Tommy's bloody cold after all. The dawn was soiled and yellow, the street lights were still on, illuminating posters announcing an imminent electricity strike. What a depressing evening with Clifford. What had he meant at the end about my hearing something? He often talked wildly, picturesquely, with a kind of rhetorical over-emphasis which led straight on into pure romancing. As for Tommy's letter with its picture of happy home life with the little ones it made me want to spew. At any rate she had not been gurgling about 'bairns', as she sometimes did. What a terrible dream that was about Crystal. Whatever should I do if Crystal died? But marriage with Arthur was as good as death. Did she really know how she felt? Did she really know what it would mean? Did she imagine that she could marry Arthur and still have me? Was I not being stupidly heroic about the whole business? Should I not simply, as I had said to Clifford, prevent it?

The haze of black thoughts round my head was suddenly pierced and dispelled. What had happened? At one moment I had been shuffling along with the crowd of other zombies, nuzzling my way through a light rain of tiny yellowish ice drops, breathing a damp air which sliced into the innards like a knife, and at the next all was warmth and brightness. It was like being lightly hit with a golden ball in a transformation scene. I had spotted Biscuit on the other side of the road, walking slowly along parallel to me, her head slightly turned in my direction. She was wearing a duffle coat with the hood turned up and it was surprising that I had been able to recognize her. Some power had felicitously led my gaze to that glimpse of a dark eye and a bony cheek. I felt sudden happiness, and with it a shock of surprise that this warm feeling was happiness, it was happiness I felt, irrational, unwarranted, baseless, doubtless quite momentary, but that was certainly what that very unusual sensation was. I walked on feigning not to have noticed her, wondering what she would do and whether she would accost me. After about twenty paces however this began to seem an idiotically wasteful procedure. I let her get a little ahead of me, then crossed the road and came up behind her, grabbing her by the wrist. I felt we had known each other for years. I squeezed the thin wrist, then pulled her arm through mine, holding her hand. She was wearing a little short woollen glove and I pulled this off and pocketed it and held her warm dry hand firmly in my cold wet one. I very rarely wore gloves. I felt the warmth of her body along my forearm and at my thigh. We walked along in the semi-darkness in the flowing rush hour crowd. I did not look into her face.

'Well, Biscuit, darling?'

'Good morning.'

'Good morning, who?'

'Good morning, Hilary.'

'You're going to have dinner with me tonight.' Tuesday was Arthur's day, but that could scarcely matter less.

'No, I can't, I'm sorry.'

'Why not? Won't they let you?'

'I can't.'

'Biscuit, are you *married*?'

'No.'

'No ring? No, no ring. But is there some man who rules your life?'

'No man—'

'Well then why can't you? After all, dear Biscuit, you are behaving like a perfect tease. I am not going to put up any longer with not knowing all about you and why you keep following me around. It is rather odd, you know. Do you live near here?'

'I cannot come tonight.'

We had reached the tube station and I was keeping a firm hold of her hand which had shown a little fluttery inclination to escape as we came to the entrance. She drew away from my arm but I pulled her on, squeezing the frail knuckles between my fingers and thumb. I bought her a ticket and fumbled for my own season. We went on down the steps onto the eastbound platform. I had decided to keep her with me now until she had revealed herself and thoroughly explained her little mystery.

'Please—Hilary—you're hurting me—'

I pulled her along the platform. There was a dense crowd in the middle of which we were totally private. Londoners, having seen everything, live in blinkers. I pushed her back against a wall, thrusting her between two people as if into a slot, and followed her, placing my hands on the wall on either side of her shoulders. We faced each other. The comparative warmth of the station made our wet faces glow, mine red, hers a faintly rosy gold. I brushed my cheek for a moment against the folds of her hood which had fallen back about her neck. A smell of warm wet wool pervaded the crowded platform, merging into a smell rather like sweat, merging into the dark rubbery smell of the Underground. A Putney Bridge train came thundering in and the crowd began to surge forward. 'Biscuit,' I said in the privacy of the people and the thunder and the wetness and the wool.

'Look, Biscuit, never mind about this evening. You're here now and I'm not going to let you go. You're my prisoner and I'm not going to release you until you've told me everything. You've bewitched me and the only thing I can do is grab you and hold on until I've got the truth. I warn you, I'll hold on for hours if necessary.' I thought, I will get her onto the Inner Circle and keep her there by force until she talks. I don't care how many times we go round.

The Putney Bridge train had gone. The platform was rapidly filling up again. An Inner Circle train began to draw in. 'Come along, prisoner.' I pulled her forward with me. The train was already full to the doors and we were the last to get on, squashing ourselves forcibly up against the reluctant crush of cringing persons within. I thrust Biscuit in in front of me, and as I inserted myself, trying to find a space for my two feet on the overcrowded floor, I loosened my hold for a second. The doors began to close.

She was outside. Quick as an eel, she had stepped off as I stepped on. The doors had closed between us. I pressed my face up to the glass. Inches away I saw her face, her mouth opening inaudibly in the clatter of the now moving train. Her frail hands lifted in an interpretative gesture. 'I'm sorry— I'm sorry—' She walked beside the train and put one hand flat on the glass. I saw the paler greyish palm and the criss-cross of lines, hieroglyph of a mystery that still evaded capture.

On Tuesdays chez Arthur supper was always the same winter and summer. (Wittgenstein would have liked that.) It consisted of tinned tongue with instant mashed potatoes and peas, followed by biscuits and cheese and bananas. I brought the wine.

It was the last day of the old world. (Only I did not know this yet.) Arthur and I were drunk. (Just for tonight I had brought two bottles.)

Arthur had a two-room flat over a baker's shop in Blythe Road. I found the smell of the bread maddening. If one was hungry it made hunger intolerable. If not hungry it made one feel sick. Sometimes it merged into a sort of yeasty fermenting smell as if the bread were turning into beer. Arthur said he was used to it and claimed he could not smell it. His flat was small, dirty and unattractive. There were various relics left by the (now defunct) person Arthur referred to as his 'mummy'. Mummy had left Arthur a green blue and brown carpet with a pattern of wavy triangles, a sideboard with rounded corners and a chocolate brown inlay of elongated fan designs, a greenish glass firescreen engraved with a representation of the Empire State Building, an armchair with an embroidery of rather dated aeroplanes, a diamond-shaped orange rug, which fought hard with the carpet, and a pair of light green statuettes of half-draped ladies in suitable attitudes labelled Dawn and Dusk respectively. There was a sort of touching whiff of ancient *joie de vivre* about this stuff which made me feel a tiny sympathy though no curiosity. Arthur's father (also defunct) had been a railway porter. Arthur, so far as he went, was another little exhibit of the liberating power of the examination system.

We had finished our supper (eaten off Mummy's plates embellished with a white cottage posed against a geometrical beige sunrise) and were (I mean I was) in the rather snappish stage of drunkenness when one realizes that it has all been in vain. Arthur who soon got tipsy (he usually drank beer) was looking dreamy. He was never snappish. He had taken his glasses off and was rather idiotically swinging them to and fro in a pendulum motion. In fact I had drunk the larger part of the two bottles. We had been having a confused conversation about the office, about the pantomime, now about Christopher Cather's 'religious' views.

'Of course,' I said, 'if you think the world is an illusion you don't care what you do. A very convenient doctrine.'

'Doesn't Christianity say—?'

'Naturally of course Christopher doesn't really believe this, no one could. He announces that people don't really exist! It doesn't stop him laying about him with his ego like the rest of us.'

'Well, I don't think we exist all that much,' said Arthur.

'Speak for yourself.'

'I think we should just be kind to each other. It's all a pretty good mess-up and if that's what Christopher means—'

'Oh, don't you start.'

'I mean one's mind is just an accidental jumble of stuff. There's nothing behind ordinary life. There isn't anything complete. Life isn't a play. It isn't even a pantomime.'

'No Never-Never Land.'

'Certainly no Never-Never Land,' said Arthur. 'That's the point.'

'So you don't see Peter Pan as reality breaking in?'

'No,' said Arthur. 'On the contrary. What is real is the Darlings' home life. Hook is just a fantasy of Mr Darling.'

'What is Peter then?'

'Peter is—Peter is—Oh I don't know—spirit gone wrong,

87

just turning up as an unnerving visitor who can't really help
and can't get in either.'

'That's rather fanciful.'

'I mean the spiritual urge is mad unless it's embodied in
some ordinary way of life. It's destructive, it's just a crazy
sprite.'

'I think Smee is the real hero. Hook envies Smee. So Hook
can be saved.'

'Only in the novel.'

'Novels explain. Plays don't.'

'It's better not to explain,' said Arthur. 'Poetry is best of
all. Who wouldn't rather be a poet than anything else?
Poetry is where words end.'

'Poetry is where words begin.'

'I think Nana is the hero.'

'Nana is the most conventional character in the whole
thing. Now Smee—'

'You must remember that Smee serves Hook.'

'You must remember that Nana is only a dog.'

'Exactly,' said Arthur. 'There's nothing bogus about Nana.
Nana doesn't *talk*. Even Mr Darling fails, he wants to be
Hook.'

'What about Wendy, does she fail?'

'Yes. Wendy is the human soul seeking the truth. She ends
up with a compromise.'

'Living half in an unreal world?'

'Yes, like most of us do. It's a defeat but a fairly honourable
one. That's the best we can hope for, I suppose. Now Nana.
She's the *truth* of the Darling home, its best part, its reality.
Nana fears Peter, she's the only one who really *recognizes*
Peter.'

'I can't think why you idolize the Darling home life. It
seems to me to be pretty dreary.'

'Oh no—what could be better—a home with—children
and—'

'I think we're drunk,' I said. 'At any rate I must be. I
thought for two minutes that you were saying something
interesting.'

At that moment fortunately the telephone rang. It was an
old age pensioner whose budgie had just died. I could hear the
old fool whining away at the other end of the line. I gathered
my things together. I knew from experience that Arthur was
incapable of terminating a telephone conversation. He begged
me, covering the mouthpiece, to stay, but I had had enough

anyway. I did not want to hear any more on the subject of happy homes and children.

Outside the crazy old English weather had done another quick change act. The clouds had rolled away and there was a clear night. In spite of the London glow a few stars were visible in the faintly reddish sky. It was a long time since I had seen the Milky Way. The great wheel of the galaxy, the gleaming fuzz of innumerable stars, the deep absolute darkness that hid other and other and other galaxies. Arthur was right. We did not exist all that much. We could suffer like mad all the same. Something was there, a wounded complex of resentment and anxiety and pain, something half crushed, something swallowed, not yet digested and still screaming. I considered the idea of going on to see Crystal. But it was the sort of thing I never did. I must keep to my routine. Besides she would be asleep by now. Supposing Crystal took me at my word and suddenly accepted Arthur? Had I not better put a stop to the whole thing by lifting my finger? It was no good trying to distract myself by thinking about Biscuit. I did try, but there was no joy in it. Biscuit was just another piece of meaningless teasing on the part of the cosmos, like poking an insect with a straw. I walked very slowly home.

WEDNESDAY

IT WAS now Wednesday, the most important day in the story so far, and one of the most crucial days in my life. It began tediously enough with a row with Christopher Cather. I had risen to find the kitchen occupied by a strange boy whose long hair was thrust through an elastic band. He had presumably spent the night. I went into Christopher's room to tell him that I would not have in the flat a boy whose hair was done up in an elastic band. Christopher said I was ridiculously narrow-minded. I also told Christopher that I objected to his wearing such a short jersey that every time he moved I could see an expanse of flesh. I desired him to keep his flesh to himself. Christopher said that the jersey had shrunk in the washing machine. I told him that I had told him he was never to use the washing machine. He said I was a stingy bastard. I replied. I left without shaving and banged the door.

The lift was still out of order. The electricity strike was on the posters again, billed to start at any moment. It was raining. I looked around for Biscuit but there was no sign of her. When I got to the office I intended to shave (I kept shaving gear there) but found I had no razor blades. I felt depressed and unclean. I sat and stared at the cobweb-smudged wall, hoping that the desire to tell Crystal to drop Arthur would soon become irresistible. I nudged it along a bit. She would see him tomorrow. Should I not see her tonight?

Mrs Witcher and Reggie came in laughing merrily. They were having a festival season to prolong their triumph. Tommy rang up (a forbidden action) and I put the telephone down. Arthur, whose assistance I needed, had rather surprisingly failed to appear. It was about eleven forty-five when the shattering thing occurred.

Reggie and Mrs Witcher normally chattered throughout the day. I suppose they did some work. I was so used to their vulgar cacophony that I was easily able to switch off from it. Sometimes I listened. I had been writing a fine little minute concerning the position of a messenger who had been seconded to another department and while there had received what was now said to be an *ex gratia* honorarium for clearing some pigeons' nests off the roof, and who, after returning to our department, had broken his leg while clearing some more pigeons' nests, which he now alleged to be part of his normal duties. I had resolved this matter elegantly and was now sitting back before starting on another case, wondering why Arthur had failed to turn up, and idly listening to the ceaseless chatter of the other two. They had been discussing the pantomime. Now evidently they were off on something else.

'You don't say Earl Salisbury!' This was Edith who was an expert on the aristocracy. 'You say Lord Salisbury, but the Earl of Salisbury.'

'Is a duke higher than an earl?'

'Of course he is, silly.'

'Is an earl the same as a marquis?'

'A woman keeps her title. She doesn't become plain Mrs when she changes her surname.'

'Well I think she ought to! But does that mean her father was an earl?'

'Let's ask Mr Know-all. Hilary—Hilaree!'

'Yes?'

'When someone is called Lady Somebody Something her father is an earl, isn't he, and she keeps her title, doesn't she, when she marries and becomes Somebody Something Else?'

'I think so,' I said, 'but you're the expert. I think if you're the daughter of the Earl of Whitebait you are called Lady Joan Chubb and when you marry a Mr Stickleback you become Lady Joan Stickleback.'

'Isn't Hilary witty. Is an earl the same thing as a marquis?'

'I don't know.'

'I thought you went to Oxford.'

'I did a secretarial course there.'

'Hilary's always romancing. I don't think he was near Oxford in his life.'

'Hilary went to the Spastics' University at Scunthorpe.'

'Hilary—Hilaree—'

'Anyway, there it is, she used to be Lady Kitty Mallow and then she married Mr Gunnar Jopling and became Lady Kitty Jopling.'

Skinker came in at that moment. 'What's the matter, Mr Burde?'

'I just dropped my ink.'

He picked up my ink pot.

Some of the ink had come out onto the floorboards. I leaned over the edge of the desk staring down at the little dark pool and breathing hard. Very slowly I laid a piece of blotting paper down on top of the ink.

'Are you all right, Mr Burde? Feeling funny?'

I gave a jerk with my hand which he understood and obeyed. He left the room and closed the door.

'It's rather flashy to be called Lady Kitty though, isn't it?' Reggie was saying. 'I mean, she can't have been christened Kitty.'

I cleared my throat.

'Yes, Hilary, dear? Did you make some observation?'

I simulated some coughing to cover the fact that I was finding it hard to breathe normally or to produce my voice. 'You said something about Jopling?'

'Yes, a man called Gunnar Jopling.'

'I've heard of him before,' said Reggie. 'I thought he was some sort of politician, but he can't have been.'

'He was head of that thing on monetary reform. And then he was something at the United Nations. I saw him on television.'

'What about him?' I said.

'Haven't you heard? He's the new head of the office. He's taking Templar-Spence's place.'

'Templar-Spence has gone already,' said Reggie. 'But Jopling won't be here for three weeks.'

'And it's his wife that's Lady Kitty, so I suppose her father was an earl or something.'

'How many earls are there?'

I leaned over my desk for a while and pretended to write. Then I quietly left the room and went to the cloakroom and put on my overcoat and took my umbrella and went downstairs and out into Whitehall. It was still raining a little. I wanted to see Clifford Larr. He never allowed me to talk to him in the office and frowned on meetings anywhere near it, but this was an emergency. He usually left the office to go to his lunch at St Stephen's Tavern at about twelve-thirty. It was now twelve-ten. I walked slowly up and down, hiding under my umbrella and keeping the main door under observation. About twenty-five minutes passed. Thirty minutes. Then Clifford emerged, dressed in his smart tweed coat and trilby hat. He was beginning to open his umbrella when he saw me and closed it again. He hesitated, then walked in my direction. We turned towards Trafalgar Square, walking slowly. I put my umbrella down.

'You've heard,' said Clifford.

'Yes.'

'Well, what do you want me to do about it?'

'I want to talk to you.'

'There's nothing to say. I've got a meeting at two and I've got to read a lot of stuff before it. You know we don't meet each other here.'

'I want to talk to you. Come into the park.'

'Good day. I go this way, you go that.'

'Come into the park. Do you want me to grasp your arm and make a scene?'

We changed direction. Clifford put up his umbrella, as a disguise no doubt. I put mine down. The rain had almost stopped. We passed in silence through the Horse Guards, crossed the parade ground and entered St James's Park, walking on the north side of the lake. The rain stopped completely and a little very brilliant pale blue sky was emerging over Buckingham Palace.

'What am I to do?' I said to Clifford.

'I don't see why you have to do anything,' said Clifford underneath his umbrella. 'You won't be meeting him.'

'I shall pass him on the stairs.'

'Do you imagine he'll attack you, seize you by the throat or something?'

'I shall have to resign.'

'Don't be so idiotic. Well, please yourself. Now I'm going back.'

'No. Please. *Please*. I heard it just now. I don't know what to do.'

'Put up with it. He'll ignore you. Or if you hate it, resign. There's no problem.'

'It's such a fantastic chance. Why should he come here of all places? I thought I'd never see him again, I prayed I'd never see him again. I hoped he'd die. I thought of him as dead.'

'That was rather uncharitable as well as rather unrealistic. He's a very successful man. And now I must—'

'Come as far as the bridge, Clifford, please, come as far as the bridge. I think I'm going mad.'

We walked onto the iron bridge and stood looking back over the water towards Whitehall. The fairy pinnacles of Whitehall Court were visible to the left of the sturdy outline of the New Public Offices, and beyond yellow island willows the gracious palace-like façade of the Foreign Office building gleamed a luminous greenish grey. A little watery sunshine was illuminating the crowded skyline against a backdrop of leaden darkness. South of the river it was still raining, and the glittering lines of the rain could be seen falling in front of the sky's thick gloom, lighted up by the pursuing sun.

'Do you think he knows I'm here?'

'I shouldn't think so. It'll be a nice surprise for him to see a familiar face.'

'I can't endure it,' I said. 'If we meet we'll—faint with—hatred or something.'

'I don't see why you shouldn't say good morning like civilized persons.'

'Say good morning! Clifford, do you think anyone in the office—apart from you—knows about—me and Gunnar?'

'No.'

'You won't tell, will you?'

'No, of course not.'

'I feel ill. I think I'm going to faint now.'

'Don't be so spineless. As for hatred, I don't see why *you* should feel any.'

'If you don't see that you need a lesson in psychology.'

'Oh I know one is supposed to detest the folk one has injured. But there are limits.'

'There are no limits to anything here.'

'Nearly twenty years have passed after all.'

'Not for me. It's yesterday.'

'You know I can't stand this sort of intensity. I've got troubles of my own.'

'He's married again.'

'Why not? He has been getting on with his life while you have been sitting there paralysed with self-pity.'

'You despise me, don't you. You are ashamed of being my friend. You feel you'd lose face in the office if you were known to be my friend. All right, clear off then. And don't expect me next Monday.'

'All right, I won't. Good-bye.'

I watched him go, then dulled my eyes so that his figure should mingle with those of the indifferent people who were sauntering, now that the rain had stopped, in the frail sunshine. I crossed the bridge and began to walk slowly back along the other side of the lake. I went on up Great George Street and turned into Whitehall at the parliament end. As I did so I ran into Arthur who had just crossed the road from the station.

'Hilary! Oh Hilary!'

One look at Arthur told the story. He was completely transformed. He pulled his woollen cap off and waved it. Joy blazed out of his head, shining out through eyes, nose, mouth. He was illuminated like a Hallowe'en turnip. Even his hair managed to look beautiful.

'Hilary, Crystal says she'll marry me. I got her letter this morning. I couldn't do anything. I couldn't come to the office—I felt so happy—I just lay on the floor—I was simply bowled over by happiness—I could hardly breathe—I wanted to shout and sing but I felt too weak with joy—I just lay there as if I'd been mugged. Hilary, you do approve, don't you? I mean, you don't mind? Crystal said you—I say, Hilary, are you angry? Oh dear—are you—you look so—'

'No, no,' I said. 'I'm delighted about you and Crystal, absolutely delighted, of course. It's just that suddenly I'm feeling very ill. I think I'll go home.'

'Let me come with you. What is it? You look like a ghost.'

'No, no. It's just the 'flu. I'll go and lie down. I'm so glad about—you and—' I hailed a taxi.

Arthur looked amazed. Then he waved me off. From the taxi, now stopped in traffic, I saw him catch up and pass me by, oblivious. As he came near, his lunatic beaming smile attracting the attention of the passers by, he suddenly began to dance, lifting his arms in the air. People passed and smiled. The taxi moved on.

At home I found the elastic band boy still in the kitchen and turned him out of the flat. Christopher, sulky for once, told me what I was and went with him. I went into my bedroom and emulating Arthur lay down on the floor.

THURSDAY

'SING ME a song of social significance!' warbled Freddie Impiatt.

It was Thursday. I had turned up at the office on Thursday morning. It was better to be there than lying on the floor at home. I was now at the Impiatts for the same reason. I had told them in the Room that I had a stomach upset and felt rotten. They left me alone. I persuaded Arthur to leave me alone too. But I could hear him singing close by in his cupboard. Now Freddie was singing and even dancing a few steps on the carpet as he poured out the drinks. His big rubbery forehead was creased up with wrinkles of self-satisfaction and pleasure. He had already spoilt several jokes by laughing uncontrollably half way through telling them. Laura in a tentlike robe with jingling ornaments, hair streaming, was watching me intently. I had changed my plea to toothache and I could see she did not believe me. Clifford Larr came in. I looked at him. His eyes passed me stonily. I wondered if I had not better go home at once.

'I hear the yen is not to be devalued after all,' said Clifford.

'Hilary, what *is* it?' said Laura.

'I told you, toothache.'

'It's Tommy.'

'It isn't Tommy. If I had no troubles but Tommy I'd sing all day.'

'So it isn't just toothache.'

'And we still say we won the war!'

We went down to dinner.

'You like artichokes, don't you, Hilary?'

'They're an occupation. Like meccano. I don't call it eating.'

'I'll give you beans and a spoon next time.'

'I don't think food should be toys.'

This rubbish with Laura was so mechanical for both of us that I could carry it on, listen to Freddie and Clifford discussing the international monetary crisis, while busy the whole time with the most lurid private reflections. I was now eating some sort of meat which had been reduced to a characterless jelly and tasted mainly of garlic. I wondered whether I should go on to Crystal's place as usual after dinner to fetch Arthur away. Perhaps not. Fetching Arthur away had no meaning any more. Yet I had to tell Crystal what I had heard on Wednesday morning. And I had to *see* Crystal and pretend to bless her so precipitate decision. She would be waiting anxiously for that. I had felt incapable of visiting her last night. Better the assumed calm of the usual mind-numbing routine. It was perfectly true that I had said 'write to him'; but I had, as I now realized, said this imagining that she would understand that I did not mean it! Had she been in such a haste because she feared I might change my mind? Or was it all some sort of stupid dreadful misconception? Should I not stop it *now*? Mingling with these reflections, vivid scenes from the far past floated before my eyes with a coloured clarity which made the occupations of the present moment into shadows. How strange that behind a smiling chattering mask one may rehearse in the utmost detail pictures and conversations which constitute torture, that behind that mask one may weep, one may howl.

'What language are you going to learn next, Hilary?'

'Sanskrit. I've met a wonderful Indian girl who'll teach me.'

'I'm jealous! I can't think why you want to learn a dead language.'

'He knows all the living ones,' said Freddie.

'No, I don't. I don't know Chinese or Japanese or any Indian or African or Polynesian language. My Turkish is shadowy. My Finnish is poor—'

'Hilary loves showing off.'

'I always thought the Tower of Babel such a sinister myth,' said Freddie. 'Who could love a God who deliberately confused mankind in that mean way?'

'One could respect him,' said Clifford. 'He knew his business.'

'I wonder if there'll ever be a real international language?' said Freddie.

'There is. English.'

'Hilary is so chauvinistic.'

'What about Esperanto?' said Laura. 'Hilary, do you know Esperanto?'

'Of course.'

'Do you think it—?'

'How can one tolerate a language where the word for "mother" is "little father"?'

'Is it?'

'The Esperanto for "mother" is *patrino*.'

'Down with Esperanto!' said Laura.

'You are quite right that God knew his business,' I said to Clifford. I wanted to communicate with him, but he still refused to look at me. 'But one needn't take it too cynically. Nothing humbles human pride more than inability to understand a language. It's a perfect image of spiritual limitation. The cleverest man looks a fool if he can't speak a language properly.'

'That's why you want to know all languages, Hilary?' said Laura.

'Naturally.'

'God wanted us to see how limited we were?' said Freddie.

'He wanted us to see that goodness is a foreign language.'

'It's one of Hilary's metaphysical evenings,' said Freddie.

'I can't think how the words of all those languages don't get all mixed up in your head,' said Laura. 'They would in mine.'

'Word pie.'

Clifford was cold and silent, unsmiling, fiddling with his sweet, a mess of pineapple covered with some sort of nasty pungent liqueur. He suddenly turned to Freddie and said, 'What do you think of Templar-Spence's successor?'

'Oh yes,' said Freddie. 'Gunnar Jopling. A good appointment, don't you think? I gather he'll be with us in a week or two.'

'I can't eat this,' I said to Laura. 'It gets at my tooth. Do you think I could have some whisky?'

'Yes, of course. Is he Swedish or something, being called Gunnar? It's a nice name.'

'No, very English. May have had a Swedish ancestor. He's been seconded all over the place, hasn't he. Started in the Treasury. Then there was that business with the airlines. Then the International Monetary Fund, then the United Nations. Such an able man. I gather he's tipped to be head of the Civil Service.'

'Wasn't there something about his wanting to get into politics?' said Laura.

'I think there was some relief in the Labour Party when he decided not to! He might have got to the top rather too fast. A man of ruthless ambition. He'll certainly be a change from that old sheep Templar-Spence. He'll shake things up a bit in the department.'

'Will I like him?' said Laura.

'Women are always so personal,' said Freddie. 'Will she like him?'

'Is he married?'

'Are you after him already, darling? Yes, he is. He married Lady Kitty Mallow.'

'Oh yes, I remember now. That deb. She must be quite a lot younger than him. Isn't she fearfully rich?'

'I hear they've bought a house on Cheyne Walk,' said Freddie. 'Duncan told me when we met at the Cabinet Offices.'

'Must be rolling. She's his second wife, isn't she? Didn't the first one—something happened—'

'His first wife was killed in an accident,' said Clifford.

'Oh yes. And his son committed suicide.'

'That was later on.'

'Poor man,' said Laura. 'I expect that accounts for the ruthless ambition. When shall we invite him to dinner? He sounds so interesting. You haven't told me if I'll like him.'

'I've only seen him at meetings. He's such a cool customer it's hard to tell. Have you come across him at all, Clifford?'

'I knew him very slightly as an undergraduate,' said Clifford. 'And I've seen him in action at meetings. But the person to ask is Hilary. Hilary and he are old friends.'

There were exclamations. I drank the rest of the whisky very quickly and pulled my feet in under me ready to rise. Clifford's malice had taken me by surprise and I was totally unprepared to produce suitable lies. I saw Laura's face, reddened by wine, surrounded by the greying elf locks, ablaze with gleeful curiosity.

'Hilary, you're so secretive, so you're his friend, what fun! Do you know Lady Kitty too?'

'We shall now see Hilary rise to power!' said Freddie, who seemed not totally pleased with the unexpected news.

'Hilary will be asked to Cheyne Walk.'

'Hilary will hear all the secrets.'

'We shall have to make up to Hilary now.'

'We aren't friends,' I said. 'I mean—I don't know him at all well—I haven't seen him for years and years—we're complete strangers—I don't suppose he even remembers me—'

'Oh come, Hilary, once seen never forgotten!'

'Hilary is so modest.'

'Nonsense, Hilary. Now tell us all about him. What is he really like? Is he nice?'

'Well, is he nice?' said Clifford, with at last the ghost of a malicious smile as I was silently trying to think what to say.

'Oh very nice,' I said. 'But really I don't know him, really. Please don't expect—'

'Do you know Lady Kitty?'

'No—look—I haven't seen him for twenty years—'

'Did you know his first wife?' said Clifford, smiling more.

'No—Laura, I'm terribly sorry, but I'm in anguish with this tooth. Do you mind if I go home?'

Laura led me up to the drawing-room, where the lights were still goldenly on and the fire was burning and there was a strange silence. She held me by the sleeve, looking intently into my face.

'Here, my dear, have a little more whisky. Don't rush off. You're looking terribly odd. Have you really got toothache?'

'Yes.'

'Drink this. I'll give you some to take home with you. You haven't got toothache at all now, have you, confess.'

'No.'

'What a dear old liar you are. I always know. It's Tommy.'

'Yes.'

'Tell me, Hilary, tell me—'

'It isn't just Tommy,' I said. 'It's Crystal. She's going to marry Arthur Fisch.'

'Aaah—and you feel that you and Tommy—Darling, you mustn't marry Tommy just because Crystal is marrying Arthur.'

'Don't tell anyone about Crystal.'

'No, I won't. I understand, she may change her mind. Oh I do feel for you. I won't even tell Freddie. But I must come soon and talk to you about it. I'll come on Saturday.'

'I must go now, Laura dear.'

'Now I understand everything. I could see you were suffering. I can read you like a book, you know. Darling Hilary, I do love you.' Standing on tiptoe, Laura put her arms round me and pressed her hot cheek against mine. The jangling ornaments pressed into my shirt. She kissed me on the side of the mouth. The whisky dribbled onto the flowing gown.

THURSDAY

I WALKED very fast, pounding along like a machine, out of Queen's Gate Terrace, down Gloucester Road, along Cromwell Road, down Earls Court Road, along Old Brompton Road, along Lillie Road. The night was raw and cold, not raining, freezing. I could feel the frost forming underfoot on the damp pavements, slippery, crystalline. As I passed the railings of Brompton Cemetery I could feel the frost in the dark within, moving, fingering the grass, fingering the tombs, a ghost vainly seeking ghosts. I walked like a fast machine, my head erect, my arms swinging, my blood pumping. I could not bear to think of the conversation which had just ceased. There was a stone in my heart which was hatred, fear.

I arrived at Crystal's flat earlier than usual. I let myself in quietly and tiptoed half way up the stairs and listened. There was total silence up above. I could see the line of yellow light under the door. Misery and rage boiled round me in the darkness, seething in and out of my head in a surge of black atoms. I bounded up the last few steps and threw open the door.

Crystal and Arthur were sitting at the table. My entry was sudden enough to catch the essence of the previous scene. They were sitting silently at the table, their chairs turned sideways, close together, gazing into each other's eyes. They had both removed their glasses. Arthur had taken his jacket off. Each of them had rolled up a sleeve and they were caressing each other's arms upon the table.

They now faced me, red with guilt and embarrassment, rolling down their sleeves hastily, resuming their glasses. They both rose to their feet.

I sat down heavily on the third chair, scraping it loudly on the floor. I had drunk a lot of whisky and the fast walk had not improved things. Golden now, the atoms continued to boil round about me. Arthur put on his jacket, then picked up his overcoat and his woollen cap. 'Sit down,' I said to him. He sat down, and so did Crystal. I poured out some of the Spanish burgundy, spilling some on the table. 'Let's have a gossip,' I said.

'What did you have for dinner?' said Arthur.

'I forget. I didn't eat any.'

'We had fish fingers and chips and Lyons individual fruit

pies,' said Arthur. He could see that I was drunk, but he had seen that before. He was so happy he could not prevent a lunatic smile from distorting his face, making it almost unrecognizable.

'How's the 'flu, Hilary?'

'What 'flu?'

'I thought—'

'I reek of garlic,' I said.

'I can't smell it,' said Arthur.

'I tell you I reek of it.'

'Is it cold outside?' said Crystal.

'I didn't notice.'

There was a silence. They were both looking at me, Crystal very anxiously, Arthur with a vague happy benevolent gentleness. Crystal took her glasses off again and rubbed her eyes. She peered at me with her naked beautiful golden eyes, as if this would inspire some more direct communication. She was watching for a merciful sign. Almost anything would have served. I did not give one.

I said to her, 'Just guess who is the new head of our office?'

'Who?'

'Our old friend Gunnar Jopling.'

Crystal drew a gasping breath. Then she slowly put her glasses on, her mouth fell open, the big lower lip moist and trembling, and a quick red flush spread over her face and neck.

Arthur, who was not looking at her, said, 'I say, do you know him?'

'Used to. Ah well. Off we go. Come on, Arthur. Good night, petkin.'

'Wait,' said Crystal. 'Please wait—Hilary, can we—' She wanted to talk to me alone.

I felt perverse and cruel. I would not even look at her. I rose. I had not taken off my coat. I helped Arthur on with his, humming loudly in a way which prevented conversation.

'Could you stay, please?' said Crystal loudly over the humming.

'Sorry. Must go now. See you Saturday.' I picked up the burgundy bottle, intending to pour out the last drop for myself, but my hand was trembling so much I had to put it down again. I gave Crystal one look. She uttered a little quick—'ach—' I pushed Arthur out of the room, not giving him time for any farewell and followed him at once.

Outside I started humming again. It was bitterly cold.

Arthur took some time, as we walked along, fixing his layers of woolly cap down over his ears. He waited politely until, at Hammersmith Road, I stopped my roundelay.

'How interesting that you know Jopling. Is he nice?'

'Charming.'

'Where did you know him?'

'At college.'

'It'll be nice for him to find someone he knows in the office,' said Arthur. Arthur was quite sincere in uttering these inane words. He actually thought a man like Jopling might feel lonely and be cheered up by catching sight of a boyhood chum.

'We aren't on terribly close terms, we haven't seen each other for ages.' It had been idiotic to include Arthur in that little scene, but I had somehow wanted to console myself by shocking Crystal and then leaving her without an explanation. At the same time I terribly needed Crystal to know. Always, all my life, it had helped me to bear dreadful things if Crystal simply knew about them. Even if there was nothing she could do, her loving sharing mind drew off some of the pain. I felt this now as I wondered what was going to happen and what on earth I was going to do about Gunnar Jopling. 'I rather annoyed him at college because I won all the prizes. I expect we shall be quite polite but reserved when we meet. By the way, Arthur, I don't want it known in the office that I know him. This is just between you and me.'

'Of course I won't say a word,' said Arthur. The fact that Gunnar Jopling had won most of the available prizes since college and I had won none must I suppose have occurred to Arthur, or perhaps his asinine tactfulness prevented the thought from becoming conscious. Arthur's mind tended to inhibit discrediting thoughts.

We crossed the road and paused under a lamp post. 'Well, good night.'

'Hilary, it is all right, isn't it, about me and Crystal? You're not against it, are you? If you were —'

I intended to say Oh yes, splendid, but instead I picked up his words. 'Well, what would you do if I were?'

Arthur was silent for a moment and for the first time that evening I looked at his face. It was red and damp and burnished with the cold. 'I don't know,' he said. He looked at me mildly, exuding a sort of quietness.

I looked at him, and his brown troubled eyes, all moist and intent and screwed up against the chill air. His absurd woolly cap gave him a foreign look, and with his moustache he looked like a French soldier in the 1914 War. Then he seemed suddenly to recede. He looked like a ghost. He vanished. I laughed, and still laughing turned away eastward along the Hammersmith Road. It was beginning to be slightly foggy and the lamp posts stretched away down the almost empty road, each one surrounded by a globular fuzz of light.

FRIDAY

IT WAS Friday morning. It was just about daylight as I reached the office. Fog had swept over London during the night, not one of the thick great fogs, but something more like a sea mist, greyish, not brown, and carrying suspended in its gauzy being cold globules of water which lightly covered the overcoats of early Londoners with a spider's web of moisture which, in the warmth of tube trains and offices, turned the said overcoats into heavy steaming puddings. The woollen smell was once again pervasive, managing to carry with it overtones of dirt and sweat. I left my wet stinking coat on a coathanger in the cloakroom and hung up my umbrella and the cap which was having its first winter outing this morning, and went on to the Room, which was in darkness as usual at this time of day, and turned on the light, bringing the two long neon strips into action. After blinking twice on and off the cold very bright light revealed the Room.

Everything was different. The first thing I saw was that now a carpet covered the whole of the floor. Then I saw that my desk had been put back into the window. Mrs Witcher's desk stood behind mine, and Reggie Farbottom's desk had been placed near the door where mine had lately been. There was even another picture, a print of the Duke of Wellington, hanging on the near wall over Reggie's desk. The Room looked almost cosy. It must have been the carpet.

'How do you like it, Mr Burde?' said Skinker's voice behind me.

I turned round. Skinker and Arthur were standing in the corridor. They must have hidden in Arthur's cupboard as I came along, waiting to witness my surprise. Arthur's eyes were shining. I took in at once what an act of bravery this was on Arthur's part and how much Crystal's love must have inspired him to make him capable of it.

I did not smile. I said, 'I can't have Mrs Witcher behind me looking over my shoulder. Please put her desk back where it was before.'

Skinker and Arthur hastened to move Mrs Witcher's desk and push it against the wall.

'Good. That's all right now.' Then I smiled. (This was for Skinker's benefit. Arthur could sufficiently read my face.)

'We thought you'd be pleased, din' we,' said Skinker.

'I am pleased,' I said.

'I want to see them two's faces when they sees the fetty-comply.'

'Wherever did you get the carpet?' I asked Arthur.

'I went right up into the attics,' he said. 'I don't know whether we're supposed to. I found several rooms just full of oddments, old bits of carpet and broken chairs and stuff. I found the Duke up there too. I hope I won't get into trouble.' The vague idea of 'getting into trouble' dogged Arthur's office life quite a lot. It was a real credit to him that he had faced the danger of it for my sake.

'Thank you, Arthur, thank you, Skinker. I appreciate this.'

Mrs Witcher came in. The three of us watched her in silence. She took it all in, then marched past us to her desk. 'Clever dicks, aren't you!' she said over her shoulder. She sat down.

Reggie arrived. 'I say, who did this?'

'We did,' I said. 'Any objections?'

'Bloody selfish bugger, aren't you,' said Reggie. 'Mean selfish bugger. Isn't he, Edith? All right, little boy, fix it your way.' Edith made no reply. Reggie sat down. We had won.

I moved to the door with my allies. Skinker departed grinning with satisfaction. I went with Arthur into his cupboard. 'Thanks.'

'That's all right, Hilary. I hope they won't mind about the carpet.'

'Of course not.'

'I say—you didn't—last night—'

'Tell you what you wanted to hear. I'll tell you now. Of course I don't mind about you and Crystal. You have my blessing for what it's worth. I've never managed to wish myself much luck. But I wish you two plenty.'

'Oh thank heavens,' said Arthur. 'I mean, I knew you didn't—but it's jolly good, *jolly* good to hear you say that. It's the only thing I need to—'

'Make you perfectly happy.'

'Well, yes.'

'That's fine then. Everything's perfect.'

I went back into the Room across to my desk in the window. Big Ben's face, still illuminated, looked at me through the fog. I had missed him.

'I hope you're enjoying your mean little revenge,' said Edith.

'Even then he couldn't do it himself,' said Reggie. 'All he could do was cry until Arthur took over.'

I started to look at a case. Soon the Room would know all about Arthur's engagement. The news would be greeted with screams.

The lights suddenly went out.

'Bloody electricians, fuck them,' said Reggie's voice in the murk. There was a general sound of chairs moving, people emerging into the corridor. Laughter.

'Candles coming!' said Skinker's voice.

I stayed where I was looking out of the window into the grey gloom. Big Ben had been extinguished too. I thought of Biscuit. Who was she and would I ever see her again?

'The candles are rather fun, aren't they?' said Tommy.

London was still in darkness. Tommy had tried to make a little feast out of it. I was the skeleton. I said nothing.

Tommy's sitting-room, with a paraffin heater, was rather cold. She had laid an Indian cloth this evening, yellow with brown commas on it. There were six candles in modern pottery candlesticks. Our supper was fillet steak and salad and a treacle tart which she had made herself. She knew I liked treacle tart. I could not eat. I drank some of the St Emilion. She provided the wine. It tasted foul, but I drank some more. I considered telling Tommy everything. I should soon have to tell somebody. But no, not Tommy. What a bond such a confession would make.

Tommy was looking her most Victorian. It was partly the ringlets. She was looking tired, which suited her. The flickering light brought out the pitting of her face, illumined against a dark background, but did not reveal the colour of her eyes. Her little nose and mouth were wrinkled up with puzzlement and concern and love. Tonight she was wearing a white lacy blouse with a jet brooch in the form of a cross, a long black waistcoat and an ankle-length black velvet skirt, hitched up a little to reveal one delicate calf and one slim ankle in white openwork stocking, and one little velvet slipper. She had small feet. Her silver-ringed hands were busy pushing her trailing hair nervously back over the high collar of the blouse whose pure whiteness the candles were celebrating. Of all this I was, in spite of everything, aware and, in the curious way in which sex can poke its preoccupying presence into almost any state of affairs, I even found her attractive this evening. For me, the tides of her attractiveness ebbed and flowed under no discernible laws. When she did attract me it was a matter of something to be got over with, something which temporarily interrupted the ordinary courtesies of tenderness and kindness. I considered stretching my hand out to her across the yellow tablecloth as she was willing me to do, but I did not. Especially as things were now, I would have to get rid of Tommy.

She was now at her most patient and ingenious. She tried everything, every sort of conversation, every sort of silence. The slice of treacle tart, drenched in cream and quietly soaking lay untouched on my plate. I drank a little more wine and grimaced. I had said nothing about Crystal and Arthur. I could not face Tommy's joy.

'Would you like some whisky, darling?'

'No.'

'What do you want for Christmas?'

'A loaded revolver.'

'What is it—Hilary—dear heart—there's something. And it's not just me.'

'Sorry, Tomkins.'

'You're like a dead person tonight, a zombie.'

'I wish I was dead.'

'Don't speak so, it's wicked. Tell me. Tell me a little. Tell it in an allegory.'

'You are a funny girl. I like you sometimes.'

'I like you sometimes. Tell.'

'I can't, Tommy. I did something very wrong long ago. And I can't get away from it ever.' This was more than I had ever said to Tommy before and she knew it. I heard her little thrilled triumphant intake of breath and I shrank from her.

'Go on. Please. You know I love you. I just want to be you. To be a place where you are—where you spread out and are relieved of pain.'

'I can't be relieved of pain,' I said. 'Sin and pain are inextricably mixed. Only Jesus Christ could sort them out.'

'Let me be Jesus Christ. After all—they say—we can be—'

'No, you can't be, Tomkins, sorry. You're just you. You've made a treacle tart which I'm sorry I can't eat. I hope it won't be wasted.'

'Treacle keeps.'

'You're the little Scottish girl who knows that treacle keeps. My trouble is cosmic.'

After a pause Tommy said, 'Aren't you thinking rather too grandly of yourself? You are just you after all, with the crinkly hair and the crooked face and the odd socks on—'

'That's Laura Impiatt's joke.'

'Why do you bring Laura in here?'

'I don't know. Not because she's relevant.'

'It's Laura. That's your trouble. Laura. Why did you bring her in suddenly?'

'Oh, Tommy, stop—I'm going home.'

'Why did you suddenly mention Laura?'

'I don't know. My mind is wandering. Of course I think too grandly of myself. Who am I to have a cosmic sorrow? Come, Thomas, be kind to me.'

'Do you promise it isn't—?'

'Yes, yes, yes. Tommy. I must go. I'm very sorry.'

Tommy got up and rushed at my knees in a way she sometimes had. She was kneeling between my knees, her hands fumbling for my hands, her hair, smelling of shampoo (she always washed it on Fridays) tumbling about over the lower part of my jacket. 'Oh little Thomas—'

'My love—oh my love—let me help you—I love you so much—'

'I can't think why. Tommy, we must part.'

'Don't say that like that when we are communicating—'

'We aren't communicating. You are in some kind of rapture. I am as cold as a caller herring.'

'You want me.'

'I don't.' I thrust her roughly away before it should become too apparent that I did. She fell backwards, sitting upon the floor. I got up.

'I hate you.'

'OK, Thomson. Good night.'

'Don't go. Tell me. Tell me what it was you did. Tell me in an allegory.'

I left her. The streets were black except for the little glow-worm lights here and there of people making their way along with torches. But there was a celebration up above. The huge

109

brilliant arch of the Milky Way was visible, rejoicing silently in Reason's ear. The stars were so crowded together, they formed the segment of one golden ring. Yet the light they gave was to each other, they seemed not to know of us, and there was no brightness here below. I knew my London blindfold however. I began to walk north. It took me nearly half an hour to walk from Tommy's flat to Arthur's. It was half past ten when I rang Arthur's bell. A moment later I was with him in his little room lighted by one candle. I had decided to tell Arthur the whole story.

FRIDAY

I WILL now tell the story which is at the centre of this story, and which it was necessary to delay until the moment when, in this story, I told it. I will tell it now, as far as it can be told by me, truthfully and as it was, and not as I told it that Friday night to Arthur. In telling Arthur I omitted certain things, though nothing of importance, and I doubtless told it in a way which was sympathetic to myself, though, since I gave him the main facts, I could not in telling it excuse myself. I also told it somewhat in fits and starts, with pauses in which Arthur asked questions. And there were details which I filled in later when, in the days that followed, I spoke of these matters to him again. I told him because he was (I now believed) going to marry Crystal, and because he was a gentle harmless being, and because I had to tell somebody, I had to let the monstrous thing out of the sealed sphere which composed my consciousness and Crystal's. It is strange to think that on that momentous summer day in the past when at that party in my college rooms Crystal had cried out 'This is the happiest day of my life', Anne Jopling was actually present. She was there in that room on that day.

I first met Gunnar Jopling when I was an undergraduate and he was a young don in another subject (he was a historian) and at another college. He and my tutor, a mild man called Eldridge, gave a class together on 'French Literature and the Revolution', and I attended this class. It took place on Tuesdays round a long table covered with a green baize cloth in a rather dark room in Gunnar's college. It was one of those rather select classes with a restricted membership and all present thought well of themselves for being there. I was determined to be the star. I already had a considerable reputation as a linguistic polymath.

This was not the first time I had seen Gunnar. The very first time I saw him was across the High Street. He was striding along, wearing his gown, *arm in arm with Anne*. Someone said, 'There's Gunnar Jopling.' 'Who's the pretty girl?' 'Mrs Gunnar Jopling.' Gunnar had some sort of special reputation, the way some people have for no very clear reason. Of course he was clever, but there were plenty of clever people in Oxford. His appearance was striking, but again not exceptionally so. He was six foot two (an inch taller than me), a big burly chap (he had been a rugger blue and was also a notable boxer), thick straight fair hair and blue eyes and a very smooth glowing pink and white complexion. His eyes were a bright summer blue with a darker mottle, rather striking. He had a Scandinavian grandparent. He was himself English of the English and very public school.

I enjoyed the class and shone, though so unfortunately did others. We were a brilliant lot, we thought. Gunnar was a good deal more picturesque than Eldridge and I wanted Gunnar's good opinion and got it. About half way through the term Eldridge, a dry man but humane, told me that Gunnar had questioned him about me. Eldridge had told Gunnar a little about my background and this had perhaps kindled a mild interest, or so I inferred from the way in which the mottled blue eyes now scrutinized me. I suppose I was generally looked on as a bit of an oddity. There was nothing very special in all this. I sought the good opinion of any don whom I respected. I always imagined that every old Damoetas would love to hear my song. I went later (I think Gunnar actually suggested this to Eldridge) to a class which Gunnar gave on the Risorgimento. I talked to him occasionally after classes, and once or twice when I met him in the street, but he never invited me to his rooms and I never especially coveted this honour though it would certainly have flattered me. When I got my First Gunnar sent a card with 'well done' written in his tiny hand. Then a little while later, when I was elected to a fellowship at Gunnar's college, he sent me a letter of welcome in pleasingly friendly terms which led me to believe that he must have been partly instrumental in getting me in.

An Oxford college is an odd little democratic society. As the fellows run the college, personalities can gain an importance which is far from frivolous. I was well aware (because such things get around) that my election had not been uncontested. There were those who held that I was merely, in the narrowest and dullest sense, a linguist. 'Burde reads poetry for the grammar,' was a *mot* of my college enemy, Stitchworthy, who had, I was of course rapidly informed, bitterly opposed my fellowship. Gunnar's good opinion must have counted for a lot. When I knew that I had been elected, that the thing that I wanted most in the universe was now mine, I trembled with joy but also with fear. I had fought every inch of the way to where I was, and I could not have done so without having a good deal of confidence in myself as a scholar. However I also knew that I was still very far from the highly desirable condition of having 'caught up'. There were huge areas of ignorance, holes into which I might stumble, lacunae which men like Gunnar or Eldridge or Clifford Larr had quietly filled up during their schooldays without even noticing what they were doing. I was terrified of making some memorable public blunder. And I was, as I entered my paradise, secretly very vulnerable to the sarcasm of Stitchworthy and his friends and correspondingly grateful for the protection of Gunnar's respect.

I settled in. My pupils took me for granted and did not fall off their chairs laughing at the idea of being instructed by me. My colleagues turned out to be less formidable (and also in some cases considerably less brilliant) than I had imagined beforehand. The younger dons made a joke of Stitchworthy, calling him Dame Stitch. I began timidly to decorate my rooms, copying heartily from Gunnar and others whom I imagined to have good taste. I began to make plans to bring Crystal to Oxford and settle her there in some elegant nest and possibly even select some very superior person to be her husband. I also began to draw up a plan for her education, which was now at last to be taken in hand. During this time Crystal and I were both mad with happiness. Crystal was still in the north where she was finishing her course in dressmaking. (Aunt Bill was dead by then, thank God.) She was, I think, a bit nervous about coming to Oxford, in case she should 'disgrace me'. She was not at all concerned about her hypothetical grand marriage, and nor in any serious sense indeed was I. What delighted her most, after my success, was the idea that now I would teach her. I would tell her to read books and she would read them. She would work for me, work to become, for me, a worthier, more useful, more presentable sister.

I began to relax a little bit more into my surroundings, to acquire protective colouration. I bought a motor car. This absolutely delighted Crystal. I was soon on fairly easy terms with most of my colleagues, but without quite making friends. I was still awkward, separatist, aggressive, touchy. Gunnar treated me as his protégé in a way which sometimes annoyed me, though he was unfailingly kind. I admired him, I wanted to be friends with him, and yet at the same time I snubbed him. We once nearly quarrelled seriously in fact over Stitchworthy.

Stitchworthy, who was also a historian, had written an article for a learned journal concerning Cromwell, in which he had included a discussion of Marvell and a reference to Horace's *Epistles*. He quoted a piece of Horace and made clear from his remarks that he had misconstrued it. When I spotted this I could hardly believe my luck. I wrote a short dry note designed for the journal in question, pointing out Stitchworthy's howler, and concluding, 'grammarians may or may not read a poem adequately, but those ignorant of grammar are not reading it at all.' I showed this little masterpiece to Gunnar, expecting him to be amused; but he was on the contrary rather annoyed and said I ought not to publish it. He said the note was spiteful in tone and that it was bad form so soon after my election, to attack a senior don in my own college, and crow over his mistakes. He said we were all capable of making mistakes. I thought his attitude was absurd and we parted angrily. I published the note. Gunnar forgave me. Stitchworthy of course never did.

Before this I had met Anne Jopling. I first met her when I was looking over my new rooms, before I had actually moved in. It was July, a blazing hot day, and I was looking out of one of the windows in a mindless daze of happiness, surveying the extremely elegant front quad of my new college, when Gunnar and Anne came in under the archway. She was wearing a flowery mauve dress of some very light veil-like material, with a broad mauve belt. She was very slim. She looked up at the window and saw me and smiled, thereby making clear that she knew who I was. Then she said something to Gunnar. He called up, 'Can we come and see your rooms?' I said yes, of course, please. 'We'll be up in a few minutes.' Then he and Anne arrived with a bottle of champagne and three glasses. 'I thought we should toast your arrival.' I was incoherent with gratitude and joy. It was one of those perfectly happy moments, which must be fairly rare in any life, when good will and circumstance glorify a human encounter. Gunnar introduced Anne, who said she had heard so much about me and had long been wanting to meet me.

Anne is not easy to describe. Her face still seems to me the most beautiful human face I ever saw, although she would perhaps not generally have been thought excessively good-looking. Her face had a secret private inward pure dewy beauty which, to me, *blazed* forth. Her hair was mousy-brown and straight and cut in a simple sort of bob. She had a large brow and a rather bony face, with slightly prominent blue-grey eyes and a long sensitive mobile beautifully shaped mouth. She never wore make-up. Her skin was very fine, as if transparent, and always seemed very slightly moist. Her eyes had a moist bright look and absolutely *shone* with intelligence. To say it was 'a clever face' would quite misdescribe it, though of course it was a clever face. It was a shining face, shining with interest and warmth and wit and a benign intelligent curiosity about everything. It shone upon me now as we drank the champagne in my empty rooms on that sunny summer day, and we chattered and laughed and were utterly happy. We were very young. I was twenty-three. Gunnar was twenty-seven. Anne was twenty-five. They had been fellow students. They had a son of four.

I said I hoped I would see them at my party, which was to take place next week in my old undergraduate rooms, the party at which Crystal was so happy, and they said they would come. (It was the first party I had ever given.) And they came and they both went out of their way to be absolutely angelic to Crystal and I could have kissed their feet. I suppose Crystal was a funny little object at that party. I daresay I was a funny object myself. During that long vacation the Joplings, lingering in Oxford, asked me to dinner. Then asked me again. They lived in an untidy large Victorian house in north Oxford, full of beautiful things but not a bit like a museum. Both their families were (as I conceived it then) well off. Their little son, called Tristram, was clever and pretty and well-behaved. (Only I did not like children.) They were obviously very happy. They were extremely kind to me. The Michaelmas Term began, my first term as a college tutor, and I saw quite a lot of Gunnar and Anne, I met them at their house, at other houses, in college.

As an undergraduate I had of course felt, in the mechanical way that men do, interested in the girls whom I saw about me. I joined no societies (I only briefly mistook my love for Russian for a love for Marx) and the sports I practised were exclusively male. Everyone else seemed much better at making friends, of either sex, than I was. I occasionally talked to the girls whom I got to know through my work (a rather clever one attended Gunnar's classes), but they tended to giggle at me and I immediately became offended and withdrew. On a few occasions I even invited girls to tea, but I found it so hard to talk to them and felt so awkward and embarrassed that I thoroughly bored. them, and indeed they bored me. And I could hardly ask them to come into my bedroom and lie down without having made at least a little genial conversation first. (Or so I thought. Perhaps I was wrong.) I remained virgin throughout my undergraduate days without feeling the anxiety which so often afflicts men who have been unable to test themselves in this respect. I was far more anxious about my exams. I was *busy*. Like a knight upon a quest I was dedicated, under orders. I had to rescue myself and Crystal, to get us out of the dark hole in which we had grown up and out into the sunlight, into freedom. I had to *win* the inalienable advantages necessary for the completion of the rescue. I had to make myself absolutely *safe*. Until this was done nothing else really mattered much. On that day in July when I stood in my new rooms and looked out of the window I felt that at last I was safe. I had pulled it off. I had done it.

To say that I then felt free to fall in love puts it too simply. That was an aspect of the matter. A pair of blinkers which had kept me narrowly to a single task had been removed. I suddenly saw much more of the world. I rested. Or at least I tried to. The habit of relentless activity is hard to break. Yes, I was ready to fall in love. But I did not fall in love with just anybody, I fell in love with Anne, in spite of there being every reason why I ought not to, because those shining clever gentle eyes somehow, and from the very first moment, looked right into my soul and I felt myself *known* for the first time in my life. Of course Crystal knew me, but Crystal and I were so much jumbled up together that it might be more accurate to say that Crystal was me. There was no element of discrimination and shaping judgment. Anne met me as a stranger, saw me as a stranger, and miraculously understood me. Her presence made me rest, every muscle, every atom, became quiet and relaxed. I lived, I saw, I was. Time, which had been a clock ticking away the dangerous moments of my urgent trial, the test I simply must not fail, suddenly became silent and huge. It was not that, at first at any rate, we had any very significant talk. Her presence simply gave me some absolute calm joy which I did not at first recognize as a form of love.

It was not until the beginning of the Hilary Term that I put it to myself that I was really in love for the first time, that this was it, that I had fallen madly in love with Anne Jopling. The discovery that one is in love is automatically delightful, unless there are very strong contrary factors. There were strong contrary factors. She was the wife of a man I liked and respected and who was by way of being my benefactor. She

116

was happily married. She was not in love with me. But since I did not envisage any attempt to seduce her or indeed to bother her at all with the news of my extraordinary condition, I felt free to enjoy it privately, to experience that amazing enlargement of the world, its mythical transformation, its beatification, which being in love brings about. Of course I was also a martyr, I was pierced and pinned, I writhed in agony. I went about Oxford in a secret daze of pain and joy, not thinking of the future at all, and certainly not even remotely meditating upon the capture of the beloved. Then one day she kissed me.

Of course this was not the first time. Grown-up Oxford kisses a lot, in a way which surprised and rather shocked me when I was first made free of that rather peculiar society. Oxford is a very hedonistic place. (I am told Cambridge is quite different.) At dinner parties, even at cocktail parties, people who scarcely know each other embrace and kiss. Anne surprised me very much by kissing my cheek on the second occasion of my being invited to dinner. I was then not yet in love, or at any rate not aware of it. I can still vividly recall the unexpected fresh touch of those lips upon my cheek, suddenly in the porch of that big house, in the summer dark nearly twenty years ago. But that, as I say, was the sort of kiss which everyone at Oxford was constantly bestowing and receiving, and meant absolutely nothing.

The serious kiss happened in my rooms on the second of March; it was the sixth week of the Hilary Term. By then it was a custom that she would come sometimes to bring me things, stuff for the rooms, curtain hooks, picture hooks, ashtrays, a little cushion. She did this for other people too, she enjoyed giving little presents and 'mothering' the younger bachelor dons. She had (perhaps unwisely? She and Gunnar often discussed this) given up her own academic career. (She too had got her 'first'.) There was only one child, though they ardently hoped for more. Anne had time and creative energy to spare. I had by now been fully in love for over a month. I had managed to do my teaching and behave like a sane person, only my social life, such as it was, had completely ceased as I had to stay in my rooms all the time in case Anne should decide to call. On this day, it was about eleven o'clock in the morning and the sun was shining. I had a pupil, but I dismissed him as soon as Anne turned up. She chided me for this. She had brought me some blotting paper. (I had once complained that somehow or other I never seemed to have any.) She had brought a large packet of sheets of different colours. She pulled the package open and displayed the sheets on my table fanwise, laughing. I offered her some sherry, and she refused, saying it was too early and anyway she was in a rush and must go now. I had not seen her for six days, during which time I had not left my room except for dashes to the dining hall. Now she had come and was at once proposing to go. We were both standing leaning against the mantelpiece, she admiring her fan of blotting paper, I staring at her. She was making some jest and laughing. Then she turned to me, and stopped laughing. Of course my expression was unmistakable and concealment was at an end. I suppose in the agony of that threatened departure, I had deliberately brought it to an end. She looked at my grim face for a moment, then she kissed me on the lips.

I became instantly mad. I grasped her violently in my arms and drew her closely up against me and held her there in a blind ecstasy of motionless passion. I held her furiously in silence for what seemed ages and ages. She was at first quite still, then she began to struggle.

I slowly let her go. I saw her face, utterly and forever changed. I was still mad. I said, 'I love you. Will you come in here, will you come in here with me and lie down? Just for a moment. I want to hold you. I've never made love to anybody. Come in with me, please, please.'

She was marvellously direct. Her restraining controlling hand was still pressed against my shoulder. 'Hilary. I'm sorry. Stop this. Is it just that—you want to find out—if you can make love?'

'I love you, Anne. I worship you. I think about you all the time. I've never loved anyone else. I love you to insanity, to death, I can't help it. Oh don't go away from me, please, don't leave me.' I fell on my knees, grasping her legs, embracing her skirt and her mackintosh, pressing my head against her thigh.

'Hilary, get up. *Get up!*'

The door had very softly and quietly opened and like a cat entering Tristram had come into the room.

I got up.

Anne, her face blazing, turned quickly and took Tristram by the hand and disappeared out of the door.

Only after she had gone did I feel, in a sort of memory hallucination, her heart beating violently against my heart. I went into my bedroom and fell face downwards on the bed and lay there biting my hands and moaning.

FRIDAY

I was to go to dinner with the Joplings three days later.
The three days were three blanks of white hell with a few
flashes of lurid joy. I had of course soon clarified the matter of
the kiss. She had just kissed me out of impulsive kindness, out
of the general happiness of her fulfilled life, out of the casual
affection which such as she could easily spare for a deprived
person such as me. The whole incident must be sealed off.
That kiss too meant nothing. Except that Anne would not
come to see me again. I was not even sure that I ought to go
to dinner. I went because I had to. I had to see her. And when
I saw her all clarification vanished. Eldridge was there and a
visiting Italian scholar. We talked Italian. Anne's was even
better than Gunnar's. She behaved as usual, except that,
when I first arrived, her eyes showed consciousness of what
had happened. It was also somehow mysteriously clear to me
that she had said nothing to Gunnar. I had not even wondered
in these three days whether she would have told her husband.
I had forgotten Gunnar's existence. When I was leaving she
kissed my cheek as usual. I pressed her hand hard, and then
regretted this because it left me uncertain whether or not she
had pressed mine.

Hell really began after that. Of course Anne would tell
Gunnar sooner or later. I would never be invited or visited
again. What was I going to do? I had now no serious occupation except thinking about Anne. I continued to teach and to
eat, but I did these things in a coma, and in any case the
term was now almost over. I avoided occasions of meeting
Gunnar in college, though when we did meet he was perfectly friendly and ordinary. Then I heard someone say in hall
that the Joplings were leaving for Italy as soon as the vacation
began. I made myself even more of a hermit. Term ended and
I sat in my rooms unable even to answer Crystal's letters. I
did not reflect or speculate or make plans. I just suffered
blankly from Anne's absence, like someone who is totally
absorbed in a physical pain. There was nothing else but this
pain; except that sometimes I would feel a teasing urge to
rush to her house and find out if she was still there. I sat in my
armchair in my rooms and suffered. I did not even wait, I
suffered. I wanted, if I wanted anything precise, enough days
to have passed for me to be sure that she had left Oxford.
Then one morning, again about eleven o'clock, she suddenly
entered my room.

She came towards me and I took her in my arms at once. I
could not speak. She was quiet for a moment, then began to

release herself. 'Hilary. Please. Just listen to what I say, believe what I say and don't think there is anything else. We're going to Italy. I couldn't just go away. I thought I could. But I kept worrying about you. I couldn't leave without seeing you again. So, I just came to say good-bye. Just that. Don't suffer, oh don't suffer, don't—Good-bye—' And she darted out of the door. I stood where I was, transmuted. Ah if only, if only she had not come! Without that visit I might have managed myself, have savaged my love into hopelessness and the saving lie of appearance. Without that, I would not have let myself believe in her *interest*, not felt again the *complice* beating of her heart with mine. As it was, I now had enough and more than enough to live on for the whole vacation. I knew now that I should see her again, that I should hold her in my arms again. I became suddenly blissfully happy. I could even work. Crystal came down and I drove her round the Cotswolds in the car. However I curtailed her visit and could not talk to her of the future. Of course I said nothing about Anne. I spent the rest of the vacation in my rooms, reading, working. I read poetry and enjoyed the grammar and the poems too. I luxuriated in Russian. I played with Turkish. I made progress in Hungarian. I prepared my lectures for next term. And *now* I waited.

The Joplings returned just before term. I met Anne in the quad. Gunnar was over near the gate, out of earshot, talking to the college organist. (He was a great arranger of concerts.) He waved to me. I waved back. I said to Anne, 'I've got to make love to you, I've got to, I don't care if I die afterwards, I've got to and I'm going to.' Gunnar approached across the grass. 'Hello, Hilary.' 'Hello. Had a nice time in Italy?' 'Marvellous. We were in Calabria. We nearly bought a farmhouse. Why don't you come in to dinner tomorrow? That would be OK, wouldn't it, Anne?' I went to dinner. I drove my ankle hard against Anne's under the table. She drew away. Three days later she came to my room.

It was on a Wednesday afternoon in the fourth week of Trinity Term that she gave in at last. She came first out of pity, so she said, and because she feared I might make some desperate move. I think if I had not told her that I was virgin and that it was bed I wanted, if I had talked more tenderly and sentimentally of being in love, she might have been able to resist. As it was, I think it began to seem to her something simple and quickly given, which she had and I needed, and which out of her generosity she would have to give me sooner or later. She wanted to show me that I could love a woman. In fact I never doubted that I could, but it helped both of us if I let her think of it in this way. I was totally in love, but I wanted to make love, to screw her, more urgently than I had ever wanted anything, and this was the role my love played to her, and the guise, which had its own sort of pseudo-innocence, in which it presented itself. Of course she understood the rest of it too and would not have consented had she not known that my whole being was her slave. But it was my pressing need that she met, not the rest. The rest could wait. We pretended that this huge love did not exist, while at the same time we knew that it was the only possible ground of our proceeding. And thus complicitly we cheated each other. In fact Anne was by this time, though she tried to conceal it, physically very much in love with me. I could hardly believe at first that this was so. What a black glory shone around when I realized it. I drew her like a magnet and she had to come to me. She flew south through Oxford, she flew to my rooms, distraught with need, dissolving into relieved joy as she entered. And still I talked simply of her kindness, my gratitude.

After the great holy enactment of that Wednesday afternoon, after we had dressed, we stood dazed, hand in hand, gazing haplessly as if we pitied each other, stunned by the immensity of the tornado which had picked us up and deposited us in another country. There was no simple thing now which was needed and could be given. We had created a maze and were lost. And now we could see the possibilities of pain, our pain and that of others. After Anne's first visit to me, after her return from Italy, I had put a complete stop to all Crystal's arrangements. Crystal had intended to spend most of Trinity Term in lodgings in Oxford. I told her it was impossible, there was no suitable accommodation, I was working too hard, everything would have to wait. Of course Crystal did not complain. I had cleared the decks for action, but what action was possible? What was there for me to do except to continue to beg a married woman to visit me in secret? In any case how much longer could it be secret? Anne visited lots of people, but it was still a fact that every time she crossed the quad dozens of curious eyes could mark where she went. We parted passionately, but without any plan. We could not bear even to talk of a plan. I heard nothing from her for a week.

At the end of the week I received a letter from her saying that we had better not meet again. I did not reply. I stayed in my rooms and waited. She came. We made love. It sounds as if it was a pretty heartless business. Any story can be told many ways; and there is a kind of justice in the fact that this one could be told cynically: a young wife and mother secretly amusing herself, a libertine deceiving his best friend, and so on. There is no escape here from damnation by the facts. I do not in any case want to excuse myself, but I do want to try to excuse Anne. It was all so complicated and it happened, not all at once, but in little movements each one of which seemed to have its own inevitability and its own sense. We were young and gripped by the awful compelling force of physical love. I was in total love from the start. Anne became so. She was sorry for me. Pity changed imperceptibly into enslaving fascination. She felt the grains of violence in me and yearned over them. I talked about my past. I told her things I had not told even to Crystal. She talked about her past. I could communicate with her, miraculously, totally. She *saw* me, she attended to me more than anyone had ever done, even Mr Osmand. It was like being seen by God. She bathed my hurt soul in a reviving dew. Yet at the same time we were both in hell. She suffered hideously. I saw her bright face changing, losing its joy, and I ground my teeth with despair and fury against the Fates. If only this woman were not married, if only things were different, if only— She did not want to come to me and yet she did and she came. She loved her husband and her son, but she loved me too and she desired me in a way in which (I suspect: she never said this) she had never desired her husband. We suffered so much together during that May and that June, and comforted each other, and resolved to part, and could not part, and wept.

Then one day she came and I knew at once from her face what had happened. Gunnar had found out. We never discovered how, but it would not have been difficult. He asked her and (as we had agreed she must) she told him. I did not ask her how he behaved. She went away from me in a misery such as I had never seen, like a dead woman walking. The next morning I got a letter from Gunnar which just said, *Please leave Anne alone. Please.* Then nothing for several days. Gunnar did not appear in College. Term came to an end. I was in a frenzy, but now there were dreadful hopes. I had no intention of giving her up. We had, as it were, waited for Gunnar's knowledge, as we had waited for Anne's surrender, treating these things as blank wall-like barriers beyond which things would have to change, beyond which it was fruitless to try to look beforehand. Now that this last one was past I knew that I must simply persuade Anne to come to me, to come to me forever, to break and abandon her marriage, and marry me instead. And I knew too, with the strength of the hold which I had at that moment on her being, that this was possible. I must, as a first move, simply take her away, kidnap her if necessary, be alone with her for a long time: for a long time without lies at last. Waiting was anguish now, since I felt that every hour which she remained with Gunnar was diminishing my power. On the fourth day I telephoned her and asked her to meet me in St John's garden. My college rooms were not safe any more. I met her and she cried for an hour. We hid ourselves in the wildest part of the garden and she cried and cried. I told her all that I felt, all that I intended. She was incoherent, practically hysterical. I was demented with distress. Nothing could be planned or even discussed.

The following evening at about nine o'clock she arrived in my rooms with a white rigid face, trembling and shuddering. I gave her some whisky and took a stiff drink myself. She said, 'I simply had to run out of the house.' This was what I had been waiting for. I said, 'I'll take you away. Come.' I seized a few things and threw them into a suitcase, then led her down the stairs and put her into my car. I was in a sweat of terror all the time in case Gunnar should turn up. Not that I feared any violence which he could put upon me, but I wanted to take this god-given chance to carry her right away while she was in a mood of absolute flight. I was trembling so much myself I could hardly start the car. Anne sat beside me in a trance, staring blankly ahead. As we careered through Headington towards the London road she said, 'Where are we going?' 'To London.' 'No—please—take me home—' 'Certainly not. I am running away with you forever. I am your home now.' She began to cry. Before we got to the motorway she said, 'Hilary, stop please. There's something I've got to tell you.' 'There's nothing more to say, darling. We love each other. It's too late for regrets now. You're mine.' 'Stop, please, I've got to tell you something. *Stop.*'

I slowed down and drew the car into a lay-by. There was a blue midsummer dusky light, the sky still glowing but the earth darkening. I turned to her in the dimness. Passing cars, their headlights just switched on, momently revealed her face.

'Anne, darling, I love you. Don't leave me. You've come to me now, don't leave me, I should die.'

She put her arms round my neck with such a gesture of

confidence and absolute love that for a moment all fear left me. Then pulling back she said, 'Hilary, it's no good.'

'Don't. I shall start the car. We've escaped, we're going on. You're mine.'

'No, no, listen. We can't go. I'm pregnant.'

I stared at her dim white face in the gathering darkness. I could not see her eyes, but I knew from the convulsive trembling of her body that she was crying. 'So soon,' I said. 'Well, surely that is it, the final bond between us. You *can't* leave me now. Are you sure?' I was however instinctively appalled.

'Yes. But Hilary, you haven't understood—'

'What—you mean—'

'Yes. It's not your child, it's Gunnar's.'

A flood of icy coldness filled my heart and my veins. I kept my voice hard and steady. 'You mean it might be?'

'No. It is. Because of the time. There isn't any doubt. I thought perhaps—but I kept wanting not to know. I only found out just now for certain—I thought it just couldn't be—and I really meant earlier to leave you—I meant to leave you as soon as Gunnar found out, I thought I'd have to—so I just—let things drift—and kept hoping it wasn't—and didn't go to the doctor—oh I've been so wicked, so stupid—'

'I see,' I said. 'You intended to leave me as soon as Gunnar found out. You never told me so.'

'I didn't intend anything. What could I do? I couldn't see what I would do. I'm caught. I love Gunnar. I love Tristram. It's my doom that I love you too. You don't know, even you don't know at all, what I've had to suffer in these last months—'

'You sound quite resentful,' I said, keeping the cool hard tone.

'I suppose I am in a way. I was so happy—before you came along.'

'Too bad. I was so happy before you came along too.'

'Then it's plain—isn't it—we must part—oh God—we must both try to be—as we were before—it's such agony—I'm sorry, my darling, I'm very very very sorry—Please will you drive me home? Oh my God, I do love you, I do love you—But it's just hopeless—' She was shuddering and wailing.

I said, 'Does Gunnar know?'

'About the baby? Yes.'

If only she had lied at that point. If only she had not told me that as well.

'So he thinks you're tied to him—because of the bloody baby?'

'I am tied.'

'No,' I said. 'I'm afraid you aren't. You're wrong there. You're coming with me, baby and all. Wherever we're going now we're going together, my darling.' Fearful rage and misery possessed my body, making it violent, mechanical, precise. I started the car again and drove on.

'Hilary, please take me home, please, please, please—'

I said nothing. We came onto the motorway.

'Hilary, please don't drive so fast, do you want to kill us both—Hilary don't drive so fast—Hilary, *Hilary*—oh please please take me home—oh stop, stop, stop, don't drive so fast—'

The car crossed the central reservation at about a hundred miles an hour. It was a matter of chance which car on the other side we hit. We hit a Bentley driven by a stockbroker and travelling almost equally fast. Both cars were completely smashed and six other cars were severely damaged. The stockbroker escaped with two broken legs. No one else was badly hurt except me and Anne. I had multiple injuries. Anne died in hospital on the following day.

I never doubted that I had behaved wickedly. That knowledge I carried away with me into the years to come. But the thing itself as we lived it was such a complex of contradictions and misunderstandings and mistakes and little makeshifts and sheer blind muddled waiting and hoping. How could we know that it was wending its way to that end? I was dreadfully in love with the sort of black certain metaphysical love that cuts deeper than anything and thus seems its own absolute justification. *On n'aime qu'une fois, la première.* I think this is true of the one and only Eros. Though also perhaps the one and only Eros is not the greatest of all the gods. Anne was dreadfully in love too, but her love was crazed, crazed with the hopelessness of it all, which perhaps she saw and I did not. She loved her husband; and I could *remember*, even at the times of blackest glory, how happy she had been when I first met her; and I could see too how destroyed she was later, destroyed by me and by my terrible love.

I thought later on, as the years passed in almost uninterrupted meditation upon the events of that summer, that I had perhaps overestimated the force of her passion. It may have been so. Even if she had not discovered that she was pregnant would she ever really have decided to leave Gunnar and come to me? What went on between them after Gunnar found out? This I did not know or want to know. On the other hand, if I had not become mad with rage at what she told me, if I had simply driven her away with me on that night, was it conceivable that she would have stayed with me, would not her tears have forced me finally to take her home to Gunnar and Tristram? Of course she loved me, that could not be doubted. Perhaps she was impressed by the force of my love; being thus impressed is as good a cause of real love as another. If only she had not come back to me after that first kiss. If only she had not told me that Gunnar knew she was pregnant. That revelation had some sort of terrible importance at that moment. If she had not told me it would all have seemed a problem, an obstacle, something to be dealt with by me, I would not have been precipitated straight into fury and despair. There are those who hold that the world is well lost for love. I did not think this. I loved Anne with a concentration of my whole being which could only happen once. But I wished forever that I had not. I wished I had never met her. For the world was lost indeed, and I had lost it not only for myself but for Crystal.

I resigned my fellowship of course. Gunnar also resigned. He went into politics for a short time, contested a Labour seat, then entered the Civil Service and began to become a successful and famous man. I was (I think this describes it) ill for years. Not really mentally ill. I never thought I would go mad. But I was simply crushed, unmanned. I had lost my moral self-respect and with it my ability to control my life. Sin and despair are mixed and only repentance can change sin into pure pain. I could not clean the resentment out of my misery. Did I repent? That question troubled me as the years went by. Can something half crushed and bleeding repent? Can that fearfully complex theological concept stoop down into the real horrors of human nature? Can it, without God, do so? I doubt it. Can sheer suffering redeem? It did not redeem me, it just weakened me further. I, who had so long cried out for justice, would have been willing to pay, only I had nothing to pay with and there was no one to receive the payment. I knew I had killed Anne (and her unborn child) almost as surely as if I had hit her with an axe. The business was brilliantly hushed up by Gunnar. (No wonder he succeeded later in high level diplomacy.) He put it around that I was kindly giving Anne a lift to London. Later my name was dropped from the story altogether. I disappeared from Oxford as if I had never existed. Much later I heard someone say that Gunnar Jopling's first wife had died by crashing her car. I imagined that I would carry the placard *Murderer* around my neck forever. But people have their own troubles and tend to forget. One is not all that interesting. Even Hitler is being forgotten at last.

Crystal of course was perfect. It was for a little while unclear whether I would live. I lived and completely recovered. Crystal sat by me for weeks and months. I did not tell her everything at once, but in the end I did tell her everything. She knew we were both done for. She was perfect. I could not work for a year, not because of my bodily health but because I was in despair. I suffered an agony of remorse about Anne which bit me physically, doubling me up for whole parts of the day. I had a problem about responsibility for the past which became a problem of identity. I mourned and mourned about the destruction of my hopes. The loss of Oxford, of learning and scholarship and improvement, the loss of Crystal's metamorphosis and Crystal's happiness. I went back to the north and lived for a year with Crystal in one room in the town where I was born. People who had known me and envied me came to survey with satisfaction the wreckage of clever ambitious fortunate Hilary Burde. (A pity Aunt Bill missed that. She would have loved it.) Mr Osmand had already left the town. I hoped he never heard. I wept over Crystal. She wept over me. She supported me by returning to work in the chocolate factory. To this day the smell of chocolate brings back the horror of that time.

It would of course have been possible to recover and to set out once more on the quest of all the things I wanted and had so largely got when I met Anne. Oxford would be impossible of course, but there were other universities where I could have set myself up, where I could have educated Crystal and lived something like the sort of life which I had coveted. It would have been possible to do this in the sense that someone else in similar circumstances might have been able to do it. I was not able. At any rate I did not do it. Paradoxically, I might have survived better alone. It was the thought of Crystal's suffering, her loss, her disappointment that was my chief millstone; and grief itself sapped the will to find any remedy. I just wanted to die, at least that was my mood. I could not kill myself because of Crystal. I wanted to hide. After the year in the north I went to London, as criminals and destroyed people do, because it is the best place to hide. And I hid. And Crystal came and hid with me. I got a job as a clerk in a car hire firm. I lost the job when I was required to do some driving. I had been banned from driving for life after the accident. I got a little job with an estate agent, then a little job in a local government office. At last I gravitated into the civil service, at the humble level at which I had remained ever since until I almost began to think of myself as an old man.

Gunnar had vanished from my life, as I imagined forever. As he became more important and successful I began to hear of him, to read about him in the newspapers, but though these reminders jabbed like daggers it was news of a stranger. Gunnar was a big international man, someone existing in Brussels, in Geneva, in Washington, in New York, never to cross my path again. I only saw him once after the accident. He came to see me in the hospital as soon as I was able to talk. (My jaw was smashed and speech was impossible for some time.) He was cold and civil and asked me, as if he were a police officer investigating some minor offence, to tell him about the accident. I told him; at least I told him the mechanical details, the speed of the car, the way it somersaulted. The crash had deprived me of consciousness and I did not see Anne after the moment of impact. He asked nothing more. He went away without any show of emotion, without any remark or look which could establish a connection between us. And at his cue I was equally cold. Later I went over and over this last meeting in my mind thinking of things I might have said. 'I'm sorry. Forgive me.' Yet how could I, without help from him, have said that? If only he had shown a flicker of emotion I could have burst out to him. But there was no emotion and no outburst. I thought later of writing to him, but I never wrote. Tristram committed suicide at the age of sixteen.

SATURDAY

IT WAS Saturday morning. It was a cold day with a lot of low scurrying brown clouds and a bitterly cold wind and a few flashes of watery sun which simply showed up how wet and muddy London was. I had had bad dreams, most of which I had forgotten, the atmosphere of horror only remaining. Would that our sins had built-in qualities of oblivescence such as our dreams have. One dream I remembered. I was in a quiet awful place beside some water where some huge crime either had been committed in the past or would be committed in the future. Not knowing which was part of the dreadfulness of the dream.

This morning I heartily regretted having told Arthur. At the time I had felt relieved to tell. There had been an almost orgiastic satisfaction in doing so. I had sent Arthur out to get some wine, and I had drunk a great deal. This morning I felt terrible, sick and giddy and disgusted with myself. I ate three aspirins and drank a great deal of water. It was not that I doubted Arthur's discretion or that I minded his knowing. This knowledge, which would have been intolerable inside almost anyone else's head, was harmless in Arthur's. It just now seemed a terrible mistake to have relived it all. All that immodest spewing talk, all those eloquent emotional drunken words, had made the whole thing hideously more vivid. Even my dull stripped flat gave back the dreadful resonance. I had stripped the flat as I had stripped my life in a vain attempt to remove from it anything which could remind me of Anne. Today, opening my Polish dictionary, I found a pressed flower, a white violet, which she had espied in her garden and given me during that charmed and innocent time when I loved her and she did not yet know it.

The day began with a letter from Tommy.

Dear heart, I am sorry I was so useless last night and please forgive what I said about Laura Impiatt, I know that was just stupid. You know I love you and I want to marry you, but I want most of all to take pain away from you and I'm sure if you would only share your woes with

me you would feel better. I can't believe that you ever
did anything really bad, but even if you did I feel that you
ought to forgive yourself. Guilt does no good to anyone,
does it? Anyway I forgive you, on behalf of God. Won't
you take that from me as a Christmas present? I feel I
love you so much that I am able (and so on and so on)

I thought it was rather touching of Tommy to offer me
God's forgiveness for Christmas, especially as she did not
know what I had done, and I realized that I was lucky to
be loved by a girl as intelligent and nice as Tommy, but she
was simply no use to me at all and I wished her at the devil.

The electricity was still off. The flat was extremely cold.
I was wearing a jersey and an overcoat and felt awkward
and bulky and still frozen. I burnt myself lighting a spirit
stove to boil a kettle. Mr Pellow knocked on the door, asking
if we could spare him a candle. I told him we could not.
Later I caught Christopher sneaking out with a candle for
Mr Pellow. I confiscated it. Christopher told me that Mick
Ladderslow had been arrested in connection with the Steal
for Chairman Mao Campaign, and would I perhaps put
up some money to bail him out of prison? I would not.
Christopher went away and started practising his tabla. I told
him to shut up. He came back into the kitchen and broke
the spirit stove by turning the handle too hard. I told him I
had had enough of him and he could clear out, but he took
no notice as I often said this. Jimbo Davis arrived looking
spiritual and carrying some evergreen branches. He took my
hand in an (or did I imagine it?) especially sympathetic
way, murmuring 'yes, yes—' He and Christopher retired into
Christopher's room where they laughed a lot, doubtless at my
expense.

Laura Impiatt arrived. I passionately did not want to see
her, but had not the spirit to invent an immediate lie. ('Oh
what a shame, I am just this moment leaving for Hounslow.')
Today, although it was not raining, she was wearing a huge
yellow sou'wester tied under the chin, a quilted mackintosh
coat and blue serge trousers pulled in above her ankles with
bicycle clips. She did not take her coat off. We sat at the
kitchen table, two bulky cold muffled up objects with red
noses. She wanted coffee but there was now no way of boiling
a kettle. We peered at each other in the gloom.

'Hilary, will you be able to bear it if Crystal marries
Arthur?'

130

'Don't be silly, Laura, just don't be silly, there's a dear.'

'I know how close you are to Crystal.'

'I want her to marry Arthur.'

'Then why were you almost mad with misery on Thursday?'

'I wasn't, I had toothache. Arthur is a splendid chap.'

'Arthur is not exactly a catch.'

'Beggars can't be choosers. Crystal is not exactly an English Rose.'

'I'm surprised to hear you talk like that about Crystal.'

'I can see what's obvious, even about my sister. She's lucky to have a suitor at all.'

'I would have expected you to be more sort of fastidious.'

'Who am I to be sort of fastidious.'

'But don't you *care*? And you can't be serious about marrying Tommy.'

'Who said I was marrying Tommy?'

'You did, on Thursday.'

'I was just saying anything that came into my head to shut you up.'

'How nice of you! You know, Hilary, you don't value yourself enough. There's so much of you and you make so little of it. It's as if you'd lost all your courage, just absolutely lost your nerve.'

'That's right.'

'But why? Hilary, you *must* tell me. It would do you good to tell it all to somebody. I know there's *something*. Hilary, let me help you. I love you, my dear, let me help. Don't just throw yourself away. I know you need a home, and you'll need it all the more if Crystal marries. Lean on me, use me. You know you have a home with us at Queen's Gate Terrace. It could be much more to you if only you'd open yourself a little. We are childless. Freddie's very fond of you—'

'Laura, I shall be sick.'

'Oh, my dear, I know you so well. I do. Just relax, you're all tense, you're so physically tense, relax, see, your hands are all knotted up—'

'It's so bloody cold.'

Laura had taken one of my hands and was kneading it enthusiastically between her own. Her hands in fact were so cold that the process, even if I had cared for it in general, would have brought little relief. I closed my eyes in an absolute gesture of despair. I wanted to scream at Laura, to terrify her. Anne's face appeared with a hallucinatory clarity in the domed darkness, as if cast by a magic lantern onto the London night sky. I must write my letter of resignation. I must do it this morning. I must be gone before he arrived. The 'I'm sorry' which I could not say to him had been said often enough since, but it did no good, there was no one to listen.

At that moment the electricity suddenly came on and the kitchen leapt into bright light. The boys cheered. I removed my hand from Laura's cold clasp.

The front door bell rang. I went to the door. It was the telephone engineer. I stared at him stupidly.

'It's the boss in person. Hello.'

'But the telephone,' I said. 'You've done all that, haven't you? There's nothing more to do, is there? It's all gone away.'

'Telephone? What's that? I'm not on duty.'

'What—?'

'This is a social call, man. I'm here as Len, not for Her Majesty.'

'You want Christopher.'

'This is where we came in.'

'What?'

'You just said "you want Christopher". That's what you said to me the first time.'

'Well, do you?'

'I think it's an indelicate question.'

I called 'Christopher!' and went back to the kitchen leaving the front door open. Christopher emerged. Laura said to me, 'I must have a word with Christopher. Freddie wants him to write some music for *It is later than you think*.'

'*It is later than you think*. Yes, indeed.'

'Why, hello, Len, how nice! Len and I are old friends!'

'Are you, Laura?'

Christopher and Len and Laura were filling the kitchen with chatter. Jimbo, still in Christopher's room, was arranging the green branches in a vase. Through the still open front door I saw Biscuit standing on the landing wearing a sari.

I went out to her slowly, pulling the door to behind me.

The sari was a plain bluish-purple with a wide golden border. She had been wearing a coat over it but had removed the coat. It was folded up neatly beside her on the floor. Her hair had been put up into an intricately woven glossy ball suspended somehow at the back of her head. This made her look older. And the sari gave her, in an odd way, a look of being in uniform, on duty. With the great erection of the hair the pale brown face looked thinner, the eyes huger, reflecting in their depths the bluish-purple tints of the gorgeous sari.

'Hello, mystery girl.'

'Hello, Hilary.'

'I'm Hilary today, am I? Why did you run away?'

I took her wrist lightly between my fingers. The bony feel of the wrist was already familiar. I moved my hand, caressing the wrist, taking her small hand, still lightly, in a full grasp. Her hand was moist and warm. It moved inside my hand like a snuggling animal.

'It's full up in there,' I said, motioning over my shoulder at the flat.

'I'm sorry. Then will you come with me? Will you come with me to a café? I have got something to give you.' The way she said 'to a café' sounded curiously foreign and the phrase had a ridiculously improper ring about it.

I looked down at her. Her hand had reminded me of Anne's hand. Or rather, her hand had reminded my hand. My hand did not know that Anne was dead and that twenty years had passed and that I was a murderer. Gunnar must have seen Anne in the hospital before she died. What had happened to her face? Did he hold her in his arms when she was dying?

'Will you come with me, please?'

'No,' I said, 'I'm busy. I've got to write an important letter. I can't play games of will you won't you with mystery girls. Just fuck off and leave me alone, will you? I've got enough trouble without being persecuted by bloody tarts.'

I went back into the flat and slammed the door. Laura and the boys were making some coffee.

I was with Crystal. She was holding my hand. It seemed to be my day for holding hands with women. I now regretted having sent Biscuit away. I would like to have gone to bed with her. Presumably that was what it was all about. It would have distracted my mind. I wondered if she would ever come back again. She had looked very beautiful in her sari. And at least she was a little separate piece of possible future. I was rather short of future at present.

The electricity, much reduced in power, had remained on all day, and was still on, although further cuts were threatened.

I had eaten a little supper and drunk a great deal of the litre bottle of Spanish burgundy. Supper had consisted of steak and kidney pudding, out of a tin, brussels sprouts and mince pies. The white lace tablecloth was on, and I had spilt wine on it again. Crystal washed it snow-white every week.

'Do you still want to see the Christ Child in Regent Street?'

'Oh—dearest—have you sent that letter yet?'

'I haven't written it. yet.'

'Must you leave the office?'

'Of course.'

'You needn't see him.'

'He'd be there. And he'd know I was there.' How awful for Gunnar, it occurred to me, to find me infesting the place as a low form of life, a sort of loathsome beetle. 'The least I can do is be gone before he comes, not remind him that I exist.'

Crystal's rather square podgy face was all wrinkled up with anxiety and grief and love. Her frizzy orangy hair was tangled as she had been twisting it between her fingers earlier in the evening. She was wearing her glasses, gazing across the room with her enlarged golden eyes, staring at the row of ebony elephants that marched upon the sideboard and holding my hand in both of hers. Laura had kneaded, Biscuit had nuzzled. Crystal held steady, firm, the way you might hold someone's hand if he were going to be shot.

'I'll soon get another job,' I said. 'And if I can't, you and Arthur can support me! I won't starve.'

'If it would help if I stopped going with Arthur—'

'Oh don't be idiotic, Crystal! If I could only be sure you were happy and looked after I'd—'

'What?'

'Oh not kill myself or anything. Not even emigrate. I might marry Tommy.'

'We'll lose each other,' said Crystal. She released my hand and turned to face me. She took off her glasses and looked at me with her beautiful truthful defenceless myopic eyes.

'Don't say that, darling. You know we can't lose each other. We are one.'

'I feel so frightened. There were funny noises downstairs last night.'

'Oh nonsense.' Crystal had never had these sort of fears before. Or more likely, she had had them but had never troubled me with them.

'Everything's suddenly so frightening. Oh if only it hadn't happened, if only he hadn't come back. I feel the past will destroy us, something terrible will come out of the past and eat us up.'

'Stop it, Crystal. I shall just take a new job, nothing else will happen.'

'I feel you're in danger. I prayed for you last night. I wish I really believed in God.'

'Your prayers will invent God. He'll have to exist just to receive them. I'll take you to Regent Street and we'll see the Christ Child, and we'll have a dinner out, shall we, like we did once. Oh Crystal, I do wish you could be happy. If I thought you could be happy I could simply cease to exist with a sigh of joy.'

'How can I be happy when I know you suffer all the time, all the time, because of *that*, and now it's come after us like a—like a sort of demon of revenge—'

'None of that, Crystal. Prayer is better. Do you know what dear old Tommy told me in a letter? She said she had forgiven me on behalf of God!'

'You never told Tommy?'

'No. And I never will. Whatever happens. But, Crystal, listen. I haven't said this to you yet. I've told Arthur.'

'Told Arthur—when?'

'Last night.'

'Everything?'

'Yes.'

'Oh dear—' said Crystal. 'Oh dear—' The big golden eyes were filling with tears.

I was appalled. 'But Crystal, I thought you'd approve, be pleased—I felt—if you're going to marry him—it was a kind of gesture—and he is so—and I had to tell someone—didn't you want him to know?'

'No. I didn't want him to know. I didn't want *anybody* to know. I didn't want it to *exist* as anything that people knew. I want it not to have happened at all. And one of the things about Arthur was that he didn't know—'

'Oh my God!' I said. I felt exasperation. Had I got to play the instrument of Crystal's sensibility forever? She was stupidly vulnerable. 'Brace up, Crystal. All these things did happen. Keeping them secret isn't going to unhappen them.

I haven't spoilt Arthur for you. Arthur's got to grow up. You've got to grow up. There are terrible things in the world. Anyway, Arthur ought to know that he's getting a murderer for a brother-in-law!'

'What did he say?'

What did he say? I had not paid much attention to what Arthur said, half the time as I was talking I was unaware that Arthur existed. 'It doesn't matter what he said. He talked some guff about forgiveness. Now, Crystal, stop crying. I don't see why I should have to put up with your bloody tears as well as everything else.'

Crystal mopped her eyes with her hands, then began to fumble under her skirt for the handkerchief which she still kept in her knickers like a little girl. 'I wish we still believed in Jesus Christ and that he could wash away our sins.'

'Washed by the Blood of the Lamb. Remember all that old stuff? Washing in somebody's blood—what repellent images one cheerfully put up with in one's childhood. Over and over like a mighty sea, comes the blood of Jesus rolling over.'

'It's the love of Jesus, not the blood of Jesus.'

'Well, since there's no Jesus it'll have to be your love that saves me, Crystal, so don't stop praying, will you?'

MONDAY

IT WAS now Monday afternoon (it looks as if nothing ever happens on Sundays, but just wait a while), getting dark, which consisted in a yellowish twilight which had persisted all day thickening into a yellowish darkness. Big Ben's lighted face had not been extinguished since morning. I sat at my desk looking at that friendly countenance and trying to compose my letter of resignation. The thought of searching for another job and doing so rather briskly, since I had no savings, filled me with frightened exhausted dejection. Someone (Reggie?) had purloined my fountain pen, and I was struggling with a steel-nibbed dip-pen which I had got from the stores, and which spluttered the ink merrily about in intervals of scratching holes in the paper.

Sunday had passed somehow. I went to the cinema twice and got drunk in the intervals. I also walked a good deal. There are so many kinds of walking. I walked a special kind of metaphysical sad London walking, which I had walked before, only I performed it now with an almost ritualistic intensity. In Russian there is no general word for 'go'. Going has to be specified as walking or riding, then as habitual or non-habitual walking or riding, then as perfective or imperfective habitual or non-habitual walking or riding, all involving different verbs. The sort of walking which I indulged in on that Sunday deserved a special word to celebrate its conceptual peculiarity.

During the later part of Monday morning one of Arthur's lame ducks who had just come out of prison and had celebrated this by getting drunk, came round to find Arthur and obtain some more money to get drunker. I helped Arthur to get him out of the building. Arthur had not returned, presumably being unable to shake off his bibulous friend, or perhaps being engaged in escorting him to a suitable place of refuge. The porter at the door, having vainly opposed ingress, reported to Freddie Impiatt, who came to see me as if it was my fault, and gave me a sort of dressing down while Reggie Farbottom and Mrs Witcher giggled in the background.

After lunch however a rather more respectful attitude became evident. When I came in Reggie was eagerly imparting something to Mrs Witcher. They fell silent when I arrived, staring at me.

'I say, Hilary, is it true that you and Jopling are old friends?'

'No.'

'There you are, Reggie, I told you it couldn't be true.'

'But you do know him, don't you, I was told you were old friends, that you were at school together.'

'They couldn't have been,' said Edith. 'Hilary's miles younger.'

I sat down in my protected nook, in the yellow beam of old Big Ben. I would miss that.

'Hilar*ee*! Don't you answer when people speak to you any more?'

'I didn't think an answer was required.'

'You do know him though? They were saying in the bar you knew him well.'

'I used to know him very slightly. We haven't met for years.'

'Fancy Hilary knowing Jopling!'

'I didn't know Hilary knew anybody.'

'We'll have to start calling him Mr Burde now.'

'Mr Burde, hey there, Mr Burde—'

And so on and so on.

I made up my mind to go home early. I could not write the letter of resignation and could not do anything else either. The work had already gone dead on me. I decided to adopt a device which I sometimes adopted when depressed, to get onto the Inner Circle and go round and round until opening time and then go to the bar either at Liverpool Street or Sloane Square, according to which was nearer. This system weighted the balance slightly in favour of Liverpool Street if I took the westbound line, and of Sloane Square if I took the eastbound line, since there were fifteen stations between Liverpool Street and Sloane Square on the former route and twelve on the latter route. I attempted to let some immediate chance decide which direction I took. The element of gamble distracted the mind a bit, though not so much as being in bed with Biscuit would have done.

I intended of course to go and see Clifford Larr as usual in the evening. He knew my tantrums and how to ignore them. I did not really believe that my outburst in the park could have ended our friendship. He had already taken a reprisal in the form of his indiscretions on Thursday, and would I hoped be satisfied, though he might still be bloody-minded enough to refuse to see me or simply to be absent. But there was always, with such a man, also the possibility of his suddenly deciding that one had gone too far and that all was over. This possibility began, as the day went on, suddenly to ache on its own, a perceptible special pain among all the others, making thought impossible, prompting flight. Soon after four o'clock I got up and glided quietly out of the room. Reggie and Edith were playing noughts and crosses. Arthur had still not come back.

I went to the cloakroom and put on my overcoat and cap. I could never bring myself to sport a trilby or a bowler; the cap provided some protection even though it signally failed to cover the ears. I could not descend to the Arthur woolly beret level. I set off down the stairs. I always used the lift to come up, the stairs to come down. The lift carried the hazards of social life. It was a concession to old age that I no longer walked up.

The stairs were, in accordance with government standards of economy, very ill lit. I had descended two flights and was descending a third when a stout elderly man turned the corner from the lower landing and began slowly to mount towards me, holding onto the banisters. We passed each other. For a second I saw his face. I reached the next landing and turned the corner. I held onto the wall for a moment, then sat down on the stairs at the top of the next flight.

Arthur was just coming up. 'I say, Hilary, what's the matter? Are you all right? Are you feeling funny?'

I said, 'Go away.'

'Hilary, can I — ?'

'Go away!'

In order to escape from Arthur I pulled myself up and went quickly on down the stairs, leaving him staring after me. I went out into the street.

I had had a flash of the blue eyes before he passed, otherwise I might not have recognized him. He was partly bald and had become stout. He had the gait and bearing of an older man, much older than me, older than his own years. He also had, even in that glimpse, the air of a grandee, a public man. Perhaps this had contributed to the effect of age. But what was even more devastating than seeing him was being seen by him. I had intended to be far away when

Gunnar Jopling came. Now: he had seen me. But had he recognized me, could he, in those few seconds, have done so? Of course I had not changed as much as he. On the other hand, he could not possibly have been expecting to see me. No, he had not looked at me. He had surely passed by, preoccupied, not seeing.

By this time I had got myself, somehow, in a state of unconsciousness, onto the Inner Circle, direction Paddington. I went over the incident again and again in my mind. It was so dark, we passed so quickly. I was wearing a cap, no, no he could not possibly have known me. But we had passed each other on the stairs, our two bodies had passed within two feet of each other. I could have touched his sleeve. I sat in the train with my face in my hands. A kindly old lady asked me if I was all right, and when I did not reply thrust a pound note into my pocket. I felt a second or two of gratitude.

Hours passed and it was opening time. The Inner Circle roulette determined on Liverpool Street, which I was rather glad of and must unconsciously have voted for by taking the Paddington direction. Liverpool Street has a terrible shoddy doomridden end of the world majesty about it, like some place out of Edgar Allan Poe. I got drunk standing on the platform, watching the trains come and go. At last I got onto a train myself and went to Gloucester Road.

There had been a glimmer from the sitting-room window. The glass panel above the door was lighted up. I let myself in with my key as usual. 'Hello, Clifford.'

'Hello.'

He was in the kitchen, chopping an onion.

'Did you expect me?'

'No.'

'Didn't you — ?'

'You said you were not coming.'

I glanced through the dining-room door. The table was laid for one. The chessboard occupied my place. I got out knives and forks and a glass and one of the sissy place mats that Clifford used and laid a second place on the shining mahogany. I moved the chessboard, problem and all.

I went back to the kitchen. 'I'm sorry I was so bloody.'

'OK.' He smiled, not at me, sweeping the chopped onion into a red simmering mess in a saucepan.

That at least was all right.

I sat down on the chair I usually occupied while Clifford was cooking. I was glad to see him. I needed to talk to him.

'Can I have a drink?'

'It sounds as if you've had one.'

I helped myself.

'I saw Gunnar this afternoon.'

Clifford was interested and turned to look at me though he did not arrest his cooking operations. 'Really? In the office? Did he pin you to the wall, incoherent with rage?'

'I don't think he recognized me—we passed on the stairs—I don't think—after all, he doesn't know I'm there.'

'He does.'

'*What?*'

'Freddie told him.'

'Oh *Christ*! And you told Freddie. That was bloody thoughtful of you, wasn't it. How do you know Freddie told him?'

'Freddie, artlessly chattering at a meeting, said he had told Gunnar about you and Gunnar had said how nice. Come, don't look like that!'

'Oh— Have you seen him?'

'Not yet, as it happens, but I expect I shall soon. He's going to be on the spot as from tomorrow.'

'*Tomorrow?* I thought it was going to be weeks.'

'Well, it isn't.'

'I'm leaving the office, of course.'

'Why "of course"?' said Clifford, wiping his hands on some ornate kitchen paper and pouring out some sherry for himself.

'Well, obviously. I can't stay around in that place meeting him on stairs and in doorways. I couldn't stand it, and I don't see why he should have to either. Consideration for him dictates my instant departure. Surely you can see that.'

'I'm not so sure. I don't think you should run away.'

'Run is exactly what I'm going to do, *run*.'

'I think you should stay at the office and sit it out and see what happens.'

'To amuse you?'

'Well, it *would* amuse me, but not just for that, for your own sake.'

'For *my* sake?'

'And for his.'

'You're mad,' I said. 'He must want to vomit at the idea that I'm in the building. Oh Christ in heaven, I wish you hadn't told bloody Freddie. If Gunnar didn't *know* it would somehow be so much easier, I could simply slip away and—'

'I agree with you, as it happens. And I admit it was inconvenient of me to tell the Impiatts, though you understand why I did it. But it does, I think, make a difference that he knows. I think it means that you must stay.'

'I don't see that!'

'If Gunnar had never known you were there or had any special cue for thinking about you, OK. But now that your continued existence has been brought to his attention it would be rather ill-mannered of you to vanish at once.'

'Ill-mannered?'

'Yes. If you whisk away after this little reminder, this little shock, you may be minimizing your own distress, but you will be increasing his. And, if I may say so, I think you are in duty bound to sacrifice your interests to his.'

'What on earth are you talking about?'

'He is a bogyman to you. And no doubt you are a bogyman to him. You said yourself that he would want to vomit simply at the idea that you were in the building. If you just vanish you produce the nausea without any cure.'

'There is no cure.'

'There may be no *cure*, but I think it might help him if he were just to see you a bit around the place and get used to seeing you and find that the world doesn't end after all. He might also like to reflect upon the difference between his station in life and yours, it could cheer him up a bit.'

'This is macabre. It wouldn't cheer me up.'

'But the point is, isn't it, that you must sacrifice yourself. It's a tiny little service which you can perform for him, and I think that you ought to perform it, regardless of your own feelings.'

'This is an insane argument.'

'It's a pretty insane situation and, as you say, for the

outsider, interesting. What will happen? How will you both behave? The unexciting answer is, I'm afraid, perfectly. But this in itself will do a tiny bit of good in the world.'

'You seem very concerned for his welfare.'

'No. I'm just being impartial. As you know I never particularly liked Gunnar in the old days. I was told he had charm, I could never see it. He just seemed to me pretentious and conceited. No, no, I'm offering you what I think is a sound moral argument. I'm not suggesting you should try to talk to each other! Of course that would be impossible. But if you can nod affably on the stairs this may be a good thing for him and even possibly for you.'

'Affably! We will hardly be feeling affable!'

'Of course not. That's not the point. You must just be there, undergo him, let him pass you by. I don't suggest that you stay on forever. But I think you should stay on for six months.'

'No,' I said. 'No.' I could see the force of Clifford's argument all the same, and I hated it. Ought I to 'expose myself' to Gunnar as to a menacing ray? Ought I to stay on to be a spectacle to him, to accept at close quarters, his silent hatred and contempt; and then at last creep away and hide? There was something hideous and frightening about this. But could it be that I ought to do it, could it be that Clifford was right and that this was a sort of small service which I could render to Gunnar, something which I could as it were, after all, give him? And even if it were so, was I prepared to give him anything? Did I not hate him for the damage which I had done him? He had wrecked my life and Crystal's.

'What's his second wife like?' I said, to divert the conversation from this awful channel.

'I don't know. Some sort of fashionable nonentity.'

'Educated?'

'I don't think so.'

'Any children?'

'No.'

I said, 'Crystal is definitely going to marry Arthur, it's fixed. She has said yes. Arthur is glorified. Arthur in majesty.'

'Oh no—' Clifford threw down the spoon with a clatter.

'Yes. I'm afraid so.'

'You can't let her—oh no, no, no— I didn't take you seriously last time—you must stop it—'

'What can I do? It may even be a good thing.'

Clifford took off his apron. 'Come on.'

'What? Where?'

'We're going round straight away to see her.'

'See Crystal? Certainly not!'

'I want to see the girl who's going to be Mrs Arthur Fisch.'

'No,' I said. 'Sorry. *No.*'

'We're going to see Crystal.'

'No, we're not. Clifford, don't be an absolute devil. You know how Crystal feels about you. I expect she daren't even think about you now. How *could* you want to upset her just when she's made up her mind? God, don't you think I hate this too? But I want her to be settled and happy.'

'And do you honestly think she will be if she marries that drip?'

'Yes. Probably. Otherwise I wouldn't let her. Arthur isn't one of the wonders of nature, but he's a decent chap and he loves her.'

'I'd like to stop it,' said Clifford.

'You keep out of it. I mean that. Keep out. Keep away. If Crystal were to set eyes on you now—'

'Why should little Arthur have a virgin? Why should he have that virgin?'

'You are touchingly romantic about virginity.'

'It still has a meaning. In this rotten greedy lolling dribbling world.'

'You promise you won't go and see Crystal or write to her or anything?'

'I never promise. How can I commit my future self?'

'But you won't, will you? It isn't as if you had anything to offer her. All you can do there is destroy.'

'Oh, all right,' said Clifford with a sudden change of mood from enthusiasm to apathy which was characteristic of him. 'It's your affair anyway, I was just thinking about you and if you regard it as marvellous then that's that. She's your property until she becomes Arthur's. It's true that I have no constructive plan. Anyway I daresay it won't happen. Now, as dear Laura would say, *à table, à table.*'

We sat down. There was some sort of eggs messed around with vegetables. Then some sort of fish messed around with fruit.

'How did Gunnar look?'

'Old.'

'We are all old, my darling,' said Clifford. His lips relaxed. He reached out his hand across the table and took hold of mine.

TUESDAY

IT WAS Tuesday morning. I arrived very early and took the lift up and scuttled to my place in the window. It was still dark and Big Ben's face was round and bright as if the moon had come visiting amid the towers of Westminster. I cowered in my corner like a frightened animal. I would have liked to barricade myself in.

Tommy's Tuesday letter had arrived from King's Lynn. It was unusual in tone.

Darling, I have been saying marry me for so long you can probably not hear the words. I begin to feel, for many reasons, that I must now make them into a real question and receive a real answer. I cannot respect myself otherwise. I must settle the future one way or another. I know you have deep troubles and I know you need me. Everything is becoming urgent. Unless we seize each other we may be swept apart. Take my hand in the rain and the storm and hold onto it, oh my dear, and let me go with you into whatever is to come. I am close to you and there is real speech between us. Recognize this and the achievement of it and the salvation of it. I must see you soon, there is something we must talk about together. I cannot wait until Friday, there are reasons why. *Please let me see you on Wednesday*. I will telephone the office on Wednesday morning.

Your own faithful,

Thomas.

My first thought on reading this high-flown epistle was that Tommy must have discovered all about Gunnar and Anne, hence this desire to save me from the storm and so on. Yet how could she possibly have found out? I was developing persecution mania. Would I ever tell Tommy all about that business? No. That was another reason why I could never marry her.

I sat in my safe window and gazed out at the gradually lightening scene. It was another of those bitter yellow days. I wondered whether or not to put in my resignation at once. Last night I had been curiously compelled by Clifford's argument. Perhaps I ought to stick it out and as it were expose or exhibit myself to my enemy. It was an odd idea, but there was some logic to it. Perhaps I ought not to run away but to endure, and let the thing become, through the simple fact that we sometimes just saw each other and nodded (but would we?), that much more ordinary. Would this, not only for him but for me, somehow reduce the nightmare? I had reflected about this after, rather drunk, leaving Clifford's flat. This morning however the whole argument seemed just jesuitical, even frivolous. In any case, much deeper and more awful reasons why I should not leave my job were beginning to come into view.

I made believe to myself that I was tough and sane and on the whole recovered. But I really knew, and knew now with an awful penetration of it into the heart, into the guts, how frail the achievement was. I did not anticipate breakdown or madness. But if I were to leave Whitehall and wander round looking for work and failing to get it, with my money rapidly running out, what condition would I soon find myself in? I remembered, and it felt hideously close, that awful year in the north, the 'chocolate year', when I lay on a camp bed in Crystal's room and pretended to be recovering from physical injuries when really I was battling with my mind. Suppose I were to give up my job and then become, even temporarily, incapable of earning my own living? Suppose I were to fall back into that black terrible slough? The deeper levels of the mind know not of time. It was all still *there*. It would have needed God to remove it. Even Crystal could not do it. Suppose I could not earn money? Suppose I had to be supported by Crystal? *Suppose I had to be supported by Arthur?* If I stayed where I was, even if I were to become for a while almost unable to work, I could at least manage, I could get away with it, no one would notice me and I would be safe.

Reggie came in whistling, eating peppermint. 'Hello, Hil. You skedaddled pretty early yesterday, didn't you? Thought we wouldn't notice you'd slunk off! Go to a flick?'

Edith arrived.

'I was just telling Hilary we saw him skrimshanking yesterday.'

'I say, have you heard? Mrs Frederickson has had triplets!'

'No!'

'She took that ghastly fertility drug.'

I settled back, pretending to work. I pretended all morning.

I decided to go early to lunch and take a long lunch hour, in spite of the witticisms which this would provoke in the Room. Walking was therapeutic. I thought I might walk as far as north Soho and have a sandwich in one of the Charlotte Street pubs, where I used to get drunk when I was younger.

I slipped out and donned overcoat and cap and made for the stairs. I hesitated. Was the lift safer? But suppose I were to be caught in the lift with Gunnar? Was he in the office today? I decided to brave the stairs. I went on down I had almost reached the ground floor when a woman who had just entered from the street crossed the hall quickly and began to hurry up the stairs. She was not an office person, not anyone I knew. She was smartly dressed. That degree of smartness in the office was unusual. She was dark, wearing a fur hat and an expensive-looking fur coat, caught in to a slim waist with a metal belt, and a bright silky scarf. I took all this in. She passed me with a whiff of perfume and disappeared onto the landing.

I stopped. I turned. I felt an immediate certainty but had to test it. I padded back up the stairs. Templar-Spence's room, and so presumably Gunnar's, was on the first floor, the *piano nobile*, a little way from the stairhead. I reached the top of the flight and came out onto the wide carpeted landing. The woman in the fur coat was standing at the door of Gunnar's room with her hand upon the handle, and looking back. I stood there for a second and she looked straight at me. She not only knew that I had turned and followed her. *She knew who I was.*

I receded quickly. I almost ran from the building. I told myself again and again that I must be mistaken. I *must* be mistaken That look had, in the second it had lasted, seemed a look of recognition. And yet it was absolutely impossible that she should know who I was. This was persecution mania, the old sickness that I feared so. I walked and walked. I found myself at the foot of the Post Office tower. I drank whisky in several bars. I could not eat anything. I considered not returning to the office. I came back about three. I had to hold onto order and routine. I must stay at my desk. I must try to do my work. I must not start wandering round London all day.

'I say, Hilo, three hours for lunch isn't bad!'

'Hilary looks as if he's had one or two.'

'Hilary, Hilar*ee*—'

I settled down again to pretending to work. I even read a new case through twice, without understanding anything. One of the Registry girls, Jenny Searle, brought the tea in, as Skinker had the 'flu. She asked me if I was feeling all right. Arthur brought in a pile of stuff. He too looked at me anxiously. He did not dare to touch me, but he put his hand down on top of the papers in a gesture which by some mystery of human sign language conveyed sympathy.

I could still smell Lady Kitty's perfume, as if some of it must have got onto my clothes as she passed me. I tried to picture her face but could only vaguely conjure up dark hair, dark eyes. Dark blue eyes? Dark brown eyes? I had by now firmly decided that what I had believed must be false. She could not possibly have known who I was. She perhaps sensed that someone had come back up the stairs after her, some curious impertinent clerk. She may not even have noticed me coming down. *She* had nothing to do with the matter. Though it now occurred to me that I had never reflected about how Gunnar must have told his second wife how his first wife died. In fact I could not bear to imagine Gunnar talking, Gunnar thinking, Gunnar *conscious*, and I tried to cloud the whole subject over in my mind.

It was already dark. My head was aching from the whisky. I was drawing intersecting circles on my blotting pad and listening idly to the interminable chatter of Reggie and Mrs Witcher. How long would it be before the whole office knew of what I had done? Would it get around in the end? There is such a terrible difference between a secret disgrace and a public one.

I heard Gunnar's name and started to listen more carefully. Now Mrs Witcher was talking about Lady Kitty. 'She's the daughter of some sort of little Irish lord.'

'I thought she was Jewish, sort of banker's family?'

'That's the mother's side, she's half Jewish.'

'Lots of lolly there I imagine.'

'Oh yes, and lots of style. You know, she's got a lady's maid, and not just a lady's maid, but a *black* lady's maid!'

'A negress with a turban? What fun.'

'No, Indian, I think, but something blackish. Of course she and Jopling have been all round the world. What, Hilary, off again? It's like living with a jack-in-the-box.'

I got out of the door and eventually out of the building. I turned up my coat collar against the damp cutting wind and began to walk randomly along Whitehall. A black lady's maid. *Biscuit.*

I was with Arthur as usual, since it was Tuesday. We had eaten cold tongue and instant potato and peas and cheese and biscuits and bananas. At least Arthur had and I had feigned to.

I had had a lot of thoughts since leaving the office. One was that I must do everything in order as I had always done. I must go regularly to work. I must keep to my 'days'. I must not become a madman walking about London and living on the tube. I had also given some rather cloudy and desperate consideration to the question of Biscuit. Was it conceivable that Biscuit was Lady Kitty's maid and that she had been sent to report on me? I decided to decide that it was impossible; I had enough troubles without envisaging anything as weird and nightmarish as that: so I terminated these reflections by an act of will. Another more immediate thing was that I must get through the evening with Arthur in as dignified and rational a way as possible, preserving what was left of my authority and status. My relations with Arthur must not break down into overt hostility or emotional chaos.

'What do you think of the wine, Arthur?'

'What?'

'What do you think of the wine?'

'Oh, fine, yes, fine.'

'It's just cheap stuff, of course, but these little blended French wines are quite good if you let them breathe a little.'

'It's—yes—it's not the stuff we drink at Crystal's, is it?'

'No, that's Spanish.'

'Hilary, would you mind if we fixed the day?'

'What day?'

'The day for Crystal and me—to get married.'

I looked at the firescreen representing the Empire State Building and at all the dust which had somehow managed to adhere to the vertical surface. 'When—?'

'I've been to the registrar and—I hope you don't mind—it could be soonish—I mean in a—week or so—'

'In a week or so?'

I heard Clifford Larr's voice saying 'It won't happen'. Would Clifford keep his half promise not to interfere?

'Yes—I'd rather it was soon, if you don't mind—'

'Do you see much of Crystal now?' I said.

'No, no, I just go the usual times.'

Poor children. This was because of me. They were afraid to shift anything, to alter anything, without my permission. Yet after that final visit to the registry office 'in a week or so' the world would be utterly different. As Clifford had said, Crystal was my property, until she became Arthur's. Ought I not to set them free, to tell Arthur now that he should see Crystal more, that Crystal needed protection? What was Crystal doing now, while I was carousing with Arthur? Sitting at home alone. What indeed did Crystal do most of the time when I was busy with other matters? I did not think about that. Was I not even now hoping that Clifford would somehow make it impossible for her to marry Arthur? He could probably do so. He could probably do it by a single visit. So let Crystal be alone, let her wait. Oh how could Arthur torment me with this frightful decision when there were so many other things making ordinary life impossible!

'You don't want to get married in a church?'

'It takes longer and—'

'You are both in a fearful hurry.'

'No. I mean—'

'Don't fix anything yet,' I said. 'I'll talk to Crystal.'

For a second Arthur's face looked disappointed, vexed, almost sulky. 'All right.'

There was a silence, Arthur picking moodily at his moustache, then cleaning his glasses carefully upon the tablecloth, I crumbling up pieces of cheese and strewing them about.

He said, 'Do you mind if I talk about that other business?'

'What other business?'

'Jopling.'

'Oh that. If you want to. I rather thought we'd finished it.'

'What are you going to do?'

'Nothing.'

'What *did* you do then—I mean after you came out of hospital—did you write to him or anything?'

'No.'

'You did nothing at all to—?'

'Of course not. When you've done something like that there's nothing more to be said.'

'I don't think I agree,' said Arthur. Perhaps the sulkiness was making him uppish. 'I think you could have written to him. I would have done.'

' "My dear Gunnar, I really must apologize—" '

'Just in order to continue the connection, to make some sorting out or reconciling or something—possible.'

'Use your imagination, for Christ's sake! "Continuing the connection" was just what was absolutely out of the question! One must have some decency and sense.'

'And now, I think you should go to him—'

'Go to him?'

'And say—here I am, after all these years, and I'd like you to know how sorry I am—or something like that—'

' "Here I am after all these years"—he'd be pleased, wouldn't he!'

'Well, he might be,' said Arthur. 'After all you aren't the only person who exists. He's been thinking about it too for twenty years. He might be glad to let you know—that he forgave you—'

'Your vocabulary is killing me. But suppose he hasn't forgiven me, suppose he wants to kill me?'

'It might do him good to find out that he didn't after all.'

'You make me want to throw up.'

'Sorry. I'm not explaining this very well. It's just that the only thing really worth doing here is something rather extreme, and it isn't just a thing between you and him, as

if it were a fight, there's a background to it, I don't mean
God or anything, but just our general sort of human thing,
our sort of place—'

'So eloquent, so clear.'

'I mean sort of possibilities of reconciliation, general ones,
like it's better to forgive than to hate. Even a few words
between you could make a lot of difference—'

'Do stop drivelling, dear Arthur. Look, it's time I went
home.'

'It's pouring with rain. Would you like my umbrella?'

'No.'

'You know what, Hilary. I think I saw Lady Kitty Jopling
in the office today.'

'Really.'

'It must have been her, she was wearing a mink coat,
at least I suppose it was mink. She was coming down the
stairs, we nearly collided. And my God, perfume, talk about
pong!'

'Good night. Arthur.'

WEDNESDAY

IT WAS Wednesday. The rain which had begun last night was continuing, descending in steady straight parallel lines, a curtain of darkness upon darkness, as the minutes dragged on towards lunch time. At about ten o'clock Tommy rang up. She started asking if she could see me that evening. I put the telephone down without replying. I tried to do some work and actually succeeded. The sheer passage of time since the news of Gunnar's return into my life had done a tiny bit of good. I had now survived for a week. Nothing awful had happened though some pretty odd things had. I was safe in my corner doing my job. It had become clear that it would be idiotic to leave. I would manage somehow if I just lay low and kept to my routine. The idea that Biscuit was Lady Kitty's maid had already begun to seem unreal, the fantasy of a persecuted mind. There was no evidence for this. Biscuit might be anybody. She might be and doubtless was just an idle whore who picked on solitary men hoping to get money out of them. She probably lived nearby. Lots of whores did. And as for Lady Kitty herself, I would in all probability never see her again. Wives were not encouraged to frequent government offices. And as this source of worry eased slightly I began to think more about Crystal. I decided I would, just for once, go and see her this evening; and if I were perfectly satisfied that she really did want to marry Arthur I ought to stop procrastinating. Oh *God*.

At this point in my reflections Tommy walked in. Or rather she burst in or flew in. There was a dark flurry and Tommy, in a very wet mackintosh, was leaning over my desk and scattering water all over my papers. She had pulled off her hat and her hair was hanging down her neck in thick wet tails like heavy dead snakes. The medusa effect was enhanced by the crude neon lighting, which showed her pitted face red and vivid, excited, wet with rain.

I was instantly rigid and nearly incoherent with anger. I spoke in a quiet biting voice just above a whisper. 'I told you never to do this, never.'

'You wouldn't speak to me on the 'phone, you hung up on me—' Tommy's voice was a good deal less quiet.

'This is going to be good,' said Mrs Witcher.

'Get out. Go on. Get out.'

'No. I want to talk to you. I want to tell you something. I'll go if you'll come too.'

'Go. *Go.*'

'Do you want me to start screaming?'

I got up and walked quickly to the door, aware of the delighted faces of Reggie and Edith Witcher.

I started to walk down the stairs. Tommy walked beside me. 'I told you never to come to the office. I cannot and will not have scenes like this in the room where I work.'

'I'm fed up with your hanging up on me every time I ring.'

'I told you not to ring.'

'I said in my letter I was going to ring this morning.'

'I don't care a fuck what you said in your letter. I'm going to see you to the door and you go out and stay out.'

'Come out for a minute and talk to me.'

'I will not talk to you. I will not be blackmailed by a stupid emotional woman. Either you do what I tell you or you go to the devil.'

Someone had passed by us on the stairs. Someone dressed today in a smart tweed coat and a white sheepskin hat. The whiff of the familiar perfume passed like driving mist. I had been speaking quietly but my words must have been audible. Tommy was saying something. We reached the ground floor and emerged into the street.

It was pouring with rain. 'Oh Hilary—darling—you're getting all wet—please forgive me—please see me tonight— you can't leave me like this, I shall cry all day—I'm so sorry to have displeased you—I just had to see you, I had to—please say you'll see me tonight—'

In order to get rid of her and because it was raining so hard I said, 'All right. Come to the flat at eight.' I went back inside. My clothes were dripping. I was soaked to the skin.

WEDNESDAY

A purely physical set-back can have a profound mental effect. This is obvious in large cases but is equally marked and more insidious in small ones. Simply because I got so wet and cold at eleven a.m. I made a decision at eleven p.m. which I would certainly not otherwise have made.

After Tommy disappeared I went back into the building and back to the Room where Edith and Reggie were gleefully awaiting my return. They began to offer the predictable witticisms but I shut them up with a ferocity which silenced even titters. It was impossible to get my clothes dry and I felt so cold and so wretched I decided about midday that I must go home and change. I intended to return in the afternoon, but did not. I got home, took off my clothes and had a hot bath. (Christopher was out cleaning flats.) I got into bed with a hot water bottle but simply could not get warm. I lay there shivering. I did not exactly feel delirious, but all sorts of compulsive lurid fantasies possessed my mind. I wondered if Gunnar would kill me. I pictured this happening. I was obsessively miserable because Lady Kitty had heard me brawling vulgarly with a woman. I had no good reason to believe that Lady Kitty knew who I was, but this did not stop me from believing it. I had no conception whatever of Lady Kitty, I had never really ever seen her face, but she suddenly seemed to loom larger and larger like a mythological figure. I reflected upon the mystery of Biscuit, and began to picture myself as the victim of some sort of enormous plot, whereby Gunnar was going to murder me and make it seem an accident.

At about five o'clock Christopher returned, and seeing my light on (I was trying to read *Pan Tadeusz* but could not keep my attention on the page) knocked on my door. He came in waving some five pound notes, a contribution towards the mounting rent bill.

'Hilary, look, lovely rent! I say, are you ill or something?'

'I think I'm getting 'flu,' I said. 'It's all round the office.' My limbs were aching. I felt as if I had a temperature.

Christopher backed away a little. 'I'm so sorry. Can I get you anything?'

'No. Thanks for the rent.'

'Wouldn't you like some tea or some whisky or something?'

'No. Just fuck off, there's a good boy.'

Christopher was looking his most pardish, beautiful and

slim and young, his pale face blazing with health, his pale blue eyes bright with intelligence and *joie de vivre*. I looked at him with disgust.

'By the way, we got Mick out of jug. He's coming in this evening.'

'Was he acquitted? Too bad.'

'No, no, he's out on bail.'

'How did you get the money?'

'Clifford gave it to me.'

'More fool he. Go away, will you. And for God's sake pull your jersey down.'

I lay now tormented by the idea that Christopher had seen Clifford. There was no sort of reasoning in this torment, it was just mechanical. The thought that Clifford had probably also provided the fivers which lay on my bedside table made things no better, made them worse. In the kitchen Christopher was singing *Who is it, waterbird, who who who? Sad am I, waterbird, blue blue blue*.

'Shut up!'

Silence.

Later on Mick and Jimbo arrived and later still there was the sound of the tabla being discreetly played in Christopher's room. Christopher let Tommy in when she came at eight. 'Mrs Uhlmeister has come.' Tommy's name evidently had some sort of comic or ritualistic significance for Christopher too.

I was feeling so intensely sorry for myself by this time, I was delighted to see Tommy. After all, a woman is a woman and it is her job to be a ministering angel. Tommy ministered.

'Why, darling, are you ill?'

'Yes.'

'Temperature?' feeling my brow. 'Have you a thermometer?'

'No.'

'You feel all chilled,' feeling my limbs. I was in pyjamas, 'and your hottie's all cold.'

'If you mean my hot water bottle, you are at liberty to rejuvenate it.'

Tommy bustled around, boiling a kettle, found another hot water bottle, inserted the two bottles in suitable places in the bed, found an extra blanket and an extra pillow, and made a marvellous steaming hot drink out of whisky and lemon. She sat beside me on the bed, half embracing me and taking occasional sips out of the same glass.

'Don't be such an idiot, Thomas, you'll get my 'flu or whatever it is.'

'I want your 'flu. I want you. I love you viruses and all.' She kissed me on the lips.

'You dolt, Tomkins. What an excellent drink you've made.'

'Are you warmer?'

'A bit. I still feel—'

'I'll warm you up properly.'

In a moment she was taking off her clothes. Shoes went flying. Blue Italian beads clinked on the table. Brown Norwegian sweater fell upon the floor, followed by blue tweed skirt and sensible woollen vest and brassière. Long red woollen knickers came off and then, more carefully, dark blue tights. Then Tommy was with me, her small vigorous glowing warm body nuzzling against me, her little hands fiddling with my pyjama buttons and exploring the black hair of my front, her wonderful long legs against my legs, then a prehensile foot pulling at my pyjama trousers.

I laughed. Then I made love to her. And in the transporting joy of love seemed to find a sudden fated issue from all the terrors that had been obsessing me. The world, for a short time, became marvellously simple and beautiful, immediate present and satisfactory. And it seemed real too, as if I had moved out of awful dreams into a plain pure reality. Afterwards we lay for a long time in silence, her head upon my chest, her lips moving slightly in the black fur in an ecstasy of affection, her thighs, her legs glued to me, her feet embracing my feet. I felt dazed and warm and not exactly happy, but with the conception of happiness, usually absent from me, present somehow as a distant buzz.

'You see,' said Tommy at last.

'What do I see, little Tomkins?'

'You love me.'

'I've let you rape me, that's all. I wasn't strong enough to resist.'

'Hilary, it does work, between us, it does. It's not just physical. I won't put up with your pretending it is. With someone like you it couldn't be. You're all mind, well not all, there's *this* marvellous thing, thank God, but you couldn't make love like that unless you loved.'

'Couldn't I? You underestimate your charms.'

'You know what I mean. Hilary, let's get married. Why not opt for happiness? I could make you happy. And you haven't been. I don't know why, but you haven't, perhaps ever, been really happy. Let me love you and look after you forever. Let's have a home, a real place, I could make it so nice. I want to give my whole life to making you happy. It mightn't be easy, but I could learn, I will learn. And you'll tell me, won't you, about that thing that happened long ago.'

I pushed her a little away from me, unglueing a clinging caressing leg. 'You said you wanted to ask me something or tell me something, didn't you? All that stuff in your letter and ringing me up and calling in in that wicked forbidden way and not waiting for Friday. What was it all about?'

'Well—there was something, but it doesn't matter now—I mean, it was nothing, nothing matters but you.'

'So it was all a pretext?'

'Well, yes— it doesn't matter.'

'You're a very bad girl.'

After a silence, Tommy said, 'Is Crystal going to marry Arthur?'

It was typical of the way I ran my affairs that no one had yet told Tommy this. I reflected. 'Yes.'

'Oh—' Her gasp of relief, her tremor of joy.

I remembered Clifford's words: I suppose if Crystal marries her dull swain you will marry yours.

Tommy was no dull swain. She was, as I could objectively see, a dear wonderful clever little girl. Was it conceivable that she *could* make me happy? If I married her I would utterly lose my life as it was now. But what was the value of my life as it was now? Nothing— It was a dim sad frightened sort of a life, and one which was burgeoning into nightmare. Could Tommy, in this crisis, *save* me? Suppose I were to leave my job. If I had Tommy to support I would have to find another job and I would have a motive for doing so. I would earn money to buy saucepans for our little 'home'. *Could* it be like that? Would I be able ever to tell Tommy about the past, to tell her about Anne in the motor car? I had told Arthur. But telling Tommy would be a very different matter. Of course there could be no doubt that my marrying Tommy would make Crystal's marrying Arthur that much easier, perhaps even that much happier. What would it be like then, the four of us? At first it seemed an absolutely appalling idea—and yet—could we not have life and have it more abundantly? I had to let Crystal go, she had to let me go. After all, it had to happen.

WEDNESDAY

'What are you thinking, my love, my darling?'

'About you. I was wondering if you could make me happy. It would be fearfully difficult.'

'I'm fearfully clever, and I love you fearfully much.'

'Let's have some more of that delicious whisky and lemon drink.'

At eleven o'clock that night I was engaged to be married to Thomasina Uhlmeister.

THURSDAY

'HERE'S to Tommy and Hilary!'
    'Tommy and Hilary, may they be blissfully happy!'
'Hooray!'

It was Thursday evening and we were at dinner with the Impiatts. 'We' were Tommy and me.

How the news had got out so quickly I was not sure and did not want to discover. Tommy was doubtless overjoyed to let our 'engagement' be announced at once, though whether she had arranged this deliberately was unclear. Somebody had telephoned somebody. Possibly Laura had telephoned Tommy. Possibly Tommy had telephoned Laura. Perhaps Laura had learnt something from Christopher. Christopher would hardly even have needed to listen at the door to get the general idea. Anyway, there we were, an officially engaged couple, sitting *à quatre* with the Impiatts, toasting our own success in champagne.

I did not let Tommy stay the night. I sent her away about twelve. On Thursday morning I felt physically restored, so presumably it was not the 'flu. I had a headache, but I attributed that to the whisky. Mentally I did not feel so good. I went to the office, I did my work. I kept up my reign of terror in the Room, and achieved quiet if not peace thereby. I heartily regretted what had occurred. It might not be too strong to say that I was appalled at myself. On the other hand, I did not regret it enough to have the will power immediately to reverse it. Not foreseeing instant exposure, I decided to let it drift. I did not really regard myself as committed. I was however impressed by the fact that I certainly *had* thought the marriage feasible, and had even, on some grounds or other which I could not now quite recall, welcomed the idea. I remembered having thought something about happiness. And although I could not now recapture my reasoning, I *had* reasoned and was by no means totally confident that today's argument was to be preferred to yesterday's. When I arrived at the Impiatts and found that the secret was out and that (surprise, surprise!) Laura had actually invited Tommy in her new role as my fiancée, I was completely stunned. I played along of course, I had no alternative, and I did not even glare at Tommy who was constantly throwing me delighted rueful humbly apologetic glances.

Joy had transformed Tommy as it had transformed Arthur. She looked almost beautiful. She was wearing an ankle-length woollen dress of blue and green check with a high neck and an imitation gold chain and locket. (The locket contained a snip of my chest hair which she had removed last night.) Her mousy ringlets had been persuaded to unravel themselves into a ripple of more orthodox curls. Her pock-marked face glowed with health and triumph. Her little lipsticked mouth and small nose thrust out at the new world, mobile and gay. The smoky-grey pure transparent eyes were huge and moist with deference and humility and bliss. Sitting next to me at table she gently put her foot up against mine. I kicked her smartly on the ankle. She began to giggle and tears of pure joy overflowed onto her cheeks.

Laura was saying, 'Tommy and I must go Christmas shopping together. Let me see, how many shopping days now to Christmas? We must go *wedding* shopping together. Will you have a white wedding, Hilary dear?'

'Don't be a dope, Laura.'

'What would you like as a wedding present?'

'A single ticket to Australia.'

'Now then, Hilary, you're not going to be allowed to escape, is he, Tommy? Men are always terrified of it, aren't they. I remember how scared Freddie was. I practically had to keep him handcuffed.'

'Nonsense, darling, it was you who were ready to bolt!'

'Will you get married on the same day as Arthur and Crystal?' Laura's promise not to tell Freddie about Arthur and Crystal had evidently wilted, perhaps under the influence of the news about Tommy and me. 'A double wedding is such fun. Will you let me arrange it all?'

'Certainly not. We haven't even told Arthur and Crystal yet—besides they may not be—there's nothing definite at all—'

'Oh come, come. I think a January wedding would be nice. There might be snow and the brides could wear fur hats.'

'And we'll have a great office party!' said Freddie. 'It isn't often that we have a double office wedding. We might even arrange it to coincide with the pantomime.'

'We might have a song about it in the panto! I'll ask Christopher.'

'What an absolutely marvellous idea!'

'You'll do no such bloody thing. How is the pantomime getting on, by the way, Freddie?' I urgently wanted to change the subject. Tommy's little foot had come back to the attack.

'Oh everything's fine except that we still haven't cast Peter. That pretty little Jenny Searle in Registry will make quite a good Wendy. But we're at our wits' end for a Peter.'

'Why shouldn't Tommy play Peter?' said Laura.

This was discussed with great animation. There seemed to be nothing against it. Tommy was an actress, a dancer. She was slim and slight enough for the part and not too tall. She was of course an outsider, but there were, as Freddie explained, precedents for this. The year before last when they did *Aladdin* Mrs Frederickson's younger brother had played the Genie of the Lamp. Besides, if by then Tommy and I were one flesh, she would not really be an outsider. And so on and so on and so on. Tommy was so pleased and so happy and drank so much champagne she became almost speechless.

When I rose to go at my usual early hour (on Thursdays I normally went on to fetch Arthur from Crystal's) Tommy rose too of course. She went upstairs to get her coat and Freddie followed her up to give her a text of the pantomime to look at. I was left alone for a moment with Laura. We were by now in the drawing-room where we had been drinking coffee.

'Laura, do ask Freddie not to tell the office yet—'

Laura was wearing another of her tents, a voluminous orange silk affair that made a formidable frou-frou. With her streaming grey hair and her saffron robe she looked like some sort of dotty Buddhist priestess. She had been exceptionally merry throughout the evening. Now suddenly her exalted face contracted, she bit her lip, and on the instant there were tears in her eyes. She was standing close to me. Without looking at me she clasped my hand and pressed it hard. She held it so for a moment, then drew it up against her thigh, and released it. I felt the slippery silk, the warm plump flesh.

'Oh, Laura—'

She shook her head and dashed the tears away with her knuckles, turning to pour herself out some brandy. Freddie and Tommy were coming down the stairs laughing.

I was aghast. I did not know what to think. Laura could not possibly be in love with me. Perhaps she just suddenly felt envious of Tommy's youth. Tommy's slim charm, Tommy as fiancée, Tommy as Peter Pan. Yet Tommy was not all that much younger than Laura, and had not Laura herself suggested Tommy for Peter? Had that been generosity or was it the perverse act of a woman who wants suddenly to heap up her own chagrin? All this passed through my head in seconds.

Freddie came in. 'I say, Freddie, don't tell the office yet, I shall be teased to pieces!'

A minute later Tommy and I were out in the street. It was raining very slightly, something more like a damp yellowish mist, the beginnings of a fog.

'Darling, you aren't angry with me? I didn't do it on purpose, honest—you see Laura—'

'OK. OK.'

'Darling, we are still—engaged—aren't we?'

'Oh leave me alone,' I said. 'I can't tell you how much I disenjoyed this evening. I don't want to see the Impiatts ever again, I hate them.'

'But darling, are we—?'

'I'm going to Crystal's good night.'

'Let me come with you. We could tell them.'

'No.'

'Will you tell them?'

'I don't know. Just stop persecuting me, will you, Tommy? I've got a lot of troubles.'

'But darling, we will be married, won't we, like you said yesterday, we will, won't we—?'

'I don't know. Maybe. How can I see the future?'

'You'll come tomorrow, won't you, as usual?'

'Yes, yes. Good night.'

I walked away briskly. When I got as far as Gloucester Road station I rang Crystal to say that I had 'flu and would not be coming.

FRIDAY

IT WAS Friday afternoon, nearly time to leave the office. I had successfully kept up appearances during the day. I had managed to do some work. Arthur came in to inquire anxiously after my 'flu, and I told him I was better, to which he replied that he could see I was not and I must be feeling terrible. He advised me to go home to bed. I could see that Arthur wanted to go on talking to me, but I gave him no encouragement and he was well trained enough not to press the matter, and retired to his cupboard. As for Reggie and Mrs Witcher, I ignored all remarks they made to me or else replied with offensive abruptness. There was some giggling, but they soon got tired of it and left me alone.

After lunch Freddie Impiatt rang up, in the best of spirits, to say that he had consulted the pantomime committee and they were all in favour of Tommy playing Peter, and would I tell her this glad news. I said I would. In spite of the horrors of last night, I was still, where Tommy was concerned, attempting to trust an insight which I had had, but which I had no longer. Perhaps it would be a good idea to marry Tommy. Perhaps I would be 'happy' whatever that was. The concept, conveyed to me briefly on Wednesday night, had gone again. Perhaps Wednesday had been simply sex and not any sort of revelation however tiny. I wondered whether seeing Tommy this evening would clarify my mind. If I just sat and stared at Tommy would I be able to read off the answer? I felt very dejected and very tired. The headache had come back. Was it the champagne or was I getting the 'flu after all?

When my watch said half past five I got up and cleared my desk. It was too foggy to see Big Ben. Edith and Reggie had already gone. They had said 'good night' and I had said 'good night'. There was no point in making quite unnecessary enemies, even if one was irritated with the whole universe to the point of screaming. I put on my overcoat and cap and decided I would go to the Sloane Square bar until it was time to go to Tommy's. I knew that Tommy would be certain to annoy me. It would be a rotten evening. I began

to trudge down the stairs. When I got to the last flight I saw
Gunnar in the hall talking to Clifford Larr. He had made a
joke and was laughing in a characteristic way, jolting himself
about and spluttering. He had his coat on and was either
coming or going, presumably going. I froze. Clifford had
seen me, and without seeming to observe me was making
some affable reply. I began to recede backwards up the
stairs. At that moment Gunnar turned. Escape was impossible.
I came back down the stairs at a swift pace and crossed the
hall making for the street door. Gunnar and Clifford watched
me in silence. As I passed them, not looking at them, I
inclined my head slightly in a sort of nod or bow. When I
got to the door I was in such a hurry I slipped slightly and
cannoned against the wall with my shoulder. I got myself
out, stumbling down the steps.

Outside the fog possessed the air. The rush hour crowds,
huddled up in their overcoats, heads down, hands in pockets,
were jostling slowly along, humpy and indistinct. Their
steps dulled, they seemed to walk on tiptoe. A damp vaporous
haze, which left visibility at about ten yards, fuzzed yellowly
about the lamp posts and thickened brownly between them.
The cold sulphurous sooty gas entered the lungs with every
breath, tormenting the throat and chilling the body. The
great concourse of motor cars, their lights blazing ineffectually,
illuminating nothing but fog, crawled one after the other
in slow cautious procession. Up above a blanket of thick fuzzy
darkness pressed down upon the scene.

I felt as if my chest would burst with frenzy and rage. I
inhaled the fog in furious gasps and began to cough. I felt
humiliated, defeated, crushed. I considered going back and
confronting Gunnar and—what? I had run past him like a
dog expecting to be kicked. I had fallen ignominiously out
of the door. I had not dared to look him in the face. I had,
however, in my first vision of him from the stairs, seen him
very much more clearly than on the last occasion. He was of
course stouter, but the impression of age which I had received
now seemed mistaken. His fair hair, now greyish-fair, fuzzed
round a bald patch. His face, which had been pink and
smooth, was browner and rougher. But in spite of a slight
stoop, the impression of energy, of burly vitality, even of
physical strength was as great as ever.

I walked along in a turmoil of indecision and rage. I felt
a kind of pure hatred of Gunnar, a desire to punch him hard
in the face. At the same time I wanted to go back and—

not punch him—speak to him—expunge the vile impression of myself as a frightened cur. I even stopped and stood there rigid in the midst of the slow hurrying homeward-bound crowd, wondering if I should go back. But suppose he were not in the hall. Suppose he had gone up to his office. Suppose I were to climb the stairs and knock on the door and go in and—I felt practically faint with emotion. I knew I could not do it. I began to walk slowly on, devouring my misery and shame.

I had reached the end of Whitehall and was waiting with a mass of other people for the traffic lights to stop the traffic so that we could cross the road to Westminster Station. A kind of reddish blur high above us was the illuminated face of Big Ben. I stood there, hands hanging, pressed upon by my fellow beings, a machine in torment. Then, just as the lights were about to change, a woman who had been standing a little behind me moved forward and was by my side. Our sleeves touched. It was Biscuit.

She was wearing her dark blue duffle coat with the hood pushed back. I caught the flash of her dark eye as she stood beside me. Neither of us looked at the other. The lights changed and we crossed the road side by side in the midst of the great trudging mass. When we reached the opposite pavement I slowed my pace and she continued to walk with me and still neither of us looked at the other. When we were quite close to the station entrance I said, 'Could you give my compliments to Lady Kitty and tell her that I can do without the attentions of her spies.'

We reached the brightly lighted entrance and I began to turn, or rather to push my way, into it. Biscuit took hold of my sleeve. 'Please. Come onto the bridge.'

I stepped back and we walked together, now a little out of the crowd, towards the embankment, then crossed the road to Westminster Bridge. We walked in silence to the middle of the bridge and then stopped. A few people were passing by, but there was a curious solitude on the bridge, we might have been in the middle of Hampstead Heath. The fog here formed a dark brown gauze cylinder, one side of it a little fuzzed by the light of a lamp. The line of brightness which was the terrace of the House of Commons made a very faint impression, a sort of almost imperceptible dint, upon the dark. So did the moon face of Big Ben far above. Wrapped up in dense air, the boom of fog horns could be heard from farther down the river, hollow and damp and sad. I turned to face Biscuit. She was looking up at me out of the dark ruff of her duffle hood, and her lean face looked eager and wet. Her hair was wet too with the attentions of the fog, its blackness misted over with little greyish drops. The thick plait disappeared down her neck, down inside the coat. She had her hands in her pockets, her head thrown back. I put my arms carefully round her damp shoulders and kissed her on her long shapely distinguished aristocratic Aryan mouth. She tasted of the fog, somehow of the sea, very cold.

'Well, little princess—'

She continued to look up at me with eagerness, with a sort of bright curiosity. Then she took her hands out of her pockets and took hold of my overcoat, holding onto my pockets by the flaps. I kissed her again.

'Well, Biscuit girl—let's go somewhere and make love. You've been chasing me around for quite a long time now. You deserve to have your reward.' It seemed to be my week for making love to girls. Most unusual.

'How did you know?' she said.

'What? Oh that you were Lady Kitty's maid. *Are* you Lady Kitty's maid?'

'Yes.'

'That was just a conjecture. Never mind. Don't let's talk about that. Let's go back to my flat and make love.'

She laughed. 'You are funny!'

'You're pretty funny, following me about everywhere, Miss Alexandra Bissett. What was your father's rank?'

'Colonel.'

'I don't believe you. Was he married to your mother?'

Biscuit's distinguished face contracted in a slight frown before she replied, 'No.'

'I'm sorry, it's no business of mine. My parents weren't married either. I hope you don't think I—Biscuit, say my name, will you?'

'Your name? Hilary.'

'That's right. It's just Hilary. Stupid old Hilary. Nobody minds him. You forgive him, don't you? Let's be friends, shall we?'

'Yes, yes,' said Biscuit, with her strange eagerness, her strange enthusiasm, 'do let's! Oh Hilary—I'm so sorry—'

'What have you got to be sorry about, my Biscuitling?'

'I'm sorry—I do wish— Look—I've got something for you—'

'So you said the other day when you wanted to lure me to some wicked café. What is it?'

'It's a letter.'

'A *letter*?' I felt suddenly the touch of the cold fog, its bitterness, its darkness. 'Who—from—?'

'From Lady Kitty.'

'A letter—to me—from Lady Kitty—?'

'Yes. Here it is. Here. Don't lose it.' She was thrusting a white envelope into one of my hands. My wet fingers closed on it. I stepped a little back from Biscuit.

'What about? Why on earth should Lady Kitty write to me? Do you know?'

'No,' said Biscuit. She added, 'Of course I don't know, I'm only the messenger.'

I stared down at Biscuit and her lovely eager thin face seemed to harden and recede and become the face of a stranger. Anger, fear, almost superstitious terror possessed me.

'Well, messenger, you'd better go then. You've done your job. Now go.'

'But I—'

'Go. *Go*.'

Biscuit turned and disappeared into the fog. I stood there alone in the middle of the bridge holding Lady Kitty's letter in my hand. After a little while I put the envelope in my pocket and began to walk back towards Westminster Station. Ten minutes later I was in the bar on the westbound platform at Sloane Square.

I was drinking gin and reading Lady Kitty's letter. People came and went in the bar and there was a constant cackle of conversation and an intermittent rattle of trains. I read Lady Kitty's letter carefully several times over. It ran as follows:

Dear Mr Burde,

I hope you will forgive me for writing to you like this out of the blue. I would not do so without a very good reason. I should say at once that my husband has of course

169

told me all about what happened at Oxford in relation to you and the first Mrs Jopling. It may seem strange to you that I should write and what I want is not easy to say. The past has remained something very awful for my husband and he has felt a bitterness which does not diminish. It seemed that there was nothing that could be done about this. (And we have *tried*.) Now it turns out so surprisingly that it seems the work of providence that you are in the same office. I think that he will not speak to you. The resentment and the pride are great, as you can imagine. But I want you to speak to him. I think that he would like to talk to you about the past, and I think if you could both just begin to talk quietly about it, it would help my husband very much indeed. I think if you only met once and talked like that it would help him. I wonder if you understand? A psychoanalist might not help him, but you might help him, and only you. I do not mean that he is unbalanced about it, not at all. He is a healthy successful man, bursting with energy and can enjoy his life. But there is all the time this shadow that will not go away. I do not mean either that it could ever go away, but a single talk with you could help to remove a sort of anger at the world, a desire for revenge even, which is with him like an endless toothache. If he could see you as a real person who has grown older and has suffered too perhaps. I know that I ask a lot of you as you may well prefer not to talk about those events or be made to think about them. But I ask this as something important which I think that you can do to help my husband. And I hope perhaps that you might like to help him. It is important that I have not told him that I am writing to you. This must remain a secret, he must not know that I asked you to approach him, as this would of course reduce the value of your coming, you see this. So please whatever happens keep this absolutely to yourself. Also, I write on my own writing paper, but please do not write to me or telephone me at Cheyne Walk. I send this letter to you by the hand of my maid. I wonder if you would be so good as to tell her whether or not you will do what I ask. You can easily go to him in the office and ask for a talk. Please excuse me for writing to you to ask this great favour.

> Yours sincerely,
> Katharine Jopling.

P.S. I have read this letter through and I feel there are more things, which it is not easy to say in a letter, which you should know before you see my husband. If you would be so good as to meet me once briefly I could explain them. I believe you like the park, and I suggest we might meet there next Monday morning about eight o'clock, by the Serpentine on your side of the bridge. Please tell my maid if you will come. I shall quite understand if you prefer not to. Please be sure to destroy this letter.

This communication put me into such a state of wild emotion that I could hardly breathe. The blood rushed to my face and my heart beat with such violence that I had to restrain it with my hand for fear it might do itself a mischief. The roar of the trains, the chatter of the people, made an undulating din in the midst of which my mind floated, dazed and separate. I sat blind with emotion, alone, rapt by pain and fear and by something else which made me want to cry, something which quite dreadfully touched the heart: and at the same time I was able to notice that Lady Kitty could not spell and to wonder if she realized that at this time of year it was still almost dark at eight o'clock in the morning.

The letter was dated a week ago and was presumably what Biscuit had tried to deliver last Saturday. It was a neatly written letter, doubtless the result of several drafts. Lady Kitty had acted quickly and yet carefully. Then I realized that Biscuit was supposed to take a message back, only I had dismissed her. This upset me very much. For of course there could be no doubt or hesitation about it. I would certainly do whatever Lady Kitty wanted. I would see her, I would see Gunnar, I would take the initiative which she said he would not take. I must do this and trust to her judgment that it would do more good than harm. Whether she was right or not was another matter. But it was not for me even to speculate about this. I simply had to do what her letter told me. As for my failure to return an answer at once by Biscuit, I must hope that this would not be interpreted as indecision. Of course there could be no question of my communicating with the house in Cheyne Walk. But Biscuit would surely come again for her reply. I was confronted, I suddenly realized with a mixture of alarm and awed relief, with an organization of almost military efficiency. There was no doubt, and as I saw this I let my head fall back against the wall in a kind of frightened admiring amaze, that Biscuit had been sent to observe me, to report on me, to see if I was the sort of person who could be trusted to receive Lady Kitty's—oh my God—so precious letter. Biscuit would turn up again to learn my answer to it, to learn if I would speak to Gunnar and whether I would be beside the Serpentine at eight o'clock on Monday.

The whole vista which now unravelled before my dazzled eyes was so extraordinary that I panted with emotion as I viewed it. Fancy, and this was the least of shocks, those two women discussing me! Biscuit must in some sense have reported favourably, yet on what evidence and in what terms? Lady Kitty would not have written such a dangerous *brave* letter to just anybody. How fantastically kind of her to write to me! And what on earth could she think about me, what image of me was there in her mind? I now realized that, with my idiotic conception of myself as scarcely existing, I had not imagined that she would ever have given me a single thought. I must have supposed, when I knew that Gunnar had married again, that he must have told his spouse about the past. Only I had not reflected. I had not really conceived that some conception of *me* had existed all these years in the minds of Gunnar and his second wife. And thus I had of course protected myself. What monster had been there all these years of which I knew nothing and which was yet a part of my being?

It was odd, almost frivolous, that I thought first about the women. But I thought about them briefly. The important thing was Gunnar. And as I read the letter through for the fourth time my imagination began to be stirred and very uncomfortably stirred. 'Bitterness . . . resentment . . . anger . . . revenge . . .' I had in truth not imagined Gunnar as *brooding*. I had conceived of him as hating me, but I had pictured this hatred as something clean, hygienic, separate and somehow essentially past, like a sharp knife put away forever in a drawer. Not that I thought that such things fade or vanish in the end. But I did not rate it among the live continuing functioning changing things of the world, partly because I did not conceive that I would ever meet Gunnar again. As far as my life was concerned it was all over. But supposing all these years Gunnar's hatred had grown, had flowered? Suppose he had meditated schemes of revenge, suppose he had wanted to kill me, suppose he still wanted to? What use was Lady Kitty's touching idea of a quiet talk in the face of a horror like that?

172

And yet she had written to ask my help. Her letter bewildered me, since it conjured up for the first time a genuinely biting image of the real Gunnar, and in the same breath spoke of reconciliation and cure as being at least worth the attempt. I had to trust her here. She must have some good enough reason to think the quiet talk a possibility. If there was really nothing for me in Gunnar except mad rage, she would not have made the suggestion—unless she was a very silly woman. But then perhaps she was a very silly woman? That had to be considered too. Altogether it was important that I should see her before deciding exactly how to approach Gunnar. It might be wisest to write him a letter. Then if he did not want to see me there need be no drama at all. All he had to do was not to reply.

But then, the imagination raced frenziedly on, what would become of me? How would I feel as the hours and the days went by and Gunnar did not answer me—or if he just replied formally that he would not see me? I measured what an immense mental change I had already undergone since opening that fateful letter. What a completely new landscape confronted me now! I had never for a moment envisaged a reconciliation with Gunnar, even the degree of reconciliation which talking would imply, as being available to me. Even God could scarcely have brought it about. Could Lady Kitty manage to do what God could not? Of course Lady Kitty had the advantage of existing, of sitting in her room at Cheyne Walk and writing this letter and handing it to her maid . . . But amazing as were her possible achievements, what she had already brought about was perhaps equally remarkable. She had totally altered my mind. I now thought it at least conceivable that I might speak again to Gunnar and be in some way at peace with him; and now that I could conceive of this, I wanted it, I needed it, with a desperation which was something new in my life. If *that* could only happen . . . How terrible suddenly to want this almost impossible thing, to realize that it could be, and yet might never be. This was a new suffering which the damned had not imagined, as if Christ should open a window into hell, look through, and then close it again.

This consideration, this glimpse of a completely new torture, brought my thoughts abruptly back to myself. Of course they had never really been away, but now all the old familiar solipsistic self-protective instincts were active, rejecting the possibility of change, the possibility of failure. I could now have faced the idea of Gunnar's murdering me more readily than the idea of his ignoring me, of his simply failing to respond to my appeal. After all, nothing had happened yet, nothing need happen, to alter the arrangements of my life. I had only to say no to Lady Kitty. It would be a reasonable enough no. No might indeed be not only the prudent answer but the right answer. I could say no and remain in safety. And yet — how could I not be there beside the Serpentine on Monday morning where in my feverish imagination I could already see myself waiting?

I rose now in sheer confused agitation and blundered out of the bar onto the platform, holding the letter still unfolded in my hand. A Hounslow train was just roaring into the station in a loud climax of dry clamour. Not knowing what I was doing I began to walk towards the escalator.

'Hilary!'

The face of Biscuit suddenly materialized. I cannoned into her, then grabbed her coat and pulled her back beside me against the wall. The people on the platform surged forward, the people off the train streamed past. Biscuit and I leaned back against the advertisements.

'Hello, Biscuit, we meet again. Why are you here?'

'I followed you.'

'Followed — you mean from — ?'

'Yes, from the bridge. I wanted to bring back the message. I was to bring it back tonight. I thought I would wait until you had finished the letter. Then I could take the message.'

'Oh, my God. And how long have you waited?'

'Not long. Only an hour and a half.'

'An hour and a half? Have I been sitting in there for an hour and a half?'

'I watched you through the window. I did not like to interrupt you as you were thinking.'

'Thinking? Was that thinking? I wondered what it was.'

'The message — '

'Oh yes, the message. What message, incidentally?'

'Will you do what Lady Kitty asks and will you meet her on Monday?'

'I thought you didn't know what was in the letter.'

'I don't. I ask what I was told to ask.'

'You're a handy girl, aren't you. I wish you were my maid. The answer is yes and yes.'

'Yes and yes?'

'Yes, I will do what she asks and yes I will meet her on Monday.'

'Thank you. Good night—then—Hilary.'

I looked down at Biscuit. She was looking up at me. Her duffle coat was dry now (had she really been sitting patiently on the cold platform all that time?), her eyes were glistening and big, but I did not interrogate them. Her bony face looked tired. In the rough shapeless coat she looked like a refugee. I kissed her lightly on the cheek.

'Off you go. How will you get to Cheyne Walk from here?'

'I shall walk, it is not far.'

'Good night, then.'

She turned and went slowly away without looking back and got onto the escalator and was carried upward out of sight. I waited a while to let her get ahead on her journey back to Cheyne Walk, where she would report, in some bright cosy unimaginable boudoir, to her unimaginable employer. Then I followed up myself and came out into Sloane Square. The night air bit with a coldness which shocked the blood into retreat. I thrust my hands deep into my pockets. The fog was a little less dense. I stood still for a while, then began to walk along in the direction of the King's Arms.

Suddenly I remembered Tommy. I looked at my watch. Biscuit's vigil had lasted more like two hours. Tommy had been waiting for me for well over an hour. I went into the telephone box outside the Royal Court Theatre and rang her number.

'Tommy—'

'Oh darling—darling—thank God. I couldn't think what had happened—I thought you'd been run over, I thought you'd been killed—I was so worried— Oh thank God, thank God—'

'Tommy, I'm so sorry—'

'That's all right, I'm just so relieved to hear your voice, oh I am so relieved—I was imagining all sorts of things—'

'I'm sorry, darling—'

'Will you come now?'

'Well, no, I can't—'

There was a silence.

'Tommy, I'm sorry, it isn't that—I mean I'm not with anyone else. I'm in a telephone box in Sloane Square and I'm just going home. I had a drink or two and forgot the time—I think I'd better—go home now—please forgive me—'

After another silence she said, 'All right—darling—I'm just so disappointed not to see you—I was so longing to see you. Will you—see me tomorrow?'

'Yes, yes, tomorrow—tomorrow morning if you like—come to the flat about eleven—we could go for a walk.'

'Oh good, oh thank you, I'm so glad—don't worry, I'll be all right, I'll sleep well. I do hope you're not upset about anything—you will tell me, won't you?'

'Yes, yes—'

'Sleep well, my darling.'

'And you too, Tommy, sleep well—good night.'

And I did sleep well. And the final thing I thought before I fell asleep was that now, at last, in the end, Lady Kitty had taken over and she would dispose of everything in the best way possible. Lady Kitty . . . would . . . arrange . . . it . . . all . . .

SATURDAY

IT WAS the next morning and Tommy and I were at the Round Pond. Tommy was happy. She knew from of old that this was a place of reconciling.

Earlier in the morning Mick and Jimbo had arrived as usual to visit Christopher. Jimbo had bought me a potted plant, a gloomy resigned growth which looked as if it had never heard of flowers. I was touched however. Did Jimbo, in the gentle sympathy of his half-feminine Welsh heart, know that I was shortly to face the flames? He gave it to me hastily and shyly, as if anxious not to display any sort of pity. Later the telephone engineer arrived and then the boy with the elastic band hair style. This contravened the rule of only three visitors at a time, but I forgave them on this occasion for the sake of Jimbo's potted plant. The telephone engineer had brought a guitar and after a while there was a cautious sound of plucked strings, then the hollow tap of the tabla and fragments of muted singing. Perhaps the Waterbirds were coming into existence after all. I did not disturb them. When Tommy came I took her away at once. I did not want to let her into the flat.

We had strolled along the vista which belongs to Watts's Bronze Horseman, and had reached the Round Pond, that centre of intense and innocent diversion, that perhaps mysterious and holy place, the omphalos of London. The quick-change artist weather had put on another show today. The fog had gone, to be replaced by a vivid russet-yellow light, cloud almost pierced by sun, which lent bright but strange colours to all things visible, the calm dark façade of Kensington Palace, the choppy metallic surface of the pond, the iridescent feathers of the ducks, the white sails of the model yachts, the red jerseys of the children, Tommy's blue mac, Tommy's grey eyes. Tommy held my hand and I let her, feeling myself like a child. I had no grain of sexual desire for her today.

Some boys were flying kites, racing along, trying to persuade strange bird-like structures to rise, to lift themselves mysteriously into the air, to tug, to be checked, to rise again, to float, to soar, until they should become high colourless spots and then vanish into the yellow sky which must after all be composed of mist. Excited dogs with sensitive spotted noses gambolled upon the glaringly green grass, mad with canine joys. Large and small beasts raced and circled in an ecstasy of motion, stopping abruptly to perform those intimate freemasonical ceremonies whereby alsatians, mastiffs, terriers, chihuahuas and pekinese all somehow recognize each other as dogs.

We admired the cunning speed of the model yachts, their owners swinging round the pond in dignified absorption to catch their vessels on the other side, adjust their sails and send them off again. We watched the diving ducks diving, and the swans swanning and the Canadian geese driving in convoy, groaning softly with excitement as they approached some bread-bestowing child. We watched an old man feeding sparrows, the tiny birds hovering like little frenzied helicopters above his fingers. We saw the beautiful feet of coots through green transparent water. Tommy laughed with happiness and squeezed my arm. I laughed too. We sat down on a wet bench. A collie ran up and thrust its warm firm muzzle into Tommy's hand.

I felt extraordinary. I was being kind to Tommy because I could not afford to quarrel with her just then, could not spare the energy for any irrelevant difference of opinion with the dear child, for instance about trivial questions such as whether or not we were going to get married. The idea of this marriage had now become utterly flimsy and unreal. The dreadful light cast by Lady Kitty's letter had made a new world, or perhaps it was an old world, a primeval world, a world in any case which had never heard of Thomasina Uhlmeister or of the man who had lain in bed with her on Wednesday night.

On the way to the Round Pond I had taken Tommy roundabout by way of the Serpentine Bridge and had inspected the place where I was to meet Lady Kitty on Monday morning. Of course I felt frightened about this meeting, but also felt, so strangely, a sort of deep calm, the almost confident calm which had accompanied me into sleep on the previous night. I was now in an interim wherein all power of action had been taken from me. I was paralysed and waiting, like a fly stung by a spider, only I was a cool resigned fly, almost without anxiety, so taken over was I by this sudden new power which had entered my life. I had been conscripted, I was under orders. Later of course I would have to make judgments, face dangers, take risks, decide and choose. But

in the pure blessed interval between now and Monday there
was absolutely nothing I could do but fold my hands and
wait. Pray perhaps, not even hope, not even speculate, but
wait. I almost wished the time was longer. I felt calm, vigorous
and in an obscure way tremendously changed. My bright
paralysed serenity communicated itself to Tommy. She
interpreted it as my brave resignation to the idea of becoming
her husband (this was plausible though wrong) and with her
intelligent tact she refrained from putting any sort of pressure
upon me. In our crazy separated ways we were almost happy,
able at any rate to enjoy the kites, the boats, the dogs, the
birds.

'Collies are so clever.'

'Are they, Tomkins?'

'I think they love us more than any other dog does.'

'Is that a sign of intelligence?'

'They communicate, they understand.'

'Do they, Thomas?'

'In Scotland you can see the collie dog on one hillside
collecting up the sheep and the shepherd a mile away on the
other hillside directing the dog by whistling.'

'Is that what you can see in Scotland, Thomasina?'

'You're teasing me, Hilary! Isn't he, collie dog?'

It was Saturday evening and I had just arrived at Crystal's
place. The evening had brought the light brown fog nuzzling
down out of the air, not as thick as last night, but gently
smudging lights and outlines, smelling of soot and burning,
not unpleasant. I shook my overcoat and laid it out on
Crystal's bed. Her little electric fire, kept on all day, had
made the room quite warm. The sewing machine was in its
usual place upon the floor, looking like a good dog. The table
was laid, the lace cloth spotless.

'Are you all right, darling?'

'Yes, yes—and you?'

'Fine. What's for supper?'

'Sausages and mashed and beans and blackberry and apple
pie and custard.'

'Oh good.' I opened the Spanish burgundy.

My enchanted Round Pond mood had undergone some modification under the gloomy challenge of the afternoon. The sheer fright I had felt in the Sloane Square Station bar had returned, the possible torture of a frustrated hope. The notion of any hope here was terrible. What could I possibly hope for? This morning I had felt almost complacent because I imagined that Lady Kitty would tell me what to do and see to it that I succeeded. Now this seemed ridiculous. Lady Kitty was some sort of blind gambler, and she was gambling with me. At least she was proposing to do so. During the afternoon (lying on my bed, alone) I had been thinking about Gunnar. About that house in north Oxford. About Tristram. About the car crash. About how wonderfully kind Gunnar had been to me. About the day when he and Anne brought the champagne. About when I saw him in hospital. About things that must not be thought about.

I tried to distract my mind by wondering whether I was really going to marry Tommy, and if so whether I ought to tell Crystal so this evening. I thought now in a resigned will-less sort of way that I might conceivably marry Tommy. I did sort of love Tommy. Our little time at the Round Pond had been for me a time of sort of love. And her absolute love for me was perhaps a gift not to be thrown away; just as Arthur's absolute love for Crystal was a gift not to be thrown away. Thus it is with some marriages and not necessarily bad ones either. Perhaps some sort of contentment might come to me somehow some day if I married little Tommy and let her try to cure my soul? I felt, as I walked through the light fog towards North End Road, tired and sad, distracted for a while from the afternoon's dread and the fear of Monday, and resolved at last to speak to Crystal about Tommy and about our possible, probable, marriage. Perhaps Crystal was waiting for this, perhaps it would relieve her mind and make her feel happier in her own choice; and if so it was for this reason worth doing. How terribly sad I felt about it now. However it did not after all matter very much to me what I did with myself.

I poured out a glass of the still rather chilly burgundy. Then I saw that Crystal was crying. A large tear had come from each eye, failed to make it over the plump curve of the cheek and rolled away on either side towards the ear. Two more tears followed.

'Oh my darling, what is it?'

Crystal quickly dispersed the tears, then went into the little kitchen and turned off the gas under the potatoes. I went after her, terrified. For a moment her face had expressed the most awful helpless grief.

'Crystal, what is it? What is it, my darling girl?'

'Nothing. It's perfectly all right. I'm so sorry, I'm just being silly.'

'What is it, tell me? Look come back in here and sit down.'

'Don't sit on your wet coat, dear.'

'*Tell me!*'

'It's just that—I've broken things off with Arthur.'

'Oh God—'

We sat at the table looking at each other. Crystal took her glasses off. More tears came out of her golden eyes and tried to go down her cheeks, but she mopped them away.

I thought, why? I thought, Clifford Larr. Had I not, in some rotten secret cranny of my soul, been hoping for just this? Clifford had decided, casually, cynically, to prevent the marriage. He had thought that he could do so by moving his little finger and he had been right. I felt distress, disgust, anger. I wondered if I should say what I thought or keep silent. I had to know, the anger was so much. I said, 'Dear heart, did Clifford do this? Did he write to you, come to see you?'

'No, no—it's nothing to do with him.'

'He didn't write or come or telephone or anything?'

'No, no, no!'

I wondered if that was true. 'Then why? I thought you'd decided, I thought you wanted it, I thought you'd be happy.'

'No, it's just—I'm so sorry—I feel I'm being stupid and awful—I just felt it wouldn't do.'

'But *why*, why did you change your mind, has anything *happened* to change your mind?'

'No, nothing, just my thoughts.'

'You haven't quarrelled with Arthur?'

'No, we never quarrel.'

'But *what* in your thoughts, why?'

'Please don't be angry—'

'I'm not! You've told him?'

'Yes, I wrote him a letter. You see, I was never really sure about it, there were so many things—'

'It's not for me, you haven't broken it off because of me, because of not wanting to leave me alone?' Oh God, ought I now to tell her about Tommy? What was I to do?

'No, no, it's not that at all. I just—it's in my own self—
I can't get married, it's too late—I'm an old maid already—
I'm a happy happy old maid—' Now tears were everywhere,
soaking her cheeks.

I pushed my chair up against hers and got her into my
arms. 'Oh my Crystal baby, my love.' She laid her head on
my shoulder and I stroked her funny frizzy hair.

'You always said we were babes in the wood.'

'Oh, Christ, yes.' How lost, in what a wood. 'Oh, Crystal,
I do so much want you to be happy, I do so blame myself,
I've wrecked your life, I know I have—'

'No, you haven't, I love you, and if I can help you and be
with you sometimes then I'm perfectly happy.'

'Over and over like a mighty sea comes the love of Crystal
rolling over me.'

Later on we calmed down and ate the sausages and mashed
and I let myself feel profound disgraceful relief at Crystal's
decision. We did not discuss Arthur or Gunnar or Tommy
and of course I said nothing about Lady Kitty. We talked a
lot about the old days, about the caravan and Aunt Bill and
about Christmas times when we were children. And I
promised to take Crystal to see the decorations in Regent
Street.

I came up in the lift, which had been mended. It was not
late. I had left Crystal before ten. She had become quite
calm and almost, in her curious way, radiant. The tears had
left her dear face quite bright. And her love for me glowed
out of it as it had always done through the long long years.
I wondered and wondered what it was that had made her
draw back. Perhaps, after all, it was just her sense that, for
her happiness, she could love no one but me? Was it indeed
perhaps her intuitive identification with me, her sense of
my tribulation, and her desire to clear the decks so as to
help me in my coming trial? She must feel that with Gunnar's
return I was in some way imperilled. And with me in trouble
how could she think of Arthur? Or rather, with me in trouble
did she not discover how little she really cared for him?

In the dreary dull electric light of the landing someone was standing outside the door of my flat. My heart sank into my boots. It was Arthur.

'Oh hello, Arthur. No one at home?'

'I didn't ring. I knew you were with—her—'

'Why didn't you ring, you dolt? Why stand on the landing?'

'I didn't want to be a nuisance—'

I opened the door and we went in.

Christopher came out of his room, looking very beautiful in a new dragon-embroidered dressing gown. 'I say, Hilary, Laura was here and— Oh hello, Arthur.'

Thank God I had missed Laura anyway. 'Did you get those candles?'

'Oh God, I forgot again, I'm so sorry! Can I make you some—?'

'No, just buzz off. And don't start any bloody music.'

I went into my bedroom and Arthur followed me and we both sat down on the bed. Arthur began to cry.

'Oh Arthur, stop, I've had such a day—'

'She told you?'

'Yes.'

'Do you think she'll change her mind?'

'How do I know? No, I shouldn't think so.' And as I saw him sitting there, his silly face all red and wet, I felt very sorry for him, but I also felt thank God that's not going to be my brother-in-law.

'Sorry, have you got a handkerchief? I don't seem to have one.'

'Here.'

'If I only knew *why*. If there was anything I could *change*, I'd do anything. I'd make myself a different person—'

'One can't. Change is impossible. If one is rejected it's no good wearing a different hat.'

'Do you think there's someone else?'

The handsome sardonic face of Clifford Larr rose again before me. No, surely that was impossible. 'No.'

'She wrote me such a funny letter, would you like to see it?' He thrust it into my hand—a piece of paper over which, upon widely spaced lines, Crystal's schoolgirl writing straggled.

Dear Arthur, it cannot be, I cannot marry you, it is no good, I am no good, I am a person who cannot marry, there are such things in my life as make it not rite, I am so sorry. Please do not come agen, I am sorry, for my sake do not, I must be alone now, I am so sorry. With loving thoughts, yours Crystal.

I shuddered at this missive which I had not been fast enough to prevent idiotic Arthur from showing me. What an odd little letter. But really there was no mystery. I had been a fool ever to imagine that Crystal would marry. Thank God that scare was over. I felt very exasperated with Arthur for the trouble he had caused us both.

'What can I do to change myself—' Arthur was going drearily on.

'Shave off your moustache.'

'Do you mean—?'

'Oh go away, Arthur, and stop crying. We've all got things to cry about. Don't you think I could drown the world with tears if I started on my own woes? You're all right. Crystal's a dotty girl anyway. You've had a lucky escape. For God's sake find yourself some normal dolly bird and get yourself a washing machine and a budgerigar.'

The lights went out abruptly. I pushed Arthur, still sniffing, to the door. I waited a moment and heard him falling down the stairs. I went to bed and to sleep.

MONDAY

IT WAS Monday morning. Sunday had been different again from Saturday. On Sunday I was simply in a sick state of anxiety and fear, as before an exam. The huge shapes of Lady Kitty, even of Gunnar, became luridly indistinct, as if something awful were shining upon me from behind them. I wished intensely that Monday morning could be over without anything catastrophic having happened, while at the same time I could not imagine what its 'being over' could possibly be like. I apprehended with vague dread that I would be tried and found wanting, or even that I was being decoyed into a trap. I anticipated some sort of débâcle which would literally drive me mad. I did not see how I could possibly behave like a rational being, not choke or faint. I of course imagined that I would oversleep and miss Lady Kitty and never ever manage to see her again. I went to three cinemas on Sunday and could remember nothing about what I had seen. I awoke at five on Monday. At seven I was walking about the park. It was now five to eight.

The sun was just rising, perhaps just risen, but had made little impression upon the scene. A hazy pall of dusk still hung over the park and the street lamps were on upon the road that crossed the bridge. It was a cold quiet morning and a grey mist rising from the lake added its veil to the dim roadway. I had already made the circuit of the area on the north of the bridge about twelve times. I had walked westward on the path beyond the Magazine, back as far as Rotten Row, down to the water on the eastern side, back across the car park, onto the bridge, back and off again towards the magazine. The place was not entirely deserted. A few cars were passing and occasionally figures loomed up out of the mist, peered at me and went by.

I was feeling sick with anxiety and terror as if I might actually have to vomit in the gutter. I regretted terribly that I had destroyed Lady Kitty's letter as now doubts assailed me about the time and place of the meeting. Perhaps it was not today, perhaps it was not here. Perhaps it was all a sort of dream anyway. No one would come, I would never see Biscuit again, never hear again from Lady Kitty. The air was intensely cold. I had dressed with modest care, allowing myself an overcoat and scarf but no cap or gloves. The omission of the cap was certainly a mistake. The chill mist seemed already to have soaked me through, laying down a penetrating film of waterdrops upon my coat, my face, my hair. Even my hands in my pockets were wet and cold. I knew that I must be looking terrible, red-nosed and bedraggled and frozen. I tried to warm my nose in my hands. It was impossible. I had no handkerchief. My quick breath was pumping clouds of steam out of dripping nostrils. I took off my scarf and could almost wring the water out of it. Then it seemed too wet to put on again and I held it helplessly in my hand.

It was now five past eight and the mist was thicker than ever. I had just run from the Magazine across the car park to the water. A few cold fluffed-up ducks were floating near to the bank. Beyond, the mist descended. There was a dreadful silence which muffled the sound of the more frequent, invisible, passing cars. I began to wonder if Lady Kitty had not by now come and gone, somehow missing me as I hurried desperately to and fro. I decided I had better stay still now for a while in what was probably the most likely place, beside the lake just east of the bridge. I waited and listened and looked. No one, nothing. It was nearly ten past eight. I could not bear the inactivity, and gasping with anxiety set off again to lope back towards the road. As I approached the corner of Rotten Row, where it turns round to run along the northern edge of the Serpentine, two riders materialized out of the mist. The horses, which had been trotting, slowed to a walk as they approached. I paused to let them turn and pass. I got an impression of two pairs of highly polished boots and took in that the riders were women. Then the horses stopped near me and one of the women dismounted. It was Biscuit.

I stood there paralysed with alarm and with a sense of outrage which I could not at once interpret. I waited for Biscuit to speak to me, but she did not. Biscuit was perfectly attired as a smart groom. Her hair was neatly piled up behind a small velvet cap. I even saw a little silver-handled whip in her hand. I saw the glowing leather of the reins, the smoking nostrils of a rather large brown horse. I saw Biscuit's face, absolutely expressionless, aloof, the face of a servant. She had already turned from me and was holding the bridle of the other horse from which the second rider was dismounting. Biscuit then withdrew, leading the two horses. She faded into the mist. Lady Kitty stood before me.

She took her hat off. I took in her smart riding habit and well made-up face. It was a strong face with rather too long a nose, dark eyes and a tumble of dark hair which emerged now from under the hat. The perfume, seeming absurdly out of place, warred with the cold air. She began to speak.

'How very kind of you to come, Mr Burde. I appreciate it very much indeed.' It sounded as if she were welcoming an honoured guest into her drawing-room. Her voice was the sort of upper class woman's voice which I particularly detested.

Emotion rose up into my mouth, into my head. Rage. I suddenly felt that I was being monstrously put upon, that the whole thing was outrageous, a farce designed to humiliate me. The arrival on horses, the masquerade with Biscuit, this woman's ghastly voice, the stupid grandness of it all. The well-cut breeches, the bloody polished boots. The elegant little leather gloves which Lady Kitty was now drawing off. I suppose (I thought of this later) that what I was feeling then was the poor man's primeval hatred of the man on the horse. It was not that I had ever coveted a horse myself, even as a child. Crystal and I never even heard of privileged children with ponies. I never conceived of riding. But now suddenly this rich woman with her horses, and with Biscuit as her servant, filled me with a hostility which rendered me for a moment speechless.

As I said nothing, Lady Kitty said, 'Mr Burde, forgive me for— Do you think we could sit down somewhere and talk?'

I said thickly, 'No, I can't—'

She said hastily, 'I'm sorry, I quite understand, it was stupid of me to ask you—'

'No, you don't understand. I don't mind talking to you. It's all this—I can't— Look, I'm sorry, I will talk to one woman, but I will not talk to two women and two horses!'

Lady Kitty hesitated. She looked round. There was no sign of Biscuit or the animals.

I went on, hardly knowing what I was saying, 'I can't talk to you today, it's spoilt. If you will come here at this time tomorrow alone and on foot I will talk to you. I'm sorry, I—' I turned abruptly on my heel and made for the bridge. When I reached the middle of the bridge I began to run.

Later on, in the office (I decided to go to the office in preference to running mad on the Inner Circle) I failed to make sense of myself entirely. I sat at my desk with my head in my hands glaring at the lighted face of Big Ben, now faintly visible. Reggie and Mrs Witcher tried to attract my attention by making jokes about my having got my lady friend into the panto, and became even more sarcastic when I failed to reply. Mrs Witcher said that if I could not give civil answers to friendly remarks I ought to see a doctor. I eventually said 'sorry' and they left me alone.

I could not conceive how I could have been so aggressive and so rude to Lady Kitty when it was so fantastically kind of her to be willing to speak to me at all. Why should she condescend to address a criminal like me? I ought to have been humble and grateful, even obsequious. I ought to have listened with bowed head to anything she thought fit to say to me. Who was I, after what I had done to her husband, to put on tantrums of stupid touchy pride and tell her to go away and come again tomorrow in a guise that suited me better? I must have been insane. Of course she would not come. I should never see her again.

I could not remember the address in Cheyne Walk, I had not noted the telephone number. I wondered if I could find out, rush round at once, demand to see her, apologize. I even thought of going downstairs to see Gunnar. The idea that he was probably at this very moment sitting in that room on the first floor, that I could talk to him by dialling the number which was here before me on the office list, that I could see him by walking down three flights of stairs and opening a door, drove me into a frenzy. I sat there with my back to the room, trying to breathe inaudibly, my heart pounding, my head swimming.

At lunch-time I walked along the embankment in a daze. It was less misty. The sun was somewhere. I walked as far as Blackfriars Bridge and back, then set off again towards Blackfriars. I could not conceive of eating anything. I could do nothing now with my life except wait in the most frightful

anxiety for tomorrow morning and then, when she did not
come, decide what on earth to do next. I went back to the
office and resumed my sulking and glaring. Arthur, thank
God, kept out of my way. At about four o'clock I remembered
that it was Monday and that Clifford Larr would be expecting
me. I felt unable to face Clifford. I supposed I ought to see
him to find out whether he had tampered with Crystal's
engagement, and if he had, to do something (what?) about it.
But I was incapable of doing what I ought. I was simply a
waiting machine. I sent Clifford a note (something which he
had told me never to do) by the now recovered Skinker
saying that I had a violent cold and could not come that
evening. I went home early and lay on my bed for hours in
torment. I was back again in the park at six a.m. on Tuesday.

TUESDAY

IT WAS Tuesday morning, eight o'clock. It was a cloudy cold morning, not raining, a gloomy twilight but little mist. I was standing near to the bend of Rotten Row, between the sandy track and the water, just on the edge of the car park. I was feeling lightheaded with hunger and emotion and sleeplessness. I was very cold and wanting the fruitless ordeal to be over. I had decided to wait until eight thirty and then go. I was wearing a cap and gloves. I looked down at my watch. A minute past eight. When I looked up again I saw a figure coming across the tarmac towards me. It was a woman pushing a bicycle.

'I hope you don't mind a bike,' said Lady Kitty, and she smiled.

Suddenly everything was quite different. It was as if a huge black lid which had been pressed down hard upon the world had been quietly lifted up. I could breathe, I could think, I could speak.

I said, taking off my cap, 'I am terribly sorry I behaved so badly yesterday, I can't think what came over me, you must have thought me an awful person. I do apologize.'

'Not at all, it is for me to apologize. I thought about it afterwards and I saw just how sort of—I mean I'm sorry, it's for me to be sorry—'

'Not at all, it's for me—'

'Well, don't let's argue. Look, I'll just shove this machine somewhere, where can I put it, here against the railings. I say, it is beastly cold, isn't it.'

'I'm so sorry, I—'

'No, no, this picturesque place and time was my choice. Now where can we sit down? I've got such a lot to say to you?

'Let's cross the bridge,' I said.

We began to walk across the bridge. The light of day now showed the slow steady movement of low grey clouds above the lake. It was extraordinary, walking with her. I felt as if I were someone in a story. It was all so strange. I kept looking about me in amazement.

Lady Kitty was fairly tall, well up to my shoulder. Today

she was wearing a sort of tweed cape and a matching hat. She had pulled off the hat to reveal the layers of falling-down hair, glossy and very dark brown. Her eyes (as I was able to observe a little later) were a dark slaty spotty blue-grey, the sort of blue-grey where the grey element is more like an injection of black. And there was the rather too long dominating nose and a large finely cut determined mouth. Not the face of a fool. Yet of her folly it was a little early to judge.

'Is it going to rain?' She uttered the question as if it were very important and as if I certainly knew the answer.

'For our purposes, no.'

'So kind of you to come. I hope you don't mind the secrecy?'

'Not at all. I must confess I was very mystified by Biscuit at first.' I wanted to hear her speak of 'Biscuit', and have done with 'my maid'.

'Biscuit enjoyed it. It makes a change from the tedium of looking after me.'

'I kept her waiting terribly on Friday.'

'Yes, she told me. She loved it.'

Mysteries, mysteries, what on earth had it been like when Biscuit told Lady Kitty how she had stood on the platform at Sloane Square station and watched me through the window of the bar as I read and reread Lady Kitty's letter?

We had reached my objective, the Peter Pan statue. Lady Kitty had walked obediently beside me, ready evidently to go on indefinitely until I should arrange for us to sit down. I dusted the frost off one of the seats with my glove. The trooping clouds were lighter, the lake water motion-less, hung with a gauze curtain just short of the opposite bank. There was no one about, not even a duck.

'Well?' I said. I had already grasped how business-like she was, or at least managed to seem. And yet this could go with a good deal of sheer asininity. Witness the unnecessary panache of yesterday. Witness perhaps the whole project.

'Well,' she said, taking up my tone. 'Listen. I don't know if I can explain clearly. I couldn't write it all. I'm not much good at writing anyway. There isn't actually any more to it except what I put in my letter, that's the essence of it. Only how it really is — the details — are so important. I mean — how it is with Gunnar.'

I flinched at the name. However it was better than 'my husband'. I said, 'Yes?'

'You see. Now let me try to put my ideas in order. It's rather extraordinary, isn't it, that we're talking at all?' She looked at me as if expecting a reply.

'Yes,' I said, 'and it may be rather unwise.'

She sat turned on the seat looking at me. I looked sometimes at her, sometimes at the water.

I regretted the remark. It was too early to insult her courage by striking a note of fear. What had I meant anyway? I meant such a lot. There was an air of sacrilege about my being with her at all. I did not express this thought however. I said, 'I may not help Gunnar at all by speaking to him. I may just annoy him.' That was putting it mildly.

'And it could be, for you, awfully distressing. I know. That's why it's so good of you to be here.' The slate-dark eyes were bright with intelligence and animation. Yes, possibly a silly woman. She found the drama interesting. Perhaps it was a change from the tedium of being looked after by Biscuit.

'Never mind me. If I can help Gunnar—' The repeated phrase struck me as ridiculous. What was I doing discussing 'helping Gunnar' with Gunnar's wife? 'Go on,' I said. 'You wanted to speak to me. Please speak.'

'Yes, yes. I must try to explain about Gunnar. It isn't easy. You don't mind if I talk about—those things—?'

'Talk about any things.'

'It's difficult to express, to tell you, how absolutely obsessed he is.'

'About—'

'Yes. He thinks about it all the time and it sort of cuts him off. No one would guess, but it is so. He's tried to stop it of course. When he was in America he tried psychoanalysis. He even went to a priest. To be dreaming about revenge the whole time—'

'Revenge?'

'That's part of it. And brooding and brooding about what exactly happened and why. To be so tied up to particular things in the past is a sort of illness. It hasn't affected his ordinary life, of course, I mean his work. He took refuge in work, in his ambitions. But it cut him off from people. Then he married me and—'

'Well, surely you can cure him!' I said. There was an ungracious bitterness in the interruption. Huge emotions were working inside me and I was concentrating on keeping calm, staring at a motionless misty willow, at a seagull on a post.

'I thought I could—I have helped him. But I can't cure him—there is only one person who can cure him—I think—'

I could not speak. I closed my eyes for a moment.

She went on. 'I may be wrong. But I think this. You see he is obsessed with you. He always knew where you were. He knew you were in the department. He always knew from the civil service list where you were.'

This was staggering news. 'But he never thought of actually trying to see me?'

'Oh no. It was just part of the revenge fantasy.'

'Part of the—I see— This cure you speak of—it sounds as if it might be rather drastic—'

'No, that's a fantasy. Really, he might, he *might*, want to talk—I thought of this before of course—'

'Did you?'

'There were too many obstacles, it seemed impossible. He has such huge pride. I couldn't, you know, suggest anything to him, and I haven't. That's why— But suddenly, it was like fate, there you were right in his path. Even then I didn't do anything about it until after he had seen you again, just literally seen you.'

I thought. 'But he didn't see me until—a week ago yesterday—and you put Biscuit on my trail before that.'

'No. He first saw you about a month ago. In the office. You didn't see him.'

'Oh God.'

'He came home absolutely shaking. I didn't press him to talk much and he didn't. But it was so important that he had just *seen* you. You see,' she went on, 'it does seem providential. As things are now, you are bound to meet now and then and that makes it that tiny bit easier to imagine talking. Only he will never make a move, I'm sure. You will have to make the move. You have no idea what it's like in his mind. You have no idea what it's like for me to see you, to be sitting here actually talking to you. That day when I saw you in the office I thought I'd faint. I knew it was you because Biscuit had described you very carefully and because of the way you behaved. When you came back up those stairs my knees nearly gave way.'

'But—why—?'

'There you are, you don't understand. You've been a sort of huge mythological figure to both of us for years, you've been *there*, behind everything. You've been a sort of fate—or a kind of awful—god—in our lives—or a huge ghost that's got to be laid, only it seemed you never would be.'

'An obstruction.'

'An immense obstruction. Not only for him but for me too. I don't want my husband to be tied up to something in the past. I want him to be entirely here in the present with me.'

Her quiet passion, her air of urgent candour, the devastating nature of her revelations, overwhelmed my mind. I was desperately trying to hold onto my wits and to carry on something like a conversation without breaking down. I said as coolly as I could, 'I have certainly been thinking about him all these years. I had no idea he had been thinking about me.'

'Well, that's stupid! How could you doubt it? Do you imagine you are the only person involved? He has thought about you. He has thought about *her*.'

There was a pause during which neither of us could speak. For a moment I thought that she was going to shed tears. Then recovering and with that brave excited air of pouring out the truth at last, she went on, 'Of course in seeking you out like this I am being selfish. I am considering myself and Gunnar here, not you. You are a sort of—'

'Instrument.'

'Yes. I want Gunnar to be able to look at you and see that you are just a—'

'Clerk in his office.'

'No, no. Just a human being, an ordinary person, not a sort of ghost or demon—'

'An ordinary unhappy unsuccessful man. Yes, indeed. But look, even if I were to, somehow, approach Gunnar, why should he talk to me at all if he feels like you say? Won't his response be just rage? I don't mean that he might attack me physically, though I suppose he might—but he hates and detests me, so how on earth can he get any profit out of talking to me?'

'Because he wants to. He never says so. But he terribly wants to. We've almost stopped talking about it, but I know. Only you must be careful and ingenious—'

'I think this requires more care and ingenuity than I'm capable of. After he saw me—in the office—when I didn't see him—did he say anything then about talking?'

'No, no, no, of course not, he just set his teeth, it was

impossible even to—oh you've no idea— But he needs you. That's why it will work in the end, I'm sure it will. Only it was necessary for me to have—nerve enough—to approach you.'

'You have plenty of nerve. He needs me, you think. Perhaps I need him even more than he needs me.'

'I've thought of that too,' she said. 'Of course I'm doing this for Gunnar and myself. But I have thought a little—about your situation—as well.'

'Kind of you.'

'I know it's a bit impertinent—'

'No, I'm not being sarcastic. And when I said "nerve" just now I meant "pluck". And I think you are being very kind.'

'You say you've thought about him—and about all that—too.'

'I've thought of nothing else ever since. That's hardly an exaggeration. I have lived and breathed it all these years.'

'And you've felt guilt?'

'Yes.'

'And you've been unhappy?'

'Yes.'

'And you feel it has ruined your life?'

'Yes.'

'Then you need help too.'

'Of course. But who can give it to me?'

'Gunnar can. Even this conversation with me can. Oh I'm so glad I saw you and didn't just write that letter! I thought at first, really until I'd actually written the letter, that I would simply ask you to see him, just like that in the letter, and then leave it all to you and do nothing more. Only the letter seemed so scanty, it explained so little—I felt I must see you—and oh how glad I am that I have!'

She was sitting very upright, the cape now thrown back, one leg tucked under her, a blue woollen dress drawn tight across her knee. The shining dark hair tumbled in a carefully contrived swirl of many-layered confusion almost to her shoulders. She was looking at me, but I did not want to meet those murky eyes, did not want my face to speak to her at all. I looked down, inspecting a nyloned ankle and a smart highly-polished but now rather muddy high-heeled shoe.

'Thanks. You are full of excellent projects. I just doubt whether any of them will work.'

'You mean you won't see Gunnar?'

Too much was happening all at once, as if destiny, having let nothing occur for years, had been storing up the events of my life. I did not want this disturbance, these decisions. I did not want to be 'used' and 'helped' by this powerful intruding ridiculously well-dressed woman. I said, 'Where does Gunnar suppose you to be at this moment? People don't usually leave their houses and stroll about at eight in the morning.'

'Gunnar is in Brussels. But even if he weren't—I often go out riding early with Biscuit. That was what the horses were about, not to impress you.'

Her trustfulness, her little eager air of truth, were irresistibly touching, shaming. I knew I should be behaving in some quite different way. I ought to have the grace to feel and express gratitude. But I could not. I felt a kind of exasperated terror, I wanted to get away. I could not bear the degree of exposure which so many hidden things had suddenly undergone. I knew too that later on I would detest this conversation and find in it endless occasions for remorse.

'I think we have said enough.'

'But you *will* see Gunnar?'

'Yes, I expect so. But I've got to think how—'

'You must help us. You must *now*, after I've talked so much, after I've said things to you which I've never said to anyone. Only you can help us. And now I see, only we can help you. I mean, Gunnar can. Why should you be unhappy? As things are you're losing both ways, you're being miserable and you're solving nothing, you're doing nothing about it. Don't you want to change your life?'

'I'm not sure. It could change for the worse. I can see that Gunnar might feel better after he'd talked to me. I doubt if I'd feel better after I'd talked to Gunnar. Gunnar can't "forgive" me, I doubt if God could, what's done is done. I don't mean anything very dramatic by that. There just isn't any psychological or spiritual machinery for removing my trouble. Gunnar feeling a bit better won't help me, it won't even, if you see what I mean, cheer me up. And seeing him will just bring it closer, drive it deeper. Death is my only solution. And I don't mean suicide. Do you understand?'

'Oh—I understand—but no—you mustn't think like that, you mustn't *think* like that—'

'You are very kind. Yes, I daresay I will talk with Gunnar,

or at least try to. My own arrangements don't matter much one way or the other. I don't actually think they could become worse. Anyway, it doesn't matter, it isn't for me to try to get anything out of this. And now I'm sorry I must leave you, I have to go to the office. Thank you for talking to me.'

'You must never never let him know—'

'Of course not.'

We stood up. Behind her upon his wet pedestal of beasts and fairies, polished and sanctified by the hands of children, towered beyond their reach the sinister boy, listening.

'Who was the woman you were with in the office?' Lady Kitty asked.

'My fiancée. Now I must go. I'm sorry. I'm glad to have met you and I'm—very grateful. I'll go quickly this way across the park. I'll say good-bye to you here.'

The presumption that we would not meet again hung between us, but we could neither of us comment on it.

I intended to say good-bye. Instead I quickly said, 'May I write to you about all this?'

'Yes. I'll send Biscuit.'

'Thank you.'

I turned abruptly away and walked fast and then ran across the wet grass in the direction of Kensington High Street.

Dearest Hilary, my usual letter, but oh how different now that we are to be married. There was always such pain in writing to you before, I felt always as if I were being sulky and importunate. My love for you, which was so pure and clean in me, became something muddy and nasty when I tried to give it to you. I could not *give* it, and that was so terrible, like a curse in a fairy tale. I felt so often that my love just irritated you. When you really love somebody you can't help feeling that you do them good by loving them. And yet I know that things between us were twisted, so that my love could not succour

you. Now all is changed. We have looked into each other's
eyes and known each other. I felt on Wednesday that
pure undoubtable communication at last. It was so different,
wasn't it, from the first days when you wanted me? We
never looked so then. You hid from me, you hid from yourself. Now you have found me and found yourself too. I
knew on Wednesday that all was well and that what
had been twisted was untwisted at last. I'm almost glad
you didn't come on Friday because Saturday was so
perfect, such a sort of seal on it all. I felt so happy beside
the Round Pond. I've never *seen* things so vividly in my
life, those dogs, those boats, all existing because of you,
the world existing because of you. You make me to see
and to be. Oh Hilary, I will behave so well, you'll see.
I won't dispute about anything ever! You shall decide
when we get married—only let it be soon—perhaps on
the day when Crystal marries Arthur? I am so happy too
in her happiness—we shall be such a joyful quartet! I
will (bold me!) ring the office on Wednesday morning
and ask you to see me on Wednesday evening! And you
will be kind to me—you will be kind to me, won't you—
now and when I am your wife. I am only your little harmless Tommy. You must love me and look after me for I
am so completely yours. God bless you and keep you. My
love to you, oh my dear. Now and forever your

Thomas.

Tommy, my dear, I got your sweet letter this evening.
I had to leave early and so missed it in the morning.
Tommy, don't ring tomorrow. I'll deliver this by hand
tonight. Tommy, I cannot marry you. You can't really
have believed I would. Your letter sounds like someone
whistling in the dark. Oh God, I'm sorry. What happened
on Wednesday wasn't true. Neither was what happened
on Saturday. I was living a lie then. I can't explain.
Nothing is your fault. What is true is what I was saying
earlier, what I've been saying for months, that it's just
no good between us. As you so cleverly said, your love
just becomes something different when it gets to me, and
something which I just don't want. I exploit your sweet
kindness by seeing you at all. Of course you want to be
exploited, but that isn't the point. It's all bad for *me*. I
cannot tell you how I despise myself for letting you console me. Tommy, it mustn't be any more. I feel some sort

of crisis in my life is approaching and I have to face it alone. You cannot really help me. You're just like endless cups of tea. I've got to be alone now. Tommy, I can never marry you. I must tell you the truth. I'm a sort of separated cursed man. And you are not the person who can save me. You can only prevent me from being saved by preventing me from being ever really serious. That is why our marriage, if it were ever conceivable at all, would be the end of me. I should die in my soul and I should hate you for it. Please believe what I say and forgive me. Don't try to see me, it would just make us both more miserable. Just please don't come near me any more. Accept a clean decent break and make yourself some other better life elsewhere. I hope you'll be happy, and you'll have a far far better chance away from me. By the way, Crystal has broken with Arthur. Only that is not the reason for this. Oh forgive me—and for Christ's sake keep away.

H.

I wrote this missive on Tuesday evening and walked to Tommy's place and dropped it through the letter box. I had already cancelled my appointment with Arthur. I gave him no reasons. He assumed, I saw it in his sad eyes, that this was the consequence of the break with Crystal. But he asked no questions. He did not ask about next Tuesday. He asked nothing. Poor Arthur. I spent the later part of the evening wandering about London, dropping into various bars. I walked as far as St Paul's and back. I came home late and went to bed. I slept well.

As I walked about in the cold yellow night I hardly thought about Tommy at all. I wrote the letter to her in a frenzy of fierce certainty after reading her letter. During the day, as I sat in the office looking at Big Ben and doing, in fact, some work, Tommy simply ceased to exist for me, she fell to pieces. How flimsy Tommy's hold upon me was had been proved by half an hour of Lady Kitty. Tommy just had to go. There was nothing crude or vulgar about this. It was not that I wanted to cashier Tommy so as to be able to think about Lady Kitty. I thought it quite possible that I would not see Lady Kitty again. (Though it was important to me that I had her permission to write her a letter.) It was just that Lady Kitty's message belonged to the deep business of my life with which poor Tommy had simply nothing to do. I now had a task, I was like a knight with a quest. I neeeded my chastity now, I needed my aloneness; and it seemed to me with a quickening amazement that I had *kept* myself for just this time. I could not confide what I had to do to anybody, and fortunately there was nobody who had any claim to know it, nobody who had any claim upon my spirit and my hours. Crystal I would perhaps tell later. No one else mattered. The half-lie of my relation with Tommy must certainly go. As I had told her, my earlier desire to end it was my true desire. And now, thank God, Lady Kitty had given me the motive power necessary to move into the truth, into my own truth, my own place, my centre from which I would be able to act.

But what exactly was I going to do and what would be, for me, the consequences? Of course, in spite of my defensive replies to Lady Kitty, there could be no doubt that I must do what she asked. What would it be like? Suppose it were simply awful? Suppose it just ended in some terrible display of Gunnar's hatred and anger? My position was indeed not as bad as it might be, I still had much to lose. I had never seen Gunnar unmasked, never *seen* his horror of me, the horror from which he could not escape and which made him brood upon revenge. What sort of Gorgon might I now, by meddling, unveil, which should appal me and drive me at last into madness? Only I had to meddle. There was no indecision in me at all. And as I thought about what I must do I wavered between this fear and a crazy tormenting hope that all might yet be well. Of course the past could not be undone. But, yet, there could be deep change. How deep that change could be I felt in myself more and more as the day went on, as if Lady Kitty had shaken me and broken something inside and I was now seeing the pieces make a new pattern and offer a new way. Lady Kitty had spoken of cure, and of Gunnar's cure, not mine, though in her grace she had glanced at mine too. She had been practical, not high-minded. It was for me to supply the rest: to give, to her practical shake-up, its spiritual sense. Why should Christ's blood stream vainly in the firmament? I could climb out of the pit in which I had elected to live and in which I had also incarcerated Crystal. I could climb up and see the light again.

What a stupid coagulated mass of indistinguishable guilt and misery I had become. How perfectly futile all my sufferings had been. If only I could separate out that awful mixture of sin and pain, if I could only even for a short time, even for a moment, suffer purely without the burden of resentment and self-degradation to which I had deliberately condemned myself, there might be a place for a miracle. And I reflected too, as I walked and walked about London, on the absolute doneness of what was done. I saw Anne's face as I had seen it that evening in the car, not glorified, not the face of what had once seemed our heroism, but muddled, guilty, frightened. If I had not killed her she would have stayed with Gunnar. Did I kill her for that reason or was it all just chaos and accident, and did it matter that I could probably never answer that question?

WEDNESDAY

O N WEDNESDAY morning I woke up exhausted and frightened. The exhilarated energy had gone. What had I got to be so animated about? A feeling of, in both senses, determination remained however. I had, it occurred to me, at last, got a job to do. Since the catastrophe I had declared myself jobless. I recalled with dull pain my brutal and as it had then seemed inspired letter to Tommy. Why on earth had I described her to Lady Kitty as my fiancée, out of some sort of instinct of self-destructive pique? Had I actually now got rid of little grey-eyed long-legged Tommy, excised her from my life after all? I had decreed for myself a sort of loneliness, but whereas the loneliness might be long, the task for which it was essential might prove very short. Could a fresh era which began thus with my violence to Tommy be in any sense a hallowed time? Did the idea of *truth* really cover me where Tommy was concerned? Was Tommy indeed a lie which I had to abjure, an encumbrance which in my new dedication I was bound to shed? It did not, in the morning darkness as I rose, seem so clear.

What was clear was that I *needed* to write that letter to Lady Kitty. Thank heavens I had had the quick wit to ask her if I might write to her. That at least, amidst all the dread, presented itself as a humane and consoling operation. I did not try myself with ideas of seeing her again. But I did so much want, and felt I somehow deserved, the *relief* of writing to her and explaining myself to her before I decided what my plan of campaign should be in regard to Gunnar. There was a kind of strange holy safety, as if I were in 'retreat', in the existence of the *interval*, the interval between my receipt of Lady Kitty's instructions and the unpredictable battle scene between me and Gunnar. The shake which I had received, the depth to which I had been as it were cracked, gave me for the present work enough. I felt I needed to brood, even to rest for a while, upon what had already happened before I ran rashly on into whatever was to come. I wanted very much now to meditate and to wait, and meanwhile take my time over the invention and writing of the permitted letter.

WEDNESDAY

The tube train was even more crowded than usual that morning. I had done the walk to Gloucester Road passing the now forever numinous place where I had met Lady Kitty, and had at first rejected her. The dawn, which had been a pale glowing primrose yellow behind the bare trees of the park, was already clouding over by the time I reached the station. Jammed body to body, we yawned and swayed, breathing into each other's expressionless faces, like forms packaged up for hell. I kept, as always, a sharp lookout for people with colds. I breathed nervously, consciously, feeling the elasticated in and out of the warm intrusive bodies of my fellow passengers. Reggie Farbottom often lauded the pleasure of being crushed against a bosomy typist. This could not please me. Female forms and faces were, in this stuffy insipid proximity, if anything more terrible. The tired heavily made up faces of girls, thrust up against mine, smelling of cheap cosmetics and expressing the vacancy of youth without its joy, seemed simply to declare the poverty of the human race, its miserable limitations, its absolute inability to grasp the real. Or were these spiritless surfaces simply the mirrors of my own mediocrity? I thought about Tommy sitting in her dressing gown over her cup of coffee. No glove puppets this morning. No joyful quartets.

The day was bleak, with a damp cold which nuzzled its way into one's clothing, up one's sleeves, down one's neck. The warmth of the office, as I came in through the doors, was welcome. No power cuts today, thank heaven, the strike appeared to be over. However the lift was out of order, not an unusual state of affairs. I began to mount the staircase. I had already decided that the best way to alleviate the teasing anxiety which I now felt was to spend the morning drafting the permitted letter to Lady Kitty. There was so much, at our extraordinary meeting beside the sinister boy, that had been assumed, hinted at, left unsaid. Had she really *understood* me? Until I had explained myself to her, exposed myself utterly to her, I was incapable of further action. And what a comfort there was in this. Beyond, there was nothing but fear and hazard.

As I reached the top of the first flight of stairs I nearly collided with Gunnar who was about to come down. I apprehended in a moment how he shied from me as he recognized me, how he shrank from me, went round me. Our eyes met with a sudden wildness. It was like a violent clash of arms. He went on down the stairs.

The idea of 'the interval' was annihilated. I stood in shock, in perfect indecision. Then came a rush of power too harsh to be called hope and yet not uncoloured by it, more like a sort of frightful urgent terror. I gripped the bannister, turned myself round and said, 'Gunnar.'

I said it not loudly, softly yet clearly, like someone calling to a ghost or speaking idly and yet eloquently to the dead.

We were alone on the stairs, I at the top, he more than halfway down. The momentum of his 'shy' from me had quickened his pace and I expected him in a moment to be gone. But he hesitated, stopped and slowly turned. We looked at each other.

Gunnar was frowning in a manner which might only have been expressive of irritation. Then he began to come back slowly up the stairs. I waited tensely as he approached me. I flattened myself against the wall. He passed me by without a glance and went back along the corridor towards his room. I felt a second of anguish until I realized quite clearly that he intended me to follow him.

He went into his room leaving the door open. Very soft-footed, as if trailing an animal, I moved after him down the corridor and slipped into the room closing the door behind me.

The rooms at this level had double-glazed windows and the traffic of Whitehall was muted into a hum scarcely more audible than silence itself. A little rain tapping on the glass with a faint insistence was louder, closer. The big square handsome room was dark except for a green-shaded lamp upon the desk, throwing a very white light upon some papers. Gunnar sat down and waited. His *waiting* was as perceptible to me as the tapping rain, the immense desk, his own form hunched in the chair. And it was frightful. I came towards the desk and stood before him. I wanted him to see my face clearly but the only way to achieve this would have been either to sit or to kneel, or else to move the lamp. I said again, 'Gunnar.'

The name was different this time, uttered no longer idly into emptiness, but with an urgency of present need and also with a sort of amazement, as if one were to meet a friend unexpectedly in a far-off place. Uttered still as a call which did not dare to be a summons.

Gunnar made a very slight movement which I interpreted as an order to sit down. I pulled a chair close to the other side of the desk and sat. I did now actually move the lamp so that it gave more light to both our faces. I caught a sudden glimpse of Gunnar, his face half illuminated, frowning, glaring.

At that moment someone knocked on the door and almost at once entered the room. Turning my dazzled eyes out of the lamplight I recognized, by his general outline in the half dark, the form of Clifford Larr.

I got up. Clifford was standing frozen, his hand still on the door handle. Gunnar had not moved. Inside a split second I reflected. Then I did what seemed the only possible thing. I made for the door, passing Clifford, who stepped aside, and went out again into the corridor closing the door behind me.

The lofty brightly lit corridor was empty. It seemed like a long hall seen in a dream and I a tiny menaced figure moving. I reached the stairs, hesitated, then began slowly to go down, holding hard to the bannister, my feet slowly taking the treads. I reached the hall, crossed it and went out through the doors into the street.

A light fine rain was now falling, the rain which had been tap-tapping discreetly upon Gunnar's window through those immensely long seconds during which I had been in his room and something had happened. *What* exactly had happened I was still unsure, but as I walked along I was already beginning to read it off the world, to see it, in the guise of passing cars and buses. I crossed through the Horse Guards and began to walk over the wide empty rain-pattered parade ground to the park. I reached the war memorial. Mons. Retreat from Mons. Landrecies. Marne 1914. Aisne 1914. Ypres 1914. Langemarck 1914. Givenchy 1914. I went on into St James's Park and along the right-hand side of the lake as far as the bridge. I walked onto the bridge and paused in its centre. The farther towers of Whitehall were invisible in the murky rain, but beyond the iron-grey expanse of pitted water I could see the Foreign Office with its line of lights. I took off my cap and let the rain gently hit my face, tap my brow and eyelids. I looked down onto the nearer surface of the lake, which brightened near to the bridge into a metallic green, and saw there black and white tufted ducks, bobbing bright-eyed upon the choppy wavelets, diving suddenly and popping up again, sleekly beautiful, perfect, new-minted by ingenious nature, enjoying the rain, enjoying their being. I watched the ducks, seeing them with a clarity which seemed like a new mode of vision, as if a cataract had been peeled off my eyes. I breathed slowly and deeply and looked at the ducks.

'Hello, I thought I'd find you here.'

Clifford Larr was beside me. I felt intense annoyance at his arrival.

'The porter said you had left the office in a sort of trance.'

I said nothing.

'I must confess I'm consumed by curiosity. Come on now, come out of your trance. Explain to me the meaning of that perfectly fascinating scene which I interrupted just now.'

'Did—Gunnar—say anything to you?'

'Of course not. He started talking shop at once as cool as you please. I should like to have felt his pulse though. Let me feel yours.'

I shook Clifford's hand off my arm and began to walk back off the bridge. He walked beside me, laughing his nervous irritating laugh.

'Was that the reconciliation scene?' Clifford was smiling, but he had come out without his umbrella and evidently regretted this and objected to his fine trilby hat getting wet. He took the hat off, gave it for a moment all his attention, ceased smiling, shook it, settled it back on his head and smiled again. I was bareheaded, my cap in my hand, my hair plastered damply to my face and neck.

'No.' It had not been the reconciliation scene. It had been mysterious, ambiguous, for hope or fear I knew not what. But it had been somehow a tremendous communication, a moment when lightning had split rocks, earthquakes had riven cliffs, mountains had been cleft in two. None of this could I explain to Clifford. I made a gesture implying that he should leave me alone, and sat down on a sopping wet seat near the edge of the water. The rain-washed park seemed empty except for our two figures. Some glittering mallards approached and regarded us with their jewel eyes.

Clifford mopped the seat a little with his handkerchief, then sat down beside me. 'What was it then? You must tell me. Something's happened, it must have happened. I shall die of curiosity.'

'Between Gunnar and me,' I said. 'Nothing has happened. I am just doing what she told me to do.'

'*She?*'

'Lady Kitty.'

'Good—God—' Clifford, staring at me, emitted several little whistles. 'So you talk to *her?*'

'I saw her once,' I said, 'at her request. She asked me to see Gunnar, that's all.'

'That's all! Why? To—well, to calm the nerves of all concerned I suppose. But will it, can it? Why, anything might happen. What boldness, hers I mean. What, when you come to think of it, bloody cheek!'

'I wanted to see him anyway,' I said, 'only I wouldn't have dared to do so without her. He doesn't know she's asked me.' I detested Clifford's tone and his language. I wished he would go away and leave me alone with my great thoughts. I also uncomfortably knew that I ought not to have mentioned Lady Kitty. Only I wanted to break his mockery, to meet his persiflage with a blank truthful simplicity.

'What a trickster!'

'Have you met her?'

'Yes,' said Clifford, 'I have met her twice, at cocktail parties.'

'What did you think of her?'

'I thought she was a saucy minx. I don't mean anything to do with impropriety. I'm sure she is a perfect picture of propriety in the strict sense. After all, she would have the wit to play safe. But she is one of those numerous women who can't stop flickering their eyelashes at anything in trousers, a compulsive flirt. She flirted with the prime minister. I suppose she flirted with you.'

'No.' How could I convey the sober serious merciful sweetness of her demeanour to me? I had no intention of trying.

'Well, I see she has purchased your loyalty at any rate. So, obedient to her commands, you went to see our friend Gunnar. And what happened?'

'Nothing. I had just come in. You arrived too soon.'

'Dear me, I'm so sorry— Did I wreck the touching scene? What did he say?'

'I've told you, nothing.'

'You will be reconciled,' said Clifford. 'I can see it all. It will be very affecting and very edifying. He will forgive you. You will weep on each other's shoulders and become loving friends forever after. You will dine at Cheyne Walk every Wednesday and have lunch with Gunnar at his club every Friday. They will exhibit you to their friends as the penitent monster—because the whole story will have got around by then of course—Lady Kitty will see to that.'

'Go away, please,' I said.

'You will have a wonderful friendship with Gunnar, he will glow with magnanimity and you will have your little pleasure of being forgiven and you will smile the smile of abasement and you will both enjoy yourselves like mad. What a bond and what a bondage! He will buy you, in fact Lady Kitty has already bought you for him. She was probably surprised to find how cheap you were. Well, are you furious with me?'

'Clifford, do go, there's a good chap. And for Christ's sake don't repeat what I've said to you to anyone.'

'Don't worry. I'm not going to be around much longer.'

'What do you mean?'

'I shall be dead.'

'Oh that. Well, fuck off and take those sleeping pills if you want to. Just leave me alone, will you?'

Clifford rose and shadowily departed. I forgot him. The tufted ducks had come back. They looked more marvellous than ever.

It was Wednesday evening. I had spent longer than usual at the Liverpool Street bar and was feeling rather drunk. I came up in the lift with Mr Pellow who told me a long story about how he had got another teaching job but had not said anything about being suspended from the previous one and how this had all come out and what the Head had said and what the history master had said and how upset the boys were when he had to go though he had only been there three days. This tale took some time and I went into his flat to hear it out and drank his whisky and sympathized, and thought about Gunnar and wondered what I ought or ought not to do next. Fearful agonizing anxiety had returned.

When I let myself into my own flat I realized at once that there was a woman there. There were noises in Christopher's room, the unmistakable sound of a woman coughing. I wondered for a moment with a sickening spasm if it could be Lady Kitty. Impossible. Biscuit? More likely to be Tommy. I was gliding back out through the door when Laura Impiatt erupted into the hall and seized my arm.

'No, you don't! You coward! No *wonder* you've got a bad conscience! I've been *waiting* for you for *ages*. Christopher has been *so kind*. He has been *singing* to me.'

'Let him sing on,' I said. I went on into the kitchen, shedding my wet overcoat as I went. Laura, clucking, picked it up from the floor and hung it on a peg and followed me. Christopher, in a long Indian robe and wooden beads and a far-away smile, his long fair hair carefully combed, began to do a sort of slow tap dance in the hall, stretching out his arms and humming.

In the kitchen, watched by Laura, I turned on the stove, took a tin of baked beans and a tin of tomatoes out of the cupboard, opened the tins and poured their contents into a saucepan, put the saucepan on the heat, winkled a piece of sliced bread out of its package, put it under the grill, took the butter out of the refrigerator and began to lay the table for one.

'I won't offer you any beans, Laura, I know you despise them.'

'Hilary, you fascinate me!'

'Oh good.' I stirred the beans, I turned the toast.

Outside Christopher was singing or rather droning in the slipshod semi-audible sub-American manner of the modern pop singer. '*Be my bird, waterbird, true true true.*'

This was one of Laura's young bright days. Her glowing eyes were misty and elated, her lips moist for some fray, as if she were about to bound onto a platform and advocate something. She was wearing a well-cut black velvet dress and had her hair tied by a black velvet ribbon at the nape of the neck and pony-tailing down her back. She closed the kitchen door and sat down.

'I'm dining at home and this is far too early anyway. Only proles and Hilaries dine at this hour.'

'Hilary is a prole, thank God. Who's coming to dinner?'

'The Templar-Spences and one of Freddie's tycoons.'

'*How can we part, dear, how can yer go away, I search my heart, dear, for somethin ter say ter make yer stay, and so I pray, waterbird . . .*'

I buttered the toast and poured the bean and tomato mess over it. I hated eating my own food with a witness, but I was very hungry, having been too agitated to eat at lunch-time. I ladled on mustard, buttered another piece of bread and sat down to wolf the stuff. Laura watched in silence until I had finished. It took about a minute.

'What's for din-dins at your place?'

'Smoked salmon. Stifados. Lime soufflé.'

'Why aren't you there cooking it?'

'It's cooked, except for the soufflé, and I do that at the last moment. I've been at a cocktail party. The Joplings were there.'

'They seem to spend all their time at cocktail parties.'

'They are *special* people, oh *special*, I love them both.'

'How nice.'

'*When my dear waterbird flew flew flew, left me without a bird, blue blue blue.*'

'Have you met her yet?'

'No.'

'She's marvellous. But listen, Hilary, I've come here from Tommy.'

'*From* Tommy?'

'*Little bird, waterbird, you, you, you.*'

'Yes, I rang her and she cried and cried and told me *everything* and I said I'd come and see you.'

'How kind.'

'Hilary, I do think you should think again.'

'Like the waterbird.'

'She may not be a dream woman but she loves you so much and it would do you so much good to get married.'

'Sez you.'

'If you're not careful you'll get old and cold the way single men do.'

'I'm already old and cold. Laura, just let me run my life, will you, dear? I'm quite a mature adult, you know.'

'This is playing merry hell with the panto, by the way.'

'Fuck the panto.'

'Actually, I never really saw you married to Tommy.'

'You're a fine ambassador.'

'*It's not so easy, dear, ter find a true lover, yer may search everywhere and not find another.*'

'Perhaps you really are one of nature's bachelors.'

'Isn't it time you went home and put out the fish knives?'

'They're out. Hilary—you know there are moments when suddenly, with someone you've known a long time, you have a breakthrough and come much closer.'

'Laura, you're drunk.'

'*Our love was demented, our love was a feud, are yer contented ter call it a mood, jus' an interlude?*'

'Hilary, I know you think I lead a silly empty social life, yes, you do. And it's perfectly true that though I have lots and lots of dear acquaintances I haven't got many friends and I *need* friends. We know each other well, you and I, but we've never really *talked*, never really *looked*, and my God as one grows old it's important—' Laura's hand came across the table and pounced on mine. I looked down at the plump red wrinkled ageing fingers, the wedding ring, sunk into the flesh. I looked up at Laura's eager ruddy face and her wide-apart mesmerizing brown eyes.

'Hilary, listen. I need a friend now. I need help. I need *you.* I need you as a dear close secret man. I must have one. Don't be afraid. There's something I want to ask you. There's something urgent that I want to tell you, only I can't tell you now—'

'*Wait a bit, waterbird, do do do. Let's not be, little bird, through through through.*'

'Oh shut up, Christopher, for Christ's sake, stop that bloody caterwauling!'

'Sorry, Hilary—'

'Laura, I—'

The front door bell rang. With a sigh of relief I withdrew my hand from Laura's firm warm clasp and got up. Christopher had already danced to the door and opened it for Jimbo who entered bearing a bunch of white chrysanthemums. Jimbo was hatless and soaking wet. I had not heard the rain. I heard it now.

'Laura, your coat—it's pouring—you'll need an umbrella—here, take mine.'

'Thank you.' She had followed me out and let me help her on with her coat. 'You can have it back tomorrow.'

'Tomorrow?'

'Thursday. Our day. Have you forgotten? Good night, Jimbo. Good night, Christopher, I'll call again about the songs. Hilary, would you come outside for a moment?'

I went out with her, closing the door and we walked as far as the lift. Laura was wearing a bulky camel hair coat. The sleeves, damp and steamy, were suddenly wrapped about my neck. Laura sighed into my mouth and kissed me on the lips. Then she pushed me away and turning her back rang for the lift. I returned to the flat.

Christopher and Jimbo were kneeling in the hall, arranging the chrysanthemums in a vase. Christopher looked up with an interested questioning expression. I went on into my bedroom and shut the door and turned off the light and lay down on the bed.

I had not written my letter to Lady Kitty. The encounter with Gunnar had temporarily blotted her out of my mind. What I could not decide now was whether the next move was mine or his. But perhaps there was no next move, perhaps it was all over? Perhaps everything needful had been done, perfected, finished in that little scene wherein he had waited and looked at me and I had said his name? Was this what reconciliation was like, a meeting of eyes, the utterance of a name? Might not more talk simply spoil this thing which had come to be? The relief, the visionary joy which I had felt in the morning with the St James's Park ducks had seemed like a guarantee that something good had happened. Later however this optimism began to seem absurd, the scene which prompted it a good deal more ambiguous and meagre. Gunnar had simply glared at me. Perhaps he had led me to his room with no friendly intent. The man had brooded on revenge for years. I did not know what he might do. Perhaps he did not.

And then, like the steadily rising moon, came the image of Lady Kitty. After all, this was her enterprise, her show. It had not been set going in any way for my benefit. I, and my satisfactions and my reliefs and my absolutions, must be nothing here. What mattered was Gunnar's state of mind, his 'cure', and on that *she* must pronounce. This view, obvious enough when it came, inspired new anxiety and also a kind of interim calm and the renewal of my intention to write to her. But not yet. Let me *rest* now, I thought, for at least a day or two. Enough has been done. If Gunnar decides to move then I must meet his move. If he does not, I must wait for Lady Kitty's instructions, and meanwhile I must write to her and tell her the many many things which I knew that I had to tell. I had a feeling, which I deliberately kept as vague as possible, of amelioration, of a new power to formulate and confront horrors which had remained for so long unapproachable in my mind. Yes, the prospect of an interval was consoling, and the sense of resting once more upon Lady Kitty's will.

I did not think about Laura. I thought about Tommy, but as if she were a historical problem separated from me by aeons of time and matrices of theory and research. It's not so easy to find a true lover, you may search everywhere and not find another. Possibly, but now I was dedicated to higher concerns. Perhaps 'love' had always been for me an *ignis fatuus*. I felt limp and wearied out. I crawled into bed without undressing. It was still raining. I slept and dreamt that Tommy, or was it some other woman, in the guise of a waterbird with beautiful eyes was battering battering battering on the glass trying to get in.

THURSDAY

ON THURSDAY evening I did not go home and change as usual, but sat in the Sloane Square bar until it was time to go along to Queen's Gate Terrace. I thought now about Laura Impiatt and the 'something urgent' which she wanted to tell me. Could it be that she was in love with me? At another time this idea would have amused and even touched me, on the assumption that nothing in the least dramatic was likely to come of it. Laura was a great one for high ideas. Now, however, this extra complication would be far from welcome. It was a time for keeping away from women. And I recalled with a pang the horrible glimpse of me feuding with Tommy which Lady Kitty had obtained upon the stairs of the office. What would Lady Kitty think of me if she got the least whiff of an impression that I was trifling with Freddie's wife? This possibility made me feel very sick indeed. It was all-important that Lady Kitty should see me, as far at least as the present was concerned, as a *clean* man. I must, I now realized, also somehow tactfully convey to her that I had broken off relations with Tommy. What an idiot I had been to say that Tommy was my fiancée. It was scarcely even true.

Later on in my reflections about Laura a new possibility came up. Suppose Laura had somehow found out about my past, about the whole business? It did not seem, from her remarks, very likely, but she might have found out something. She had said she wanted to ask me a question. In any case, sooner or later a being so consumed with curiosity was likely to sniff out something odd about me and 'the Joplings'. This was another reason for keeping aloof from Laura. Yet also of course I wanted to see her in order to find out what it was she wanted to ask and to tell.

It had been a strange day at the office. The weather was cold and raw, a little misty, a fine rain fell, was still falling. I sat at my desk, doing my work, wondering whenever the messenger entered the room whether he might be bringing me a note written in that tiny handwriting which I had last seen saying *Please leave Anne alone. Please.* But no note came. Contrary to custom I had lunch in the office canteen. I met Clifford Larr on the stairs and he ignored me rather more pointedly than usual. Tommy rang up three times and on each occasion I put the 'phone down.

Now feeling very wet and cold I was approaching the Impiatts' door. Laura had bagged my umbrella, I was in a fair way to being soaked through. Full of thoughts, I had walked all the way from Sloane Square without noticing until too late how copious the downpour had become. My cap was a soggy mass upon my head, my overcoat was heavy with water and an ominous clammy penetrating dampness was spreading upon my shoulders and my back. I was looking forward to the bright fire in the Impiatts' drawing-room and a large beaker of gin.

Freddie opened the door and welcomed me, exclaiming suitably about my bedraggled appearance. I was about to make some facetious remark about his wife having stolen my umbrella when it occurred to me that perhaps Freddie did not always know when Laura paid me visits. The idea was disagreeable. I spotted my umbrella in the hall stand, however, and resolved to remove it quietly at the end of the evening. I was talking to Freddie, who was laboriously hanging my soaking coat up on a hanger, when I heard in the drawing-room the booming voice of a man, followed by a woman's voice, and realized with a crippling spasm of anguish that my fellow guests for the evening were Gunnar and Lady Kitty.

I sat down on a chair in the hall, in order to breathe, pretending to wring out the wet ends of my trousers. I quickly considered whether I had not better leave the house instantly on some pretext? Nothing would be more calculated to put Laura's bright curiosity onto the right track. Did Gunnar know I was coming? How was I to greet them? How would they behave? Would concealment be possible? Then with a jolting shock I remembered, only just in time, that I was not supposed ever to have met Lady Kitty before!

'Come on,' said Freddie. 'Come and bake yourself at the fire.'

I rose and slowly followed him into the bright drawing-room, very conscious that I looked like a drowned rat and had not only not changed but had slept in my clothes last night.

The first thing I saw was Laura's face and it seemed to me fairly to shine with knowledge.

Laura was all streaming hair and streaming gown. She

was wearing a garment rather like the one Christopher had been wearing yesterday, together with a lot of jangling ornaments made of what looked like polished steel. As she approached me with both arms outstretched, I saw over her shoulder the suddenly frozen faces of my fellow guests. It was evident that Laura had planned a jolly surprise for all concerned.

'Hilary! How splendid!' She kissed my cheek with possessive ostentation. 'I believe you and Mr Jopling are old friends. Have you met Hilary Burde?'

The latter question was addressed to Lady Kitty, who made a vague gesture and shook her head.

'Hilary Burde. Lady Kitty Jopling. I expect you two have met in the office?' This question, another poser, was addressed to Gunnar.

'We just said hello,' I said. 'It's been a long time.' These just adequate words were uttered rather wildly.

I felt my face burning, blazing. I had, as I entered the room, had place for the hope that Gunnar would not perceive his wife's distress. I need not have worried. Lady Kitty had already recovered, perhaps a little too rapidly on the assumption that she had just been unexpectedly confronted with her husband's famous enemy. Her reactions should of course have been the other way round, first blandness, then amazement. However Gunnar's own agitation seemed great enough to preclude any observation of his wife's behaviour.

Gunnar's big frame had run to fat but still towered, topping six feet, the slight stoop making him seem now about the same height as me. What chiefly made him unlike his old self was the podginess of the face, the cheeks plumped out and with a ruddiness which was not that of youth, the brow fleshy with some wrinkles. His fair hair had become a sandy grey hinting at baldness, but there was still plenty of it, and the mottled blue eyes, between tired stained lids, remained clear and bright and brought back the clever attractive athlete who had been loved by *Anne*. It was strange how between us at that moment her name was suddenly there like a flash, like a physical manifestation. It rang out, and our former selves appeared like ghosts and her ghost was with them. Perhaps it was simply being able to see his eyes. But Gunnar now reminded me so intensely of Anne that it was as if the physical scene was darkened and nothing was there between us except the flame of her presence, her radiant face, beautiful and young. Between us: for I knew

216

for certain that Gunnar in that same instant was thinking of her too.

All these apprehensions however lasted only a moment or two, during which time I did not look at Lady Kitty. Laura had bustled towards me, now back again. Freddie was coming up from behind exclaiming, 'Hilary's soaked.'

'Why so he is!' cried Laura. 'He's been walking in the rain again, the bad thing. Look at his trousers, and look at his back all dark with wet, just feel that!' And she began patting my back as if inviting the others to do so too. 'Hilary, take off your jacket at once! Freddie, get him one of yours. Hilary, let go! Don't be naughty or we shall take your trousers as well! Now sit down here with your back to the fire. Why look at him, he's *steaming*!'

Rather than indulge in the playful scuffle which Laura doubtless wanted I did as I was told and sat down on the floor with my back to the fire. My vest and shirt were adhering damply to my shoulders from which steam was indeed rising up. Cool drips of water from my wet streaky hair were now finding their way down my back. I realized with dismay that below the statutory two top buttons my shirt was buttonless and also had a conspicuous tear which, stuff it downward as I would, I could not conceal inside my trousers.

Freddie had left the room. Laura was fussing round, petting me and calling me 'Hilo', a name which she had never used before and which even as an office usage was, thank God, rare enough. Lady Kitty had moved aside and sat down on my right in a chair remote from the fire. She was wearing a green silk evening dress with a lot of white embroidery. Her long nose and long, full, now pouting, lips gave to her face an animal-like intensity, the sort of unnerving 'brilliance' which a fox's face possesses. Gunnar, opposite, had leaned back against some bookshelves and was staring not exactly at my face but at the whole of me, his eyes turned almost into blue rectangles by an intent fastidious frown. Then Laura stopped feeling my hair, and saying 'I must fetch a towel', vanished from the room.

There was a perceptible almost audible gasp as the three of us were left suddenly alone together. To decrease the tension I shifted, knelt, then sat cross-legged gripping my trouser ends. I felt an agonizing desire to make some sound, to groan softly since I could think of no possible words. I also very much wanted to turn to look at Lady Kitty whose gaze I could feel burning my right cheek, but I kept my face resolutely towards Gunnar.

Gunnar kept on looking at me with the intent yet somehow sightless, somehow horrified, glare. He was holding in his hand a copita of sherry, now almost empty. Then as he looked he tilted the glass, spilling the remains of the drink upon the carpet, and bringing up his other hand he snapped the glass in two at the stem.

I got up. So did Lady Kitty. With a quick singing flurry of the green dress she came forward between us. She put her own glass beside Gunnar upon the shelves. She took gently out of his hands the two halves of the broken glass and retreated, releasing them into the folds of her skirt with a gesture of extraordinary deliberate grace. As Freddie re-entered the room Lady Kitty was picking up the broken glass from the carpet. 'I'm terribly sorry I have broken it.'

Freddie told her not to worry and began to help me on with a voluminous jacket of his own. Laura arrived crying '*A table!*', screamed at my ludicrous appearance and would have towelled my hair briskly only I snatched the towel from her in time. Lady Kitty passed me without a glance, moving away into the hall in obedience to Laura's summons. Laura followed. Freddie said to Gunnar, 'This is Hilary's day for seeing us, you know. Did Hilary have "days" when you first knew him?' Gunnar said, obviously not having the faintest idea what he was being asked, 'Oh yes.' As he turned to the door our eyes, drawn irresistibly, met for a second only. Gunnar's face contracted and he turned his head abruptly away. I went last from the room.

As I came into the hall, where the others were still talking, the front door letter-box was pushed open and a letter flew in and landed with a plop upon the mat. Laura went to pick it up. 'Why, Hilary, it's for you. Oh dear me, it's from her!' She put the envelope into my hands and I saw my name in Tommy's writing. 'Don't mind us, my dear, you just read it now.'

The Impiatts' dining-room was in the basement next door to the kitchen. Freddie was already leading Gunnar down. Laura went on after, ushering Lady Kitty to follow her. I tore open Tommy's letter. *Oh my darling, I can't bear it, I am dying of pain. Please please see me. I will wait for you tonight at the flat. T.*

'I must just fetch my bag. I left it in the drawing-room.' Lady Kitty's voice.

THURSDAY

I lifted my head and looked straight into the brilliant dark slaty-blue eyes. The shrill singing of the *frou-frou* passed me as she entered the drawing-room, pounced on her bag and emerged again. As she passed me the second time she murmured, 'Biscuit will come on Saturday morning.'

I followed her down the stairs to dinner. (Watercress soup, *bœuf Stroganoff* and *crêpes Suzette*.)

FRIDAY

Dear Lady Kitty,

I hope that you will think that I have done right. As Gunnar will have told you, I spoke to him on Wednesday. I had intended to wait longer but I met him on the stairs and suddenly I could not bear to pass by without a word. I went to his room, but we had no time to talk as someone came. To be precise, I said his name, once on the stairs once in the room. He said nothing. I would so much like to know, only I realize I have no right to ask questions, what he felt about this encounter. I felt then that it was good, that it was like some sort of parley. Now this idea seems absurd. And I don't just mean because of the incident with the sherry glass in which you intervened. The talk at dinner, our awful juxtaposition, my sense then of Gunnar's mind, made peace between us seem inconceivable. One does not suddenly get over hating somebody, people do not forgive, it is impossible. I cannot tell you how clear this became to me at that dinner which was, though I am sure Mr and Mrs Impiatt noticed nothing, a time of horror. I am sure you understand. I felt then and feel now how hopeless it all is, and have considered whether the best thing for me to do would not simply be to vanish. I shall certainly see to it that you are never again embarrassed by my presence as a fellow guest. As I trust you realized, I did not know beforehand that you would be there. However, having spoken of vanishing let me assure you at once that I have no immediate intention of doing so. The time for vanishing will come, that I understand, and when it does you will hear of me no more. But meanwhile I recognize my plain duty to stick it out and to try my best. If my trying can in any smallest way help Gunnar, ease any tension or soothe any pain, then I am obliged to persevere and I will do so. And let me say: I would and will do anything that you ask of me.

May I for a moment speak about myself? It is a relief to do so. This is the only context in which I can speak, you are the only person to whom I can speak. I have carried this thing silently and alone all these years and the burden has not become less. I am not even sure what the name of the burden is. Naming might help, only words are defeated. Guilt, sin, pain, repentance, remorse? Not repentance, for repentance would somehow change the thing, and it is its unchangedness which utterly spoils life and precludes joy. Forgive this exercise in self-pity, which may seem hideously out of place. What claims have I here, what can I hope to be but the merest instrument? And yet as I reflect, and especially after the *horror* of Gunnar's presence at that dinner, I feel that if sense is to be made of this I must consider my own needs too, they must be *there*, accepted as part of my motives. Accepted: yet by whom? I can hardly ask Gunnar to 'accept' them, to allow that the thing which may do him good may do me good. It would be too much to expect that his pity for me should heal both of us. I cannot, somehow, even expect him to *know* that I have suffered— and suffer and will suffer. So I suppose the person to whom I address this plea is either God or you. Therefore you. Please forgive me. It is already some infinitesimal kind of alleviation to be able to say to you that this thing is to me like yesterday, and that it has ruined my life down to its last details. It may seem 'cowardly' to have let such devastation come about, and now to force the unsavoury spectacle of it upon someone who should particularly be spared it. Yet such things happen to men, lives are thus ruined, thus tainted and darkened and irrevocably spoilt, wrong turnings are taken and persisted in, and those who make one mistake wreck all the rest out of frenzy, even out of pique. Only your gracious kindness to me, your notice of me, your, dare I say it, *need* of me has made a place where this statement can be made, this gruesome truth at last paraded. For a moment *light* can fall upon an obscene and awful wound. And for that, whatever happens, I am grateful to you, and by that, whatever happens, I shall be helped.

I dare to say these things to you because of the extraordinary opportunity which you have, it seems knowingly, given me, and also because our meeting is of necessity something absolutely momentary, so momentary as scarcely to exist as a meeting of two people, although it enormously exists as an *event*. Obviously no 'friendship' can ever be between me and Gunnar. So much has happened in my mind since we talked in the park. I believe at first I imagined that there could perhaps be a 'relationship'. I now see that this is impossible. I will do whatever you want, I will do if I can what is needful, and then I shall disappear. I shall pass like a comet. I think in fact, now in my later clearer vision of it, that there is little, though there is possibly something, that I can do for Gunnar. (And, alas, little that Gunnar can do for me.) And I certainly do not expect that you will remember me with gratitude. I shall, soon, have gone. Only an event will have occurred, an event which your grace and your courage made to be. And I will remember your kindness to me and even if there is nothing else for me to carry away I shall carry that away—and it will be precious to me in the long years to come and the horror, the dreadful wound, will perhaps, who knows, become a little better after all.

One other thing, since I feel that as I write this I must keep nothing back. I have broken off my engagement to Mrs Uhlmeister. In fact I was never really engaged to her at all. You may not even recall this matter, but I thought that I would mention it as Mr and Mrs Impiatt were rather jocular about it during dinner.

Please please forgive this letter. It is, I am sure, the only letter I shall ever write to you. The relief of writing it has been immense, cosmic. You have already done so much for me. To do your will, to be of service to you and Gunnar, is the only wish of a man destined to vanish. Accept my gratitude, my homage. I will await your instructions about what to do next, and I will do whatever you tell me. I hope with all my heart that Gunnar will be willing to see me again, or at any rate has not decided that he will not. I do not expect any communication from him of course. If you think it best I will again approach him in the office, or else write to him. Your good wishes are as prayers in the light of which I can now almost pray myself.

> Yours most sincerely,
> Hilary Burde.

It was three a.m. and I was sitting up in a damnably cold bedroom in a small hotel near Paddington. I was in a frenzy. My heart was beating so hard that I had at times to press my two hands against it as if this were the only way to prevent it from breaking through the flesh. My blood raced, my head swam. I had decided, well it was scarcely a decision, not to go home and face Tommy. I went early from the Impiatts and telephoned Crystal from Gloucester Road to tell her not to expect me. I did not say why and she did not ask. Her voice on the telephone echoed sadly, echoed with loneliness, though she spoke only words of love. I took the Inner Circle to Paddington and went at random into one of the cheap hotels in Sussex Gardens. I got some writing paper from the porter and then sat in my room composing.

I wrote the letter several times over, perhaps five times, making additions and minor changes of wording. I wrote fast, there was no lack of inspiration. The first draft was full of colons and semicolons which I excised in the second draft in favour of dashes, and then in subsequent drafts changed most of the dashes into commas and reinstated a colon or two. I noticed (I was not exactly drunk but had drunken symptoms) that I had scarcely mentioned Gunnar at all in draft one. I felt divinely possessed but also profoundly confused about what I was supposed to be doing and what all the commotion was for. It was as if there was no one in the universe except me and Kitty. (She had, in fact, been 'Kitty' in my thoughts for several days now.) Something terrible had happened, yesterday, years ago, before the world began, but what was it? Something had to be done, there was some ordeal, some service to be performed, but what? All I knew was that she had ordained it. I was to do her will and then die. I was a man destined to vanish, and in vanishing to achieve my all: to serve, and then to disappear into solitude.

That I was in love with Kitty and that this was a love letter was clear to me well before one o'clock. I had, I suppose, been in love with her for some time. The beginnings of love are always temporally baffling. I had seen her now, including this evening, five times: twice in the office, once in the park with the horses, once in the park alone, and now at the Impiatts. I suppose I could not really have fallen in love with her at first sight, yet when I talked to her at Peter Pan my veneration, my adoration was already old. Writing to her was like writing to an old friend. 'Forgive this letter, my dear' I had thoughtlessly written in the first draft. My darling. Of course the letter reeked with self-pity, it was full of absurdities, even pomposities, 'the only wish of a man destined to vanish' and so on. But however undignified, the eloquence was necessary, the self-revelation essential. This was the only chance I would ever have to express these things.

Was I destined to vanish? Was this the only letter I would ever write to Kitty? These questions concerned a future which, to my three a.m. mood, was inconceivably remote. I had a deep relieved happy consciousness of surrender to her will. She would decide everything. She had already decided to send Biscuit to me on Saturday, and before the far future of Saturday came there was the wonderful whole of Friday to be lived through in her service. And perhaps Biscuit would bring me another precious letter from her mistress. The light shed by this conception quite sufficiently blotted out the yet farther distant time when it should be incumbent on me to vanish.

At about half past three I went to bed and to sleep, and the thought of Kitty spread a tent of quietness above my dreaming head. She was so kind to me, oh she was so kind.

In the morning (Friday) I had breakfast in Paddington main line station, at the buffet on platform one, eating toast and marmalade at a table out on the platform, near to the most moving war memorial in London which represents a soldier of the first war, dressed in his trench warfare kit with his greatcoat over his shoulders, standing in a calm attitude and reading a letter from home. I sat there on the platform for some time and watched the departure of the seven-thirty for Exeter St David's, Plymouth and Penzance, the seven-forty for Bath, Bristol Temple Meads and Weston-Super-Mare, the eight o'clock for Cheltenham Spa, Swansea and Fishguard Harbour, and the eight-five for Reading, Oxford and Worcester Shrub Hill. I felt now much less exalted and much more frightened: not frightened really of anything that could happen in the world, but frightened of my own mind, of sudden vistas of new kinds of pain. How could I so *love* someone whom I could never see or know, the person indeed who was of all the farthest from me, the most ineluctably separated? What awful suffering, not yet felt, not yet revealed, would this involve? Was this the punishment, the expiation, the end, the dark hole into which I would finally disappear? Yet even then I knew that from myself I would not disappear. I would go on indestructibly, day after day, week after week, year after year, and I would not break down and no one would ever hear me scream. That was the worst of it. And with this worst was interwoven the fact and miracle of love with all its gentleness and its vision and its pure joy.

I tried desperately to keep these terrors as vague as possible, and I was helped in this by the idea that today was Friday, and tomorrow was Saturday and tomorrow Biscuit would come. Even here there was already the calming pattern of a routine. Ought I then to give Biscuit the letter which I had written last night? Somewhere outside the great arched galleries of the station the daylight was trying to come, but within was a yellow darkness penetrated by electric light and the smell of sulphur. As the inevitable trains departed one after another I reread and considered carefully the final draft of the letter. Ought I to send it, should I rewrite it, ought I not to sober it up considerably? To me at any rate the ecstasy was visible, the stretching out of uncontrollable and yearning arms. Was it necessary to be so picturesque about my ruined life? And could I really tell Kitty quite so baldly that I had broken with Tommy? Was this not undignified, gratuitous, mean, manifestly indiscreet and unkind? Why should it matter whether or not Kitty thought of me as 'engaged'? Of course it mattered frightfully, but did this mattering matter? Why should I assume that Kitty would be interested in this sordid information? Would it not make a bad impression, this eagerness to assert my solitude, ostentatiously to shake Tommy off? The Impiatts' silly witticisms at dinner had seemed to make it essential. I could not bear to let Kitty imagine me as involved in a vulgar brawl or lovers' tiff yet unresolved. Better the awkward truth than that. I had to let her know that I had regained the purity of being alone. I decided to let that stand, I decided to let the whole letter stand. I had written it in some sort of mad inspired state. Let Kitty have it and, in her wisdom and her mercy, make of it what she would.

The dinner table had indeed been a place of horror. Freddie had started up at once talking to Gunnar about the pantomime. He had then realized with embarrassment that, given my latest non-relations with Tommy, this was not a tactful subject. He tried to change it, but Laura picked it up and with manifest intent began to tease me about Tommy, whom she called my 'young woman', implying that any coolness between us was of course momentary and that Tommy would act in the pantomime as planned. 'Hilary insisted on bringing his young woman in.' 'I didn't.' 'Hilary is the most fearful liar, but of course you've known him for ages.' 'We can't have Hilary quarrelling with our star, can we, Freddie?' The Impiatts could not intermit their custom of making me a butt of simple-minded jokes, and I could not slip out of my role of clown, however agonizing it was to play this role to this audience. 'What do you bet Hilary's wearing odd socks again? Hilary, show your socks at once!' It was Hilary this and Hilary that until I was red and boiling with embarrassment and grief and rage.

Reflecting upon it afterwards, Laura's behaviour was in fact tiresome to the point of oddness. She was uneasy, excited, drinking and laughing more than usual, and seemed almost to be anxious to make a fool of me in front of her guests. She certainly went out of her way to present me as a man with a long-established mistress. 'Oh we know all about your quarrels with Tommy and how long they last!' This was particularly exasperating and cruel as there was nothing which I could say in reply. Laura was in a positively malicious mood which I could not interpret. Perhaps after all she was a bit in love with me? A possessive woman will warn another woman off her territory, however unlikely it is that the other may prove a rival. The process may be almost mechanical. It was in any case impossible that Laura should not see Kitty as a richly endowed competitor for Laura's little world. Was Kitty being informed that, contrary to appearances, I was not a lonely accessible bachelor, and that in so far as I belonged to anybody other than Tommy I belonged to Laura? Or did Laura's weird state of mind conceivably arise out of some knowledge of my former relations with Gunnar? The notion that Kitty might become friendly with Laura came to me suddenly during the *bœuf Stroganoff* and made me choke. Supposing Kitty were, at least, to take Laura into her confidence? Why not? The idea of Kitty receiving Laura's picture of me made me feel very ill indeed. Not that Laura, in reality, disliked or despised me; but she would inevitably make me appear absurd.

It was Kitty who (seeing my pain?) rescued the pantomime

conversation by making it more general. Gunnar, who had either become pompous through being grand, or was so now out of nervousness, made a speech to Freddie to the effect that of course *Peter Pan* was about parents and being unwilling to grow up, but what made it sinister was that childishness had been invested with spirituality. 'The fragmentation of spirit is the problem of our age,' Gunnar informed Freddie. 'Peter personifies a spirituality which is irrevocably caught in childhood and which yet cannot surrender its pretensions. Peter is essentially a being from elsewhere, the apotheosis of an immature spirituality.' Gunnar addressed himself to Freddie, sometimes to Laura. So far as possible he ignored me. I was sitting between Laura and Kitty. I did not know what to do with my eyes or my hands or my feet. My head ached with not looking at Gunnar. Laura, making jokes, more than once laid her hand on my knee. The green silk was inches away.

And now I was sitting on Paddington platform one, watching the departure of the nine-five for Birmingham New Street, and thinking, as it was about time to do, about Gunnar; and as I thought about him I felt my racing mind becoming quiet, as someone who after appeals and hopes contemplates as a reality his irrevocable sentence at last. I could have no dealings here with dreams. In this sterner context my 'feelings' about Kitty were indeed the *merest* feelings and I knew that I could be harsh with them. They existed as something beautiful but totally irrelevant, like a flower one might notice on the way to the gallows. Nor must I even tell myself that my task here was one which Kitty suggested and imposed. This flattery too must be denied me. Life, or truth, something deep and hard which could not be evaded, suggested and imposed this task. And the only hope which existed for me at all was one which I could not pursue, should not perhaps even conceive, and which must be merely a by-product of my striving, the hope, which I had mentioned in such melodramatic terms to Kitty, that I might be able by helping Gunnar to help myself.

Yet could I help Gunnar? How was it to be done? Was the fundamental problem one that concerned him or one that concerned me? The origin of it all was that I had done something. But what had I done? Had I punished myself simply because I had been so terribly punished by fate? I had been extremely unlucky. If Anne had got out of the car on that evening and gone home to her husband . . . What might now seem in retrospect a small sin had become a monumental sin by what seemed in the strictest sense to be an accident. A death is the most terrible of *facts*. This fact lay between me and Gunnar, poisoning my life with guilt, his with hate. And nothing could take that fact away. Time could not do it. Had time done anything, changed me so that I was a different person? Was I still and forever the person who . . .? Even a law court lets you off at last.

That I should never forget the fact was something for which I must almost pray. Had I begun to forget it? In the years that had passed I had not forgotten Anne. Her face even now, her moist lips, her radiant eyes, hung before me upon the foggy curtain of the sulphurous air. Oh Anne, oh my darling, I have not forgotten you, my heart at this moment beats for you, my hands tremble and move as if to embrace you. But the fact—have I forgotten that I killed her, have I changed *that* into something huge and dark, wrapping it round as the years went by with my misery and my guilt: the burden which I had told Kitty that I could not name? Was this the thing which, for Gunnar, I must unwrap? The thing which he too had wrapped about, with misery and hate and empty dreams of revenge.

Anne had never really been a part of my life. Gunnar's life had been ripped apart, and I had done it, entering from outside as a cruel ruthless invader. If God had existed and we could have stood together in His presence and looked together without falsity at what had been done, and then looked at each other, might not some miracle have occurred? 'This is what I did.' 'I know.' But there was no such scene, only two sodden semi-conscious psyches wrestling with each other in the dark. Could anything ever be clarified, could anything be really *done* here? Had not my feelings, whatever they were, for Kitty simply misled me with a momentary vision of a new heaven and a new earth? I had wrecked my life and Crystal's by a guilt which was itself a kind of sin. Could that be cut away? The idea of forgiveness, pardon, reconciliation, seemed here too fuzzy, too soft for what was needed. If Gunnar and I could be even for a moment simple, sincere, together . . . But that was the way of hope, and there must be no hope, only a task, only the truth itself if one could but discern it and hang on.

I took the Inner Circle to Westminster and went to the office.

SATURDAY

'I THINK it was perfectly bloody of you,' said Christopher. It was Saturday morning, about nine o'clock. The weather had changed. It was a clear frosty day with the sun shining. I was shaving. I had spent Friday night at the same hotel, returning home only on Saturday so as to be in position for Biscuit. I could not have endured a meeting with Tommy. Or rather, in my present state of mind Tommy simply did not exist, a tornado was blowing through my life which had swept poor Tommy right away. I reckoned that she would not turn up at the office, nor did she. She rang up once, but I put the 'phone down. I returned to an unexpected barrage of moral criticism from Christopher.

'She stayed here on Thursday evening from nine-thirty until one in the morning, and last night she was here at six and stayed till two. She sat on your bed and cried. I've never seen a woman cry so.'

'Tough on you,' I said, scraping away.

'How can you treat a poor bird like that? And you were in bed with her last week.'

'How do you know?'

'You made such a bloody row, the place was rocking.'

'Have you never left anybody? Tears must flow.'

'Tears must flow, but you might at least do it honestly, not just fail to turn up when you know she is waiting.'

'I have done it honestly. I've told her a hundred times over that it's no good. I wrote her a long letter about it. Is it my fault if she hangs around and gets in a frenzy?'

'Yes, it is your fault. You ought to have seen those tears and not just run away from them. Her tears are a fact. And you caused them.'

Another fact. Only I was not interested. I had no intention of feeling guilt about Tommy. 'We're all sinners. We all hurt each other just by existing.'

'That's right, blame God or the cosmos or something. You said you'd marry her.'

'She dreamed it. Losing me is something a girl should be congratulated on.'

'Sure losing you is something a girl should be congratulated on. But somehow all that crying, it just bugged me. It suddenly seemed like the rotten way it all is, people homeless or hungry or half mad, or lying on the pavement outside Charing Cross Station—'

'Look, Tommy isn't lying on the pavement outside Charing Cross Station—'

'OK, we're all sinners and we cause it all the time, but we can avoid being bloody cynical and bloody cruel. She expected you, she couldn't *believe* you wouldn't come—'

'More fool she.'

'She sat waiting for you like a little child and when you didn't come she thought you'd been run over. Jesus!'

'No such luck.'

'You're bloody lucky to be loved by that nice girl, you don't deserve love.'

'You're telling me.'

'No one does, I mean. Of course there are muddles but it was so cruel just to let her wait, you knew she was there—'

'I didn't—'

'Well, you didn't bloody think then. The trouble with you is you're a snob, it's all that rat race competition, all you can think of is getting away from your working-class background, you hate yourself so you can't love anyone else—'

'Oh shut up, will you.'

'That poor girl—'

'Well, why didn't you console her yourself? Or do you only like scraggy boys in tight jeans?'

'That's a lousy thing to say.'

'If you want to stay in this house you can bloody well hold your tongue. I'm fed up with being lectured by a yapping little drop-out who can't do anything but smoke pot.'

'At least I haven't given up. I try to be kind. You've just given up. You simply tread on people. You're a destroyer, a murderer—'

I had put the razor down. Christopher, still in pyjamas, was standing in the door of the bathroom, his golden hair in a frizzy globular tangle, his light blue eyes screwed up with passion. I clenched my right fist and grasped Christopher's shoulder with my left hand, digging my fingers violently into the flesh. He remained perfectly still. His face relaxed into a sudden mildness. I let go of him and took the tumbler from the bathroom shelf and hurled it past him into the hall where it broke into fragments. Christopher continued to look at me mildly for a moment; then he turned and began to pick up the pieces of glass and drop them into a waste-paper basket.

I leaned over the basin closing my eyes. I was so frightened. I was frightened in case Biscuit should not come, I was frightened in case she should bring a message which would terminate my quest, I was frightened of myself and of the impossibility of what I wanted to do and of the horrors which awaited me if in the tiniest way I failed or slipped. There was no clarity now, no exhilaration, no hope, only dread. And Christopher's words, presenting facts, accusing me of murder. And my violent desire to hit him, to hurt him, to trample him under foot. And Gunnar breaking the sherry glass. And women's tears.

'Sorry, Hilary—I'm sorry—I shouldn't have—I'm sorry.'

'I'm sorry too,' I said. 'Better use a brush to sweep that stuff up, you'll cut yourself.'

I went into the bedroom and put my tie on and looked at myself in the glass. I was glaring like a madman. I lay down on the bed, and I thought about Kitty's green silken thigh inches away at the dinner table. My mind surged and boiled and I lay there rigid and clenched my fists with the force of blind inner violence. Time passed. The bell rang.

I was with Biscuit in the park. When she arrived I came out to her at once. I said, 'Wait till we're in the park.' We entered near the Broadwalk and I turned to the left, striking out across the grass in the direction of Speke. The sun shone from a brilliantly blue sky and the thick crystalline tufty hoar frost was piled high upon the motionless boughs of the bare trees. Smoke from a bonfire of leaves rose straight upward in an unswaying column. There was not a breath of wind. It was very cold.

I led Biscuit across the grass into the middle of nowhere, a space between huge trees, then turned and faced her. I feared that her message would be in some way fatal, in some way good-bye. I touched in my overcoat pocket the long letter which I had written to Kitty and for which now there might be no place.

'Well, Biscuit?'

Biscuit was wearing blue tweedy trousers and black lace-up boots and the shabby blue duffle coat with her plait tucked in behind. The cold air made her sallow-golden cheeks glow with a strangely darkish red, making her cheek bones stand out as blobs of colour. For a moment her huge dark eyes gazed up at me with an unsmiling intensity which was almost hostile. Then she drew an envelope out of her pocket and held it to me in silence with a gloved hand.

I could not conceal my emotion. I had no gloves, and my hands, red and moist, bitten to the bone by the cold air and trembling into the bargain, fumbled clumsily to open the slim missive. I got it open at last. There was a very short note. *Hold fast and don't worry. Could you see me at Cheyne Walk at six this evening? I shall be alone. K.J.*

This was so unexpected and so perfect, so wonderful, so beyond my dreams, so filling the future with joy, that for a moment I simply did not know what to do with myself. I wanted to shout or caper or spin like a top. I did not want Biscuit to see my face, so I turned abruptly and began to walk in the direction of the Serpentine. The grass was thickly encrusted with frost, laid out in an elaborate flattened criss-cross pattern of spidery glassy fibres which took our foot-steps with a crisp dry sound. The distant traffic was a quiet murmur. Beneath the cloudless sky and the almost trans-lucent frosty plumage of the trees a great winter silence possessed the scene, in which I could hear Biscuit's light footsteps as she followed after me.

I stopped and let her catch up and we faced each other again. 'Biscuit—'

'Yes?'

'Tell Lady Kitty that I will come this evening.'

'Yes.'

'And—will you—give her this.' I took my plump letter to Kitty out of my pocket and handed it over. Gazing up at me expressionlessly Biscuit put it away.

'Biscottina.'

'Yes?'

'Look at our footprints in the frost.'

We looked back at our two tracks, absurdly wavering, stretching away behind us across the frost-lacquered grass, my large feet and Biscuit's little feet.

'Biscottinetta.'

'Yes?'

'Can you play leap-frog?'

'Yes!' She loosened her duffle coat.

I moved a few paces farther on and leaned over to make a 'back'. A moment later I heard the crunch crunch of her running steps and with the lightest possible tap of her fingers upon my spine she soared lightly over me and bounded onwards, her toes dabbing the frosted grass in a line of little round holes. She leaned over for me. I ran and went over her with a light spring, touching the stuff of her coat with the gentlest flying caress of one hand. There seemed to be no gravity in the park that morning. I ran on and leaned again for her. I pumped in hope and happiness with the cold air. Kitty's note had released me into a carefree world.

Her words could scarcely have been more reassuring and had the wonderful effect of creating another *interim*. I seemed to live in these days by interims. Until this evening I had nothing to fear, no decisions to make, nothing to do but enjoy myself. The prospect of seeing Kitty at six turned the universe into a glorious mish-mash of sheer joy. No wonder I could fly like a bird. Moreover this was not just a private selfish delight at the thought of being with Kitty, it was a sort of spiritual bliss, an explosion of confidence. Somehow the whole plan would work. I would do what Kitty wanted, I would help Gunnar, I would help myself, there would be reconciliation and tears of relief. I would be able to change my life after all and live like an ordinary man. I would educate Crystal and take her to Venice and make her laugh with happiness. I would at last be able to do all the things which had seemed impossible. All would be well and all would be well and all manner of thing would be well. More strangely still, this great hope of good coexisted, without losing a tittle of its power, with all the old realistic terrors, the fears of a false step, the fears of Gunnar's anger and Gunnar's revenge; it even coexisted, strangest of all, with my perfectly commonsensical awareness that Kitty was not really a saint or a prophetess, but an ordinary and possibly rather silly woman who liked a mystery and the exercise of power. Such are the remarkable faculties of the human mind, such was my mind that morning in the park as it expanded and rejoiced.

By now our leap-frogging had brought us near to the Serpentine and we stopped breathless and laughing. I took

Biscuit in my arms and hugged her as one child hugs another, feeling the frailty of her thin body inside her bulky coat.

The frost, which had so mysteriously appeared during the night, had balanced itself inches high upon the branches of trees, upon the iron railings and the backs of seats. It seemed indeed organically connected with these terrestrial surfaces, as if the world had begun, during the hours of darkness, to exude a minutely complicated crystalline plumage which, precariously still, rising high upon the thinnest topmost twigs of the immobile trees, appeared a silvery grey against a sky by contrast so blue as to seem indigo, to seem almost brilliantly leaden.

We had come out into the open beside the water. Not at Peter Pan, my carefree running steps had had the awareness to avoid that; we were in the next bay, the nearest one to the bridge. The Serpentine was frozen along its edges and the thick dust of the frost upon the ice was crisscrossed already with the footprints of waterbirds. Some ducks, in single file, were walking on the ice as if for a wager and finding it quite hard to keep their feet. We came to a seat and I dusted the frost off with my sleeve and we sat down and I put my arm along the back of the seat, knocking off a solid little wall of frost, and drew Biscuit up close against me till I could feel her warmth through the surfaces of two very damp overcoats.

'Well, Lady Alexandra Bissett, and how are we today, Lady Alexandra?'

'All right, Hilary. It's such a lovely day.'

'It's one of the great days. Tell me something, Alexandra. Was your father really a British colonel?'

Biscuit pushed me a little away so that she could look up into my face. I contemplated her reddish-black eyes, the refinement of her long thin wary mouth.

'No.'

'A private?'

'No.'

'Was your mother a Brahmin?'

'No.'

'Were you born in Benares?'

'No.'

'Were you born in India?'

'No.'

'Are you a dreadful little liar?'

'Yes.'

'I shall be jolly sorry if it turns out that your name isn't even Alexandra Bissett.'

'Oh it is, it is!' she said eagerly. 'My name is Alexandra Bissett. I was called after Princess Alexandra.'

'So even if you aren't a princess you were called after one. I thought you couldn't possibly really come from India.'

'Why?'

'Because of your voice. You're a little Cockney girl, aren't you? You were born in, let me see—Stepney?'

'East India Dock Road.'

'Not Benares.'

'Not Benares.'

'My dearest little London Biscuitula.' I kissed the thin intelligent mouth. It gave a little responsive motion but did not try to detain my lips. It was very cold. I thought, here I am kissing Lady Kitty's maid, and not for the first time either. That seemed all right. As I would never kiss Lady Kitty I might as well kiss her maid. After all I too belonged to the servants' hall. It did not even make me feel sad. In the pure interim of today nothing could make me feel sad.

'Was your mother English?'

'Yes.'

'But you had an Indian father? Who was he?'

'I don't know.'

'My father was a mystery man too.'

'I think he only knew my mother for a short time. She said he was a Pakistani, but she called everybody a Pakistani.'

'Milk chocolate Biscuit. Here, give me your hands.' Biscuit had taken her gloves off and now her two little skinny warm hands had burrowed into the sleeves of my overcoat and were holding onto my wrists. 'And your mother?'

'She died. She was a waitress.'

'And how did Lady Kitty manage to acquire you?'

'I was a cleaner, I did cleaning in houses, I did in her house when she was a young lady. I was fifteen. She thought I was pretty and she wanted me.'

'She saw you and she wanted you and she got you?'

'Her parents gave me to her as a Christmas present—'

'Dear Biscuit!'

'To be her little maid, like giving her a toy or something to play with.'

'A playmate.'

'A plaything.' She spoke entirely without irony, without bitterness or any intent to wit, in the curious objective open

235

truthful-sounding manner which I now seemed to know so well and in which she could utter both truth and lies. Her voice had indeed the flat twang of east London, but her speech had some more ancient simplicity or perhaps it had just been in some way maimed or gutted as a result of living for so many years among educated people without being one of them.

'But you don't mind, Biscuitine, you aren't unhappy? You must be devoted to her—'

'Of course I am devoted to her,' said Biscuit, in the same even oddly authoritative voice, and she withdrew her hands from my sleeves. 'She does with me what she will.'

'I expect she does that with most people.'

'But one day I shall go away.'

'How will that be?'

'I will meet a man who will take me away.'

'Poor Biscuit. Have you been waiting for him all these years, your prince, poor disinherited princess?' The words were cruel, as I knew when I had uttered them. And yet her enigmatic dignity did not evoke pity. Suddenly I thought and uttered my thought. 'Not me—darling Biscuit—I can't be him.'

'I know.' She got up. 'You see, you love her. They always do.' She began to walk away towards the bridge.

I went after her and caught the sleeve of her coat. 'Biscuit, don't spoil things.'

'What things?'

'Don't— Don't— It's such a lovely day.'

A quartet of Canada geese whizzed under the bridge and took the water with a noisy checked flurry.

'Biscuit, has Lady Kitty talked to you about me? Has she told you why she wants to talk to me? It's not perhaps— what you think at all. Has she told you anything?'

'No.' We watched the geese fussily settling their wings. 'I think nothing. She has told me nothing. Why should she. I am a servant.'

'A plaything. A toy. Come! Biscuit, I may not be the prince but I do love you. I do. Is that any good?'

She smiled, first at the geese and then at me. 'No.'

It was exactly six p.m. I had not returned to the flat for I feared an invasion by Tommy. I would have liked to shave again but by six o'clock this did not matter any more. I had been walking the embankment since five and was sick and faint with anxiety. It was a cold clear night and some stars were visible over the river. My limbs were restless and twitching with a chill ague, and I was fidgety and nervous with dread. I had resisted the temptation of the King's Head. I had eaten practically no lunch. This was no moment for seeking alcoholic inspiration. I must be chaste and cool. As it was I had reduced myself to a shuddering wreck with hunger and with cold.

My teeth were chattering. I pressed the iron gate and walked up to the door and rang the bell. Biscuit opened the door and a rush of warm air came out. Biscuit could not possibly have been wearing a white apron and a white starched cap and streamers, but the effect was somehow the same. She looked at me coldly. 'Will you come in, please? Madam is upstairs.'

'Come off it, Biscuit.'

'Put your coat here, please. Madam is upstairs.'

'Well, kindly tell Madam to come down,' I said. 'I am not coming in.'

Biscuit turned expressionlessly towards the staircase, leaving me standing in the doorway. After a moment's hesitation I drew the door to without shutting it and went back down the path and through the gate and waited on the pavement. I looked up at the well curtained windows of the first floor where a little line of golden light was showing.

I had thought this out beforehand. I could not possibly enter Gunnar's house. My presence there without his knowledge would be an outrage. And how could I possibly talk to Kitty while listening for Gunnar's key in the door? I would be in continual fear in his house, suspecting his presence in darkened alcoves or behind screens. It was not that I rationally imagined that I would be walking into some sort of trap. I just did not want to step onto his territory at all. And I did not want to see his wife in the context of a conjugal home. Better the blasted heath for whatever conversation we were to have together.

I waited for what seemed a long time. Then Kitty slipped

out of the door and closed it behind her. She was wearing the magnificent fur coat, pulled to her waist by the metal belt, and a scarf over her head. She came swiftly down the path, smiling, as if my refusal to enter had been the most usual thing in the world. 'How kind of you to come.'

'How kind of you to ask me.'

'Shall we walk on the embankment?'

'Yes, if you will.'

'You needn't be afraid to come in, you know. Gunnar is dining at Chequers.'

'I would rather talk to you out here.'

'I quite understand.'

We went through the garden and across the road and approached the embankment wall. The tide was in and very full, upon the turn, and the black water moved slowly just below the wall, turning back meditatively towards the sea.

I did not want to stay near the house, and we walked on a bit in silence until we reached a wooden jetty which stretched out into the river, with one or two launches moored and bobbing beside it. There was a light halfway down the jetty. We passed the light and moved on into darkness. The water was all about us now, we could hear it splashing below our feet, gently slapping at the structure of the jetty.

'What a pleasant region of London you live in,' I said. The shuddering and chattering had quite gone. I felt perfectly calm, even warm. A thrilling current of sheer joy came from the woman beside me and warmed my whole body and made it tingle with well-being. I could look at her, at the gorgeous soft coat with its turned up collar, at the slim waist and the way her pulled-in scarf had made her face seem thinner, more hawk-like. I could smell her perfume. Our steamy breaths, pumped out into the night air, mingled.

Hands in pockets she replied, 'Yes, it is delightful, isn't it. I used to live in Chelsea when I was a child.'

When she had coveted a little Indian girl and received her as a Christmas present.

We were silent for a moment, not awkwardly, looking at each other. I could just make out her face, her long nose, the flash of her eyeballs, in the dimness.

I said, 'How is Gunnar? Does he want to see me?'

'That's just the question,' said Kitty. 'That is what I want to talk to you about.' As if there might have been hundreds of other possible topics of conversation. 'Gunnar is in a frenzy.'

'Oh God.' She was going to tell me it was all no good, and then to say good-bye.

'He is in a perfect frenzy. He cannot think about anything but you.'

'Does he want to kill me?'

'Sometimes.'

I thought to myself, suppose I were to offer myself to Gunnar's rage, like a hare jumping into a fire? Was that what Kitty wanted? Was she pleased that Gunnar wanted to kill me? Perhaps. Women could be like that.

I spoke coolly. 'Am I then to assume that our little meeting in his room was not a success? He told you of it, I imagine?'

'Yes, of course. But he is in a frenzy, he is totally confused and obsessed, he doesn't know what he wants, or what he will do. He didn't then. When you spoke to him he had to see you, but—'

'He didn't know whether to talk to me or to strangle me?'

'Exactly.'

'Well, what am I to do now? You said I should try to see him. I have. He hated it. What next, if anything?'

'Please don't be so impatient, Hilary.'

Her use of my name nearly sent me spinning off into the water. I wanted suddenly to turn right round like someone in a dance. I think I gave a sort of gasp.

'I may call you "Hilary", mayn't I?'

'Of course. I'm not impatient. I'm prepared to hang on indefinitely if it's any good. But what can I do? Have you discussed it, have you tried to persuade him to see me?'

'Oh yes, we've immensely discussed it, we've had such long long talks about you.'

What a vista.

'You see,' she went on, 'as I told you, we've been thinking about you for years. That's partly why I called you "Hilary" just now.'

Partly? And had they been thus bandying my name in their long talks 'for years'? I felt a mixture of humility and exasperation which made me want to bow my head and moan, but the coolness persisted. We were still facing each other like two antagonists. She had thrown her head back and the scarf had fallen to her shoulders releasing the tumble of dark hair. Her hands were still deep in her pockets.

I did not pick up any of these fascinating matters. I said rather brusquely, 'Well, I came here for instructions and you seem to have none.'

'I am frightfully sorry. I know the whole thing is a terrible imposition, a terrible—impertinence.'

What a ridiculous word. I felt I wanted to laugh with despair. I was spending these privileged minutes of my life in her presence and I was behaving like a stolid churl and we could not communicate and she would never and could never know how I felt and had perhaps even the impression that I was annoyed with her. Wanting to scream I stood very still. The traffic rumbled along the embankment but the plopping meditating tide-turning river spoke of silence.

'Lady Kitty,' I said, 'it is for me to be sorry. I will do anything I can to help you and Gunnar. Shall I try to see him again? Shall I write to him?'

'No, no. Just wait. The fact is that—things are now in motion. It is very good that you saw him in the office, that was brave of you and I am so pleased. It was a fearful shock, but good. You see, he is moving now, it is sort of dynamic, he can't rest, he'll decide something soon, he'll have to, it will be too much for him not to, he will have to see you in order to break the spell.'

This was not altogether reassuring. It also occurred to me that so far Kitty had had nothing to say to me which could not have been conveyed in a note via Biscuit just saying *Wait*. I wondered if there was more to come. I certainly hoped so. I dreaded her now saying good-bye. Soon, in any case, there would be between us a good-bye which was good-bye forever. Perhaps it was this one, which was now in an instant coming. I clenched my fists, trying hard to think of something important to say.

'I wanted to talk to you,' she said rather abruptly, as if we had not hitherto been talking.

'Anything you will.'

Kitty began to pace to and fro, her shoes striking the frosty boards with a muted hollow sound.

'You see,' she went on, 'the strange thing is, well I suppose it's not strange, that you're the only person I can talk to about certain things. Of course I've talked to Gunnar, as I told you, but between us there's only a sort of narrow area— I mean, we discuss the same things over and over, about how Gunnar feels, about whether time makes any difference, whether he feels better than he did a year ago, whether seeing

240

this or that psychiatrist has done any good and so on and so on. It's been like living with a disease. Can you understand? Am I boring you?'

'Don't be silly,' I said.

'I'm sorry, I didn't mean it like that, I mean that in some awful sense it is boring, dreadful but boring and somehow hopeless. Any deep obsession is boring. One is always in the same place saying the same things, going round and round in the same routine, and one wants to break out, one wants a huge absolute change and that's just what's impossible.' She paused but I said nothing. 'When we met at Peter Pan I told you—I think—you see I've talked to you in my mind and I'm not sure what I've told you really and what I imagine I've told you—I've lived all these years—under her shadow.'

'Yes.'

'But we never really talked about her, Gunnar and I, we couldn't. At least I could have, but he couldn't. We talked about *it*, his obsession, his illness, but her name could not be mentioned. And yet she was there, she is there.'

'Yes.'

'I've been living with a ghost—well, with two ghosts.'

'Two?'

'Hers, and yours.'

'Of course. And you must lay them both.' It had never come to me more clearly that it was not only my destiny but also my duty to vanish: to perform the necessary rites and then to crumble to dust and, in their lives, walk no more.

'It seems an unkind way to put it, but yes. You see, I've never had it really straight with Gunnar. He keeps saying it isn't fair to me and that I married a sick man. Our love has always been crippled, damaged, because I could not get in to the place where he was suffering and help him. And I want, oh more than I can express to you, to see him let go of the past, became free, able to come forward into the future with me with a whole heart.'

I was rigid, every muscle hard, like a man about to be shot who keeps conjured before his eyes his absolute duty to the cause which brought him to that moment. Bitterness here could break all, was a more dangerous enemy than any kind of softness. There was a narrow comfortless line in the centre to which I must keep. I said, but it was not out of bitterness, 'She existed.'

Kitty was silent. She did not answer this, but said in a few moments, still pacing, 'What was she like?'

'Has Gunnar never told you?'

'Never in the world. You obviously haven't *understood*. Nothing could be more impossible.'

I reflected. 'I don't think I can tell you either, not just like that.'

'Say something. Please. Anything. What colour was her hair?'

'Mouse.'

'But she was beautiful?'

'She had lovely—bright—clever—eyes. I'm very sorry but I can't—I can't—'

Kitty sighed deeply and stood still gazing out over the dark now faster moving tide of the river.

'You never saw a photograph of her?' I said after a moment.

She shook her head. I wondered if she was beginning to cry, but I could not now see her face.

She spoke again in a firm voice. She had evidently decided to leave that subject. 'You told me that this—business—had wrecked your life.'

'Yes. And my sister's.'

'You have a sister?'

Kitty's discussion of me with Gunnar could not after all have been very detailed if even this had not emerged. I did not know if I was pleased or not.

'Yes.'

Kitty did not pursue the sister. 'Well, as I think I said then, ought you not to see to yourself, try to cure yourself as well, or get cured and better and so on?' The words were awkward and could not but sound cold.

'Ghosts don't get cured. They just fade away.' This ought not to have been said.

She replied, perhaps even a trifle more coldly, 'You know that's silly. You must try, you can try. And if you help Gunnar you will at least have done something to sort of rescue the past.'

'Yes. I suppose so.' With desperation I felt the current of communication between us drying up, ceasing. In a moment now she would tell me to go, and I could think of nothing to say to stop her. And I was behaving as if I resented everything she said. How could I remove this impression without seizing her hand and crying out? I said abruptly, 'You got my letter?'

'Yes, of course. Thank you—thank you for writing at such length—'

242

Silence. The letter had been a mistake, everything I did here was a mistake.

Kitty spoke again, sounding a little now as if she too wanted to 'save' our conversation. 'You mustn't worry so.'

'Worry? Well, one does rather!'

'Sorry, my words are all going wrong this evening. I mean —you think everything's your fault, but it isn't.'

'I can't see whose else's fault anything can be here!'

'Well—his—even mine—'

'Scarcely yours!'

'Yes, mine. I haven't—at least—brought him luck—I haven't been able really to help him—another woman might have—and I've had no children—and he so much wants—'

'I expect he does, after losing two, but I don't see—' I felt now as if I were plunging around in the mud.

'Two?'

'Yes—' Then I covered my mouth with my hand.

'How do you mean *two*?'

'Oh well—I suppose—there might have been—I don't mean anything—'

'Why *two*, you said *two*?'

Kitty had stopped in front of me. Her glaring eyes shone with passion. There was no escape.

'Anne was pregnant—his—'

'He never told me.'

I moved away from her. I did not want to see her face, I wanted to cover my own.

Kitty too had turned away. It was as if a bell had rung to separate two fighters. Or as if two planes peeling off east and west were suddenly separated by the whole sky. She sat down upon the edge of the jetty, the expensive coat trailing in the mud.

I had never felt more a victim of the past. I said, 'I am very sorry—'

'Please go away now.'

'May I—'

'Please go. Thank you for coming. Now please go.'

I went slowly away from her in the direction of the embankment.

It was only seven-thirty when I reached the North End Road. I had of course in the previous days, and even during today, and even somehow in Kitty's presence, not forgotten that I was to see Crystal on Saturday evening. Saturday was Crystal's day and unless I told her I was not coming she would expect me. When I telephoned her on Thursday evening I had heard that lonely echo from the private inwardness of her sad existence. Of course I knew that Crystal had stripped her life for me, that she was alone because of me. How I had planned once to surround her with friends, with sources of joy, to make up forever for those horrible childhood years! It would have been possible, even easy, if I had been happy myself. As it was she lived in poverty and solitude and of the two friends whom I had brought to her one (Clifford) had caused her misery and the other (Arthur) she had surrendered because of me. Did I measure her loneliness or try to imagine it? No. I never reflected on how she passed the long hours and days between our meetings.

I was always profoundly relieved and glad to come to Crystal, though this never, in the harsh chemistry of my soul, set going any wish to see her oftener, and this evening I needed her with a blind passionate hunted frenzy. In the certain hope that everything would be absolutely as usual I bounded up the stairs to her room.

Everything was absolutely as usual. The lace tablecloth was laid for two and the parchment shaded lamp with the galleon on it was switched on in the corner, for decoration only, since the bright centre light revealed the shabby room but too well. The sherry was on the table. The wine I had brought with me, bought at the usual nearby pub. Crystal was sitting beside the table and sewing. She read my face at once, threw the sewing down and came round the table. We embraced and held onto each other tightly, eyes closed. As I am six foot one and Crystal scarcely five feet two an embrace was always some sort of ingenious compromise. I sagged, she stood on tiptoe. It was very easy to sag on this occasion, I felt ready to fall to the ground as soon as her hands touched me.

I let go of her and sat down heavily on her bed, rumpling the green satin bedspread. She stared at me for a few moments, as if touching my head with the tender sensitive antennae of her loving thoughts. Then she poured out some sherry and put it on the table within my reach. I peeled off my coat and pulled the wine bottle out of the pocket.

'What's for supper?'

'Fish cakes and grilled tomatoes and chips and strawberry trifle and cream.'

'Good.'

Crystal began to open the wine bottle, as she always did at this stage, still watching me.

'Are you all right, Crystal darling?'

'Yes, fine.'

'Have you seen Arthur?'

'No.'

'You haven't changed your mind about chucking him?'

'No.'

I looked up at Crystal. Her beautiful golden eyes were hidden by the thick glasses whereon all sorts of reflections were playing as she moved her head, dealing with the bottle. Her frizzy orange-tinted hair hung heavily down as if a small thick mat had been laid upon her head. Her moist jutting lower lip expressed anxiety and concern. The nostrils of her stumpy upturned nose moved in and out.

I was drinking my sherry. I needed that drink.

Crystal said, 'Have you seen Tommy?'

'Yes, but that's all over, finished with.' It seemed a hundred years since I had dismissed Thomasina from my life and my thoughts, and it only now occurred to me that I had not hitherto had time to inform Crystal.

'I know. She came here.'

'Tommy came here, bothering you? Blast her. What did she say?'

'She cried.'

'She cries everywhere.'

Crystal was silent. She placed the wine bottle carefully upon the little decorated cork mat which awaited it upon the table. Words were not necessary to tell me that although Crystal sympathized a bit with Tommy she was glad that I was not going to marry her.

'Give me some more sherry, darling.'

For both of us, that was enough about Tommy. I had decided as I came along to tell Crystal everything. Well, almost everything.

'Have you cooked the fish cakes?'

'Yes, everything's cooked. It's in the oven. We can have it when we like.'

'Good. Sit down, dear heart. Near me.'

She sat down on an upright chair near to the bed, holding her sewing on her lap. She was wearing a shapeless old woollen dress with blue and green stripes which used to belong to Aunt Bill, and which Crystal had altered, more than once, to fit herself. Crystal's wardrobe went on and on forever. Nothing was ever thrown away.

'Crystal, listen. I have seen Lady Kitty. You know, Gunnar's wife.'

A dark red-purplish flush rose into Crystal's face, making it look for a moment almost leaden.

'Have you seen Gunnar?'

'No. Well, literally yes, but I haven't talked to him. I don't know if I will—it's all—oh it's all so complicated—' It struck me now for the first time that, feeling as I did about Kitty, perhaps I ought not to see Gunnar, ought not to proceed another step along the road where a woman's well-meaning rashness was leading me. I had accepted Kitty's picture of the situation with naive faith. But why should I trust her judgment of what was needful?

'How was it you saw Lady Kitty?'

'She asked to see me. She sent her servant to me. I talked to her twice. Gunnar doesn't know.'

'Gunnar doesn't know you saw her?'

'No. You see—' How absurd it all seemed now that I was trying to tell it. 'You see, she feels I might be able to help Gunnar. I mean, he's been obsessed all these years with what happened, he's been hating me and wanting revenge and she says it's—it's like an illness—and if he could just see me and—it wouldn't really matter much what we said so long as we talked—'

'But if he hates you, if he wants revenge?'

'He might stop, if he saw me. He might feel differently—anyway it might become less of a—'

'He might hurt you.'

'Don't be silly, Crystal. These are mental things.' Were they?

'I don't want you to see him,' she said. She was pulling the piece of sewing between her two hands, pulling it apart. In the moment of silence I could hear the threads breaking. I took it from her and put it on the table.

'No need to get as red as a turkey cock about it. It can't do any harm.'

'It can. I don't want you to see him or to see her again.
I don't want you to have anything to do with them at all.
We were all right. Why did they have to come? Why can't
they leave us alone? Please, Hilary, change your job, get
away from him, please. Then we can be like we were before.
And now there's just the two of us again. If you see him you
will be hurt, you will be badly hurt somehow, I know it, I
know it—'

'Dear child, dear love, don't be so bloody irrational. And
try to think of me, well I know you're thinking of me, but
think of me a bit more intelligently. Suppose I want to see
Gunnar? Suppose I feel it might help *me* to have a talk with
him? He's not the only one who's obsessed, he's not the only
one who's got the horrors about—that—'

Crystal was silent for a while, looking down, away from
me. 'Do you want to see him?'

'I don't know. I want to do what she wants.'

'What Lady Kitty wants? Why?'

'Because she's— Because I love her—I can't help it—'

This was the bit I had decided not to tell; but once I
had started it was impossible to hold it back. Without it, in
any case, the story scarcely made sense.

'I see,' said Crystal after a moment. She picked up her
sewing again and began to fiddle with it, drawing her finger
along the seam. Then she found her needle and began with
remarkable neat rhythmical quickness to sew.

'I love her,' I said. 'Yes, I love her.' It was something vast
to say it, it seemed to open up a great dark dome above me
blazing with stars. 'But of course—'

'Have you told her?'

'What do you take me for? Of course I haven't.'

'Does she love you?'

'Don't be idiotic, Crystal. I'm sorry I told you, you're
getting the wrong end of the stick at once. It's not like that.
Quite probably I shall never see her again. They want to
get on with their lives, I'm just a sort of instrument. She
doesn't care for me, she just wants me to see Gunnar so as to
help him and she doesn't want him to know she suggested it.'

'Why not?'

'Because it would make it less sort of efficient, efficacious.'
Was that the reason? I had not really reflected on the reason.

'Well, he might not be pleased—' said Crystal, her needle
flashing.

'Oh do stop sewing, Crystal, my nerves are shot to pieces!'

'Would you like your supper now?'

'No. Give me some wine.'

Crystal put the sewing down again, poured the wine.

'Have they got children, Gunnar and her?'

'No. Look, Crystal, my loving Lady Kitty is just a fact, it's just an irrelevant fact—'

'You said it made you want to do what she told you.'

'Yes, but I'd do that anyway out of a sense of duty. If there's the faintest possibility of my being able to help Gunnar I've got to try, can't you see that? This isn't the beginning of anything. I'm not going to be a friend of the family, how can I be? I'll just see Gunnar once, twice maybe, then I'm done. I certainly won't be seeing *her* again, I may not even see her again at all, as I said. Do try and understand.'

'I think I'll have some sherry,' said Crystal. This was unusual. She said, 'I don't want you to see him. I don't want there to be anything between you any more at all.'

'But why? I wouldn't have looked for him. But now he's here. We meet on the bloody stairs!'

'That's why you must change your job.'

'Oh don't keep saying that! It's not so bloody easy. Maybe I will later on. I can't see that far ahead. But the immediate thing is—'

'I don't want you to see him.'

'So you've said six times, but why? You can't seriously think he'll murder me!'

Crystal was now silent for such a long time, staring at her sherry and not drinking it, some new sort of alarm began to break in on me. She was behaving in a strange way, as if some other harder form of being were coming about within her.

'Crystal, what is it?'

At last she spoke. 'My darling, I must tell you something.'

'What, for Christ's sake? Have you got cancer or something?' Utter panic squeezed my heart.

'No, no, it's about the past, things that happened then.'

'You swear you haven't got cancer?'

'I swear. Listen now. I never really told you about that time, about what it was like for me at that time.'

This was perfectly true. We had never discussed the accident, what had happened before it and what had happened after it. I told Crystal enough for her to be able to make sense of the business. That is, I told her that I had been having a love affair with Anne. Apart from that she had to rely on telepathy. Neither had I ever asked what those days had been like for her, while I was lying in hospital smashed up and half dead. Silence was better. Crystal and I had been through so many horrors together in our childhood, we had formed a tacit pact never to inquire, never to 'go over' what had happened.

'Do you want to tell me now? Why? Whatever can be the point? I'd rather you didn't.'

Crystal was silent again for about a minute. Then she said, 'I think I must tell you. I think there is a point. It's becoming too awful not to.'

'*What*, for God's sake? You're driving me mad with your hints.'

'Wait. I'll tell you. Only listen. Please be patient. I think it will be easier for me if I tell it all in order so as to show the whole of it. Listen now. The first I knew was I got a telephone call from the college. They said you had had a serious car accident and you were in the Radcliffe Infirmary. That was on the Tuesday night, in fact it was very late, about midnight or after, I had gone to bed. What time was the accident?'

'About ten.'

'Well you were by then in the hospital and they telephoned me and of course I went at once to the railway station but there was no train until five. So I waited and I got that train to Birmingham and then I got the train to Oxford and I got to the hospital about eleven and the first person I saw was Gunnar. Anne was still alive then.'

I poured myself out some more wine. My hand shook violently. Crystal's face was transformed, hardened. She was looking at the floor.

'Gunnar told me that you were "both" badly hurt, and I could not understand him at first, but then I gathered that Anne had been with you in the car. I tried to see you, but they wouldn't let me, they were operating on you. Anne was somewhere else in the hospital. Gunnar came along to see how you were. I think he didn't know then how bad Anne was, perhaps they didn't tell him, or perhaps they didn't know. I was sitting on a chair in a corridor and I was feeling very faint, and he said hadn't I better come back to his house and lie down, as there was nothing we could either of us do just then by waiting, so I went back with him to his car and we went to his house which you remember it's just — quite close — and we went there and he wanted me to eat something only of course we couldn't either of us eat. The little boy, the child, I can't remember his name, wasn't there, I think he was away with some relations. And I lay down in a bedroom upstairs and he went back to the hospital, and he told me of course he would find out how you were. That must have been about two or three o'clock and I was feeling very collapsed. Then I sort of fell asleep or went into a kind of coma, I lay there and everything went strange. Then I woke up again in the most fearful terror, it was about six o'clock and I was alone in the house, and I got up and began to go downstairs, and as I was on the stairs the front door opened and Gunnar came in and said "Anne is dead", and he went on into a room at the back and sat down at a table. I heard what he said and I took it in but I could really think of nothing but you and I asked him "Is Hilary dead?" and he said nothing, he just sat there looking at that big window and the garden and he was as still as a statue, like paralysed, and he would not answer, and I went to the telephone and I wanted to telephone the hospital only I couldn't remember its name and I was crying so I couldn't see the numbers anyway, so then I just ran out of the house. I knew which way the hospital was and I began to run along that way, crying. Then someone just grabbed me, it was Gunnar, and he just pulled me and led me back to the house and of course I went, I was almost hysterical with fear, and he got me inside and put me to sit on a chair in the hall and he telephoned the hospital and got through to the ward where you were and he spoke so calmly and clearly, and they said the operation had been successful and you were resting, and somehow the word "resting" was so wonderful just at that moment, but I was still shaking with fear, and Gunnar asked if I could see you, and he spoke so calmly and clearly, and they said yes maybe, and then he led me out, he really led me, and he pulled me along by the sleeve, and he put me into the car and drove me to the hospital and led me up to the ward, and I did actually see you, though you didn't remember afterwards, you were just coming round from the anaesthetic and your jaw was all bandaged up but your face was quite all right and your eyes were open and you looked at me and somehow you looked so whole and so like yourself and I was weeping with relief and the nurse said that you'd get perfectly well again, though I don't suppose she knew really, and then I went out and Gunnar was waiting outside and I told him, and we went down and got into his car and went back to the house, and then he sort of collapsed and we sort of changed places. And the telephone was ringing and it was Anne's mother, you remember, well I suppose you never knew, that they couldn't get hold of her in the morning, she was on holiday in Spain, and she rang up from Spain, and I made Gunnar talk to her, and after that he asked me to deal with the telephone or if anyone came round, and just tell them what had happened and that he didn't want to see anyone. And a few people did ring up and one or two came to the door and I told them and all the time Gunnar was sitting in the back room again, just sitting there quite still at the table and looking at the window. And oh I felt so relieved about you, I was able then to be so sorry for him and so sorry about Anne, they had both been so kind to me, so awfully kind, kinder than anyone, and I went into the kitchen and I began to feel hungry, and that was so wonderful too, and I made some toast and opened a tin of beans, and I wanted Gunnar to eat something only he wouldn't and he wouldn't move, he just sat and sat, and I ate the beans, and then I found out where the drink was kept, you see he had offered me brandy in the afternoon only I had refused it, and I got out the brandy and the whisky and the glasses and I put them on the table, and I put out, funny I can remember it so clearly, I can *see* it all so clearly, a plate of chocolate biscuits. And I gave Gunnar some brandy and I drank some whisky myself, I think I felt then that whisky was somehow less extreme than brandy, and Gunnar drank the brandy and then he began to cry terribly, with huge tears on and on and still staring, and then at last he began to cry less and he ate a chocolate biscuit and then he began to talk, and it must have been about ten o'clock or later. And it was such a strange thing, he talked about his childhood and about his mother who was half Norwegian and about how he visited his grandparents on some farm near some lake and how he once went to Lappland and saw reindeer, and he talked a lot about reindeer and about how, so funny, they like the smell of human water, urine, and how they eat this special moss, and what it was like in the north where there was no night for months and then no day for months and he talked about the northern lights. And all this time we were drinking and I think he drank all the brandy in the bottle, and I drank a bit of whisky and felt very strange, and I kept saying he ought to go to bed, but in an odd way we didn't either of us want to go to bed, we just wanted to make it go on and on and sit on and on and go on and on talking forever in that strange way, it was as if we were in a trance. And then at last we were so weary and he started to cry again and that showed that that was at an end and he got up and started to go up to bed, still crying. And I went up too and I felt so exhausted and so peculiar, and I went into the room where I had been lying down in the afternoon and I undressed and put on my nightdress, because I'd packed a little case when I came away, just night things, and then I went to see what Gunnar was doing and he was just lying down on his bed, and I told him to get undressed and get into bed, and he took his shoes off and his trousers and he was sort of falling about. I suppose it was the brandy. And I pulled back the clothes for him to get into bed and he got in and then said in such a—such a terribly sad miserable way, Don't leave me! So I stood there beside him for a while and he was sort of moaning and then I pitied him so much I got into the bed beside him and I took him in my arms and then he made love to me.'

'*He made love to you?*'

'Yes.'

'What on earth do you mean, Crystal?'

'Just like that, like it is.'

'Do you know what you're talking about?'

'Yes.'

'You mean that on the night of Anne's death Gunnar fucked you?'

'Yes.'

'It's not possible.'

'Yes. But try and understand what it was like. It was not like—it was not like for real—I mean it was real—you see he didn't know I was a virgin—well, I suppose he must have done but he seemed surprised—but it all happened—as if it were in a dream—somehow as if it had to and without talk—and yet it was not a dream, and I was very awake, very conscious, and—'

'And you *let* him?'

'Yes, of course. I would have done anything for him on that night—I felt so—you see, you were alive and Anne was dead—and in some strange awful way the fact that she was dead made you that much more alive—I felt somehow I owed something to Gunnar. I owed him the world—and I was so sorry for him, I wanted to hold him and hold him, and he had been so kind to me, so awfully kind—and of course it was the brandy and the shock and—of course it wasn't me just as me, he—it was like for absolute forgetting, for blindness—it was like someone might look at an awful dirty magazine because it sort of takes the attention away from everything else—I don't think in a sense he knew what he was doing, though in a sense of course he did—'

'Wait a moment, Crystal, describe this properly. Oh God, oh *God*! He made love to you. How long for, and what happened afterwards, and did you stay the night in his bed?'

'I don't know—how long for—' she said. 'I don't know. I was— After it he fell asleep and I went away to my own bed and I went to sleep too. When I woke up in the morning he was already up and dressed and downstairs and talking on the telephone. He was arranging about the funeral.'

'Christ. *Christ*. What did you do then?'

'I dressed and packed up my things and I went downstairs and he put down the telephone, and do you know he had already earlier rung up the hospital to find out how you were, and he said you had had a good night. And I asked him if I could help him and he said no and we were standing there in the hall, and I said could I make him breakfast and he said no, and he offered me some and I said no, and I had put on my coat, you see, and I had my case. And I thanked him and said I would go to a hotel, and he said he would drive me, and I said no and he didn't insist and he opened the door. And I said good-bye to him and I stretched out my hand and he kissed it and I went out and after that I didn't—see him—any more at all.'

'Do you think he remembered what happened in the night?'

'I'm not sure. I suppose so. Otherwise he would not have kissed my hand, would he?' She added after a moment, 'You know, he is the only man who ever did that, kissed my hand.'

'Crystal, I wonder if you know what this is doing to me?'

'I had to tell you,' she said, still not looking at me.

'Much better not.'

'I had to. If he had not come back I shouldn't ever have told you. But with him there, so near, and now—you've seen *her*—and you asked me why—I didn't want you to see him—' Tears suddenly broke out of Crystal's bent face.

'You've changed the past,' I said. As I moved away from her and sat at the table opposite to her, watching her cry, I felt that hundreds of things had changed which I had not yet had time to notice. 'Oh why did you, why—'

'I loved him.'

'What on earth do you mean.'

'He was so kind to me, and that day at the party, he treated me—like someone important—'

I recalled the day of the party, the day which Crystal had said was 'the happiest day of her life'. Was that because Gunnar had been kind to her?

'You don't have to love everyone who's kind to you,' I said. And I thought, well, why not, when there have been so few? Gunnar. Clifford. Arthur. 'You never told this to anyone else, did you, Crystal?'

'No, of course not, of course not! I broke off with Arthur because I knew I could never tell him.'

And I had thought she had broken with Arthur because of me, to support me, to be with me, to be entirely beside me in my ordeal. But in reality she had broken because of Gunnar, because— 'Crystal, you don't *still* love Gunnar, do you?'

'Yes.' She was still weeping, but quietly, mopping her eyes rhythmically with a handkerchief.

She had broken with Arthur so as to be alone, to be there, ready, waiting, in case Gunnar should remember her, should need her, should want to see her. What a pathetic illusion! She had broken with Arthur for the same reason that I had broken with Tommy, to be available. But even as I thought these vile lunatic thoughts I knew that they were mad. Crystal could not seriously think that Gunnar could need her any more than I could seriously think that, except as a mere device, Kitty could need me.

'You're insane,' I said. 'You're behaving like a hysterical unbalanced woman. It's meaningless to go on "loving" somebody like that, somebody you'll never see again. Anyway, you don't love him. You don't know what the word means in that sense. I don't exactly blame you for what happened, it was like a sort of brainstorm—but you must have wits enough to imagine how Gunnar must have felt afterwards, how he must have hated himself and you. For him it's just a terrible disgusting memory. You don't imagine he's going to come round again to kiss your hand, do you?'

Crystal just shook her head, still mopping steadily at her steadily weeping eyes.

'I'm sorry,' I said. I knew I was being cruel, but it was such

254

an unexpected blow, I felt sickened, frightened. The idea of this curious, weird relationship, which for Crystal at least was still alive, between her and Gunnar made me feel some awful primitive pain. (Jealousy?)

Crystal was making an effort to compose herself. She said, now looking at me timidly, 'Dear—it doesn't make any—difference—does it? I mean you aren't so shocked and so—that you hate me? It is all right, isn't it, as it's always been? I thought I just had to tell you because— But it is all right, isn't it?'

I thought, no, it is not all right, it will never be all right again, something is lost and spoilt and ruined forever. Oh Crystal, Crystal, my pure darling, how could this awful thing have happened to us? I said, 'Yes, it's all right, of course.'

'You don't hate me, do you? I shall die.'

'Don't be silly, Crystal.'

'Well, will you—please—have your supper—we could have supper now, couldn't we? It's fish cakes like you like—and nice—tomatoes and—'

'Supper after this! No thanks. I couldn't eat anything.'

'Oh, please, please—' She began to cry again.

'Oh stop it, Crystal! I've got enough without your tears.'

'I don't want you to see him.'

'I don't see why not, if you're still in love with him!'

'He might think—'

'Might think what? Do stop blubbering and talk clearly. Might think I wanted to bring you together or something? Oh Crystal darling, return to reality! Gunnar isn't interested in you. You're just a nasty obscene incident in the remote past. It's me he's interested in. And I've got to see him. I've got to. What you've told me makes me feel absolutely sick, but it doesn't alter the situation, it doesn't alter my duty.'

'Are you going to see *her* again?' Crystal was sitting upright, staring at me, squeezing her handkerchief which was now so soaked with her tears that drops of water were falling from it onto her woollen skirt.

'I don't know, I told you, I don't know, you're tormenting me!'

'You said you were in love with her.'

'I was raving.'

'You'll hate me now, you'll hate me because I told you, I won't be able to be any more a place for you to come to, we can't be together any more like when we were children, it's all gone, it's all gone, oh why did I tell you, oh why—'

'Don't, Crystal, you're killing me.' It was indeed as if some bond with childhood had been broken, some bond which had lasted crazily preternaturally long, some innocence. 'Look, I'm sorry, I'm going now.' I felt I wanted to get out, I wanted to breathe purer air, to *run*. 'Don't be upset, nothing's spoilt or changed, it can't be, it's just that I'm under such awful pressure. Forgive me. You eat the fish cakes. Don't worry, don't worry.'

I was pulling my coat on. She said nothing more and did not try to stop me, but watched me quietly, her face swollen and almost unrecognizable with weeping. I stopped on the way to the door.

'Crystal—there hasn't ever been anybody else—ever—like that, has there?'

Her cry of denial was like the wild scream of a bird. I stumbled out of the door and down the stairs, and when I reached the street I began to run.

SUNDAY

IT WAS Sunday morning. It was raining, and a rackety wind was sweeping the rain in little wild gusts across the windows, as if bombarding them with tin-tacks. I was lying (fully clothed) upon my bed, and Tommy was sitting on a chair beside me, knitting.

Sunday had of course brought Tommy, who was at last lucky in finding me at home. With an exercise of the considerable intelligence of which she was capable, she had taken in immediately that I was abstracted, obsessed, miles away, scarcely able to apprehend her, and she had refrained from tears or questions, had gone into the kitchen and made some coffee, which she also distributed to Christopher, Mick, Len and Jimbo. She tidied things, washed things, and watered the gloomy plant which Jimbo had given me.

Kitty had said, 'Oh, you have a sister?' So (unless she was deliberately deceiving me?) Gunnar had not told her about what happened on the night of Anne's death. This was not improbable. She had said they had never discussed *that* time in detail and Gunnar might well have felt this piece of nightmare reminiscence to be unnecessary. He must simply detest the memory of it. That is, if it really happened. But had it happened? Hysterical middle-aged women, especially virgins, sometimes imagined such tales, that a man had broken in, that they had been seduced, raped, something perhaps which they both feared and wanted? I could not see Crystal in that light. Yet how far, for any purpose, could I see her objectively? Had she really got her head screwed on? Had she not every sort of reason and excuse for being, in lonely middle age, rather dotty, a somewhat peculiar virgin? And yet if it was true, so strangely not one. There was indeed something here which I could not bear. The loss of Crystal's innocence, a tie with childhood, a refuge, a pure unsullied place? Crystal mixed up with Gunnar, tied right into the middle of that hellish business, no. Gunnar had not told. Did this mean that it had not happened, or did it mean that it was for him too potent a source of nightmare?

Tommy was knitting because I had once said to her, just in order to utter some vague sugary nonsense, 'I love to see you knit, it looks so domestic.' This was not even true. I hated to see her or anybody knit. It reminded me of foul Aunt Bill. It made me feel wolfish. It conjured up images of complacent family life which made me want to vomit. Tommy was knitting an obviously large jersey, designed obviously for me, only I had not given her the pleasure of answering a question about what it was she was knitting. Today, Tommy sitting there quietly click-clicking with those needles while I stared at the ceiling gave me a sense of being an invalid. I was ill and Tommy was my nurse. I was in prison and Tommy was visiting me. Tommy had kidnapped me and was waiting for me to confess. Getting rid of Thomas was proving embarrassingly difficult. I had not the strength or the will to decide even how to get her to leave me now, to get her out of the room, let alone how to induce her to go away and stay away forever. However it did not seem urgent since this was another interim. About Tommy, for the moment, I felt conscienceless. I had told her to go often enough. If she still stayed, her suffering was her affair. She had timidly suggested that we should go to the Round Pond. I had simply shaken my head.

I knew that I ought to go and see Crystal again. That was important. What was she doing now, crying, regretting? I had trained her so well that I knew she would not communicate with me, would not alter the routine one iota. But I ought to go and see her, I ought at least to ring her up. I had left her in the midst of desolation. I had felt, I still felt, a horror of her which I could not control and which I had been unable to conceal. The picture of her stay in Gunnar's house had added a new dimension of horror, a great room, a great space, to my memory of that awful time. Gunnar coming in and saying, 'Anne is dead.' Crystal getting into her nightdress. I would have to live with these images forever and I could not forgive Crystal for imparting them to me. There was only one thing now which seemed to prevent utter misery and ferocious madness from overwhelming me (the sort of ferocity, for instance, which could send Tommy running away screaming) and that was my attentive agonizing anxiety about Kitty and when I should hear from her and when if ever I should see her. Until that awful pain, in which there were deep mysterious grains of joy, was altered by certainty into some other pain (for there was no escape from pain) I had no time to deal even with Crystal and with the urgency of her despair. My whole occupation was waiting.

SUNDAY

The front door bell rang. Laura? Biscuit? Kitty? I was off the bed in a single spring and reached the door. It was Biscuit.

Without interrupting the movement of opening the door I emerged onto the landing, closed the door behind me, and strode towards the stairs. Biscuit followed. I went down the stairs two at a time and on through the hallway and out into the street. The wind was propelling a fine rain. I had neither hat nor coat. I began to walk on down the street, not looking back. I turned the corner and stopped. Biscuit caught up with me. 'Well?' I said.

Biscuit was wearing her duffle coat with the hood pulled over her head. Her little sallow thin face inside looked like a boy's face, a child's face. She fumbled in her pocket and brought out *two* letters. I took them, the soft flung rain already blurring the writing. My name was written on each envelope. One letter was from Kitty, the other from Gunnar.

My head was bursting with anxiety and terror. I wanted to get rid of Biscuit with a violence which could have made me strangle her. I said, 'Good. Now clear off.'

I turned from her and began to walk along fast in the direction of Bayswater station, holding the two letters in my hand in my jacket pocket.

When I reached the station I went to the door of the bar, but it was not yet open. I leaned against the door, my wet shoulders glued to the glass.

Biscuit came in. She saw me, threw back the hood of her coat, took a ticket from a machine, and went on towards the ticket barrier. As she passed me, without turning her head, she said, 'Good-bye'. She passed the barrier and disappeared down the stairs towards the westbound platform.

I was fumbling frenziedly with the letters. I opened Kitty's first. It said, *Do as he asks, please. He must never know I saw you. Thank you and good-bye. K.J.* Then I opened Gunnar's. Gunnar's note was a little longer. *I would like to see you and talk to you, once only, and I hope you will agree to meet me. I suggest this evening, Sunday, about six o'clock at the above address. G.J.*

So Gunnar too used Biscuit post. I put the letters away in my pocket and unglued myself from the door. *Thank you and good-bye.* The end of the quest was in sight, the Lady had already gone. I took a fivepenny ticket and went on down towards the eastbound platform. Sightless, breathless, I waited for an Inner Circle train. Bayswater, Paddington,

SUNDAY

Edgware Road, Baker Street, Great Portland Street, Euston Square, King's Cross . . .

Once again I was an hour early at Cheyne Walk. I had not returned to the flat. I spent most of the day on the Inner Circle. At lunch-time I stopped at Sloane Square and endeavoured to eat a sandwich. I drank a cautious amount of whisky, then mounted the train again. About four thirty I was back at Sloane Square. The rain had stopped, but a cold east wind was blowing. I was still, of course, coatless. I walked briskly along the King's Road and then down towards the river, passing Gunnar's house at about five o'clock. A light showed above the curtains on the first floor. I wondered if Kitty and Gunnar were there talking about me. I wandered a bit in the gardens and inspected a statue by Epstein representing a woman tearing her clothes off. I went into Chelsea Old Church and wandered about in the half dark reading the memorial tablets and wondering if when I was alone with Gunnar I would faint. At six o'clock exactly I rang the door bell.

Gunnar opened the door. A sort of gust of emotion came out of the house together with the warmth of the central heating.

'Good evening. Nice of you to come.'

'Not at all.'

'Will you come upstairs?'

These astounding words were uttered.

I followed him up the stairs. The place smelt of solid well-to-do warmth and expensive furnishing and Kitty's perfume. I followed Gunnar up into the drawing-room.

The beautiful room was as menacing to me as if I had passed under a portcullis. Or perhaps it was more like the sultan's palace where you cross the marble courtyard and pass by the fountain and walk in under the mosaic colonnade to the room full of soft hangings where you are to be strangled. I had an instantaneous vision as I came in of Gunnar and me locked in frightful combat staggering about breaking

260

vases and plates and lamps. A room to bleed in, a room to die in.

It was indeed a beautiful room. I had seen a number of well-appointed drawing-rooms by this time, Laura Impiatt's for instance, and Clifford's, but this room was the most casually gorgeous I had ever entered. By comparison, Laura's taste was pretentious, Clifford's was cold. This was a big room with big confident furniture in it, lit by many lamps upon many tables. A large Chinese lacquer cabinet dominated one end, a carved marble mantelpiece with an immense gilt mirror over it the other. The carpet, which appeared to be Aubusson, strewed the centre of the room with roses inside an elliptical yellow medallion, and stretched away into shadow beneath tables, desks, bookcases. It was a grand man's grand room: a far cry from the muddled prettiness of a room which had existed once in north Oxford.

There was a marked silence. The windows must have been double-glazed. The embankment traffic was the faintest murmur, merely perhaps a vibration. Gunnar walked and I still followed to where a small fire was burning beneath the festooned marble of the mantelpiece. On a low table was a tray with bottles and glasses and cigarettes in a malachite box.

'Would you like a drink?'

'Thank you, yes. Whisky and soda.'

'Do you smoke?'

'No, thank you.'

'Didn't you have a coat?'

'A coat? No.'

After this piece of conversation Gunnar busied himself with the drinks. He filled a cut glass tumbler with whisky and soda, then went on holding it for a moment, looking into the fire and breathing hard, before handing it to me. He poured out some whisky for himself. He took a cigarette, then threw it back. He did not ask me to sit down. Then he began to look at me. We looked at each other.

It was an odd looking, like a sort of staring through time. As sometimes the cinema plays with a man's features, wrapping them in mist, then changing them from age to youth, so we looked. Gunnar, in the subdued golden glitter-laden light of his own drawing-room, looked younger than I had seen him look since his return into my life. In fact he seemed to have been getting steadily younger since that first moment when I had passed him upon the stairs. He had an outdoor

261

look, only now more that of a sea captain than of a rugger blue. His face was weathered, larger but without flabbiness, more commanding, his bigness formidable still. He was wearing a soft dark tweed suit and a radiantly white shirt with a surprisingly gaudy tie. I was wearing my shabby greasy everyday office suit which had not been improved by a lot of lying about on beds and travelling in the underground and being rained upon. We stared at each other, standing there with a tense quietness which could have been the prelude to the reeling wrestling death struggle which I had been picturing just now.

Gunnar's look, however, was curiously objective. It was not angry, it rather expressed puzzlement, curiosity, perhaps a fastidious distaste. It was obviously going to be extremely difficult to begin the conversation. I was rigid with emotion, only my lower jaw had a slight tendency to tremble. I kept turning my drink round and round, feeling the criss-cross pattern on the glass. I had no conception of anything to say and had deliberately throughout the day avoided the invention of any possible speech. I wanted to be ready for anything, for incoherent fury, for emotional breakdown. I had not expected quite this awful coolness.

'Thank you for coming,' said Gunnar.

'Not at all.'

We had said that before.

Gunnar began to walk to and fro, a step or two to the window curtains, a step or two back to the hearth rug, rather as Kitty had paced upon the wooden jetty. Where was Kitty now? Was she at the door listening? This quietness could not last. What outburst would end it?

'I wanted to see you *just once* and talk about the past,' said Gunnar. 'Just once, because I think that will be enough. More would be an imposition. And I don't imagine you particularly want to see me.'

'I imagine you don't particularly want to see me, in general that is —' I felt suddenly that I was going to be stupid, and the idea of appearing stupid to Gunnar filled me with a black ferocious misery. He would say to Kitty, and perhaps this would be the great moment of relief: after all, he is a little stupid man.

'No, of course. And obviously here there can't be any sort of ordinary — conversation — or,' he sought for the word, 'armistice'.

'Or — reconciliation — No, of course not.'

262

But why not? Was not this the only thing worth striving for, the only thing that really mattered? I felt the anguish, the tongue-tied stupidity, the sense of being gripped by a relentless and mocking past.

'I daresay you detest me,' said Gunnar. 'I messed up your life and one naturally hates people one has injured.'

'Naturally.' It was as if Gunnar were putting the words into my mouth. And yet the old hatred and anger spoke for me with an authority which no gentleness could shake. 'I messed up *your* life.' Stupidity.

'Quite. But look—this is a—almost a technical question. You know, it has done me a lot of good just to see you.'

This could have been a humane remark, but in the context it sounded almost clinical.

'You can perhaps have no idea,' Gunnar went on, 'how obsessed I have been with the past. Some people can get over tragedies in their lives. I have never managed to get over this one.'

'Neither have I,' I said. 'I have never stopped feeling guilty and—' My words lacked conviction. What place could there be in this conversation run by Gunnar for any sort of asking of pardon?

'I don't think I want to know about your feelings,' said Gunnar. He said it judiciously, not vindictively. 'I have been entirely selfish in demanding this conversation. And it is not without its risks.'

'You mean we might fight?'

'No, no, of course not. I mean, where old awful things in one's mind are concerned, a mistake or an accident could have serious consequences.'

'A mistake or an accident?'

'Yes. All our words are so loaded. You could say something which I could never forget.'

'I must be careful what I say then, mustn't I,' I said. He was cool, I was becoming cold. I thought, he has grown old after all, he has become a pompous ass. He has taken this risk, but he will not allow anything violent or truthful to emerge. And I cannot tell the truth, I have almost trained myself not to. And we are not in the presence of anything which can compel truth from us. What would it be like anyway, that explosion? The room would clatter and break after all.

'Quite,' said Gunnar. He was silent for a moment. We had both put our glasses down on the table without drinking.

'But can you not formulate what you want? Do you want actually to discuss the past?'

Gunnar was silent again for a bit. Then he said, 'No. I don't think so. I used to think I wanted to. Do people who have been in concentration camps together reminisce? I doubt it. I have spent years in deep analysis. I have talked about it all so much—'

The idea of Gunnar describing all *that* to some enigmatic man in Hampstead or New York made me feel sick. I said impatiently, 'What do you want then?'

'I thought I wanted to talk about Anne,' said Gunnar.

The name quivered in the room, seeming to make it tremble and ring.

'But you don't want to?' Did I? I desperately wanted something, which I could now as if for the first time glimpse and which could only be got here, and which I was not going to be allowed to receive.

'Possibly it is enough simply to utter her name in your presence.'

'You have done so,' I said. 'What else do you want to do in my presence?'

'It is as if,' said Gunnar, ignoring my remark, gazing at the fire, 'I wanted at last to get rid of Anne. That may seem a terrible way to put it. But—you see—it isn't the real Anne of course. The real Anne is dead.'

There was a silence in which I could hear my own heavy breathing, as if I were gasping for air, and his too.

'She is dead,' said Gunnar, picking it up as if it were a line in poetry, sighing, 'and gone from us and we must respect her—absolute—absence. *She* is out of this. What remains is a sort of a—foul ghost. I have felt this especially—because it has been so—awfully unfair to—to people one lives with now.'

I was silent, spellbound. I wanted now to hear where his eloquence would lead him.

'Her ghost,' he said slowly, 'not her at all, but something else, made up out of the vile stuff, the rags and tatters of my mind, and sopping up somehow, blackened and stained by, all that awful hatred and passion for revenge—'

'Hatred of me?'

'Yes. I somehow—made her carry it. Do you understand?'

I was not sure. But I felt the hatred and it paralysed me.

He went on, 'If she had been killed in an aeroplane crash or had died of cancer, I would have been shattered with

264

grief but I would have recovered. But since she died—as she did die—I have never been able to divide—in my soul—that grief from a sort of living burning hatred and a—wickedness which is so deep—it is the deepest thing of all—'

Is there nothing deeper than wickedness then, I wondered. But I did not say this because it was dawning on me, and with a terrible final sense of despair, that really Gunnar did not want me to talk at all. As he had said at the start, he did not want to know about my feelings. I had said to myself, I had said, oh God, to Kitty, that I was to be merely an instrument. This was surely the perfection of penance, of restitution, to work mechanically for the wronged one, to work in silence as on a treadmill, asking nothing for oneself. But I had never, even when I spoke of it, pictured an operation which, for me, was to be so totally profitless.

'How will talking to me help this?' I said coldly, stupidly, playing my role.

'It is no good talking to an analyst,' said Gunnar as if he had not heard me. 'In fact I have never said *this* to an analyst. I have only just really been able to formulate it since you came into the room. I have got to get rid of her, not of *her*, but of this filthy ghost thing—and let her alone and let her be alone as the dead should be—at last—and doing that means—getting rid of *you*.'

It sounded, in that faintly sighed-through silence, like the announcement of intention to commit murder, and it occurred to me with a strange poignancy that if Gunnar were now to try to kill me I should not resist. There would be no raging and wrestling to and fro, only the blood upon the Aubusson carpet. I said coldly, almost nastily, 'Well, I'm quite ready to be got rid of. At your service. How do we set about it?'

'We are doing it,' said Gunnar. 'You see, I imagined you as—as if you were a sort of—dreadful being—a sort of vile cruel malevolent—killer.' His voice trembled.

'I suppose I was.'

'No. That's the point. You were just a—just a—'

'Poor fish, victim of chance, muddler, little lecherous adulterer—'

'Well—'

'And now you can *see* it.'

'And now I can see it. And that brings with it—a sort of pity for *her*—which enables me—which may enable me—to leave her alone. You see—what was so awful was that I blamed her too.'

This was a simple enough idea but as he said it I realized that though I had perhaps conceived it I had never felt it. Poor Anne, oh poor Anne. If only I could utter those words. But the cure was not for me, nothing here was for me. I had simply to be quiet and to run the hazard of the 'mistakes and accidents', those things which might be said and never forgotten. I was there to be exhibited, to be despised, to be seen at last, not as a murderous villain, but as a small mean semi-conscious malignancy, a cog in the majestic wheel of chance.

'It was a muddle,' I said. 'There was — an accident.'

'Yes,' said Gunnar softly, still not looking at me, 'if I could only see — and feel — that.'

'Do you want me to — ?'

'Of course not.'

There was a short silence, he staring at the fire, moving his head gently to and fro, his blue eyes vague, as if some gentleness were coming to be in them. But not for me. I felt exasperation, misery, fear, the trembling in the lower jaw, coldness.

Gunnar picked up his glass and gulped a little. He said, 'It is remarkable.'

'What is?'

'The effect of saying certain things, of simply thinking certain things, thinking them perhaps for the first time, in your presence. It's a remarkable — catalyst.'

'Hadn't you better hire me on a permanent basis to sit in the corner of the room like a dog? Your guests wouldn't mind, would they?'

'It's better than — my God — all those years of analysis, all those conceited analysts, how I hated them, all those tens of thousands of dollars — One of them said this actually.'

'That you should see me?'

'Yes. "Why don't you just go and have a look at the guy?" he said.'

'You've looked. Has it done the trick? A little early to tell.'

'It is early to tell,' said Gunnar, and his eyes were very dreamy now. 'But I think — that — whatever can be done is done — and I won't be waiting for it any more. And after all when it comes it's something very simple, a dialectical change, the end of a nightmare, the breaking of something which can now naturally fragment away.'

'I don't quite understand,' I said, 'but I hope you're right. How do we continue the treatment?'

'Oh, there will be no need for me to trouble you again,' said Gunnar.

'I know you said "once" but I— It now seems to me— It's certainly no trouble to me—I'd be very glad to turn up—'

'No, no,' said Gunnar. 'It's much better left as it is. Another meeting would weaken it—'

'And of course there are the risks!'

'Yes. I am sorry to be so enigmatic and self-centred but I have been forced to live very much inside my own mind.' He hesitated. 'Of course I am being perfectly selfish—'

Was this a cue? I could not think, I could not feel, and the moment passed.

Gunnar was being objective again. 'This much I suppose I learnt from analysis, to pull emotion, feeling, what lies deeper and more awfully close to the live heart, out into the open a bit more; to apprehend connections and let terrible things own their feelings without disguise. To let the dog see the rabbit, as we used to say, and let the rabbit also see the dog. Only this is awfully hard to do. This is why the analyst helps, and why—'

'I have helped.'

'You have helped, just by standing here like a—'

'Deaf and dumb child or a bedpost or—'

'Yes, yes. I am most grateful. Something has certainly changed, and such changes are usually irreversible. One's deep mind is indifferent to time. You are here, you will be here, the efficacy will not fade—'

'Except that I will not be here.'

'You will not be here. After all, that would be impossible, wouldn't it?'

'Impossible.'

'I mean—'

'Naturally I am going to resign from the office,' I said. 'There is no need for you to run the risk of meeting me on the stairs. Since I shall be timelessly available in your mind as a curative agency, it would be a pity, would it not, if the real me were to intrude.'

Gunnar smiled at the fire. 'I am glad,' he said, 'that you have turned out to be this sort of person. It has made this exercise of pure egoism on my part so much easier.'

'What sort of person have I turned out to be?'

'I feared—oh—emotions—appeals, sentiment, something—mushy. I feared *you* might need help.'

'How do you know I don't since, as you say yourself, you are unwilling to investigate my feelings?'

'Well, one has one's impression. Of course you have resented being used. Your annoyance may even have been valuable.'

' "Annoyance"?'

'I mean, it has kept the temperature down. That is what I needed. I am very grateful. There was something else I thought of asking you, but I think after all—I needn't. Thank you. Thank you.'

'Success of exhibit A.'

'And I do appreciate what you say about leaving the office. Of course I expected you to go. May I offer you my best wishes for your next employment?'

'Thank you.'

'And now—I believe you said you came without a coat?'

I moved towards the door. As I came out the smell of Kitty's perfume seemed exceptionally strong. I walked down the stairs with Gunnar's heavy tread behind me. I reached the front door and opened it. The cold air reached in and grabbed me.

'Well, that's all, is it? I'm glad it was satisfactory.'

'Yes,' he said. 'I think we did well, yes, as well as possible in the circumstances.'

'I shall be leaving the office at once.'

'Good. Thank you. Good-bye then.'

'Good-bye.'

Neither of us moved to shake hands. I marched out and the door was promptly shut behind me.

I walked on into the embankment garden, then turned to look back at the house. Did I imagine it or was there a face looking out from a darkened window on the second floor? I walked on and crossed the road to the river. The tide was in, high against the wall, smelling cold and faintly rotten, carrying its jostling debris almost to within reach of my hand. The wind was blowing in sharp cutting gusts. I began to walk along in an eastward direction, then turned north towards the King's Road.

Gunnar had had his revenge after all. This was better, far better than physical assault, better than smashing my face in or breaking my ribs. I felt I had suffered a sort of spiritual evisceration. I had had the ass's head of a mean and petty cynicism placed upon me and I had worn it. I closed my eyes and ground my teeth at the thought of the things I had said and the tone I had used. And how I would remember and remember! Gunnar had claimed to have me timelessly available: and I too had with me forever this image of the thing that I had seemed, that I had been. I had accepted Gunnar's implied assumption that I did not care deeply, that I had become a little smart hard sarcastic resentful man. Did he believe this of me? Probably, and this was the ruthless logic of the matter which I must endure, it was not really necessary to Gunnar to form any view of my state of mind. If he was prepared to make the after all considerable concession of admitting that I could help him, he had surely the right to use me as he pleased. He need not trouble himself to make out what I thought. He may even have felt that it would be indelicate to do so. It had suited him, in the light of his paramount need, to regard me as a cynic, and I had done everything I could to confirm his view. And he had said good-bye. They had all said good-bye now, Biscuit, Gunnar, Kitty. The whole extraordinary business was over. And I was back where I belonged, where my childhood had condemned me to be, alone, out in the cold without a coat.

MONDAY

'WHAT'S the matter with Hilary?' Edith Witcher asked Reggie Farbottom.

'He's moping about his girl.'

'What's she done, got pregnant?'

'No, got slung out of the panto.'

'Poor old Hilo, after all that intriguing. No wonder he looks as if he was going to be sick.'

'He does look green, doesn't he.'

'Perhaps he's got the 'flu as well.'

'Shall we try and communicate with him?'

'It's like sending a space probe to Mars trying to communicate with Hilary.'

'Never mind, let's try. Hilary!'

'Hilar*ee*! Yoo-hoo! Hilo!' .

'Yes?' I was at my desk and they had been talking behind my back. It was a cold yellow morning, now Monday, Big Ben visible.

'Hilary, are you receiving us?'

'Yes.'

'Are you all right? Have you got the 'flu?'

'Yes. No.'

'What does he mean, yes, no?'

'Yes, I'm all right. No, I have not got the 'flu.'

'Hilary —'

'Yes?'

'What are you writing there? I bet it's not office work.'

'It's a letter to his girl.'

'As a matter of fact, it's my letter of resignation.'

'Of course, he couldn't possibly stay on after his girl had been slung out of the panto, he's got some dignity!'

'We are in luck, this is one of Hilary's witty days.'

I sealed up my letter of resignation and sent it off by Skinker, who also asked me, but more kindly, if I was feeling all right. Skinker had recovered from his 'flu, and told me all about it, but Arthur was apparently now down with it. This was good news since I could do without seeing Arthur at present and also he would not be expecting me tomorrow since he knew how I felt about virus infections. I had now one month in which to find another job. It would not be easy.

I felt desperately tired and did not even try to work. I had come back to the flat about midnight. I did not inquire at what time Tommy had given up waiting for me. I left the office at about twelve and telephoned Crystal from a call box near Scotland Yard. I very rarely telephoned her although I knew that she would be made glad by hearing my voice, and that she was sitting there at home sewing, lonely and thinking about me.

'Hello. It's me.'

'Oh—good—darling.'

'What are you doing?'

'Sewing.'

'What are you sewing? Is it the cocktail dress for the new lady?'

'No, I've finished that.'

'Is it nice?'

'Smashing.'

'What are you sewing?'

'I'm altering a child's coat for the woman next door.'

'Oh. Crystal—'

'Yes?'

'You're not being unhappy about that—what you said to me last time?'

Silence. Crystal's tears gathering. 'No.'

'Don't be. I'm sorry I was awful. I'm sorry I didn't stay and eat the fish cakes. Were they nice?'

'I didn't eat them then. I ate them cold for Sunday lunch. They were nice.'

'I'm glad. Crystal—'

'Yes?'

'Don't be sad, I couldn't bear it if you were sad. It doesn't matter, nothing in the past matters. I mean, of course it matters, but I should be so wretched if you—'

'I'm all right. Don't worry about me, darling, I'm perfectly all right. Really. Really and truly.'

'That's my good girl.'

Silence.

'Crystal, could I come to supper on Wednesday evening?'

'Yes—yes, of course—'

'Good, usual time. See you then.'

She would never ask to see me. She would wait, always, she would wait.

I ate my lunch at the Sherlock Holmes, or rather I drank my lunch accompanied by a few potato crisps. I returned to the office about half past two. Edith was not there. I could hear Reggie's voice in the Registry, upraised in some passage of sexual badinage.

I went to my desk and glanced mechanically at my in tray. A letter from Gunnar was lying on the top.

I seized it and pulled it open, leaning forward over the desk and gasping.

There is one other thing I want to ask you and then I shall cease to trouble you. It will take two minutes only. Perhaps you will step down to my room some time this afternoon. G.J.

I sat down and for about ten minutes concentrated on breathing normally. Then I got up and began to walk down the stairs towards the first floor. I wished heartily that I had not drunk so much at lunch, but I could not possibly have waited, I had to see Gunnar at once. I passed Clifford Larr on the stairs. We ignored each other.

As I reached Gunnar's door I had another crisis of breathing. I stood for a moment, then fearing to be observed I knocked, heard the murmur within, and entered.

He was alone, sitting as before in the semi-dark, behind the big desk with the green-shaded lamp. His shoulders were hunched up in a defensive attitude and I could see his eyes anxiously peering. He looked so vulnerable that for a moment I felt as if last night had been wiped out and we were to have, after all, another chance. However he spoke very coldly, and with the same slightly mocking, slightly contemptuous and absolutely constraining politeness.

'I am sorry to trouble you again, it will not take much of your time. I mentioned yesterday that there was one other relevant thing into which perhaps I need not go. But I find it is necessary to do so after all if I am, from my own point of view, which is all I know or wish to know anything about, to clear this matter up.'

Standing in front of him, also in darkness, I watched his large formidably clean right hand, moving nervously on the desk in the circle of light, shifting papers and trailing about. 'Yes?'

'This may seem a curious request, but — I wonder if I could just once, I repeat just once, and just briefly, visit your sister?'

This was completely unexpected. I felt a confused frightful emotion and total uncertainty about how to answer. Was

Gunnar assuming that I knew, or that I did not know, about what had happened, if it had happened? I said, 'Why?'

'I want to see her. Not at my house. Preferably at her flat or wherever she lives.'

'Just like you wanted to see me?'

'No,' said Gunnar, 'not just like that.'

'What makes you think she isn't married and living in New Zealand?'

'I found her name in the London telephone book.'

I was silent for a moment or two. He was examining his hands. I said, 'I'll ask her.'

'Will you? That's good of you. And let me know by letter one way or the other, either in the office or at Cheyne Walk. I am free on Wednesday evening, or next Monday.'

'I'll let you know.'

'Thank you.'

The words were dismissive. I stood a moment, then, as he still did not look at me, I turned on my heel to go. I stopped at the door. 'By the way, I have sent in my letter of resignation.'

'That's good. It remains for me to repeat my good wishes and say good-bye again.'

'Good-bye.' I went out.

I hurried straight on downstairs and out of the office, once more coatless. The east wind was cutting through the yellowish murk. I reached a brightly lit telephone box.

'Crystal. Hello. It's me again. It seems to be telephone day.'

'Hello, my dear.'

'Crystal, listen. I've seen Gunnar.'

Silence.

'Listen, he wants to see you.'

Silence.

'He says briefly and just once. Shall I tell him to go to hell?'

'Did you talk about —?'

'No, of course not. He didn't say anything and neither did I. But, Crystal, darling, you don't have to see him. I felt I had to tell you, it would have been wrong not to, but really there's no point, is there, and it would upset you —'

'Does *she* know?'

'No, she doesn't know.'

'Are you sure?'

'Yes. She said— Never mind, I'm sure. And Gunnar doesn't want you to come to his house, he'd come to you.'

'He'd come *here*?'

'Yes, why not, he's not God. But really I think—'

'Yes, I'll see him.'

'Crystal, you don't have to—'

'I want to. When will he come?'

'Oh Christ. He said would Wednesday evening—or next Monday—'

'Tell him Wednesday.'

'But you're seeing me on Wednesday.'

'I must see him, darling—and I couldn't wait till Monday— I'd like to see him—the earliest he can come—'

'Oh, all right. I hope you know what you're doing. I'll say between seven and eight on Wednesday.'

I rang off and stood rigid and paralysed in the lighted box until an impatient person waiting outside began to tap on the window. Ought I to have told her?

I went slowly back to the office. There was an official letter accepting my resignation with regret and pointing out that since I was under fifty I would forfeit my pension rights. I wrote a note to Gunnar giving Crystal's address and saying she would see him on Wednesday between seven and eight. Reggie and Edith were playing battleships. Out of sheer kindness of heart they asked me if I would like to play. I must have been looking terrible.

At five o'clock I left the building. The cold yellow day, which had never had any real daylight in it, was thickening into a misty fog. Great waves of gauzy yellow obscurity were rolling in from the river. I was beginning to walk along with the usual mob in the direction of Westminster station when I became aware that I was being followed by Biscuit. When I reached Parliament Square corner, instead of turning towards the station I crossed the traffic onto the big island in the middle of the square where the statues are. I walked along, away from Churchill, and sat down on a seat at the far end, opposite Big Ben, underneath the statue of Dizzy (I always loved Dizzy because of Mr Osmand). For a moment I thought that this manœuvre might have lost me Biscuit, but she appeared, padding through the gloom, and sat down beside me. The traffic encircled us, the fog hid us, nobody was near. Big Ben struck the quarter hour. I gave a groan and put my arms around Biscuit and laid my head on her shoulder, nuzzling beneath the dropped hood of her duffle coat, feeling with my cheek through the rough material the frail prominence of her collar bone.

'Biscuit, I'm done for, I can't stand it any longer, they're killing me.'

'No, no—'

'I've even lost my job. Look, Biscuit, how much do you really know about this business?'

'Nothing. How can I, I am a servant. But won't you tell me? Perhaps I could help you.'

'I'm a servant too. Maybe I could get a job as a butler. Perhaps Lady Kitty would take me on.'

'Please tell me, Hilary.'

'I bet you know all about it, you secretive oriental girl. Why are you here anyway? I thought we'd said good-bye.'

'I've brought you a letter.'

'Oh no!'

'Here.' She brought the envelope out of her pocket and thrust it into my hand. Kitty's writing.

'Look, Biscuit, you stay here, will you? I'll just take a turn and read this.'

I left her and walked away along the path. Big Ben's bright hazy face said five-twenty. I stopped beside some gloomy bushes with seemingly black leaves which stirred a little in the wind, dripping water. A lamp across the garden gave a little light. I opened Kitty's letter.

That meeting you had with Gunnar was no good at all, it was worse than useless. I listened at the door, I hope you don't mind. It has not helped him at all, he is absolutely wild as if he might go mad. You must see him again, you simply must, and you must not let him run the conversation, you must somehow break him down. I am very upset. I will explain. Please come to Cheyne Walk at six on Thursday. Gunnar will be elsewhere. Do nothing until you have seen me.

K.J.

I put the letter away and raised my face to Big Ben, and Big Ben shone upon it. London, which had been an inert listless noisy mass of senseless dark misery about me was suddenly taut, humming, clarified. There was a road again from me to Kitty. She needed me. I would see her again. I would see Gunnar again. All would yet be well.

I walked slowly back to where Biscuit was sitting, legs

outstretched, hands in pockets, gazing expressionlessly at the moving mass of passing cars. She turned and looked at me as I sat down. She had put her hood up again. 'You are pleased with your letter.'

'Yes.'

'You look quite different.'

'Yes. Tell her—just—that I will come.'

She began to get up but I pulled her back, and thrust the hood away from her face. In the light of the distant lamp, in the light of Big Ben I saw her pale little face looking up, all wet and glistening with the damp fog. And now suddenly she looked so tired, almost old, a little old woman from the East. I put my arms round her and laid my lips against her cold mouth. Then the next moment she was struggling fiercely in my grasp like a wild animal. Her feet slithered on the wet pavement, she got up, thrusting me away, then as I began to rise and she turned to go she hit me hard across the face. Something struck my coat and fell to the ground at my feet. Then Biscuit was gone.

I sat down again. The blow, though perfectly deliberate, had been mainly the swinging impact of damp duffle coat sleeve, rather resembling the proverbial slap in the face with a wet fish. I began to peer at the ground to see what it was that had fallen. There was nothing there but a stone. I picked it up. A blackish smooth elliptical stone. I stared at it. It was the stone which I had given to Biscuit in the Leningrad garden, years and years ago, on the first occasion when we met. I put it in my pocket. I pondered. I found myself, for some reason or other, thinking about Tommy. There was no doubt that I was a failure. I had been cruel to Tommy. I had lost my job. Biscuit had slapped me. Possibly, to leave aside more serious failings, I was a cad. But at six o'clock on Thursday Kitty would be waiting for me at Cheyne Walk. I got up and made my way slowly to the station and took the train to Sloane Square and sat in the bar. After a whisky and ginger ale peace descended. I had an occupation: counting the hours till Thursday evening. I felt almost happy.

MONDAY

It was a little more than an hour later and I was inserting my key in the door at the flat in Lexham Gardens. The heavens might be falling and the earth cracking but it was Monday and Clifford Larr would be waiting for me and the table would be set for supper.

I opened the door. The table was set. Clifford was in the kitchen stirring something.

'Hello, darling.'

'Hello,' I said, taking off my overcoat.

'Is your cold better?'

'What cold?'

'The one you allegedly had last Monday.'

'Oh that. What's for supper?'

'Lentil soup. Chicken casserole. Stilton cheese.'

'Good.'

'Tell me something.'

'What?'

'Anything. I'm bored.'

'A girl just slapped my face.'

'Excellent. Tommy?'

'No. Lady Kitty's maid.'

'You are *in*, aren't you, having your face slapped by the maid. I suppose you tried to kiss her?'

'Yes.'

'You behave like a lout. I suppose it is early conditioning. What does Lady Kitty think?'

'She doesn't know.'

'What makes you imagine that?'

What indeed? Did Biscuit tell Kitty of my stupid kisses? I was surrounded by terrible dangerous mysteries. I felt exasperated, frightened shame. 'That's all I'm fit for, kissing maids behind bushes and getting slapped. I've resigned my job.'

Clifford whistled thoughtfully on three notes, still stirring. 'Why?'

'Gunnar.'

'You've seen him again, since our talk in the park on Wednesday.'

'Yes. I saw him yesterday.'

'And he told you to leave the office?'

'More or less. It's not a bit like you thought.' I poured myself out a glass of sherry and sat down on my usual chair.

'Didn't you have a touching reconciliation after all?'

'No.'

'A fight?'

'No.'

'Then what on earth?'

'We had a clinical interview.'

'I am fascinated. Describe it.'

'Never boring, am I. Can I have some of those nuts?'

'Yes, but not too many. Go on.'

'He hates me,' I said, 'and it's, for him, not part of the treatment to stop doing so. That's just the thing I didn't foresee. Like you, I thought it would be either a reconciliation or a fight. And as I don't think he's a complete fool I imagined that if he asked to see me it would be for some sort of reconciliation.'

'You didn't say that on Wednesday.'

'Like you, I don't always say what I think.'

'I didn't know you were so optimistic.'

'I wasn't. But I suppose I hoped—I don't know what I thought—'

'Your behaviour is so unlike mine that sometimes understanding simply fails. You *hoped*, did you? Can you still do *that*? Surely you saw that it was totally naive to expect reconciliation—humility, sincerity, all play-acting of course, but still a lot to ask from a successful man of the world like Gunnar?'

'But on Wednesday you said you thought there would be just that, that I'd be shown off as a sort of prodigal son, you said "I can see it all".'

'As you recently observed, I do not always say what I think.'

'Ah. You feared it?'

'You are a slow man, but you sometimes arrive.'

'Well, you needn't have feared any friendship between me and Gunnar. Nothing could be more impossible.'

'I find that satisfactory. But you have not described this clinical scene.'

'It was all set up by one of Gunnar's analysts. He just wanted to see me to sort of get rid of emotions, like making a bomb safe by a controlled explosion. Only there was no explosion. We were both as cold as ice.'

'Come on, this is getting dull again. Tell me something that he said.'

'He said it did him good to utter Anne's name in my

presence. He said his hatred of me had sort of kept her going as an awful ghost.'

'Ah yes'—said Clifford thoughtfully, staring at me. 'That makes sense. I can understand that.'

'I'm not sure that I can. That was about it. He did all the talking. I behaved like an exceptionally stupid and callous zombie. He made me into one.'

'I can understand that too.'

'Then he said good-bye forever and told me to go.'

'After having instructed you to resign your job.'

'Yes.'

'However you saw him again today.'

'How did you know?'

'I followed you back down the stairs. What happened today?'

I was certainly not going to tell Clifford that dreadful story about Crystal and Gunnar. 'Nothing much.'

'You lie. Does he know you've seen his wife?'

'No.'

'Have you seen her again, since Wednesday?'

'Yes.'

'Are you in love with her?'

'Yes.'

'Of course you would be. You really are stupid. You are an absolute novice about human nature. A woman like that could do anything with you. And she isn't even clever. She's simply spoilt and confident. She's a silly romantic female who likes involving men in little mysterious plots. Have you kissed her?'

'No!'

'Only the maid.'

'Only the maid.'

'How do you see the maid, incidentally?'

'The maid brings the letters.'

'Typical. I expect she spends all her time trotting round London delivering secret notes. You don't imagine you're the only one, do you?'

'Yes, I do,' I said. 'In this sense. No one else is related to Gunnar and to his wife in the perfectly extraordinary way that I am related.'

'You sound quite proud of it. When are you going to kiss Lady Kitty?'

'Never! Look, you haven't understood. I may see Gunnar once again, I may see her once again. But neither of them

279

wants me around. I'm just a curative agent, a catalyst. Lady Kitty isn't interested in *me*, she's interested in curing her husband's obsessions.'

'You could be very wrong about that,' said Clifford thoughtfully. 'And how about Crystal?'

'How do you mean, how about Crystal?'

'Crystal must fit in somewhere.'

'Crystal doesn't fit in anywhere. Crystal is as unconnected with real life as a saint on a pillar.'

'Quite a nice image. But no. Perhaps there will be cosiness. I should like to think of Lady Kitty going to visit Crystal with a canikin of hot soup in a basket.'

'Shut up, Clifford, will you.'

'Can't you see that you're being entangled?'

'I wish I was being entangled! I'm not, I'm being amputated! Christ, I'm leaving my job, I'm moving right away into a different world. What more can they want? I'll have served my purpose and I'll go.'

'What is your new job?'

'I haven't got one! I only resigned today! I don't know if I'll be able to get one! I'll probably end up on National Assistance or selling matches. I'm really done for now, can't you see that, I've been going steadily down hill, now I'm really heading for the gutter, where, as you so often point out I began and belong!' I had not, till this moment, seen it so clearly myself. I would see Kitty once again. And after that, absolute smash.

'How interesting,' said Clifford. 'Perhaps you will take to drink and become a familiar shambling figure, sitting on the steps of the Whitehall offices, begging your ex-colleagues for pound notes.'

'Little you bloody care.'

'Is that a personal appeal?'

'You've done nothing but needle me since I arrived, you never do anything but needle me.'

'Don't break that glass, it's one of my better ones.'

'I'm going. As you so clearly suggest, it's time for me to disappear from your elegant set-up. And you can find some nice quiet little queer to visit you on Mondays henceforth. All right, I'm not going to break your fucking glass. *Goodbye.*'

I jumped up. Clifford moved quickly between me and the door and took the glass out of my hand. He held my hand. 'Darling. Stop it. Darling.'

I sat down again.

He said, 'Can't you understand human conversation? Can't you *read* it, can't you read *me*? I should have thought it would be easy enough.' He touched the side of my head gently.

'All right. Sorry.' This sort of thing had happened before.

We went into the dining-room and started on the lentil soup. It was excellent.

TUESDAY

My dearest, it is me again. I feel I am such a drag in your life. I waited on Sunday till five and Christopher was so tired of me then and I was so tired of myself, I went away. I suppose you left like that again on purpose to hurt me and make me realize at last that you really don't want me. And yet when I was sitting beside you and I was knitting and you were lying on the bed, we were so quiet and peaceful together like two married persons and I could not but believe that I was a comfort to you. I know you are in trouble, but it seems that I cannot help. I can only annoy you, and this grieves me so terribly. I am in such pain. And it can't be very nice for you to love another man's wife, surely you see there is no future in it. I expect the rumour must be all over the office by now. I told Freddie definitely that I would not play Peter, so you are free of me on that score. Only I cannot cannot believe that things are over between us. I feel as connected with you as if I were your mother. You cannot get rid of me. You will recover from your trouble and you will find me waiting. I love you. Forgive all my mistakes. I will expect you on Friday as usual.

> Your loyal loving Thomas.

It was early Tuesday morning and I was sitting at my desk in the office, the others having not yet arrived, and reading Tommy's usual Tuesday morning letter from King's Lynn. The reference to 'another man's wife' turned me cold with horror until I realized that of course poor Tommy meant Laura Impiatt! This belief was something of a convenience and I had no intention of dislodging it from Tommy's silly little head. The notion that I loved Laura was an innocent blind, a trivial tepid cover-up of the dreadful truth. Let it stand. The fact that Laura, in her dotty way, loved me, or thought she did, would help to make the useful fiction more plausible, and may even have led Laura to hint to Tommy that I loved her! No harm would be done. Whereas the monstrous fact of my love for Gunnar's wife would, if it ever emerged, wreck my mind, wreck the universe. Would I see

282

Tommy as usual on Friday? It seemed very doubtful. Friday was very far away and huge events loomed between.

I had come to the office, although I knew I would not be able to work, because it was my obligation to turn up for a further month and also, and more terribly, because I could not think what else to do. I must find other employment. But how? How was this done? I had never greatly enjoyed my job, but it had been safe and mildly amusing. Could I now sell myself outside the Civil Service in the wicked world of free enterprise where a brilliant Oxford 'first' would cut no ice? Should I try something quite different, such as school teaching? Perhaps it was not necessary to resign from the Service at all, would it not do if I simply got a transfer to another department? Why had I been in such a desperate hurry to resign? Reflection told me however that I had been right. To negotiate a transfer might take months and months, during which time I would every day be running the risk of offending Gunnar with the sight of me.

Had Kitty's note of yesterday altered the situation? No. I might talk to Gunnar once again, or I might not. But I did not think that another talk with him would make any difference to our relations or to the advisability of vanishing. Herein I differed from my darling. Kitty, whose silliness, as delineated by Clifford, I could perfectly credit, though I loved her, still imagined that Gunnar would 'break down', that he would need, to put it crudely, to forgive me for the sake of his own peace of mind. Kitty still believed in the 'reconciliation scene'. I had stupidly, surreptitiously, self-deceivingly believed in it, until lately, myself. But now no more. In fact, my attitude to Gunnar was in process of hardening a little. I had been ready to enact my guilt for his benefit. He was not interested. All right. If he could play it cool, so could I. We could, at any rate, feign a coolness which would leave the deep things untouched and enable us to disengage from each other without hideous drama. Was this after all the shabby best? I did not know nor did it just now concern me. Two things, for the moment, dominated the world: that tomorrow Gunnar would see Crystal, and the day after I would see Kitty.

The more I thought about it the more I detested the idea of Gunnar going to see Crystal. Why had I agreed to it? I had still felt, even then, as if I were somehow under Gunnar's authority, under his orders, bound, because of the past, to do his will. Today I felt rather less subservient. I could simply have said no to him. There was no need to slavishly report his wishes to Crystal, or to comply with her nervous desire to meet him once more. What good could come of it? Crystal, whose serenity was as precarious as my own, might be deeply, permanently, upset by this encounter. And the idea of it horrified me in deep places, as if I actually feared (only this was insane) that Gunnar might make love to Crystal again. Had he ever really done so? The fact that he had asked so improbably to see her was evidence in favour of her story. Perhaps he wanted—what? To beg her pardon, once more to kiss her hand? The whole idea filled me with disgust and the wish somehow to spoil his enterprise. I felt it was too late now, now that Crystal was expecting this weird visit, simply to forbid it. Should I insist on being present myself when Gunnar came? That would certainly wreck things. I decided however upon a milder form of sabotage. So when I had finished tearing up Tommy's letter I wrote a note to Crystal, to reach her by post tomorrow morning, which ran as follows:

Dearest, I am worried about your seeing G. Do you really want to? If you decide during the day that you do not, ring me at the office. If you don't ring I will come round to your place before seven and I will wait, I won't come in, and I will let him see me waiting outside. If you want me you can open the window and call. I hope you won't let him stay long. I shall want to talk to you immediately after he is gone. Much love. H.

I had just finished writing this when I heard someone enter the room and turned round. It was Arthur. He had evidently recovered from his 'flu. He looked rather pale. He came and took Reggie's chair and put it beside me and sat down.

'Hello, Arthur, I didn't expect to see you today. 'Flu better?'

'Yes, I'm fine. Hilary, is it true that you've resigned?'

'The news has got round has it? Yes.'

'The porter told me. Why?'

'You know why.'

'Oh dear, oh dear. Whatever will you do?'

Arthur's sympathetic soupy face was all crinkled up with concern, his moustache working. I wanted to hit him. 'Go to Australia.'

'To *Australia*? With Crystal?'

'Hilary, it's not *true* that you've resigned?' Edith Witcher.

'We thought you were joking yesterday!' Reggie Farbottom.

Arthur got up. He said, 'You will come this evening, won't you? I'm not infectious.'

'Hilary, why on earth have you resigned?'

'Mind you let Edith have your desk, no interlopers allowed.'

'But, Hilary, *why*?'

'I wanted a change,' I said, facing them. Arthur had moved to the door. I could see in profile his sad face as he pictured Crystal setting off for New South Wales. 'I'd fed up with leading a little monotonous life.'

'Well, I suppose we all are—'

'I decided it was time to shake things up a bit. Launch out on something new.'

'But what?'

'I'm going to start a hairdressing business!'

'In Australia,' said Arthur.

'Hilary's going to start a hairdressing business in Australia!'

'What's this?' said Freddie Impiatt, coming in. 'Hilary, are you really resigning? Why on earth?'

The others, who now included Jenny Searle and Skinker, respecting Freddie's lofty rank, gave ground. He took the chair beside me vacated by Arthur. It was like a visit from a doctor.

'Just wanted a change.'

'But why—there's no need to— Perhaps we could talk about this—'

It occurred to me that Freddie thought I was resigning because of Laura! Did he suppose I loved her? Or that she loved me? Let him suppose.

I put on a funereal face. 'I just felt it was—time to move on—'

Freddie looked very worried. He was a decent humane silly man. 'You mustn't do anything in a hurry. You know you'll lose your pension rights? I do hope— Look, we'll see you on Thursday as usual, won't we?'

Thursday! 'Yes, of course,' I said, to get rid of him. He went slowly away. The others crowded back.

'Hilary, are you really going to Australia?'

'Hilary is a hero.'

'We'd all like to go to Australia only we haven't Hilary's courage.'

'Hilary is a great man.'

'Goodness gracious, Arthur, whatever have you done?'

It was Tuesday evening and I was round at Arthur's place. I had come via a longish session at Sloane Square. I avoided Liverpool Street on Tuesdays for fear of meeting Tommy coming back from King's Lynn. The usual grub was ready and waiting on the table; tongue, mashed potatoes and peas, biscuits and cheese, bananas. I had brought the wine.

Arthur had, since I had seen him in the morning, shaved off his moustache. It improved his appearance remarkably. He looked younger and more intelligent.

'You suggested it.'

'Did I?'

'Yes. I said could I change myself, and you said I could shave off my moustache.'

'I wasn't serious. However, I think you look better without it. Don't you? Why, what's all this stuff?'

Arthur's shiny sideboard and *art déco* aeroplane armchair were covered with gaily coloured travel brochures. Sydney harbour, Sydney opera house, miles of sunny beaches, water ski-ing, surfing, kangaroos . . .

'I don't feel stuck here,' said Arthur. 'I thought I might consider coming too, if you didn't object.'

'Coming where?'

'To Australia.'

I began to laugh. I felt, for the moment, curiously free, carefree, with the freedom and insouciance of despair. The thought that I would see Kitty on Thursday, even the thought that I would see Kitty for the last time on Thursday, cast a lurid life-sustaining radiance. Another blessed merciful interim. And after that let the world end. I felt too an odd grim satisfaction at the prospect of playing policeman to Gunnar tomorrow. Gunnar might feel that he could exorcize Anne by seeing me and exorcize Crystal by seeing Crystal, but he could not get rid of and had not yet exorcized me. I was still there. Perhaps we should end up fighting after all.

'That was a joke too,' I said. 'I'm not going to Australia.'

'Oh,' said Arthur, looking relieved. 'I've been thinking about Australia ever since.'

'Well you can stop now.'

286

He began to collect up the brochures and stack them neatly on the sideboard. We sat down to supper.

I felt a kind of relief in Arthur's presence. It was partly the feeling which I had had last night that in spite of horrors in one's life a routine could persist. It was Tuesday, I was with Arthur. And there was something more. Arthur was a little untalented unambitious man, destined to spend his life in a cupboard, but there was in a quite important sense no harm in him. He was kind, guileless, harmless and he had had the wit to love Crystal, to *see* Crystal, to see her value. I felt, for this, a pure gratitude to Arthur which shed a little light upon him. More practically, he was someone to whom I could talk of my situation. Indeed he was the only person to whom I could talk of my situation since with Crystal it was too painful and Clifford only made spiteful jokes.

'How's Crystal?' said Arthur.

'Fine.'

'I wanted to say to you—don't worry, I won't go on about it—I'm still hoping, I can't help it. I'll always be there. Will you tell her just—Arthur will always be there?'

'Yes. Sure.'

'Do you think there's any chance—'

'Well, no—'

'I suppose—ah well—I wondered—I don't know whether you want to talk about that other business, how it's going?'

'That other business is going sensationally,' I told him. How was it going? There could be many different ways of explaining how it was going, many different tones. With Arthur I decided to use the sensational. Why? I felt the need of a crude cleansing briskness. There were lingering residues of sentiment and weak regret, the 'mush' to which Gunnar had alluded, illusory rubbish to be cleared away, rubbish towards which Arthur's silly sentimental innocent mind was already homing.

'Oh—do tell—'

'I saw Gunnar.'

'Oh good—oh I'm so glad—so glad— And you made it up?'

What a phrase. 'Made it up? Made *that* up? Don't be daft.'

'What happened then?'

'We established comfortably that we detested each other.'

'But you don't detest him. You like him, anyway you wish him well and you want him to forgive you. If not, what's it all for?'

What indeed. 'A lot has happened since I told you that story, in fact the story's old hat by now. Shall I put you in the picture? I saw Kitty—'

'Lady Kitty?'

'Yes, we're great friends, we meet and discuss Gunnar. Gunnar doesn't know of course. I've quite fallen for her.'

'I suppose this is another of your jokes?' said Arthur.

'No, it's not a joke unless everything is. She sends me secret letters by her maid. We have clandestine meetings beside the river. We're having one on Thursday. It's ever so exciting. I suppose that's another reason for detesting her husband.'

'Hilary, you can't mean this—' Arthur threw down his fork.

'She's a marvellous woman. Gunnar was vile to me when we met. It wasn't a meeting of human beings. He simply wanted to use me. He made it clear that he hated me and that he didn't propose to stop. There's nothing more natural of course, nothing to be surprised at. But if he hates me what's the use? Kitty says he's been obsessed with the past, obsessed with dreams of revenge. He's had analysis and all that crap. I think she imagined that if he saw me it would all fall away. Perhaps it has, but not in the way that I expected, I thought there'd be something in it for me, I didn't realize it would be like a bloody clinic. Kitty still thinks I can do something wonderful for him, but that's because being a woman she wants some sort of feast of the emotions, and because being a woman she believes in magic. But all her magic has done so far is make me fall in love with her. No, it's all over already between me and Gunnar. I was a dolt to imagine that we could help each other in *that* way. I've learnt a good deal in this last fortnight, I can tell you. I've jettisoned a lot of sentimental nonsense that I'm better without. I don't really feel sorry about the past at all, one can't, it's bound to be false or mixed up with a hundred other things. Regret, remorse, that's the most selfish thing of all. I wanted some sort of soothing experience, some sort of symbolic reassurance, I wanted him to say, "It's all right, Hilary, it's all right." But how can he say that? Perhaps if I could have imposed my will on him I might have got something, some suitable little drama. As it was he imposed his will upon me, and of course I had to let him. That was in the contract. Really there's no live connection with the past, the past is gone, that's obvious when you come to think of it, it doesn't exist any more. What remains are emotions which can be manipulated mechanically. That was

288

what my meeting with Gunnar was, an exercise in mechanical manipulation. I only hope he found it satisfactory.'

'But, Hilary, perhaps you were wrong to let it happen, perhaps you should have been more positive, more sort of inventive—'

'Inventive?'

'Yes, I mean thinking what to say to him, to appeal to him, to touch him, to help him—I mean, why should he do it all— I mean, imagine what it was like for him meeting you, he wasn't to know what you felt—'

'He didn't want to know. He said so.'

'He said so, but people often say what they don't mean, especially—'

'No, no, I've had Gunnar. The thing that's really happened to me is Kitty, that's something, that's alive all right.'

'But that's terrible, and you can't—He doesn't know you meet her?'

'Kitty adores secrets.'

'But, Hilary, no, you can't, you *can't*—' Arthur pushed his chair back, his younger-looking face pink with emotion. 'You know you oughtn't to meet his wife secretly.'

'Why? Because nobody ought ever to meet anybody else's wife secretly.'

'There are things one mustn't do—and think if he found out —you mustn't destroy your chance to do some good here. You say it was almost mechanical when you met but I bet it was your fault, you probably became dry and sarcastic—'

'Like I usually am. Well one has to defend oneself.'

'Why? You said it was in the contract that he should decide things, I'm not even sure about that, but wasn't it also in the contract that you should be open and simple with him and sort of humble and—'

'Don't make me sick, Arthur. And do you imagine it's easy to be open and simple when you're being shot at—?'

'You haven't even tried, and you've got to try. Why don't you write to him?'

'Saying what?'

'Saying you're sorry and—'

'Oh really—'

'Well, why not, isn't that the main thing? Of course emotions are mechanical, but one's got to get past mechanism. It's worth having a go. You say your life's been wrecked. You say he's been to analysts. No one goes to *them* unless things are *awful*.'

'Things have been awful for him it seems.'

'Then you must try. Reconciliation must be possible, it must be.'

'Why must it be? You talk like a bloody theologian. You believe in a sort of *thing* called reconciliation. Perhaps I believed in it once. I don't now. You think there is a sort of place reserved where reconciliation happens. That seems to me like belief in God. But there is no God. And that's the point. It's not a negative thing, it's a positive thing that there is no God.'

'All right, I don't believe in God either. But I think one should try to stick to simplicity and truth. There may be no God, but there's decency and—and there's truth and trying to stay there, I mean to stay in it, in its sort of light, and trying to do a good thing and to hold onto what you know to be a good thing even if it seems stupid when you come to do it. You could help yourself and Crystal, you could help him, but it can only be done by holding onto the good thing and believing in it and holding on, it can only be done sort of—simply—without any dignity or—drama—or—magic—'

'You are eloquent, my dear Arthur, but not very clear.'

'And you mustn't imagine you're in love with his wife.'

'I'm not imagining it.'

'Yes you are, that's rubbish, that's irrelevant, it must be—'

'A lot of things "must be" in your arguments.'

'You mustn't discuss him with his wife and see her secretly, it's not your place to do that, it's not your job, it can't do good, don't you see it makes the other thing impossible, you mustn't have muddles and secrets, and—and excitement—you must only have faithful sort of—good will and—truthfulness and— some sort of simple old idea like—you know—but you're just running away from it into a sort of complicated—'

'I like your "simple old idea", my simple old dear fellow.'

'You're deliberately destroying your power to make things better, like a soldier deliberately making himself unfit for duty, it's a crime—'

'Perhaps I am a gentleman volunteer after all.'

'If you could only go to him quietly—'

'It's just that, precisely that, Arthur, that illusion, that simple old fiction, which is sentimentality. Gunnar has given me a jolly lesson in causation. You speak of truth. Well this is a matter of science, and science is truth isn't it. There are no miracles, no redemptions, no moments of healing, no transfiguring changes in one's relation to the past. There is nothing but accepting the beastliness and defending oneself. When I was a little child I believed that Christ died for my sins. Only of course because he was God he didn't really die. That was magic all right. He suffered and then somehow everything was made well. And nothing can be more consoling than that, to think that suffering can blot out sin, can really erase it completely, and that there is no death at the end of it all. Not only that, but there is no damage done on the way either, since every little thing can be changed and *washed*, everything can be saved, everything, what a marvellous myth, and they teach it to little defenceless children, and what a bloody awful lie, this denial of causation and death, this changing of death into a fairytale of constructive suffering! Who minds suffering if there's no death and the past can be altered? One might even want to suffer if it could automatically wipe out one's crimes. Whoopee. Only it ain't so. And in all my thinking in all these years about Gunnar and about that whole business there was just a tiny grain of that sentimental old lie still left, not that I could do anything with it, I couldn't use it to change my life or Crystal's, which isn't surprising, you can't make any good use of a fib like that, but when he turned up again, Gunnar I mean, it all blazed up into a sort of stupid hope—'

'It's not a stupid hope—'

'Into a sort of stupid hope of somehow being rewarded at last for having been so unhappy, for having had one's career ruined and one's talents wasted—that's what it came to, I suppose—no one could really help me except him, no one could really help him except me—and I somehow imagined that we could get together and say hey presto and the bad stuff would all fall away and be changed in the twinkling of an eye like in the Jesus Christ story, only life isn't like that, it's too deep, it's too causal, we're too old. Of course it seems ridiculous now, it seems *stupid*, to have suffered so much because of something so accidental and sort of frail which didn't have to happen and so very nearly didn't, and of course guilt is irrational, that was partly what made me think it would all vanish. But the irrationality is of the essence, it goes all the way through, it isn't any sort of fulcrum or escape route, it's the lot—I was destined to suffer stupidly, my mother suffered stupidly, my father suffered stupidly, my sister suffers stupidly, it's what we were made for—Gunnar was just a mechanical part of my destiny just as I was a mechanical part of his—'

'Wait, stop, Hilary, stop, you're saying it all wrong, you've been drinking too much, you often do, you went to the pub before you came here—'

'You make me feel I'm back in the north, back in the old Precious Blood Mission Hall. You're drunker than I am. Look at that wine bottle.'

'It isn't like that, you make it as if it's got to be all one thing or all the other, you're all muddled—'

'You sound pretty muddled too if it comes to that. All right, you tell me what to do.'

'Stop seeing Lady Kitty. Write and tell her you won't come on Thursday. Tell her you feel it isn't right. That's one step, and if you take it you may see another. She'll understand, she'll respect you for it. She must know herself that—it's a sort of false thing—it'll lead to something bad—'

'As for bad, we're knee deep in that already. Bad breeds bad. I can't think why you attach so much importance to this. Of course it's important to *me*—'

'She's a silly bad frivolous woman.'

'Come, come, Arthur. You don't know anything about her.'

'I've seen her in the office.'

'I see. That's what's behind all this moral tirade. You took against her. Or are you in love with her yourself?'

'She's a coquette, a sort of classy flirt, one can see it, she wears perfume—'

'And a mink coat. Really, Arthur, I regard myself as a simple unsophisticated boy from the provinces, but you are being perfectly childish. She is a beautiful stylish woman, the sort of woman you and I would never normally come within a hundred miles of, there's nothing wrong in that, there's no need to hate her for it!'

'I don't like that sort of vain upper class woman, she's spoilt and silly and I wouldn't trust her—'

'How much do you know about women, my dear Arthur? Well, I suppose Crystal's rather blunter simpler charms are more up your street.'

'Please don't speak like that about Crystal.'

'Well, she is my sister and I wouldn't at all mind seeing her in mink, some decent clothes might do something for her appearance. I suppose I'm allowed to be realistic enough to see that she dresses like a guy and has a face like the back of a cab. If I realize she's ugly that doesn't mean I don't love her.'

'She isn't ugly!'

'Your illusion is touching. Now Kitty—'

'I won't have you talking here about Kitty this and Kitty that—I won't have you speaking of that woman in the same sentence as Crystal—'

'It wasn't the same sentence, it was a different sentence. As I was saying, now Kitty—'

'Get out, please, get out.'

'What?'

'*Get out.*'

Arthur had risen. He was scarlet, trembling, his mouth jerking convulsively about. I got up slowly and took my cap and put on my coat. I stood for a moment staring at Arthur with curiosity. I had never seen him look like that before. His breath was audible as if at any moment he might begin to sob. It appeared, then, that I was not the only one who was living under strain.

I went quietly out of the room and down the stairs. The sour-sweet smell of yeast from the bakery greeted me in a warm wave and I went through it and out into the street. Some bright London-pink clouds were illuminating the sky. I put on my cap and turned up my coat collar. Arthur's uncharacteristic explosion had shaken me thoroughly and I was suffering from shock.

I felt rather drunk. (Arthur had been right about that.) I also felt uncomfortably that I had said a lot of rather shoddy things which I did not really mean. Perhaps there had been something worth explaining, but I had certainly not explained it.

Then as I walked along I began to think about Kitty: not to think anything special about her, but rather perhaps simply to think her, as a mystic thinks God with a thought which goes beyond thinking and becomes being.

WEDNESDAY

IT WAS Wednesday evening, ten minutes past five, and I was at home at the flat, having left the office early. I had come home for one simple and practical reason, to fetch a pair of gloves. The weather, which had seemed to be as cold as it could be, had suddenly become even colder and the sky had assumed a thick gathered grey congested awfulness which betokened snow. If I was to spend time (how much time?) pacing up and down the road outside Crystal's house, embarrassing Gunnar and curtailing his visit, I would need a pair of gloves, not usually a part of my equipment. I also picked up a thick woollen scarf. I also, for psychological reasons, shaved. I was now ready to set out again, only it was too early. I had spent a long alcoholic lunch-time and decided that it would be wiser not to wait out this particular interim in a pub. I was becoming too dependent on alcohol. Better to stay here for a little, better anyway not to arrive tipsy. Not that I proposed to speak to Gunnar. I would simply let him see me marching to and fro like a sentinel on the other side of the road.

Foraging in the pockets of my overcoat I had discovered there the black stone which I had given to Biscuit and which she had returned to me. Why? After what thoughts? Where had she kept it in the interim? The business was full of mysteries. I also found, in another pocket, Biscuit's little woollen glove which I had drawn off and appropriated on the second occasion when I met her. I put the stone inside the glove and put both these ambiguous trophies away in a drawer. How long the struggle had already lasted, how many phases it had already been through! I felt that, like the Guards War Memorial, I could even now produce quite a respectable list of battles: Leningrad Garden. Office Stairs One. Westminster Bridge. Peter Pan. Office Stairs Two. Cheyne Walk Jetty. Cheyne Walk Drawing Room. Parliament Square . . . How many more before the war should be finally over?

I was now lying down on my bed and reflecting about the day. And as I lay back and composed my hands behind my head my heart was beating Kitty tomorrow, Kitty tomorrow. This time tomorrow I would be walking the Chelsea embankment. I tried not to think about it, but it was the heart-beat background to all other thoughts. I turned my attention to Arthur. I had quite forgotten Arthur when walking home last night. I had gone straight to bed and slept well and dreamed of an elephant who turned to pick me up and take me to the dance. The morning had brought a painful recollection. I felt thoroughly shaken by Arthur's attack on me with its emphatic and violent climax, and the more so because I uncomfortably felt that some of what he had to say made sense. I had chosen to act an unsavoury role and Arthur had taken me seriously. It turned out that I cared, a little at any rate, what Arthur thought about me. I had been guilty of cynicism, coarseness, vulgarity. Cynicism is coarseness, is vulgarity. How could I have said that about Crystal, why did not love strike me across the mouth and stop me? I had stupidly, instantly, resented Arthur's words about Kitty and I had deliberately tried to hurt him by sneering at Crystal. Of course it was crazy to meet Kitty in secret. And of course, and this was the hardest thing of all, there was a truth somewhere which denied Kitty, only I loved Kitty more than that truth, and that was a truth too. It was impossible not to see Kitty tomorrow, impossible, impossible, impossible. Doubtless I knew, in some still sober part of my mind, that this could not 'go on', that my time of meeting Kitty was nearing its end. She was not 'frivolous', though she might be 'spoilt'. Crystal and I could have done with some 'spoiling', it could even have helped our characters, it could certainly have helped mine. Kitty was a madcap romantic, but she was not irresponsible, she was not totally daft. She must know that since I would simply go on doing what she told me it was up to her to decide when enough was enough. She would soon see that there was really nothing more to 'discuss' and would terminate our conversation with a gay ruthlessness for which much later I would be grateful. I only knew that, for my own peace of mind at that later time, I could not end this thing myself. That at least was absolutely clear. She must end it, and she could well do so tomorrow. I closed my eyes on that pain. But at least tomorrow was still there with its fruit of her presence and there was still a future.

I had in fact been amazed at Arthur's nerve, at his sheer courage, in throwing me out. He was evidently amazed at it too. He was in the office before me, waiting for me, waiting to approach me with anxious humility. He begged my pardon. I begged his. He accused himself of having been drunk. I

accused myself of having been drunk. With Arthur the reconciliation scene ran on wheels. After that I asked him if he
would mind doing my work, and he agreed with alacrity and
took away the contents of my in-tray. I played battleships
with Reggie. He and Edith now treated me with studied
gentleness like someone who has been bereaved.

I was just looking at my watch and thinking it was not yet
quite time to set off for the North End Road and wondering
if I should perhaps have a cup of tea, when there was a ring
on the door bell. I got up like a jack-in-the-box and ran out.
Biscuit with a letter cancelling tomorrow?

It was Laura Impiatt. She was wild-haired, having pulled
off her cap, and wearing a military-style ankle-length belted
overcoat and boots. I was not glad to see her. An atmosphere
of silly pretence and affectation, more powerful than Kitty's
perfume, came through the door with her. I suppose she was
a nice harmless person, but I felt that just then I had no time
for her. She pounced on me.

'Hilary, is it really true you've resigned from the office?
Whatever are you thinking of?'

'I just need a change, that's all. It's nothing personal,
Laura. With me things rarely are.'

'With me things always are. Everything's personal. Anyway
I don't believe you. Christopher, did you know that Hilary's
chucking his job?'

'Why, well done, Hilary!' said Christopher, who had
emerged from his room dressed in a long purple robe and
wearing a necklace of brown beads and a matching bracelet.
'I didn't think you had it in you.'

'Christopher thinks you've become a drop-out.'

'I have.' I went into the kitchen and put on the kettle.
Laura followed me pulling off her coat. Through the open
door of Christopher's room I could see Jimbo Davis lying flat
upon the floor.

'But seriously, Hilary, whatever will you do?'

'Teach grammar to little children.'

'You are well known never to tell the truth. Well, we shall
see, won't we, Christopher? It will be perfectly fascinating.
Don't you think that Christopher ought to grow a moustache
and beard and look exactly like Jesus Christ?'

'No.'

'What on earth are you doing with that kettle?'

'Making tea.'

'*Tea?* Hilary must have gone mad.'

'Have some cake,' said Christopher. Jimbo had risen and was now in the kitchen too, gazing at me with his sympathetic mournful eyes. Christopher put a Fuller's walnut cake, already cut into slices, upon the table. I took a slice and munched it while the kettle boiled. Then I made the tea and began to eat a second slice, ignoring the others. I was feeling hungry after a lunch of potato crisps and whisky. Laura was chattering to the boys. A little time passed. Laura was eating some of the cake. Christopher and Jimbo were giggling.

I was looking at the kettle. I had never really noticed it properly before. It is odd how one lives among things and fails to notice them. Yet each thing is an individual with a deep and wonderful being of its own. The kettle was shiny and blue, glittering like a star in the bright electric light. It was a strange blue, injected somehow with black, reminding me of something. I had never noticed before how black a blue could be and yet remain blue, it was a wonderful achievement of nature. In fact the kettle was both black and blue all over at the same time which I had been told was impossible. Only of course it was possible since the colour was not really *in* the kettle. Whoever thought colours were *in* things? Colours surge out of things and stray about in clouds, in waves, yes in waves, is not everything supposed to be made up of waves. I could see the waves. The kettle was glowing and vibrating rhythmically and I was glowing and vibrating with it.

I swayed a little and put out my hand and caught something. It was Christopher's shoulder. I turned and looked at Christopher's face and it had become the face of a beautiful young girl. I lifted my hand and touched the shining blond hair and swayed again. Then I was in Christopher's room, I had moved thither with a curious ease, and it was as if my feet did not touch the ground. It was quite easy after all to walk upon the air, only no one had ever told me. I was sitting on the ground now with my back to the wall and Laura was sitting nearby and Jimbo was lying on the floor and Christopher was playing his tabla and there was a fragrant ineffable sense of togetherness as if all our minds were lightly glued together, hanging together like a clutch of angels beating their wings in the air just a little above our heads in the centre of the room, only somehow all this was sound, wonderful sound, the huge rhythmic beat of the drum which had become a Tibetan gong, an immense cavern of sound like a great mouth opening and shutting. It was cosmic and beautiful and yet also very funny. The universe was funny, fundamentally funny, and this was fundamentally important, that nothing was deeper than the funniness, nothing. Not evil, not good, not chance, the funny was deepest of all, oh what joy! Now I was turning over and over like something gently unravelling or unrolling. I was a wall of light gently unrolling itself through immense empty areas of space and time. And then I saw Mr Osmand. Somehow Mr Osmand was there too in the cavern which was also the mouth which was also the unrolling light which was also me, and Mr Osmand was like the universe, fundamentally funny. I tried to tell him so but little sugar cakes kept coming out of my mouth instead of words. I wanted to offer him some of the cakes but they danced lightly about and then floated away. Mr Osmand was crawling about on the floor like a beetle, he was a beetle with a huge head and the head came towards me and the huge beetle eyes looked into mine and the eyes had a thousand facets and each facet had a thousand facets. Mr Osmand was very beautiful and very funny and I loved him. *Amo amas amat amamus amatis amant amavi amavisti amavit amavimus amavistis amaverunt amavero amaveris amaverit* . . . Everything was love. Everything will be love. Everything has been love. Everything would be love. Everything would have been love. Ah, that was it, the truth at last. Everything would have been love. The huge eye, which had become an immense sphere, was gently breathing, only it was not an eye nor a sphere but a great wonderful animal covered in little waving legs like hairs, waving oh so gently as if they were under water. All shall be well and all shall be well said the ocean. So the place of reconciliation existed after all, not like a little knot hole in a cupboard but flowing everywhere and being everything. I had only to will it and it would be, for spirit is omnipotent only I never knew it, like being able to walk on the air. I could forgive. I could be forgiven. I could forgive. Perhaps that was the whole of it after all. Perhaps being forgiven was just forgiving only no one had ever told me. There was nothing else needful. Just to forgive. Forgiving equals being forgiven, the secret of the universe, do not whatever you do forget it. The past was folded up and in the twinkling of an eye everything had been changed and made beautiful and good.

THURSDAY

I SEEMED to have been asleep, only this was not like waking from sleep. Of course I knew what had happened. I knew it quite early on when I was looking at the kettle, only it had already not seemed important, just rather sweet and funny. I looked laboriously at my watch. It said twelve. But what did twelve mean? I looked about me, breathing regularly and deeply and feeling how pleasant simply breathing was. Gradually the world assembled itself into accustomed shapes. I was in Christopher's room, lying flat with my head on a cushion. Christopher, dressed only in his underpants, was lying on the pile of cushions which he used for a bed. Jimbo Davis was stretched out on the floor face down, one hand flung out above his head. Laura was lying at right angles to Christopher with her head resting upon his bare stomach. Her dress was undone to the waist and she had pulled her arm out of one sleeve revealing a plump shoulder and a straining brassière. Her eyes were closed and she was smiling. I looked at my watch and it said one. Was it day or night?

The door bell rang. I listened to it thoughtfully. It went on ringing. I began to get up. It was difficult. I got to my knees, to my feet, and stepped over Jimbo. I felt all right, rather well really, only a little odd spatially. My jacket had disappeared and my shirt was open and hanging out of my trousers. My mind functioned. The bell was ringing again. I opened the door. It was Freddie Impiatt.

By this time I was fairly in control of myself. I stood there looking at Freddie and pushing my shirt in. Freddie was red-faced and hatless. He said in a tense choking voice, 'Is Laura here?'

I reflected. She had better not be. I said, 'No. Sorry.'

'I've been here before, I kept ringing the bell only no one answered. I could see the light was on. I don't know where she is.'

'Sorry.'

'I believe she's here. I'm coming in.' He put a foot through the door.

'Sorry, Freddie, not now. The boys have freaked out. I can't. Anyway it's the middle of the night. It is the middle of the night, isn't it, it's not the day? I mean it's not one o'clock in the afternoon, is it?' I began to push Freddie's foot with

299

my foot. My foot pushed harder. 'I'm sorry,' I said. I managed to shut the door.

I started to look round for the telephone so as to ring the speaking clock to find out if it was day or night, only the telephone seemed to have disappeared. Somebody loomed up. It was Jimbo. I held onto him.

'Are you all right, Hilary?'

'Yes, are you?'

'I didn't take anything, I was just asleep. Don't be cross.'

'That was Freddie looking for Laura. I told him she wasn't here. I didn't want him to come in and see this.'

Christopher was still lying on his back with his mouth open. Laura had shifted, turning on her side, her head now resting on a cushion up against his shoulder, her bare arm extended across his chest. They were both slumbering reposefully, deeply.

'We'd better try to wake her up,' said Jimbo. 'Come on now, wake up, time to go home.'

We pulled her into a sitting position and pushed her arm back into her sleeve and buttoned up her dress. She was heavy and floppy and warm. She opened her eyes, still smiling, and rose quite steadily, holding onto Jimbo's hand.

I said to her, 'It's late, Laura, off you go. Freddie was here looking for you. I said you weren't here, but you were. Take her home in a taxi, will you, Jimbo?'

I went into my bedroom. The light was still turned on. I lay down on the bed. I heard Jimbo talking to Laura, helping her on with her coat, leading her out of the front door. Of course it was night as everything was dark outside. I did not feel at all sleepy, just rather relaxed, and I lay back on my pillow and meditated. I had not been very intelligent with Freddie. Laura would presumably tell him the truth, which was not after all in any way discreditable, and all I had done was make something which was innocent look like something which was not. I had also prolonged poor Freddie's anxiety about his wife. Yet surely it was also right to keep him out of that room. What a difficult situation and how naughty of the boys to drug us! I hoped that Freddie would understand.

Then suddenly I remembered, first that there was something I ought to have done, and then what it was. I was to have gone to Crystal's this evening to supervise Gunnar's visit, and to go in to her immediately after it was over. This evening. But it was now nearly two o'clock in the morning.

I sat up abruptly and put my feet on the floor. Crystal would have expected me, waited anxiously for me. Gunnar had been with her, and there had been no one to protect her. I stood up and held my head. I wanted to telephone, to run to her at once, but after a moment this seemed absurd. She would be asleep by now. I would go to her in the morning at breakfast time. I sat down again, filled with anxiety and pain. The sense of a 'good dream', which had been with me, was fading and my ordinary consciousness, my ordinary misery, were reasserting their rights. I had failed to be there to look after Crystal, to watch over her. What could she have imagined, what feared, when I so shamefully failed to turn up? I had slept, I had dreamed, when I should have been standing sentinel against the enemy.

I heard the quiet sound of Jimbo returning. He came and tapped on my door.

'You took her home?'

'Yes, he was waiting up. He was very glad to see her.'

'Well, I hope that was all right.'

As I spoke I was staring at a little rectangle of white upon my bedside table. I wondered what it was. It appeared to be a printed card. I picked it up, and read *Neville Osmand, Educational Consultant*. I stared at it uncomprehendingly.

'Where on earth did this come from?' I said to Jimbo.

'He left it.'

'*He?*'

'Yes, the chap who came last night, he said he'd taught you at school.'

Then it came back to me, a strange strange image of Mr Osmand as some kind of beast, peering closely into my face. Yet it seemed like a dream.

'He came, he really came? But I saw him in a dream. He can't have been here.'

'You were under the influence. He tried to talk to you, he went down on his knees and looked at you. I said you were on a trip.'

'What did I do? Did I talk?'

'You giggled a lot and you recited some sort of gibberish.'

'Oh Christ. Oh *Christ*—'

'Sorry, Hilary— Look, it wasn't my idea—'

'Did he leave an address, did he say he'd come back?'

'No, he just left the card with his name on.'

'Oh God. Go away, will you. Go away and turn the light out.'

THURSDAY

I lay there staring into the darkness. So, after all these years, Mr Osmand had managed to track down his prize pupil, his creation, his great achievement, Hilary Burde. What a proud moment.

THURSDAY

IT WAS Thursday morning. I was with Crystal before eight
o'clock. She seemed quite surprised to see me.

'Why, darling, hello, I didn't expect you now.'

'Why didn't you expect me now? You expected me last
night I suppose?'

'Yes, but when you didn't come I thought you'd been
detained.'

'Detained?'

'We looked out every now and then—'

'*We?*'

'Gunnar and I.'

'You mean you told Gunnar—?'

'Yes, I told him you were going to walk up and down outside, only we looked out several times and you weren't there
and then I'm afraid we forgot.'

'You forgot?'

'Well, yes. Then when he went away—'

'What time did he go away?'

'It must have been nearly midnight.'

'You mean he was here from seven till midnight?'

'Yes. I gave him supper. I didn't expect him to stay so
long. I had the supper here for you. But he ate it.'

'He did, did he. What did you give him for supper?'

'Fish fingers and peas and apricot tart. He liked it. He said
he'd never had fish fingers before.'

'God! Don't you want to know why I didn't turn up? I
thought you'd be worried stiff.'

'What happened?'

'The boys drugged me. They gave me a cake with some foul
stuff in it.'

'Are you all right?'

'Yes, but I had a jolly weird evening. I didn't come to till
after midnight.' I did not tell Crystal about Mr Osmand, it
was too painful. It had certainly been a weird evening. What
I remembered of it was not really like a dream, it was more
like an experience, as if I had actually been taken somewhere
and shown things, which I could not now recall quite clearly.
I could see Mr Osmand as a beetle walking. I could remember

303

the gentle good beast who was everything. But there had been something else which was important, a sort of mathematical equation or something, but what had it been?

'Make some tea, will you, darling? What on earth was it like, what did Gunnar have to say, he didn't sort of make advances to you, did he?'

'No, of course not! We talked.'

'What about?'

'Oh, about everything. About the past, about you, about his job, about what it was like living in New York, about a dog he'd had in New York, it was called Rosie, and this dog—'

'Stop, Crystal, stop, you're driving me mad. You mean you and Gunnar sat here and ate fish fingers and talked in a quite ordinary way about quite ordinary things? I don't believe it.'

'Well, of course it wasn't ordinary. It was very strange. I felt so frightened before he came I thought I'd faint. But he was so kind, *so kind*. After he'd been in the room a minute I felt better, oh so much better, and I feel better now—'

'And you chatted about his dog in New York.'

'We talked about all sorts of things, it all felt quite easy. He wanted to know what we'd been doing since he last saw us.'

'That must have made a glittering tale.'

'And he asked all sorts of things about you.'

'Such as what?'

'Whether you'd been unhappy, whether you'd ever had psychoanalysis—'

'I hope you told him I hadn't had that!'

'Of course I did. He spoke of you so gently and kindly—'

'He was sorry for me, that was nice of him!'

'Yes, it was, wasn't it—and I said it was so kind of him to see you.'

'What did he say?'

'He said it had done him good.'

'Oh, Crystal, Crystal. You don't understand, this is all dust and ashes. Give me that tea, for Christ's sake. He just came to despise us, to despise you, to see our poverty and find out what a lousy life we'd had. He came to triumph over us.'

'He said that you ought to be in a better job.'

'He looked at this room, he looked at your dress. That's not kindness, it's revenge. You can't think it's kindness. If you do you're bloody thick.'

'It was kindness,' said Crystal, 'it *was*. You don't know, you weren't there. He was so gentle.'

'And did he kiss your hand again?'

'When he was going, yes.'

'How touching. And when is he coming round again for a feast of fish fingers and apricot tart?'

'Never,' said Crystal composedly. I was drinking the tea and she was sitting opposite me, her hands folded upon the table. She was wearing a rather dirty overall over her dress. Her frizzy thick hair was strained back behind her ears, her face was big, greasy, defenceless, her moist lip pouting, her wide up-turned nose a little red. The room was cold. She took off her glasses revealing the weak peering golden eyes.

'Never?'

'We shall never meet again.'

'He said so?'

'Yes.'

'He thinks he's God. Did he say anything about seeing me again?'

'He said he might want to see you once more, but he'd have to think about it.'

'How gracious of him.'

'Hilary, I think we should leave London.'

'Did he suggest that?'

'Yes.'

'Crystal, I shall have a fit.'

'He said it in the nicest way, he was thinking of our welfare. He said he thought you should be able to get a job in a provincial university. We might start a new life somewhere. Exeter or Glasgow or somewhere.'

'Crystal, darling, I know you aren't very intelligent, but can't you see the difference between kind concern and bloody impertinence?'

'It wasn't impertinence, it wasn't, we were so open, he was so sincere, I've never talked like that, we were so frank, we said what we thought, we discussed everything, and it was needed, it was good, not just for him, but for me, he understood that so well, so wonderfully. I told him all about being in love with him, when I first felt it and—'

'*What?*'

'I was in love with Gunnar, I told you, how could I help it, he was so kind—I still love him—'

'Crystal—did he know—*then?*'

'I told him—on that night—I would never have let him—otherwise—oh he knew—and he remembered—'

'How kind of him to remember. Crystal, you're killing me.'

'But I told you—'

'I didn't take it in, not like that. Never mind. So you chatted about that memorable night and he thanked you and you thanked him and you said good-bye forever.'

'Not just like that. You're trying to make it all sound different from what it was. He was very upset, I mean he felt things, he came here to feel things, and it was a help to him to tell me, I know it was, and I was very glad, oh so glad, to help him—and now we've both helped him and—'

'Hail and farewell.'

'How could we go on knowing him—'

'Christ, I don't want to go on knowing him!'

'It wouldn't be possible. It's much better to do what we can and say good-bye. We shall both feel much better, ever so much better, and perhaps it will change things, I feel already that things could change. Couldn't we really leave London and live somewhere else and have a new life somewhere else? I'd so love to live in the country. I feel suddenly that it's possible now, a new life, a better life—'

'Let's go to Australia.'

'Well, why not? I'd go anywhere with you—and I could work anywhere—'

'Crystal, you don't know what you're saying. It's just as well I didn't turn up last night. I might have killed him. I think I intended to.'

'But why—oh why—when he was so kind—'

'Don't use that word again or I shall scream.'

'It has done good—it has done me good—seeing him—'

'You certainly seem very calm and pleased with yourself.'

'I'm not calm,' said Crystal, 'I'm not calm at all.' Huge tears came out of her eyes and spread all over her broad cheeks and continued to well up. 'Do see him again,' she said. 'Do see him just once more and be kind to him, please do, just to make it perfect.'

'It can never be perfect. He can never forgive me.'

'That's not the point,' said Crystal. 'What you must do is forgive him. That's what will make it perfect. If you forgive him then there'll be—a kind of open space—and he'll be able—'

At that moment I recalled what the equation had been which had seemed to me last night to be so important, the secret of the universe. Forgiving equals being forgiven. Now in sober daylight it seemed just a piece of verbal nonsense.

I drank my tea. Crystal went on crying.

Once more I was on the Chelsea embankment at five o'clock for six. A little snow was falling in tiny pinpoint flakes which hovered about in the still air uncertain whether to go up or down.

All day in the office I had felt fit to scream with joy and pain. I reclaimed some of my work from Arthur but could make nothing of it. Already it seemed incomprehensible rubbish. Had I ever understood and enjoyed all these intricate trivialities? Arthur and I rather avoided each other by mutual consent, and I was relieved when one of his junkies rang up and he went apologetically away. It looked as if after all I could not really pardon him for daring to chuck me out, and he could not really pardon me for insulting the woman he loved. Of course I was more to blame than he was but that was highly irrelevant. It appeared that this business of forgiving and being forgiven could be pretty tricky even in the best of cases.

The office day was now interminable, but I managed to struggle through it without losing my mind. I was invited into the Registry by Jenny Searle to play desk-top football. Now that I was known to be going I had suddenly become quite a popular figure, in demand everywhere. Two men, whom I did not know at all, from distant divisions, even turned up to question me about Australia. I attempted to reflect on my future, but the object in question was a blank. It was kind of Gunnar to suggest that I might join the university at Exeter or at Glasgow, but even if I wanted to do this I knew that my chances of getting an academic post, at my age and with my record, were nil. Who would write me a testimonial? Gunnar? As Stitchworthy had observed long ago, I was not really a scholar. I had nothing but my little versatile grammatical talent, my kinship with words, and of that I had, in all these years, made precisely nothing.

The only constructive thing which I did during the day was to write a letter to Mr Osmand, care of the school. I also wrote to the Headmaster, saying I was trying to trace Mr Osmand. I knew that he had left years ago, but I trusted that they would have an address. My letter to Mr Osmand said that I was very sorry to have been in such a deplorable condition when he came, that the drug had been given to me as a joke, that I hoped soon to have an opportunity of seeing him again and talking about the old days. I assured him of my continuing gratitude to him for all that he had done for me, and expressed the hope that he was well and happily situated. The letter was stiff, a letter to an old schoolmaster. I was thoroughly distressed by the incident, but I could not really concentrate on what I was writing. As for my final 'hope', it seemed on reflection a vain one. How could things possibly be well with Mr Osmand? He must be well over sixty, doubtless alone. 'Educational Consultant': what did that mean? Something tragic no doubt. He was evidently no longer a schoolmaster and what else in the world could it give him pleasure to be? Had he retired, or had he at last been sacked for patting one boy too many on the head and stroking his arm after prep? I had probably been his best pupil and look what had become of me. Of course I had never explained to him why I gave up Oxford. I wonder what he thought?

I left the office at half past four and went straight to Chelsea. I had suffered no ill effects from the drug. I had forced myself to eat some lunch. I felt weirdly clear-headed and vibrating with power. I felt as if I could have cleared the Thames in a leap. I tried hard not to think beyond my encounter with Kitty, and on the whole I succeeded. It was very possible that it would be our last meeting. Even if I were to see Gunnar again, tonight might be the last I saw of her. Or would she want a further conference after I had seen Gunnar, if I saw Gunnar? Should I even suggest this? These reflections did not get very far, burnt up as the day went on in the annihilating sense of her approach.

At fifteen minutes to six, after I had passed the house about eight times, looking up at the line of golden light in the drawing-room windows, I could bear it no longer and went and rang the door bell. I noticed at the same moment that the door was ajar. I put one foot inside and listened.

'Come on upstairs, you know the way.' Kitty's voice.

I went on up, treading softly on the thick carpet, past a

lot of glimmering things on brackets and an immense number of little pictures like glittering eyes, through the warm haze of new furnishing smells and Kitty's perfume, and entered the room where I had talked with Gunnar. An exotic sight met my eyes.

Kitty, with a towel round her shoulders, was sitting on a low satin chair near to the fireplace. A small fire was glowing in the grate. The innumerable discreet lamps were shedding their accumulation of diffused discreet light upon various trinkets on various tables. The yellow medallion on the carpet was glowing like a jewel. Kitty, wearing a long peacock-blue woollen evening dress with a pendant hood, was gazing at me. Standing behind her and holding a brush, with which she had evidently been brushing Kitty's hair, was Biscuit. Biscuit was wearing a magnificent sari, a dark brown shot silk with golden borders. Biscuit's black shining hair was unplaited and falling in a single straight torrent far down her back. As I stood there at the door, and after looking at me with expressionless attention, she began to pluck some hairs from the brush, twirl them into a little ball with her long thin fingers, and project them into the fire. Then she stood there, seemingly patient as an animal, gazing down towards the hem of Kitty's dress. She touched the back of Kitty's head very lightly with the brush, and stood there immobile waiting presumably, with lowered eyes, for Kitty's order to depart or to continue brushing.

Kitty with the dark tumble of hair brushed right back from her brow, and in the clear light of a lamp which was perched above her on the mantelpiece, presented me her most exposed face so far. Her brave audacious rash beautiful face. I could see the colour of her eyes, big, very dark slaty-blue, the large nose seemed more dominating, the mouth fuller, pouting with vitality and purpose and radiant animal self-satisfaction. I stared at that face, and the universe seemed to circle round quietly like a great bird and come to rest.

'You're early,' said Kitty, not a bit discomposed. She lifted a hand behind her and thrust Biscuit's poised brush away. With the same movement she pushed the towel off onto the floor. Biscuit picked it up and put it over her arm.

'Sorry.'

'Biscuit—'

'No need to send Biscuit away,' I said, 'I'm not staying.'

'Not staying?'

'This is the place where I talk to your husband. The place where I talk to you is outside on the jetty.'

'Biscuit, please—'

Biscuit, bearing brush and towel, moved to the door. I noticed that, beneath her sari, she was barefoot. I stood aside. A glittering strand of inky-black hair had fallen forward over her shoulder and as she twitched it back I saw the swing of long jewelled ear-rings. She passed me without a glance, with a faint frou-frou of silk, and I heard her almost inaudibly pad away, mounting the stairs behind me.

'It's very cold out there,' said Kitty. 'Has it started to snow?' She had bundled her hair forward and was combing it with her fingers and vigorously massaging her scalp. The unselfconscious confidence of the gesture disconcerted me.

'Yes.'

'Then wouldn't it be more sensible to stay in here?'

'Please yourself,' I said. 'I'm going outside.' I left the room and went downstairs and out of the house closing the front door quietly behind me. I crossed the road and made my way towards the jetty.

The place was deserted. The embankment traffic sizzled quietly along over a roadway slightly dusted with snow. The little flakes were falling sparsely but steadily. I was very cold and I was glad of my scarf and gloves. I had put my cap in my pocket. The tide was half in, a line of stone-strewn mud visible and gleaming in the dim light from the jetty. A darkened launch plopped gently, nuzzling the wood. I began to feel that I had been a perfect fool. The little scene with Biscuit had distressed me and I had been stupidly aggressive. Now if she did not come I would have to go tamely back to the house. But supposing she were offended, supposing she would not see me? I spent five minutes of knuckle-biting anguish. Then she came.

She was wearing a black woollen cap, and a huge overcoat which, I realized with renewed chagrin, must belong to Gunnar. The long dress swirled beneath it. She came towards me, to where I had stationed myself at the end of the jetty, and I waited for her to come.

'I say, it *is* cold, isn't it?'

'I'm sorry. I do hope you don't mind coming out? You see, I really don't want to be in your house without—without his knowing.'

'I quite understand.'

'He doesn't know—anything—does he?'

'Of course not.'

'And he's not likely to—'

'No, no, he went off to Brussels this morning.'

I was ready to bet Gunnar had not said anything to Kitty about Crystal. It seemed a moment to find out.

'Where was he last night? I thought I saw him in Whitehall about eight.'

'You might have done. He was dining with a friend at the House.'

There was no doubting the sincerity of her tone. So Gunnar lied to his wife. So much the worse for Gunnar. I felt a sense of power which I knew to be pointless, useless, but it pleased me.

'I'm glad you didn't speak to him,' she said. 'I wanted to see you first.'

'Am I to see him again then?'

'Yes. Once more. You know, it's odd, but this morning he seemed so much better, so much calmer.'

Crystal's doing. Who had been lecturing me about 'simplicity'? Crystal had it. Gunnar had benefited.

'Shall I write to him and suggest a meeting?'

'No. He will write to you.'

A silence. Was this all? We had walked to the end of the jetty where in a total privacy of cold the few tiny snowflakes were coming down out of a very dark darkness. The snow had blanketed the stars, even the great glow of London; all was covered and we were alone. The white flakes diamonded Kitty's black cap and her face glowed in the dim light, in the frosty air. I sought for words to detain her, another two minutes, another minute.

'What should I do when I see him again? I mean, have you any special advice?'

'I think you will know what to do. Tell me what was wrong with the last time.'

'With my last meeting with him? But you heard it all.'

'Yes, but I want you to tell me what was wrong.'

'Everything was wrong. He was too cold, I was too defensive. He assumed it was a kind of technical problem. I let this idea shut my mouth. We never met as human beings.'

'Exactly. And you must meet as human beings, mustn't you?'

'I'll try. It's not so easy to find the words—'

'If you will only *begin*, set him off as it were, the words will come rushing, like they rush when he talks to me. I promise I won't listen this time.'

'Good. I'd rather you didn't. I meant to tell him I was sorry or something like that, only in the face of his huge sort of intellectual grasp of the whole business there seemed no place for anything so stupidly simple.'

'Yes, yes, exactly, you are so right, but it's just that intellectual grasp that you must somehow break. He's thought about it so much, he's discussed it so much with those psychologists, he's made it into a sort of vast inflexible *thing*.'

'I know. But if he's willing to see me again that's a good sign, isn't it? And you said he seemed "better". Of course I'll try—I'll try, if necessary, again and again.' Spend my life trying, if only you want it, if only I can see you again.

'That won't be necessary,' said Kitty. 'I think one more meeting should be enough.'

'Of course I was not envisaging anything in the nature of friendship between us, naturally that would be impossible.'

Silence again. Snow. A kind of awkwardness which I felt in her, as if she were waiting for me to help her to terminate the interview. I desperately did not want to terminate it, but out of sheer mechanical nervousness I found myself saying, 'Well, is that all?'

'Yes, I think so. Gunnar will write to you. I'm so grateful.'

'Not at all. I'm grateful.'

We both stood still, motionless. I waited for her to move, to begin to go away. I felt it was my last chance in the world. I said, 'Shall I see you again?' It was impossible not to make the question sound desperate.

She said nothing. As the silence lengthened and as she continued to stand there some divine ferocious thrilling power out of the centre of the earth began to reach me, to rise through me. For a moment I was intensely giddy, as if I might fall. Then I put a hand on her arm. I felt the rough cold snow-dusted surface of the coat sleeve and can feel its texture this moment as I write. We stood absolutely still, arresting, arrested.

Then she made a little sound, it was a kind of sigh, a kind of groan, as if she were too choked to speak, the most wonderful communication in the world. She took a step as if to move away. I turned with her and took her in my arms and drew her body closely against mine. Her face was pressed against my shoulder and I heard the sigh again. We stood perfectly quiet.

I released her. I was almost sobbing myself, each breath came in an audible gasp. My heart was rending me with its violence.

'Oh Kitty, Kitty, I love you.'

'Hilary—'

'I love you, I'm terribly sorry, forgive me, I can't help it, I love you, I worship you—'

'Hilary—my dear—' She had come back to me. I put my arms round her shoulders and kissed her, first hastily, then slowly. It was impossible that this could really be happening. I kissed her, I opened my eyes, I saw her spangled cap, her dark creeping hair and beyond the snow now steadily falling. We moved apart again. With a distracted gesture she drew the cap off and tossed her head, then stood there gazing at me.

'Kitty, I love you, listen, I love you. I thought I'd never be able to say it. I can. I love you. I don't mind if I die now.'

'Hilary, I am so sorry—'

'I know it's hopeless, I know it's mad, I know it's wicked, I know you don't care for me, how could you. But I'm so grateful to you, just for this, just for tonight, even if we never meet again you've made me happy to the end of my life. I'm so glad you're there in the world, oh my God, oh Kitty, it's so wonderful just to say your name, I feel as if I could faint and lie at your feet and die, if only I could die now, if only I could drown—'

'Hilary, please—'

'All right, I'll stop, I'll go, I know I don't exist for you—'

'But you do, you do—'

'Oh Kitty—'

'Of course you do. I've felt so sorry for you. And I've been thinking about you for years and I thought I'd never meet you. And then suddenly you were there and you were so sort of complete and real, and I pitied you so much and you had thought so much about it too, about the past, and suffered so much, and you were so honest and so helpless and like a child, and I couldn't help—'

'What couldn't you help, Kitty?'

'Caring about you and wanting to— Oh I so much don't want to hurt you. I want to make things well for you, to take the nightmares away from you—'

'You do, you will. Oh Kitty, Kitty, thank you, you pitied me, thank you—'

We stood staring, arms hanging limply down, dazed by the suddenness and the strangeness of what happened. I was panting with anguish and with joy, pumping my steaming breath out into the cold air, feeling the snow now upon my hair, upon my eyebrows, upon my eyelashes.

'I don't know what it means,' she said. 'Forgive me—'

'Don't say that—you've been so—so gracious—so kind—'

'I must leave you now. I shouldn't have— Oh my dear dear Hilary—'

'But I'll see you again, won't I, I must see you. Just let me see you again—'

'I'll write to you.'

'You're not angry with me? I'm so very sorry I—I couldn't help myself—'

'I'm not angry. God bless you, God bless you—I must go—'

'But you will see me again?'

'I'll write—'

'Oh Kitty, I'm so happy—even if the world ends I'm happy—'

'It mustn't end,' she said. 'I mean, you must be all right, you must be. God bless you. Good night.'

And she was gone. I stood for a while groaning aloud in an ecstasy of torment. Then I knelt down in the snow, covering my face.

The time was now five minutes past eight, and I was at the Impiatts' house as I always was at this time on a Thursday. I was in the drawing-room. Laura and Freddie were there. Also Christopher.

I had no memory of leaving the Chelsea embankment. I found myself in the King's Road, walking very fast, dodging people, my face blazing. There is a sense of one's own face as stretched, as thinned, which goes with extreme joy. I felt as if my face were simply a stretched skin, the features vanished, the pure radiance blazing through. Of course it was terrible, of course it was agonizing, of course it was possible that we should never meet again. But I had kissed her. I had told her I loved her. I had heard her speak my name and say that she cared for me. Of course this was simply pity and the fanciful romanticism of an idle woman. But she had spoken so kindly and she had let me kiss her and she had not said that we must never meet again.

I reached Sloane Square station and took a fivepenny ticket and went down onto the westbound platform and into the bar. I ordered a gin. I sat down. I felt that I had received, somehow, the truth itself, the touchstone itself, as if this were something simply and unconditionally handed over. Yet what I had received was also impossible. I did not want to dwell upon the impossibility, I did not want yet to think, I wanted just to enjoy my new possession in a glorified untroubled present. And it occurred to me after a while, as the mechanical habitual part of my mind soberly reminded me that it was Thursday, that the best way to continue in a state of pure unexamined joy was to be with other people, and thus the obvious thing to do was to go along as usual to dinner at the Impiatts.

I rang the bell and Laura let me in, but without saying anything or even looking at me returned at once to the drawing-room. I took off my coat and shook it—it was very damp and a little speckled with snow flakes, though in fact the snow had now almost ceased—and hung it up on a coat hanger. I dried my hair on a dry end of my scarf. I went into the drawing-room.

'Hello,' I said. 'It's almost stopped snowing.'

I realized that I had entered into the middle of a tense silence.

Freddie, looking very grim, was standing with his back to the fire. Laura was staring at him with a peculiar bright-eyed intensity. She was wearing an ordinary day dress, not one of her robes. Christopher, wearing a suit and tie, was very red in the face, staring at the floor. Freddie, who was looking at Laura when I entered, now looked at me. He said, 'Why have you come?'

'It's Thursday, isn't it?'

'Have you forgotten what happened last night?'

The extraordinary thing was that I had. Dreams have an inbuilt tendency to be forgotten, an ingredient of oblivion. Perhaps certain drug experiences have this too. I could now clearly remember both the great gentle beast and the metaphysical equation, but I had completely forgotten that Freddie had arrived at one in the morning and that I had told him that Laura was not there and that I had subsequently sent Laura home in a taxi with Jimbo.

'Oh of course,' I said, 'I do remember now.'

'Yes, I suppose you do!' said Freddie.

'I was drugged,' I said. 'I'm very sorry. Christopher, will you explain?'

'Well—er—' said Christopher, looking at his feet.

'There you are,' said Freddie.

'He was drugged,' said Laura. 'So was I.'

'He seemed perfectly normal when I saw him,' said Freddie, 'except that he seemed recently to have had his clothes off!'

'I shouldn't have said you weren't there,' I said to Laura. 'I see that now.'

'I think Christopher had better go,' said Freddie. 'I can't think what possessed you to invite him.'

'I didn't think Hilary would come.'

'I'm sorry, Christopher, no one blames you for anything. I'd like to talk to you again about the pantomime, but not tonight.'

'I want Christopher to stay,' said Laura. 'Christopher, you are to stay.'

'I didn't go to bed with Laura,' I said to Freddie. 'Did I, Laura? Is that what you think?'

'I'd better go,' said Christopher.

'Christopher, I forbid you to go,' said Laura.

'Are we going to have any dinner?' I said. 'I'm fearfully hungry.'

'I don't care what you did or didn't do,' said Freddie, 'I don't want you in this house again.'

'Am I to go now, then?'

'Hilary, I forbid you to go,' said Laura.

'Freddie, you really have got hold of the wrong end of the stick.'

'You've been coming here for years,' said Freddie, 'you've been a bloody nuisance with your Thursdays. We've refused hundreds of invitations because of you. We've entertained you, we've fed you, we've stayed in to be bored by you, and it's never occurred to you in all this time to offer us as much as a drink.'

'A drink? You mean round at my place? I didn't think you'd want to come.'

'That doesn't matter,' said Laura, 'about Hilary not—'

'Freddie, I'm terribly sorry, if I had thought for a second that you wanted me to invite you round—'

'I didn't!' said Freddie. 'Don't worry!'

'But I thought you said—'

'I think I'd better go,' said Christopher.

'Nobody is to leave the room,' said Laura.

'Laura,' I said, 'do tell Freddie that it's not like he thinks.'

'You've been coming here for years,' said Freddie, 'and drinking us out of house and home, and taking it all for granted and never uttering a word of thanks and then you start intriguing behind my back. I know it's not important, Laura has told me all about it—'

'I haven't,' said Laura.

'I know it's not important, but it's disgusting and I won't have it. Thank God you've at least had the decency to resign from the office.'

'I didn't resign because of Laura!'

'You're not even gentleman enough to admit it.'

'A gentleman doesn't have to admit what isn't true, even in a situation like this one.'

'You're a rotter, a complete cad. I can't think why I didn't realize it before. I might have expected this—'

'From someone who came out of the gutter.'

'That has nothing to do with it.'

'Of course proles who haven't been to public schools don't know how to behave themselves.'

'I suppose I can excuse you for falling in love with my wife—'

'But I haven't, I didn't—'

'The sheer meanness of this denial—'

'I'm not in love with Laura!'

'You told Tommy you were.'

'I may have let her think it just to shut her up. Tommy was dead keen to imagine there was another woman—'

'Hilary,' said Laura, 'how can you tell such awful lies.'

'Which lies, what—?'

'I know you're trying to help me but it's very much better at this stage to tell the truth, and that's what I suggest we all do.'

'I really must go,' said Christopher, 'I'm sure you can explain everything very much more easily if I'm not there.'

'But Laura, dear, I am telling the truth!'

'I agree with Christopher,' said Freddie. 'I suggest he goes and we sort the matter out between the people involved.'

'But he is involved.'

'We don't need "witnesses". I don't want to know what Christopher saw.'

'He didn't see anything.'

'I'm going to have another drink,' said Laura.

'Can I have a drink?' I said. 'I haven't had one yet.'

Laura poured out some neat whisky for herself. I went and helped myself to a generous dose of gin and vermouth. I suddenly saw that Christopher was trembling.

Laura was wearing a smart unobtrusive dress of blue tweed and her hair, though undone, had been neatly combed down her back. It was not anything like as long as Biscuit's. Laura's prominent brown eyes were horse-wild and her emphatic voice a trifle higher and louder than usual. She looked partly like an experienced hospital matron taking charge of an accident, and partly like an ageing actress playing Lady Macbeth with studied moderation. She drank a measured amount of the whisky as if it were medicine. 'I am to blame,' she said.

'Come, come, Laura,' I said, 'don't let's exaggerate. No one is to *blame*. Freddie has simply made a mistake.'

'No, he hasn't.'

'I wish I had,' said Freddie.

'I think I had better explain everything,' said Laura. 'I'm sorry. But it is for the best. Especially as I feel that, after all the muddle which has occurred, Hilary must be exonerated.'

'Oh, thanks.'

'No one is to blame but me.'

'Look here, Laura—' Christopher began.

'Be quiet, Christopher, leave this to me. I just want to state a few facts.'

'Often a mistake,' I observed, 'but thanks for the exoneration.'

'Perhaps after all,' said Freddie, 'we needn't—'

'Yes we need. To begin with, of course Hilary is in love with me.'

'I'm not!'

'He thinks his denial will help me, but it's quite immaterial. Of course he has been in love with me for some time, but equally of course nothing has happened since I am not the least in love with him.'

'But I'm not—'

'I have felt sorry for Hilary, we all have, he is a lonely unhappy man. And let me say here that I never felt he ought to invite us back. Those who have rich lives should help those who have poor lives and not expect a return.'

'Oh never mind about that,' said Freddie. 'I don't know why I mentioned it.'

'Hilary isn't well off and his flat is a slum—'

'I wish I had invited you, I would have if I'd thought—'

'He isn't the sort of person who is capable of entertaining, anyway.'

'I hope you didn't think I was ungrateful—'

'I felt sorry for him and I thought that his loving me at a distance was something quite harmless. Perhaps that was unwise of me.'

'Look, Freddie, I am *not* in love with Laura.'

'Yes, you are,' said Freddie, 'anyone can see that with half an eye. But I don't blame you for that, I—'

'Hilary isn't to blame at all. I suppose we ought to have stopped inviting him—'

'Exactly,' said Freddie.

'As soon as it was clear how he felt, but it seemed a shame to deprive him of his only really happy bit of social life.'

'What do you know about my social life?'

'As far as Hilary goes, I was perhaps guilty of imprudence, but—'

'You say I bored you, well you've certainly often bored me! I have plenty of happy social life, I don't have to rely on—'

'Hilary, be quiet.'

'Please don't get the idea that I'm not grateful for all those expensive meals and all the drink I've lapped up, as Freddie pointed out—!'

'Oh shut up. The fact of Hilary loving me isn't important.'

'It's not only not important, it's not a fact!'

'Of course I never really thought that you were in love with Hilary—' said Freddie.

'What is important,' said Laura, 'is that I fell madly in love with Christopher.'

'Oh no,' I said. 'Oh no—look, really—'

Freddie said, 'Laura, are you serious?'

'Yes. But listen—'

'With Christopher, with this boy, with—?'

'Yes, yes, old enough to be his mother, such things happen—'

'Laura, don't exaggerate,' said Christopher. 'Please let's—'

'Don't exaggerate! Well really! However as I was saying—'

'Laura, please—'

'As I was saying, nothing happened in this case either because Christopher was never in the least in love with me.'

'Of course he wasn't, and neither was I.'

'You keep out of this, Hilary,' said Christopher.

'After all, how could he be in love with me? Look at me.'

'Oh, I don't know, Laura—' I said.

'What I want to know,' said Freddie, 'is what happened yesterday.'

'Nothing happened yesterday,' I said. 'That at least we can establish.'

'What happened yesterday,' said Laura, 'was just what Hilary said and what I said. Christopher and Jimbo thought it would be funny to hide some dope in a cake, and we all had a trip. At least Hilary and Christopher and I had a trip. Jimbo didn't take any, he looked after us.'

'He fell asleep actually.'

'Hilary came round when you had come back for the second time.'

'The fourth time.'

'And because he didn't want you to see me lying there stoned he said I wasn't there, which was very stupid of him, but he was still a bit stupefied. Then I came round and Jimbo brought me home—I can't remember any of that—the first thing I remember is sitting here and talking nonsense to you.'

'Then nothing really happened?'

'No, of course nothing happened! Only silly Hilary loved me, and your silly wife had an infatuation for a boy who could be her son. And now thank God it's all over. I'm sorry, Christopher, I didn't intend this embarrassing scene when I asked you here this evening. I didn't think it would be necessary. But I had to show Freddie he was wrong about Hilary. And the best way to do it was to tell the whole truth. In fact when one really starts to tell the truth it's indivisible, it all has to come out. And not only does that make everything plain, it—it sort of—destroys everything too. I'm sorry, Christopher, that you've been annoyed by the affections of a silly middle-aged woman. Not that you really ever noticed me at all! It all just happened in my mind. Anyway it's over now. I've come to my senses. I think you'd better go now, and Hilary too.'

'Laura,' I said, 'you're magnificent. Perhaps I love you after all.'

'But then why did Hilary resign from the office?' said Freddie.

'Because I was thoroughly bored.'

'Hilary may not have been to a public school,' said Laura, 'but he is a gentleman.'

'Thanks, Laura, but—'

'So you had this infatuation with Christopher,' said Freddie, 'but he did not return it?'

'No. Did you, Christopher?'

'No.'

'In fact, he couldn't take it seriously, he just laughed.'

'And nothing happened?'

'No, of course not! How could it? Some foolish emotions ran about, mine, Hilary's, Christopher behaved throughout like Jesus Christ.'

'I'm sorry,' said Freddie, 'I see now—'

'So it's all clear and I feel *ever* so much better, and honestly, it's all over. Thank heavens for that!'

'Perhaps you two had better go,' said Freddie.

'All right,' I said. 'I hope you really don't blame me. I'm sorry I said that about being bored here. I've hardly ever been bored actually. I just said it because—'

'And I hope you'll understand,' said Freddie, 'if we now discontinue these Thursday invitations.'

'No more Thursdays?'

'No more Thursdays.'

'What about the panto?' said Christopher.

'I won't need your assistance,' said Freddie.

Laura, who had been standing in the middle of the room with eyes blazing now sat down beside the fire. She began to cry quietly. Freddie went and leaned over her, his hand upon her shoulder.

I moved to the door and out into the hall. My overcoat was still wet. I shook it and put it on and went to the front door. I could hear Christopher coming after me. I left the house and went a little way along the pavement in the direction of Gloucester Road and, without turning round, waited. Christopher caught me up.

'Hilary, I'm terribly sorry.'

'What for?'

'Using you as a front.'

'Using me as a *front*?'

'Laura thought that as you were in love with her—'

'I wasn't!'

'She could make a sort of joke of it and then no one would notice her thing with me.'

'And did she make a sort of joke of it?'

'Well, yes—'

'So I suppose everyone imagines I'm leaving the office because of Laura!'

'I say, I'm terribly hungry, aren't you?'

'Yes. I wonder what if anything was for dinner there?'

We went into a pub and got ourselves sausages and mashed and beer. We sat down. Throughout all these absurdities in the Impiatt drawing-room I had not for a second stopped thinking about Kitty. The thought of her now filled out about me like a great vibrating sphere.

'What I can't understand,' I said, 'was why Laura had to tell Freddie about *you* at all. Why make such a thing of it? Freddie obviously had some crazy idea about me which had to be dealt with. But why drag you in, why couldn't she just have kept quiet?'

'She wanted a drama, a smash-up. She wanted it to end with a bang, to sort of sacrifice herself. As she said, she wanted to destroy it by talking about it.'

'But if there wasn't anything to it except some dotty idea in her head—'

'Oh but there was,' said Christopher.

'You mean?'

'I've been Laura's lover for nearly a year.'

'Oh—God—'

'We met when she was starting to write about the drug scene. Then my lodging with you was jolly convenient, because your habits were so regular—'

'Christ. But why on earth—I can see why Laura might fall for you, but how on earth could you want her—or were you just being kind or—?'

'Well, you're in love with her, you ought to know.'

'Let's start skipping this bit.'

'I did love her,' said Christopher, 'I just did. I couldn't help it, she was so sweet to me. I met her just after my bust-up with Clifford.'

'With—Clifford—'

'Well you knew about my bust-up with Clifford.'

'Oh, of course.'

'She picked up the pieces. I was grateful. Next thing we were in bed. These middle-aged women can be absolute sex-maniacs. Not that I'm complaining, it was good. But, you know—another man's wife—we both felt guilty. I suppose it ran its course—we kept saying it had got to stop. And she'd been having this joke about you all the time—and then when yesterday Freddie started thinking you and she were having an affair—'

'She ended it all with a bang, as you said.'

'Yes. I suppose she felt she had to get you out of it. And she finished me off at the same time.'

'Aren't you relieved?'

'Yes. Very. In a way. But I shall miss her like hell. Not sex, just seeing her, talking to her—' Tears suddenly welled up into Christopher's pale blue eyes. He sat staring at his beer mug and weeping silently. He suddenly looked about fourteen.

'What a horrid mess,' I said. I got up. 'Well I must be off. Christopher, one thing—I'd be awfully glad if you'd find somewhere else to live.'

'Oh Hilary—you're angry with me—don't be—I'm terribly sorry—it wasn't my idea.'

'I'm not angry,' I said. 'We'll stay friends. But you know— I'd just rather you lived somewhere else from now on.'

'I'm sorry,' said Christopher. 'Of course I do understand. Feeling as you do about Laura—'

I left him. The night was cold, still thickly dark but snowless. The thought of Kitty brought no relief now, no joy. I had had my glimpse of heaven, but there would be no more. Powers which I had offended were gathering to destroy me.

FRIDAY

IT WAS Friday evening and it was once more nearly six o'clock and I was once more approaching the door of the house at Cheyne Walk. I had received a note from Gunnar soon after I arrived at the office. It said, *Let us try again. Could you come to Chelsea at six this evening? If I hear nothing I will expect you. G.J.*

It was windless, freezing, one could feel the frost descending, gently fingering the twigs and the leaves in the gardens, outlining them. My breath steamed about me. I rang the bell.

Gunnar opened the door. I came in and took off my coat and followed him upstairs past the numerous pictures through the now familiar smell into the now familiar room. I was sick with the proximity of Kitty, glad she had promised not to listen. I felt desperately anxious not to fail now, for her sake, for Gunnar's sake, for the sake of some last lifeline of sanity which seemed to be left to me.

I walked on towards the fireplace and turned. Gunnar carefully closed the door. He said, 'Hilary—'

Everything vanished, even Kitty vanished. There was nothing but his utterance of my name. It was like a voice calling the damned, recognized as coming from elsewhere, from a place which they thought they had lost forever.

'Oh my God—' I said.

'Thank you for coming.'

'Gunnar— Look, do you think we could have a drink?'

'Yes. I want one too. You know I saw Crystal.'

'Yes. I'm so glad.'

'She's an angel.'

'Yes. Thanks.'

'She says she told you about that night.'

'Yes.'

'Can you forgive me?'

'Me—forgive you—?'

'It was an awful crazy thing—I won't try to explain it. It was one of those extraordinary moments when human conduct sort of shoots off at a tangent.'

'I know, I know. Crystal loved you.'

324

'Yes. She touched me so much, you know, in those old days.'

'You pitied her. You were so kind to her. Hardly anybody ever has been. Hardly anybody has ever properly *noticed* her.'

'It wasn't just pity. She was such a funny brave little thing. And—oh—an angel—'

'Gunnar, I am so terribly terribly sorry about what happened—it was so awful—I did so much damage—if it's any consolation to you I wrecked my own life—I've never really even tried to salvage anything—'

'It's no consolation *now*,' he said.

We looked at each other.

It was hot in the room. Gunnar seemed to be sweating. His jacket hung open, and he had pulled his tie down and partly unbuttoned his shirt. I could feel my face damp and burning from the sudden transition from cold to warm.

'This is better than last time,' I said.

'Why did you let last time happen?' said Gunnar.

'Why did you force it on me? I felt I had to do what you wanted. But let me say again now—God, it sounds so frail after such a thing—what can words do—'

'It's strange, I never thought I'd care a hang. I have hated you so much, perhaps you can hardly imagine such hatred and how it can eat a man up—'

'But you don't now—?'

'No, I don't *think* so. Can it have gone? Maybe Crystal made it go. It was just—amazing—that time with Crystal on Wednesday. Did she tell you about it?'

'Scarcely. She said she gave you fish fingers. She said you'd never had them before.'

'Fish fingers, yes! And I cried.'

'She didn't tell me that.'

'I haven't for years. It was extraordinary. And Crystal quoted the Bible.'

'What did she quote?'

' "Whatsoever things are true, whatsoever things are honest, whatsoever things are just" —'

' "Think on these things". She's full of Biblical lore. It's all she knows.'

'Last time you behaved as if you hated me.'

'I was angry. I felt you despised me, I felt I was just being used. And I suppose I was disappointed.'

'Disappointed?'

325

'Yes. You know—when I heard you were coming—I had a sort of wild hope that after all it would somehow be made all right. That sounds mad, as if one could change the past, but— And then—'

'Anne is so awfully far away now,' said Gunnar.

'You said your hatred of me had made her into a ghost.'

'Yes. It wasn't really her at all. And I've felt—just in these last days—as if the ghost was crumbling—and there she was, the real Anne, very very far away—and somehow safe, out of it—'

'I loved her so much, I loved her dreadfully, otherwise I wouldn't—'

'Yes, yes. You have loved since?'

The image of Kitty burnt me, as if a red-hot burnished plate had been put in front of my face. 'Like that, no.'

'I didn't mean to pry, I just wondered if you had somebody—'

'No. I'm alone.'

'Why don't you get back into the academic world, get back into teaching?'

'How kind you are,' I said, 'how remarkable it is to talk to you, how it changes the world—I thought you'd want to kill me—'

'Yes, I know. There can be too much hate, there can be too much guilt. One must try to drop these burdens at last. Do you mind if I go on talking about Anne?'

'No, no.'

'You didn't do it on purpose?'

'You mean—crash the car?'

'Yes. I didn't ask you in the hospital, I couldn't. But I've thought about it so often—'

'No. Not on purpose. I didn't crash on purpose, but I drove dangerously on purpose.' I had never before put it to myself so clearly.

'And why did you drive dangerously?'

We were looking straight at each other now.

'Because I knew I had lost her. She was going to abandon me and stay with you.'

'Did she say that?'

'Yes.' I hoped Gunnar would not ask me if Anne had said she was pregnant. He did not.

'You know—all these years—I've thought that perhaps—that night—she was running away.'

326

'No, no, no. She thought I was going to drive her home, she kept telling me to stop, she wanted to go back to you—'

Gunnar gave a long shuddering sigh, half turning aside, and we were silent for a moment.

He spoke again, in a tired resonant reflective tone. 'You know—it's a pity you didn't write to me—then—I can see that perhaps I myself made that seem impossible—or that I didn't ask you then—not because of my feelings about you— they were beyond any help—but because of Anne—I have had it in my heart to blame her, almost to hate her—no, that's too much—but there was a gentleness which should somehow have covered the fact of death—which sometimes— only sometimes—failed. I see it differently now. There is so much accident in all things—I suppose in the end all things must be forgiven. I wish we could have had this talk years ago.'

'It might not have worked years ago. If it has worked.'

'Has it done something for you?'

'Yes.'

'Would any form of words help?'

'Don't—'

'But you know—?'

'Yes.'

'I hope to God all this will last, do you think we can keep it up, do you think we're acting above our station?' Gunnar suddenly began to laugh.

I could not laugh, but I smiled. I was trembling with relief.

'What a perfectly—extraordinary—negotiation—' Gunnar laughed. It was more like weeping. The big mouth opened and shut convulsively, a little saliva dribbled over the lip, the blue eyes closed as if in anguish.

I felt an awkward almost embarrassed anxiety that all should have gone well for him, that he should be well served and satisfied.

I said, awkwardly enough, 'Is there anything else you'd like to ask me?'

'No, I don't think so, we seem to have covered the programme! Oh Lord! Hilary, I wish you could get yourself a decent job, you're obviously not getting anywhere in the office.'

'I don't want to get anywhere.'

'But you must, for your own sake, for Crystal's. You have these marvellous linguistic gifts. You must stop wasting yourself.'

'Maybe things will be different now.'

'And Crystal—she's never thought of getting married?'

'No. There was a chap but she broke it off.' Had Crystal known that Gunnar would need her, would need that talk, did she realize how much she had done for him, did she dream that at some time in the future he might need her again?

Gunnar did not pursue the matter. He stood now gulping some whisky, staring into the fire, grimacing, frowning and smiling at the same time, moving his lips as if talking to himself, and as if he were already alone. The interview was at an end and now I must help him to dismiss me.

'I should go,' I said. I wanted to say, but was afraid to say: Shall we meet again?

Gunnar, looking up, seemed suddenly also aware of the unasked question. He drew in his breath, but whether in a sigh of indecision or as a preliminary to an answer I was not to know. He turned to look at the door. Kitty had come in.

Kitty tonight was wearing a canary yellow trouser suit which made her look rich and idle. Her dark hair was particularly Dionysian and glowing; perhaps Biscuit had been brushing it again this evening. Kitty's face was so bright with interest, curiosity, even pleasure, that it was hard to believe that its owner could possibly practise any form of discretion. I was very taken aback, frightened, almost angry. There was something dangerously frivolous in this manifestation, in her evident wish to see these two men together. For a second I imagined that Kitty might actually blurt out our secret, or that she had already done so.

Gunnar, also a little disturbed, said, 'Ah Kitty—you remember Mr Burde—you met him at the Impiatts' place.'

'Hello,' said Kitty, and stretched out her hand.

I took her hand and felt its warmth, its not quite conspiratorial grip. Her face was hidden by a haze. I was now desperately anxious to get out of the house.

'Good evening. Glad to see you again. I'm afraid I have to go.' I made for the door and almost fell down the stairs.

I was relieved to find Gunnar just behind me when I got to the street door. I hoped he had not noticed my confusion.

'Thank you,' I said. 'Thank you.'

'Thank you. Good-bye, Hilary.'

We shook hands. It seemed at that moment like a final farewell. I was not sure if I was glad or not.

I went out through the gardens and across onto the pavement beside the river and began to walk slowly along. The frost was glittering on the paving stones, marked with footprints. So many confused emotions were darting and flashing about, I felt as if my head were wrapped up in a sort of sparkling gauzy veil, positively bundled up with intense feeling. I also felt rather sick.

I had not walked very far when I heard the lipping padpad of feet behind me, a woman's feet. I stopped and turned. Biscuit, duffle-coated and hooded. I walked on and she walked beside me, as she had done, as it now seemed, so many times before. I felt that we were weary, Biscuit and I, like two faithful retainers who had grown old together. 'Well, little Biscuit?'

She produced a letter from her pocket and held it towards me. I could see Kitty's writing. Written when? This afternoon, during my talk with Gunnar, in rushed haste after it? My curiosity was detached. It floated away.

'No,' I said. 'Take it back to Lady Kitty.'

Biscuit pocketed the letter. We walked on a bit until we came to the corner of Flood Street. Here we stopped.

'Biscuit dear, you mustn't be angry with me, I'm so shipwrecked. Let's say good-bye here. Let me kiss you.'

I pushed back the hood of the duffle coat. I could not see her face. When I stooped and touched it with mine it was strangely warm and, as I realized the next moment, covered in tears. I held her, not kissing her, just clutching her close against me while her hands gripped onto my overcoat. Then we let go and she turned back and I went on towards the King's Road. I was already bitterly regretting having refused Kitty's letter.

SATURDAY

THE NEXT day, Saturday, began with four letters. The
first, delivered by hand late at night or early in the
morning, was from Tommy and ran as follows:

Darling, I set the table and waited for you, I was so sure
you would come, I made a hot-pot and a treacle pudding,
I was so sure you would come. I have cried so much for
you. Oh, if you would only give me a child. You know I
want to marry you, but I would accept less. I just can't
face a life without you and I must have something. Could
you not just give me a child and we would live near you
and you could see us sometimes? Is this a crazy idea? I must
have something from you. And for that there is so little
time left. I was so unhappy waiting for you and your not
coming, I wanted to die. Please give me something to live
for. Will you think of it please, will you *think* of it? Your
Thomas.
P.S. I know it's my month-day to see Crystal but I won't
come unless you ring me.

The second letter came by post from Laura Impiatt. It ran
as follows.

Dearest Hilary, I owe you so many apologies and explana-
tions, but perhaps a simple 'I'm sorry' is best! I have been
in a terrible muddle for a long time and am profoundly
thankful that it's over. I wonder how much you guessed?
Now that I am, I think, out of the wood, I can see everything much more clearly, I can see *you* much more clearly.
Contrary to what you may have believed (you are absurdly
humble!) your love has helped and supported me a great
deal. I want you to know that. Will you come round and
see me? You must be glad that all *that* is over, and that
now we can have a *long talk*. I am staging an illness, I have
actually retired to bed, but will shortly rise anew! Could
you come for a drink on Wednesday evening? Freddie will
be out at a meeting. Wednesday I know is not one of your
booked days. Perhaps it could be *my* day?! I could give

you regular times now. Of course you must not stop your Thursdays, Freddie is not really against you. Only let a little while pass, better not come this Thursday. I'll expect you about six on Wednesday if I don't hear otherwise. Much love,

Laura.

The third letter was from the headmaster of the ——— Grammar School. (——— was the town where I was born.) It read

Dear Sir,

Mr Osmand

I have received your letter re Mr Osmand who has some years ago left this school. I write to inform you that your letter addressed to Mr Osmand has been redirected to the school where he taught after leaving here. (The address followed.) I have also taken the liberty of forwarding to the HM there a copy of your letter addressed to me. Mr Osmand has however to the best of my knowledge left that school also. Hopefully they will have a forwarding address.

Yours faithfully,

J. P. Bostock.

The fourth letter was from Kitty.

I understood your refusing to accept my letter, but this is another one. I must see you. Could we meet tomorrow Sunday morning at Peter Pan at eleven? I want to ask you something very special. It is most important. It is something for Gunnar not for me. I shall expect you. K.

Kitty's letter was delivered at about nine o'clock by Biscuit, after I had read the other three. The flat was strangely quiet and it had taken me a little while to realize that Christopher had already departed. I looked into his room. All his silly touching gear had disappeared. He had gone. I felt sad and a little frightened. An era was ending.

There was now nothing to stop me inviting Biscuit in. We sat in the kitchen drinking cups of tea. The servants' hall atmosphere was overwhelming, the air of idle menials gossiping about their betters.

'Tell her I'll come.' My main feeling on receiving her letter was profound relief. My gesture of yesterday had been idle. I would have to see Kitty now even if the heavens fell.

'Yes'

'Talk to me, Biscuit, tell me this and that. I wonder how much you really know about what's going on? I bet you know plenty.'

Biscuit had shed her duffle coat on the floor. She was wearing narrow serge trousers and a blue padded jacket, a more wintry version of what she had had on when I first saw her. Her long plait was inside the jacket. She looked tired, very little and thin, her face so narrow and frail. I put my hand upon the table as if coaxing a bird and she put her thin hand into it and let me caress her fingers.

'I know some things.'

'Really? Lady Kitty told you?'

'No, not Kitty, Gunnar.'

'*Gunnar*,' I withdrew my hand hastily. The use of the names shocked almost as much as the information.

'Why not? I have lived in his house for years. Do you think I am invisible?'

To him, yes, I had. 'But —'

'A man, two women. We have been everywhere together.'

'Biscuit, you haven't told him —'

'About you and her? Of course not! I would not hurt him with that.'

'Be careful. If you know some things you must know that there is nothing bad here, it is all to help him. I may see her once again —'

'You and your onces. You be careful too.'

'What do you mean?'

'He wanted to kill you.'

'You know why?'

'Yes.'

'But he doesn't any more, he was kind to me yesterday, we are friends now.'

'Why should you trust them?'

'*Them?*'

'People can pretend.'

'What on earth — ?'

'A plot, a trap, it would be a good way to finish you.'

'Biscuit, you're *mad*.'

'I must go now.'

'Will you kindly explain —'

'Good-bye.'

'You're joking. A rather stupid joke. Good-bye then, until the next letter.'

'I will bring no more letters, I am leaving them.'

'Leaving Lady Kitty?'

'Yes. Be careful. If you hurt him I curse you.'

'I won't hurt him! All right, off you go, I'm sick and tired of riddles.'

She picked up her coat and was out of the door like a flying shadow.

It was Saturday evening and I was with Crystal. (No Thomas of course, since I had not telephoned.) Outside the snow was falling steadily in big woolly flakes. We had had our supper: sausages and fried eggs and beans and tinned peaches and custard.

'Don't go to her,' said Crystal, 'don't go.'

I had spent the day at home alone in a prostrating agony of reflection. I lay on my bed and literally writhed with doubt and anguish.

Biscuit's extraordinary riddles had upset me profoundly and made me feel menaced and polluted as by a ghost. The spirit of revenge is not so easily exorcized. I was disturbed and muddled and could not afterwards remember exactly what Biscuit had said, let alone what she had intended. Had she hinted that the whole thing was an elaborate plot between the spouses to lure me on, and then, in a hideously appropriate situation, punish me? To make me re-enact my crime and to unmask me in it? Would I end up slaughtered by Gunnar at Kitty's feet? Were there women who could use their wiles for such a purpose, find pleasure and excitement in such a drama? Of course there were. Could Kitty conceivably be one of them?

I was not long in deciding this to be impossible. However there were other possibilities. There was the ambiguity of Biscuit herself. Because Kitty trusted Biscuit I had trusted her blindly. Could both trusts be misplaced? What secret loves and jealousies lurked unsuspected here? How much did Biscuit really know anyway? She was capable of lying. The hazard of Biscuit had however to be accepted, now as it had been at the start, and I felt fatalistic and almost uninterested in what Biscuit might or might not do. There was perhaps more danger in other quarters. Kitty might, on some truthful impulse, tell Gunnar that she had seen me. What was the significance of her suddenly appearing in the drawing-room and interrupting our talk? Had she wanted somehow, in some incoherent and illogical way, to mitigate the falsehood by seeing me in his presence? She might be suffering some guilty discomfort by which she might be prompted to tell him everything. Or she might (foolishly, but she was foolish) come to feel that since after all she had been asking me to help Gunnar it did not matter all that much that we had met clandestinely. She might tell Gunnar, she might already have told him, not thinking he would mind, not realizing how, however carefully she described it, the thing might look. Had Gunnar then shaken the whole truth out of her, the kiss upon the jetty, her feelings, mine? Or had he perhaps led her on, and involved her without her knowledge in just such a plot as Biscuit had seemed to suggest?

The strange thing was that after a while, after perhaps hours, I could look at this possibility with fairly calm eyes. Even if this was so I must see Kitty. It was almost as if, especially if this was so I must see her. I felt the forces of destiny quite sufficiently mustered round about me. Was I being lured on, fascinated, not by Kitty but by Gunnar himself, to make perfect his revenge? If there was a plot must I not connive, a trap must I not fall into it? Did I then *want* Gunnar to kill me? Of course I recognized these thoughts as half mad. They were, I suppose, a frenzied working over, in the interests of a resignation which did not divide me from Kitty, of the plausible terrors which Biscuit had conjured up. I must go to Kitty even if it were to my death, and even if she too had willed it.

I seemed at last to come, in these matters, to some sort of conclusion, and I was able to set them aside. More important, deeper, were considerations which once more cast doubt upon what I ought to do tomorrow. No, I could not believe that Gunnar had been play-acting on Friday. Of course sincerity is not indivisible, he could have been sincere and not sincere. But that talk had been something real, something momentous and genuinely achieved. Surely something good; good at least if only I and he could maintain the peace of mind necessary to let it *work*. Gunnar had hated me, he had wanted to kill me. Then suddenly because of his indelible generosity,

334

because there are righteous spirits in the world, we had been able to communicate in gentleness, to forgive ourselves and each other. It had all seemed to 'come right'. And, I now realized as I lay there writhing on my bed, how *happy* all this would have made me if it had simply happened by itself, if it had simply existed between me and Gunnar without the shadow cast upon it by Kitty. And there were moments when I cursed this spoiling of my enjoyment of a perfect thing. If only Kitty had not meddled. Yet it was through her meddling that the thing had come about.

I tossed my body and my thoughts to and fro, and as the hours passed it seemed more and more as if everything was taking place after all against a huge fated background which was, because so fated, somehow calm: my love for Kitty. Being in love has its own self-certifying universality, it informs and glorifies the world with an energy which, like a drug, becomes a necessity of consciousness. Without it, the scene is dark, without that throbbing communication, dead. A mad state, perhaps an undesirable one, inimical to justice, benevolence, common sense. But, for its slaves, it justifies itself as, for the ordinary unsaintly man, nothing else ever does. Of course I would see Kitty again. My love for her was a great unexpected extra gratuitous good thing. It was good that I should be changed, shaken, my bones severed, my mind devastated by this experience. How could I wish it otherwise or unwish any suffering it would bring me? About her feelings for me I dared not think, about the future I did not think. I assumed there was none. I had no 'hope'. There were, as I obscurely saw it, various 'goods'. If I could only endure and keep them separate and hope nothing and plan nothing and be prepared for any degree of misery then at last somehow perhaps there would be some merciful dispensation and all would ultimately after all in some as yet undisclosed sense be well.

'Don't go to her,' said Crystal. 'I am so afraid. That woman will lure you to your doom.'

'Don't be silly!' I said. 'You know nothing whatever about her.'

We were drinking wine, at least I was. Crystal had brought her chair near to mine and was staring at me intently and urgently with her enlarged yellow eyes. I was feeling electric, restless, twitching with anxiety and desire for Kitty and love and the magnitude of recent events.

'Darling, don't see her. Leave well alone. I'm so terribly

glad you saw Gunnar and it was all so good. Leave it there, leave it like that when you've got some good out of it all. Don't see her, and don't see him again either. Let's escape now when we can. I'm so glad you're leaving the office. Oh do let's go away somewhere else.'

'I can't get a university job now, Crystal, that's just a dream.'

'Well, any job, we can both work, we've always been poor, I want to go away.'

'Where to, dear?'

'We could go back to ———. I heard from—'

'Crystal, I will not go back to ———! You know that! Don't be insane.'

'Please let's break away now before something happens, Hilary. I wish we could change our lives.'

'So do I. It's not so easy.'

'We've been so unhappy all these years and it hasn't been necessary, it's been bad, we've been unhappy in a bad way.'

'You may be right,' I said, 'but it's a bit late to change that.'

'It isn't too late. I blame myself, I've let you decide everything—'

'That was pretty daft of you, wasn't it!'

'I've let you brood and worry about—that—without end, and I should have told you to stop. We should have tried to be happy.'

'Maybe. But this is all vague stuff. Human minds are relentless things and strong. You can't just turn a switch and decree merriment.'

'Now that you've had this wonderful talk with Gunnar—it's time to go—please, please, for my sake, I've never said this before, never begged you before—I do now—please don't see her—you needn't go to the office any more—let's go away on holiday, go away anywhere—'

'Don't be so silly, Crystal, anyway we haven't got any money. Where do you want to go, the South of France?'

'I'd love to go to France,' said Crystal, 'I'd love to. It seems to me now I've been stupid. I shouldn't have let us get like this. I've lived all these years like a mouse—'

'The dearest goodest little mouse that ever was!'

'In a hole, just sitting here and waiting for you to come and see me, that's what it comes to, it isn't a life—'

'I know, I know, I know, don't tell me, don't torment me with it! I wanted to make you happy, when we were young
336

I thought of nothing else, I wanted to succeed for you, I wanted to be rich for you—and look what it's all come to.'

'I've never complained—'

'Maybe you should have done, if you feel like this!'

'Maybe I should have done. Sometimes it's wicked to be unhappy. Please let's go on holiday. I'll make myself some dresses. I'd like to stay in a hotel. I've never stayed in a hotel.'

'Crystal, darling, stop it, you'll make us both cry, like you used to do in the caravan! We can't go on holiday, (a) because we've got no cash, (b) because I've got to stay here and finish various things. I've got to work my month at the office, I need the time, I need the bloody money. Gunnar may want to see me again. I—'

'You want to see her. That's the only thing that's keeping you.'

'Don't be so bloody spiteful.'

'I'm not spiteful, I'm terrified. I think I shall see Arthur again.'

'See Arthur? I thought we'd finished with Arthur.'

'Dearest, I so much want a child. I've got nothing in my life. Of course I've got you—'

'I agree that amounts to nothing.'

'I want a child. A child could change everything for me. You don't want me to sit here forever becoming bitter and old? I've never complained, but I'm complaining now. Perhaps that's the beginning of being bitter and old. I must have things different—'

'Things could be different and worse.'

'I know you don't like Arthur—'

'I don't mind Arthur. I just think he's a nonentity.'

'Well, I'm a nonentity—'

'Crystal, you're not, you're my sister. Now stop moaning.'

'We could all go away—I'd so much like to live in the country—'

'You mean you and I and Arthur? Count me out. I'm not going anywhere with you and Arthur. He was all set to follow us to Australia!'

'Australia?'

'Oh never mind. He still loves you, he's still waiting. I suggest you and Arthur go to Australia and have six children.'

'Hilary, don't be angry—'

'I'm not angry, or if I am I ought to be shot. Crystal, don't *bother* me with these things just now, will you.'

'I'm sorry.'

'Just don't torment me at present, you torment me! I've got so much to think about, so much to decide, so much to do. I've got to bloody find a job apart from everything else. Probably the best thing for me to do is to commit suicide. Then you can live happily ever after with Arthur.'

'Oh darling—don't speak like that—you know Arthur doesn't matter—you're the only thing that matters to me—'

'My dear heart, I know it's awful, and I know we've lived stupidly. You're absolutely right, it's a sort of moral cowardice, pure obsession, there has been nothing good in it. I see that now, but what am I to do? I think I mixed up some idea of expiation with a sort of self-destructive disappointed anger against everything—Christ, I even made you suffer—it was probably something to do with the ghastly revengeful sort of religion we were brought up in.'

'Don't say that. If we've gone wrong we've misused our religion.'

'I won't argue. The darkness deepens, Lord with me abide.'

'Don't see her.'

'Crystal, I've got to.'

338

SUNDAY

IT HAD snowed all night. Now the sun was shining. I was with Kitty in Kensington Gardens. We had met at Peter Pan and walked up to my 'Leningrad garden'. Here there were few people about. Some well-padded individuals were exercising their dogs, watching with absurd pleasure at the dogs' amazement at the snow, their play, the doggy footprints. The stone basins were frozen and some ducks, with comical caution, were slithering about on the ice. The fountains were bearded with opaque white icicles. We had carried a couple of chairs into the little stone pavilion at the end and were sitting there in a corner. The pavilion, heaped over with snow, was enclosed and private, our corner almost obscure. The snow had dulled the traffic noise, muffled the world about us, arched us in. Every now and then a dog ran up to the doorway, sniffed and ran off, wild with snow-joy, and a smiling wool-clad owner plodded by. No one else came. Straight ahead, between two stone nymphs, the lake curved away, goldened with willows, and the cloudless glittering blue sky arched over the snowy park. There was not a breath of wind.

The meeting with Kitty was a climax of quiet joy. There had been anguish, fear, indecision, then gradually the brightness of her presence cast beforehand, obliterating all else. Then I was with her and there was a strange blankness, an utter calm of delight. Suddenly, down into the furthest crannies of being all was well. It was all so strangely simple too, with a blameless simplicity as of childhood. Even Peter Pan, heaped up with snow, a scarcely decipherable crystal mound with streaks of polished gold, seemed for once a monument to innocence, as unsmirched as the very children who came to dig with little woolly mittened hands for the rabbits and the mice whom they knew so well. And Kitty and I too were like children, we laughed, we swung along together.

'Oh Kitty, I do love you, I'm sorry, I do, I just love saying it, it's my song of praise to the world, you don't have to do anything about it, I love your coat, it's so expensive and it smells so nice, I love your nose, I —'

'Hilary, stop, dear Hilary. You talk as if we could really be light-hearted.'

'Let's be. So much has happened in my mind since I last saw you—'

'Yes, yes. And in mine. Oh dear—I care for you so much, I care so much what happens to you, you've no idea what a figure you've been in my mind all these years—'

'A horrible figure I should have thought.'

'Of course I was curious.'

'You must have expected to hate me.'

'It's odd, but I never expected that.'

'You pitied me. That was prophetic. And you didn't just take on Gunnar's feelings.'

'I tried to be detached. And his feelings were never all that clear, I mean they were such a battlefield—'

'He was so wonderful to me on Friday, so generous, so simple, it was suddenly all sort of clarified and easy like it should be in heaven.'

'You think it will be easy in heaven?'

'Oh Kitty, I do just love talking to you, talking's so natural, babbling's natural, I don't usually babble. Yes, but heaven can only be on earth. Everything falls away, some crystal of personality that is most of all you, which perhaps you never knew existed, understands it all clearly at last and you pardon everything, not even that, that's too personal, everything *is* in the light of God—'

'I'm so terribly glad you talked like that with Gunnar, he's been a different person since.'

'Really somehow better?'

'Yes, yes, yes.'

'You didn't listen, did you? Why did you come in at the end? I nearly fainted when you came in.'

'It was rather sort of—rash—but I wanted to be with both of you together—to sort of—establish that it was possible—'

'Oh my dear— Am I to see Gunnar again?'

'Wait, wait, I've got a lot of things to say—'

'Kitty, I can't waste this love, I can't, it mustn't be wasted, poured away upon the face of the universe, you must help me—'

'You have helped me so much—'

'Helped *you*?'

'Yes, and not only by helping Gunnar. I feel, you know, it sounds a bit weird, she's gone away at last.'

'Anne—'

'You did love her very much, didn't you?'

The idea that Kitty might be jealous of Anne because of me flickered luridly, then burst like a kind of rocket. 'Yes.'

'I'm glad you did—I mean, otherwise it would all have been—'

'Even more awful.'

'You know, it's a sort of strange experience, a strange pain, to have her coming at me now through you, as if differently made in a new life, a new Anne—'

'The same Anne, dear Kitty. Gunnar and I both loved her and she's dead. If there was any ghost it was something that Gunnar's anger invented and it's gone now.'

'Yes, I heard him say that. He had to suffer of course. And so did you. But my sufferings were idiotic, I mean my sufferings because of her. I was jealous of her as if she were still alive.'

'We can be jealous of the dead, but we must remember that they are dead—there's a sort of inevitable pity mixed in.'

'Yes. I feel the pity so much now, I feel all pity, as if all the resentful things were going away.'

'You said when we first met that you wanted your husband to be entirely here in the present with you, not a haunted man.'

'Yes, and I think it's happened, or at any rate it's happening—'

'Then my work is done.' The phrase had a disturbing ring. I said quickly, 'This is the first time I've ever been able to look at you properly.'

'In a good light! I'm not young any more, not like her—'

'Sssh.'

In the shadowed corner the reflected snow-light was soft yet very clear. We were sitting half turned to each other, our knees almost touching. Kitty was wearing the mink coat, which she had thrown open, and underneath it a mousy-brown woollen dress and some pearls. Her high black leather boots were wet with melted snow. A big dark fur hood concealed her brow and her hair. Her face blazed with vitality and response to the cold, her cheeks red with a deep cloudy mantling of colour, as of a poured and mingling liquid, her long resolute mouth red too, where she kept drawing in her lips in little *moues* of emotion. The spotty stone-blue eyes were a little moist with the cold, as if the stone of them was sea-wet.

341

I kissed her cheek. It was exceedingly cold and smooth, like kissing a frozen fruit. I quickly kissed her lips, which were moist and warm. She continued to look at me but she did not stir.

'Kitty, we're mad, anyway I am. I'm yours. Dispose of me. I wish I could be your servant, like Biscuit.'

The mention of Biscuit's name carried some sort of unpleasant aura and I half remembered yesterday's scene. I also remembered someone (who?) saying that of course Biscuit was busy carrying Kitty's letters around to half the population of London. I could not ask Kitty how many slaves she had. It was not for slaves to ask such things. I said, to parry the idea of Biscuit a bit, 'Has she gone?'

'Who?'

'Biscuit. She said she was going to leave you.'

'Oh, did she talk to you?'

It seemed a little quaint of Kitty not to conceive of this possibility, or did she imagine that Biscuit delivered her missives in respectful silence? The memory of having kissed Biscuit more than once raised an inconvenient and accusing head.

'No, of course she hasn't gone,' said Kitty. 'She's always talking about leaving me. She never has and I daresay she never will.'

Kitty did not seem to like the subject of Biscuit either. Perhaps there were tales which Biscuit could tell. I felt, and could feel Kitty feeling, that we must, between us now in this precious time together, keep to essentials and communicate only what was necessary and clear. For my salvation, I prayed, for my salvation.

'Listen, Hilary,' she said, and she drew off her glove. Her hand warmly sought my gloveless hand in the gaping sleeve of my overcoat. 'You said that we were mad. Perhaps we are. But let us be mad to some purpose. I have two special things to say to you, two enterprises to suggest. One is a little crazy and will need a good deal of courage, the other is very crazy and would need a vast amount of courage.'

'For courage,' I said, 'I'm your man.' And as I held her wrist, edging her warm dry firm hand further up my coat sleeve, I loved and desired her so much I could have moaned. I added, 'I notice you distinguish here between "will" and "would".'

'What—?'

'You say the first enterprise will need courage, the second

one would need it. So it seems we shall certainly carry out the first, but the second is doubtful.'

'About the first one perhaps there is nothing surprising. I am very happily married to Gunnar, we love each other deeply.'

I very gradually released her hand and she very gradually withdrew it.

'I say this because it must be the background to what follows.'

'To the enterprise.'

'To both enterprises. You said—that you loved me—and that you did not want to waste that love, you wanted it to live—'

'I couldn't prevent it from living, it's the most living thing in the universe, you know how rare absolute love is—'

'I told you I wanted to stand with you and Gunnar in the same room just to see if it was possible. It was possible.'

'The world didn't end. The stars didn't crumble.'

'You see—to use your word—I don't want you to be wasted either.'

'You want me to be—around?'

'Yes.'

'But Kitty, aren't there lots and lots of people in your life, everyone must love you—' It was as near as I dared come to the question of all those other letters.

'No. You're special. You've lived so long in my mind. It's hard to explain. It's as if you've always been necessary, always in some strange way a part of my marriage. I fell in love with Gunnar when he was telling me about you and Anne.'

'Oh God!'

'I felt so sorry for him. I felt so sorry for you. And I've lived with this. I've lived. I've been lonely really. Not only because of Gunnar's depressions. He and I come from very different worlds and I've lived with him in his world. Love, I don't mean love affairs, I mean love, has been rare in my life. So you see—'

'I'll do whatever you want.'

'Don't say that yet. You haven't heard my second idea. The first one is just this, that we should all three of us be friends. There. It's simple, isn't it?'

'It's sublime,' I said, 'but is it possible? Gunnar, of course, doesn't know you've ever met me except at the Impiatts' and on last Friday—'

'Of course. And I shall never tell him. I saw you only for his sake. There was nothing wrong in that. And equally I

343

think there is nothing wrong in concealing it. This part of our friendship will soon belong to the past and it must remain a secret between you and me, a place where we meet in memory very privately—'

I pictured this place. Unfortunately Biscuit was there too, only that was doubtless immaterial.

'I want us now to move forward very slowly and carefully and bring it all gradually out into the open—'

'All?'

'Except for *this*—I mean you will come to see us as a friend, and then later if I see you alone Gunnar will know of it, and there will be nothing to hide, everything will be—'

'Innocent.' I felt giddy. I pictured regular dinners at Cheyne Walk. They could have Wednesdays. Lunch *tête-à-tête* with Kitty at the Savoy. She would have to pay. It was, as she said, mad. But what was the alternative? 'All right,' I said.

'Are you brave enough?'

'Yes. But you'll have to do everything, organize it all, control it all—' A large number of important questions occurred to me concerning this state of affairs, but a choking flow of hopes and fears kept me silent. If only I somehow need not lose Kitty after all. Better let her talk, let her imagine, let her lead.

Kitty was reading my thoughts. 'Don't try to see too much of the future, I can't see it either. Rest upon the simplicity of our needs. There is a love which I selfishly want to keep, which I don't want to have to throw away—'

'I will rest upon your selfishness then.'

'Good. Now let me tell you about my second idea. And hold your breath a little.'

'I'm holding it. Oh you brave wonderful woman! You know I admired you so much on that first day when we met at Peter Pan, you were so—so statesmanlike—'

'That's a wonderful compliment! Listen now. Gunnar and I are childless.'

My heart grew cold. For a second I saw Anne's face as I had seen it that evening in the car, frightened, pleading, begging me to stop so that she could get out and return to her husband.

'We are childless and this has been a great cause of grief to us. The fact is—I am now telling you something which hardly anyone knows, not even Gunnar—Gunnar cannot have children.'

'He — ?'

'He had an operation, oh some time ago now — and one result — was that. The doctor told me, and I decided not to tell Gunnar. He doesn't know.'

A sort of cold logical dew seemed to descend upon me as if suddenly everything had been made very orderly and very clear and very dreadful. I stiffened as if for that bullet in the chest.

'We both desperately want children. And Gunnar doesn't want to adopt, he wants my child. And I am over thirty.'

I seemed to have heard this bit before.

'Hilary, I want you to give me a child.'

The logical dew was helping me. I felt, myself now, very orderly and very clear and very dreadful. I could even smile at her. I said, 'We agreed that I was just an instrument, a tool, but this is taking the matter rather too literally! Dearest beloved darling Kitty, you are indeed mad, gloriously mad. You have laid before me the most wonderful beautiful mad idea with which I have ever been presented. I feel as if you have given me the Taj Mahal. All I can do is fold it up very small indeed and give it you back. Perhaps I can just tuck it into your handbag.'

'Of course it would be in every way as if it was Gunnar's child. Hilary, be serious —'

'I am, I am. Kitty, dear heart, oh I do love you so, use your sweet wonderful mind. How do you think Gunnar would react if —'

'He wouldn't ever know. How could he ever guess at anything so strange? The very madness of the scheme protects it. It's a terrible thing to ask of you, I realize that, and I couldn't ask it of anybody else — you are the only one — I can ask it of you —'

'Because of the special relationship.'

'Yes. Because of the past. You owe me —'

'I owe Gunnar a child.'

'I wasn't going to say that, but yes if you like — you said you'd do anything for me. You ought to do anything for him.'

'But this is a rather particular thing, Kitty, which not every man likes another man to do for him.'

'It would have to be done —'

'Perfectly. Oh yes. But some things by their nature can't be done perfectly.'

'I realize that the burden of silence upon you —'

345

'Oh I could manage the burden of silence. I just don't want to be murdered.'

'But—'

'Suppose your little baby turned out to bear a curious resemblance to me? Wouldn't that give poor old Gunnar something new to brood about? Gunnar is as fair as a Viking, well he is a Viking—'

'I'm not.'

'Suppose the little dear had hazel eyes?'

'My father had hazel eyes. In fact, now I come to think of it, my father looked remarkably like you.'

I began to laugh, throwing back my head and sticking out my legs and thrusting my hands deep into my pockets.

'Hilary, what—?'

'A terribly funny idea has just struck me,' I said. 'It's divinely funny, in fact it's just what's needed to make your wonderful scheme quite perfect.'

'What?'

'I never knew who my father was. Did your father ever visit the north of England?'

'Yes, I think so.'

'Did he ever go to ———?'

'I don't know.'

'What did he do? I mean did he do anything besides being a lord or whatever?'

'Yes, he was an engineer, an inventor. He invented all sorts of big engines—he used to visit, oh, iron foundries and—'

'There is an iron foundry at ———.'

'Hilary, you aren't suggesting—'

'No, no, of course not, not seriously. How could your father have met my mother, it's inconceivable. It's just that if, as well as everything else, we turned out to be brother and sister it would somehow—well, it really would be the Taj Mahal!'

'Hilary, please stop laughing.'

'Dearest Kitty, I can't do it, you know I can't. Objectively it would be a terrible crime against Gunnar, and even if we got away with the consequences, which we wouldn't, I should be driven mad by the crime. I've done enough to him without fucking his second wife, even with the highest motives!' But as I said this I could not help thinking how wonderful it would be and hang the motives. In any case, *ought* I to take Kitty's idea seriously, *ought* I to? How does 'ought' work in such outlandish regions? She was leading me

346

far, ought I not to go far, to risk the crime and the madness
after all?

'Please try to understand—'

'You couldn't stand it either. Your emotions about it
would wreck you. You'd confess it to him in the end.'

'This would be something absolutely special, not like anything anyone else could ever do or think of. It is only possible
because of you, only possible between you and me. I couldn't
ask this mad thing of anyone else. If you don't help me, help
us, nobody can.'

'Oh I know. I'm the dedicated one, the anointed one, the
sacrificial victim if you like. But I doubt if these high con-
ceptions would impress Gunnar if he were to find out.'

'But he wouldn't find out, he couldn't, this idea would
never occur to Gunnar in his wildest dreams, that you should
be the father. Just think of it! So we would be quite safe.'

'Oh Kitty, darling sweet, you are living in a fantasy world.'
And I am living there with you, and please please let it last
just a little longer.

'Don't decide yet,' she said. She was looking at me with a
fierce hardened desperate face which I had not seen before.
I took her hand again, holding onto her as if in a whirlwind.
I could feel that a sense of time had returned to us both, time
as terror, time as death. Kitty looked quickly at her watch.

'Must you go?'

'Not yet.'

We stared huge-eyed at each other. The lightness, the joy,
even the craziness, were gone. I felt the chill touch of an
inevitable doom: nothing dramatic, only the slow blundering
crushing force of the many circumstances which every day
announce impossibilities in human lives.

'Hilary, don't say anything final. Just think, will you,
about both the things I've said, both the plans. It's all so
difficult and complicated, we can't decide anything quickly,
we'll have to think, and meet again, and—'

'Yes, of course, whatever—yes, yes, we must think and meet
again— But Kitty, darling heart, you do see, don't you,
that your two plans are incompatible? This piece of logic had
only just that moment become clear to me.

'Incompatible?'

'Yes. We can't do both these things. Perhaps we can't do
either, but we certainly can't do both.'

'Why?'

'Kitty, see it, think. If I were to become your lover, for

whatever high and holy and Gunnar-directed a purpose, how could I then meet him as a friend? How could I come to your house, as you so charmingly envisage, if I had that secret under my belt? It would be impossible, I should detest myself and—no. If we are to meet all three together as friends, I cannot be your lover—and surely you didn't imagine this as any part of your first plan—no, no. But if I were to try to give you and Gunnar a child then I must vanish forever from your lives when the thing is done.'

Kitty looked away from me, looked down, shifted her boots around in the pool of melted snow which they had made upon the floor. The sun was still shining outside, we were still alone in the bright dim snow-lit cave within.

She said nothing. I felt that she was going to cry.

I said quickly, in an attempt to bring the craziness to our rescue, 'Of course, it would be a marvellous finale, wouldn't it? Like the end of *Hassan*.'

'Like what?'

'Never mind. But it does look as if, my dear dear love, you will have to choose, we will have to choose, between, well, everything for a short time and very little for a long time, whether to live dully or die gloriously. Not that I admit that either plan is feasible, I don't know what to think, I don't know what I want—Oh Christ, oh my dear, how mad, what madness encompasses us! You say that because Gunnar couldn't conceive of anything so wild we'd be safe. You mean you'd be safe. I would have vanished for ever, I would have had to. How long do you think it would take me to make you pregnant? How long would you let me make love to you if you didn't become so? Seven times? Seventy times seven?'

'Hilary, don't. We mustn't see it as madness. I don't think I agree with you anyway. I'm sure there's some way—'

'To have everything? No.'

'I don't know either what I think. Only don't suddenly decide against us.'

'Against us? Against whom? You and me? You and me and Gunnar? You and Gunnar and baby? You're looking at your watch again.'

'Hilary, I've got to go. I have to be back for luncheon.'

'Who's coming to "luncheon"?'

'Oh, some Liberal M.P.'

'What's to eat?'

'Oh—curry—'

348

'I suppose you have curry every day. All right, my dear, off you go. Mustn't keep the bigwigs waiting, must you?'

'Please—try to—'

We stood up. Then suddenly we grabbed each other, rushing together as if our bodies and our souls would join, trying desperately to overcome the awkwardness of two clumsy overdressed material objects. Kitty's fur hood fell off onto the floor. I felt her boot jar against my trouser leg. I was trying to open my overcoat and feel her breasts and get an arm well round the mink coat all at the same time. Our cheek-bones ground together, her hair slid across my mouth. I drew her very close up against me and kissed her and felt her answering kiss, as if her lips were burning. Then I felt her withdraw, saw her hand swoop to pick up the fur hood, saw her reddened fingers trembling as she did up the buttons of her coat.

'Oh Kitty, I do love you. Forgive me, forgive me—'

'I love you too. I can't not.'

'Kitty, let's not lose each other, if only we can somehow not lose each other—'

'We mustn't. Look, we needn't do anything in a hurry, we shouldn't, let's think—'

'When can I see you again?'

'Come—come to the boat jetty on Tuesday at six.'

'I'll be there. Go now, darling, darling—'

She was gone. I stood there for some time, my heart pounding, my breath coming in little gasps, my flesh shuddering in a plucked torment of desire. The sun, shining in through the door of the pavilion, was making the damp floor steam gently, and now I could hear the melting snow trickling off the roof in a steady stream. Some water had found its way down the wall and had soaked the back of my coat without my noticing. I put my cap on and twitched my shoulders against the dampness. I was just then desiring Kitty so fiercely that it really seemed that her 'final solution' would be worth anything, the best of all. To possess her utterly, and then to go, to die. That would be, somewhere in one's life, a piece of perfection.

And yet, a little later, as I walked slowly out into the stony garden and looked away past the fountains where the jagged white ice had become soft and wet and grey, towards the dazzling blue arcade of the sky above the lake, it came to me: of course after all the difficulty was a very much more difficult difficulty than we had either of us yet made out. There were not two possibilities, there were four. I could become Kitty's lover and vanish, I could become her and Gunnar's friend and stay—or I could become Kitty's lover and continue to visit Gunnar's house. A secret life with her, a public life with both. Such things could be. Was that perhaps what she herself would want in the end? Or the fourth possibility was total vanish, now. Nothing more. No more meetings, no more 'thinking what to do'. No more Kitty, no more Gunnar, nothing. Had I not, as I told her, done my work? Was it not all over? That was the last choice. And as I looked at the vibrating sky and the sparkling water I began to have a terrible little idea somewhere in my mind that I would soon know pretty clearly which of these choices was the right one.

'Where's Christopher?' said Tommy.

I had found her waiting, wrapped up in a tartan cape, outside my door when, after a long time, I returned to my flat.

'He's left me.'

'I thought at least he'd be here to let me in. I've been freezing to death out here.'

'They've turned the heating down again.'

I opened the door and let her into the flat. It was not much warmer inside.

'Have you had lunch?'

'Yes,' I said. I had had half a sandwich in a pub where I had continued my ruminations.

'Well, I haven't. Do you mind if I eat something?'

'Go ahead.'

She went into the kitchen and began fumbling noisily among the tins in the cupboard. I stood for a while staring into my bedroom. Then I came and sat at the kitchen table. Tommy had made some toast and had opened a tin of spaghetti and tomato sauce and was heating it up.

'Will you have any?'

'No, thanks. Well, yes I'll have a little.'

'Is there anything to drink?'

'There's half a bottle of Spanish burgundy, unless Christopher took it.'

I ate a little of the spaghetti and drank a glass of wine. Tommy, in silence, made a more extensive meal. It did not take long however.

'I'm sorry you came,' I said.

'Why?'

'It's no good, you know.' It suddenly struck me as comic, and I had an impulse to tell Tommy, that I was now being badgered by three childless women in their thirties, two wanting me to present them with a child, the other wanting me to sanction her marriage. Child-hunger seemed to be the thing just now.

'However, I'm glad to see you,' I said. It was true. Tommy was the accustomed. She was a dear girl, and today she was looking especially fetching in her silly little way. She was wearing a long blue and green kilt and one of the long brown jerseys and an insipid Scottish silver ornament in the shape of a sword. She had on, and had evidently forgotten, a ridiculous little blue woollen hat like a night-cap, standing straight up on her head, with a long tassel hanging down her back. Her brown suede boots were much darkened by the wet. Our muddy footprints covered the kitchen floor. Tommy was now trying to erase them with a piece of newspaper. Yes, Tommy was a dear. If I were going to choose desolation she could be, at least, a crumb of comfort. But was I going to choose desolation, *could* I?

'Are you?' said Tommy. 'Thanks.' She was staring at me, her eyes screwed up in a peculiar way, the corners of her mouth turned down.

'Cheer up, Thomas. Have some more wine. It's a mad world, Thomas.'

'I've come to tell you various things,' she said.

'Carry on. I hope they're amusing and nice. I could do with some amusing and nice things in my life.'

'I don't know whether you'll think them nice. Perhaps you will. I'm giving up my job at King's Lynn.'

'Are you? Why am I supposed to be interested? I'm not going to support you in idleness, my dear, so don't imagine it!'

'I don't imagine it,' said Tommy, staring at me. 'I shall be supported in idleness by my husband.'

'By — ?'

'I'm getting married — Hilary.'

I looked at Tommy's screwed up staring face. 'What on earth are you talking about?'

'I'm going to get married.'

'Who to?'

'To a man at King's Lynn.'

'Who, what man?'

'There are other men in the world,' said Tommy, 'beside you. He's one of the teachers there. And he's an actor. He sometimes acts in the rep. He's been in love with me for ages. His name's Kim Spranger. We're going to get married in January. We're looking for a cottage.'

'Tommy, you don't mean it—'

'Why not? Aren't you pleased? I should have thought you'd be pleased. You kept saying it was no good, you said so just now. You kept telling me to go away. Well, I'm going away.'

I reached across and took her wrist in a fierce grip. She winced with pain but remained motionless. 'Why didn't you tell me about this? You mean all this time you've been carrying on in secret with somebody else?'

'Let go,' said Tommy.

I let go.

'I haven't been "carrying on",' she said. 'I loved you and I wanted you. I didn't want Kim, and he knew I didn't. There wasn't anything to tell you. Only now it's different. I've given up hope of you. I've accepted him. And I'm very happy.' Two small tears came out and trailed slowly down her cheeks.

'You look the picture of happiness,' I said. 'You can't love this man.'

'I do love him,' said Tommy, dashing the tears away with a fierce gesture. 'He's a very very nice man and he loves me and he wants to marry me and to look after me forever and—'

'Don't tell me, and you're over thirty and you want a child.'

'He's a widower and he has a sweet little boy of five.'

'A ready-made family. Of course, I can't compete with that. No wonder you're in such a hurry to desert me just when I need you.'

'You don't need me,' said Tommy in a dead voice, examining her hands. 'That's just what at long last I've realized. You don't. There's no good fighting it any longer. You just don't.'

'If you leave me now—'

'I'm not with you so I can't leave you. You left me.'

'If you leave me now you'll drive me to an act of desperation. warn you.'

'It's too late for your warnings,' said Tommy. 'I haven't been anything to you for ages except a nuisance. If I'd had a scrap of pride I'd have cleared off long ago.'

'It looks as if you did. You had a secret liaison with this spranger.'

'I didn't! There was nothing secret.'

'You never told me he existed.'

'You never asked. You never asked me a single question about what I did at King's Lynn or who I met. If you'd asked me I would have told you. You never wanted to know what happened to me except in relation to you.'

This was true. I felt the more furious. 'You deceived me.'

'No! Besides, you were always deceiving me.'

'What do you mean?'

'I never did anything with Kim. I told him I loved you. never lied. But you've been in love with another woman, God knows what you've been doing, and you never told me, suppose you thought it was a dark secret—'

'I'm getting a bit tired of this legend about me and Laura Impiatt.'

'Oh well,' said Tommy, suddenly limp. She stroked her eyes and her cheeks and gave a long sigh. 'I suppose it doesn't matter now. I can't exactly complain if you prefer someone else to me, even if she is married. That's your affair. I thought I'd better come directly and tell you about Kim. I thought I'd write a letter, but it seemed more honest to come like this and—say good-bye.'

'Tommy, I can't believe what you're saying, you love me.'

'Do I? It doesn't necessarily go on, you know. Eventually it's just rags and tatters. It's worn through, worn away. I'm so tired, Hilary, I'm so *tired*, and I'm not as young as I was. I hate my job, well I don't hate it, but it has no meaning for me any more. I'm tired of living in a little lonely horrid London flat and wondering when I'll see you. I want a home of my own and a man of my own and maybe a child of my own, and anyway there's little Robin and he's sweet—'

'Oh fuck little Robin. Tommy, you belong to me.'

'I don't. Face the truth. I don't. What could that mean? Belong to you, like a possession you put away in a cupboard

353

and look at once a week? No. It's good-bye, Hilary. Make it easy for both of us, please, please, at least spare me now. I'm going and I'm absolutely going. I won't write you any more of those stupid letters, you obviously hated them and you were right. People mustn't persecute other people like that, it isn't fair. I won't write you any letters any more. I'm going to Kim now, I won't be in London. I don't want to see you or hear from you ever again. I've promised Kim I'm giving you up completely. That's reason. I've got to be his from now on and I'm going to be his. I'm starting a new life and I want to be happy, I want to have a go at happiness before it's too late. I loved you, but what did we ever make of it, with me bleating about marriage and a home and you making sarcastic remarks? Have we ever had any happiness out of it, either of us? You felt caught and I felt excluded. It was no good, it was just no good, I see that now. Kim loves me and I can make him perfectly happy. He's perfectly happy now, he's singing with happiness, it's wonderful to make somebody so happy, it's probably the best thing I've ever done and I'm not going to spoil it out of any sentimentality about you. Half-in-half things are no use. He's a fine decent man and he's so happy he'll make me happy soon. If I give myself to him and to his son and to his home we'll all be happy. And that's what I want. And that's a good deal more valuable in the world than hanging around you and annoying you and driving myself into a frenzy. Don't touch me, Hilary, I'm going now. I loved you dearly, I probably love you dearly, but it's no use and this is good-bye. I wish you well and I wish you happiness, though it doesn't seem to me very likely that you'll get it. Anyway I wish it to you. Don't touch me. Good-bye.'

I stood up. The front door opened, then closed quietly. I sat down again at the kitchen table. Well, that was that. Tommy was gone. It was roses round the door for Thomasina Uhlmeister. She had vanished from my life at last.

I sat perfectly still, not twitching a muscle, for a very long time. Some part of myself which was almost a stranger to me was very very sorry that Tommy was gone. Some little narrow deep comfort had been taken from me. Was it true that that little deep loss would prove the last straw which would break the barrier against desperation, against total reckless madness? Time would show.

MONDAY

'HELLO, darling.'
  'Hello.'
It was Monday evening. I was entering Clifford Larr's flat as usual.

The morning post had brought a letter from the head-master of the school to which my letter to Mr Osmand had been forwarded, saying that Mr Osmand had left the school some time ago, but my letter had been sent on to his last recorded address.

I made a token appearance at the office. The excitement about my resignation and the accompanying rumours about me and Laura seemed to have died down. The latest wonders were that Edith Witcher was in hospital after falling off a ladder while putting up Christmas decorations, and that the pantomime had been cancelled. Instead, Finance Division were putting on a show of their own which had matured in secret, called *Robin Hood in Whitehall*. Reggie Farbottom was to make a guest appearance in the role of a comic taxman.

Clifford was in the kitchen stirring some brownish mess.

'What's for din-dins?'

'Veal escalope and braised endive, ice cream and fudge sauce.'

'Oh goodie.'

'The latter is a concession to your childish tastes.'

'How kind of you!'

'How are you, darling?'

'Fine.'

'How is your exciting life?'

'Thrillinger and thrillinger.'

'Tell.'

I watched him stirring for a while until his quizzical cold eyes came to quest into mine. 'Well?'

'Christopher has left my little world,' I said. 'Perhaps he is back in yours?'

'Back? That word implies a misunderstanding.'

'Really?'

'As a matter of fact, I am going to give Christopher some

substantial financial help. He is trying to get this pop group
going.'

'The Waterbirds?'

'Yes.'

'What selfless generosity.'

'What's the matter with you, darling, are you jealous?
I'm not doing it to oblige Christopher and certainly not *pour
ses beaux yeux*. I'm simply investing my money. I like making
profits. I just think I shall get a better percentage out of the
Waterbirds than out of Turner and Newall. Any objection?'

'No, none.'

'Have I relieved your mind?'

I smiled, watching the brown mixture thickening in the
saucepan. I raised my eyes a little to Clifford's very clean
striped shirt, unbuttoned, and the glimpse of his furred front
where the signet ring hung down upon the chain, slightly
moving in the thickish greyish hair as he stirred.

'I wonder who that ring belonged to.'

'You can wonder, dear.'

'I wish you'd invest in me.'

'What's the return, darling?'

'Don't forget you're leaving me the Indian miniatures in
your will.'

'Tell me more things, the thrilling ones.'

'Tommy's left me.'

'She's always doing so.'

'She's getting married to a chap at King's Lynn. We've said
good-bye forever.'

Clifford stopped stirring. 'Are you sorry?'

'Yes. However it certainly clears the deck.'

'What for? Come, let's sit down and drink some wine. I
don't want to eat yet, do you?'

We sat at the table. Clifford poured out some *Châteauneuf*.

'Have you seen Gunnar again?'

'Yes.'

'It's becoming an addiction.'

'It was for the last time.' Was it?

'A lot of last times seem to be happening in your life. Is
this the last time we shall sit together at this table?'

'No.' I stretched my hand across and he gripped it. I
resumed my wine.

'What happened with Gunnar? Was it the great reconciliation scene this time?'

'Yes.'

'How touching. Describe it.'

'We talked together quietly like two sensible decent human beings.'

'Reminiscing. It must have been fun.'

'Do stop mocking. You always mock. It was good. He was kind to me. He saw it was partly accident, muddle—'

'Not wickedness.'

'I don't believe wickedness in that sense exists.'

'A convenient belief.'

'Anyway he—'

'Forgave you.'

'We forgave each other. And don't say "how touching".'

'I wasn't going to. I was going to say are you really such a pathetic dolt as to imagine that sentimental gestures of this kind mean anything at all?'

'Yes.'

'Have some more wine.'

'We talked about Anne. I told him she wanted to go back to him on that evening. We talked about dropping the burden, about how her ghost would go away—'

'Ghosts aren't so obliging. He hates you.'

'I don't think so.'

'And her. Have you seen her again?'

'Yes.'

'You've had a busy week. And letters via the servant, several?'

'One, two.'

'How enjoyable. And what did her ladyship want you to do?'

'She wanted me to make her pregnant.'

'*What?*'

I could not resist the temptation to startle Clifford out of his sardonic calm. Besides I wanted to rehearse the whole extraordinary business in someone's presence, and for these purposes Clifford was my only possible confidant. Arthur would have fainted.

'You're not serious?'

'She and Gunnar are childless. He can't have children only he doesn't know. She wants a child, so does he. I am a rather special agent in their lives—'

'You mean he'd *know*?'

'No, of course not! It would be a secret. But—because I'm me—because I'm a sort of—'

'Priest? I see the quaintness.'

357

'I can't think what, a sort of dedicated instrument, a tool—'

'A tool indeed!'

'Someone who owes them so much. It could be conceived of as a sort of reparation.'

'I shall scream. A reparation? Did she use that word?'

'No, but that's how she sees it. It's not so crazy as it looks at first sight, not quite anyway.'

'But Hilary, darling, my friend, my dear, you are not seriously considering presenting Gunnar with a child by this time-honoured method?'

'No,' I said. And I saw that of course I could not, it was impossible.

'I'm glad of that. I like my dear ones to be rational agents. So what will you do instead?'

'I don't know. She also suggested that we should all three be friends.'

'Dine together and play scrabble?'

'Yes. But I don't think that's really possible either.'

'Of course it isn't! So?'

'I think I shall just clear off.'

'There's a further possibility,' said Clifford. 'An old-fashioned secret liaison. Just for the fun of it, not for Gunnar and his progeny. Isn't that what the lady really wants with all this fishing about? She's a whore like the rest of them.'

'I considered this, I mean that that was what she wanted. No, I don't think so. I don't think she's reflected that far.'

'She must be pretty slow then. But will you?'

'Have a secret liaison? Certainly not.'

'So you're having a final parting with Lady Kitty too? When is it to be?'

'Tomorrow at six at Cheyne Walk.' I had now, with Clifford's help, seen it all. There was no other possible solution. As for Kitty's 'second plan', I had simply by telling Clifford of it revealed it as a lunatic fantasy. But now my heart ached terribly, and I knew that not far away, dulled for the moment by the wine, by Clifford's presence, by my own talkativeness, there was the sharpest and most crippling pain.

Clifford was looking at me with his head on one side. 'Poor child.'

'Me?'

'Yes. You are so simple, so stupid. I told you what that woman was like. Most women are like that, silly, destructive.

358

only hope the whole thing may have done you some good,
knocked some sense into you.'

'I'm glad I talked with Gunnar anyway. He was so wise.'

'Wise! Gunnar is a pretentious self-important ass. Between
you you've inflated something which had very much better
have been left alone. All right, a tragedy, a death—but one
must cut such things off and let them drift away.'

'Sounds easy. Have you ever done so?'

'*Yes.*' Clifford's hands were twisting the chain, his little
finger passing into the ring. 'One should at least digest one's
pain in silence and not parade it. I always despised Gunnar,
ever since Oxford. He has, what I cannot forgive, a thoroughly
inflated sense of his own value. We are nothing, nothing,
nothing, and to imagine otherwise is moral conceit. Did he
say anything about me?'

'About you? No. We didn't mention you.'

'I despised him. All right, he despised me. One of his stupid
rugger-playing friends called me a "bloody pansy" and he
just laughed. I always regarded Gunnar as a four-letter man.
You were always mad keen on him at Oxford, I can't think
why.'

'So was Crystal,' I said.

'*Crystal?*'

'Yes. She was in love with him.'

'Crystal in love with Gunnar?'

'Yes. She only told me just now. You know, something
absolutely amazing happened. On the night of the day when
Anne died, Crystal was round at Gunnar's house and they
went to bed together and made love.'

'Crystal and Gunnar?'

'Yes, made love—you know—'

'*It's impossible.*'

'No, it really happened. He talked about it too.'

'He talked about it?'

'Well, yes. Wasn't it extraordinary?'

'So she's not a virgin—'

'Well, technically not, but—'

'It can't be true,' said Clifford. He had stood up. 'Women
invent things. It simply can't be true. You shouldn't have
believed her. And—and—you shouldn't have told me!' He
was stammering with emotion.

'Look, don't be—'

'Then I suppose they often—if she was in love with him—'

'No, of course not, only that once! Who'd want Crystal—'

'If she let Gunnar do that to her she's probably been to bed with half the neighbourhood. You've been pretty naive about her, haven't you?'

'Clifford, wait, where are you going?'

'I'm going to see her. I'm going to ask her if it's true.'

He was out of the flat and already clattering down the stairs before I reached the door. I grabbed my coat and cap and carrying them began to run down after him, calling his name, calling on him to stop.

The front door of the house slammed in my face, and it took me a moment in the dim light of the hall to find the catch. As I got the door open I heard Clifford's car starting.

'Clifford, wait, stop, wait for me!' The car moved out, then moved past me. I ran after it, pulling on my coat as I ran. I hoped that I might catch it up in the thick traffic on the Cromwell Road. However as I saw at once, Clifford had avoided the main road, his tail lights just disappearing to the right along Pennant Mansions. Here there was little hope of a traffic jam, but I followed all the same, running as far as Marloes Road, where there was of course by now no sign of his car. I ran back to the Cromwell Road and along it eastward upon the northern pavement, hoping I might meet a taxi bound for the Air Terminal. Once I saw one on the other side of the road, and nearly got run over racing across, but someone had taken it before I arrived. By the time I had reached the railway bridge I was panting painfully and had to slow down to a quick walk. Sheer emotion destroyed my ability to run, and the pavements were hard and very slippery with the remnants of frozen snow. I could have wept at my folly. By now Clifford would have been ten minutes, fifteen minutes, with Crystal, torturing her, Clifford whom she loved, and who had always been with her so miraculously gentle.

When I got there Clifford's car was standing outside the house. I raced up the stairs gasping for breath and burst into the brightly lit room.

Crystal was sitting on her bed crying desperately. Clifford was standing with his hands in his pockets, frowning and watching her.

I stumbled across the room. My fist, propelled with all my force and with the impetus of my entry caught him on the shoulder and he crashed against the wall, then sat abruptly on a chair. Crystal screamed, 'No, no!' I sat on the bed and took her in my arms.

'Go away,' I said to Clifford, 'I never want to see you again, I mean that, get out unless you want me to throw you down the stairs.'

Holding his shoulder with one hand Clifford got up rather unsteadily and, without looking at Crystal or me, made his way to the door. A moment later his car could be heard starting, then receding down the road.

Crystal was weeping so much she was inarticulate, her face, her hands, the front of her dress, wet with tears. She was quietly hysterical, the sobs developing into wails and dying away rhythmically into gasps. I had not seen her cry like this since the caravan. After a while I stopped holding her and went and sat at the table where her sewing machine was set out. She must have been using it when Clifford burst in with his unspeakable demonstration. I watched Crystal's tears, saying every now and then, 'Do stop, Crystal, my darling, do stop crying, my heart.'

Gradually the mechanical rhythm of the hysteria gave way to a desperate soft childish sobbing which was in some ways more dreadful.

'Crystal, stop, just for my sake. I can't bear it. *Stop.*'

'I'm so sorry. Oh you hurt him, you shouldn't have hurt him—'

'I wish I'd pitched him down the stairs.'

'You shouldn't have hurt him, it wasn't his fault.'

'What wasn't his fault? He came rushing round here on purpose to upset you, didn't he? What was he saying?'

'He called me a bad name.'

'Then I wish I'd killed him.'

'Oh no, it wasn't his fault—but oh it was so terrible, so terrible—'

'Stop it, Crystal. He doesn't matter. He's a poor fish, a poor wretch, he's half crazed up himself. I only wish I could have arrived sooner. How can I not be angry when I see you crying like this? But it's over now. There, there. We've had a hard time, we mustn't mind a few rough words at our age. Forget him. He hates Gunnar. It was his own misery speaking, he was just raving.'

'He was so unkind. And he was always so kind. And I loved him so much. And when he came into the room tonight just for a second I felt such joy—and then—'

'Let it go, Crystal. It's over. Better not to think about it. Maybe you're right that it wasn't his fault. Let's say that anyway. He's a lonely man who lives in his mind with his

361

own strange fancies. He'll be sorry. If you like I'll make him beg your pardon on his knees.'

'No, no —'

'Let him go, let him go. Oh Crystal mine, I'm so glad to see you, I'm so unhappy.'

I came and sat beside her again and we hugged each other in silence for a while.

'Did you see her?' said Crystal into my overcoat.

'Yes.' I pulled the coat off and got up and began to look for some wine. There was a little left in an old bottle. I poured out a glass for myself. Crystal shook her head. 'And will you see her again?'

'Yes, tomorrow. But that will be the last time.'

'Really?'

'Crystal, I mustn't see her any more. I mustn't see him any more. It's clear at last. You were quite right. It was wrong of me to see her in secret. I've done all I can for him. He's done all he can for me. After this it might all go terribly wrong.'

'I'm so glad. I don't want you to go to them. I'm so afraid for you. Oh darling, need you see her tomorrow?'

'I must just see her to tell her, to say good-bye. And I said I'd come.'

'Can't you write her a letter instead?'

'Letters are dangerous, and— No. I must see her.' That too was clear. I had said that I would see her tomorrow at six and I just had to be there. And there was the terrible terrible fact that only the idea that I would see her tomorrow was now keeping me sane.

Crystal, with her telepathic knowledge, saw this too. She was almost calm, uttering long weary sighs of physical recovery. 'You want to see her. You don't really believe you'll say good-bye. Please write to her. Please don't see her. I feel she's a terrible woman.'

'She isn't terrible, Crystal mine. No one is terrible. Well, hardly anyone. We're all muddlers. The thing is to see when one's got to stop muddling. I can see what I've got to do, don't worry. And I have to see her tomorrow, I just have to.'

'Please—'

'No more of that, Crystal, I don't want to talk to you about her. She's almost gone, and I'll live without her, you'll see.' I sat down beside her once more and she leaned against my shoulder.

'Hilary, I want to tell you something.'

'You're engaged to Arthur again.'

'No. I haven't done anything about Arthur. I've decided I won't. It's too late, I'm too old, I don't want to, I'm better as I am. I wanted to tell you that I've absolutely decided not to.'

'Oh good. I mean—Crystal, dear little one, I want to tell you something too. I saw Tommy yesterday. She came to say good-bye, she's marrying someone at King's Lynn.'

'Oh, she's marrying Kim? I'm so glad!'

'Christ, did you know all about it?'

'Yes. She asked me not to tell you. And I didn't tell you because I thought you'd be jealous and you might marry her out of jealousy. I kept praying and praying that she'd marry Kim.'

'Well, well, well. So we're both back on the shelf, my darling.'

'I like being on the shelf with you. Oh I'm so relieved— Please don't be angry with me—'

'Crystal, you're right, we ought to leave London. Let's go right away and live somewhere together. Not in the north. We could live in Wales or Bristol or somewhere.'

'Or in Dorset or Devon, I'd like that. Oh Hilary, I've always so much wanted to live in the country. Do you think we could?'

'Why not? I could get some sort of job in local government or as a clerk somewhere. We're used to roughing it, aren't we, darling?'

'I'd find a little room—'

'No, Crystal,' I said, 'no. No more little rooms.'

'You mean—?'

'We'll live together.'

'Oh my darling—' Crystal's tears flowed again. 'Oh I feel so happy,' she said, and burrowed her funny frizzy head of hair against me. I put my arm around her.

'There, my chicken, there, my little one.'

'We'll live in the country, in a country cottage.'

'And you shall be my little housekeeper.'

'I'll work so hard, I'll keep the house so nice, I'll do dressmaking too—and we could have animals, couldn't we, some chickens and a dog?'

'Of course. And at weekends I'll dig the garden and we'll grow all our own vegetables. And we'll have a log fire and on winter evenings when the wind is whistling round the house we'll sit and listen to the radio.'

'Oh yes, yes! And you'll learn Chinese.'

'Yes.' Would I, as the wind whistled round the house? How much of me would be left by then?

'And you'll teach me French, like we said long ago.'

'Yes, yes. It will be so, Crystal, my darling, it will be so, and we'll be happy, yes we will, just you wait and see.'

TUESDAY

TUESDAY dawned at last. I had hardly slept. The unusualness of insomnia was a physical torture. The house seemed empty and sad without the boys. I heard the lift rattling in the night and it had such a lonely sound. I rose early and made tea and sat over it shivering. They seemed to have turned the heating off completely.

The first post brought a letter in an illiterate hand with a ——— postmark. Deciphered, the letter read as follows.

Dere Sir,
    I got yr letter to Mr Osmand as was here, he was my loger, he died last week, it was his sleepin pills the doctor said, I have sold his bokes to pay the rint, he ode me fir months rint and is still owin, the bokes was nothing the shop man said, and there was the expins of the funerel, the assistins grant went nowher, I pade up from my own pockit and did it proper too, and there was a wash basen as he broke fallin agenst it, cost pounds to repare and the carpit made filthy, it went to his stummick, as you are some sort of relativ and he has none other, no one visited him, I make bold to sind you the bill for outstandin rint and cost of funerel and the carpit and basen as here enclosed, hopin to here from you by retern post, I am takin legil advise,
                          Yrs truly
                                    J. Parfit (Mrs).

I screwed up this missive and kept my thought resolutely away from the picture of Mr Osmand's end which it conjured up. What desperate last minute dash for help had his visit to me represented? Better not think about that.

There was no question of going to the office. I just had to get through the day. I paced around for some time, then went out for a walk. The frozen snow had made slippery iron grey ridges upon the pavements. I went into the park but the image of Kitty with her rosy face inside her dark fur hood was waiting there for me and I wanted to go to the Leningrad garden. The brown leaves were frozen into what was left of the snow making the grass jagged and brittle. I walked about slowly and aimlessly. Doubtless the park was spoilt for me forever. It was just as well I was leaving London.

The intense cold drove me home at last, and I tried dutifully to eat something, but the act of opening a tin of beans conjured up so much of the ordinariness of life, just when there could be no more ordinariness, I nearly wept. I had not wept for years and years and years, and I did not then. But such a sadness flooded me, such a sense of wasted life and happiness which might have been and could not be. And very strangely in the midst of this utter desolation of soul there remained the glow of Kitty's once more and for the last time approaching presence. Or was it for the last time, some insane voice murmured every now and then very far away.

About three o'clock the front door bell rang. I could hope nothing from a visitor, but some sort of idiotic hope bounded for a second. It was Jimbo Davis.

I stared at him. 'Christopher's gone.'

'I know. I've come to see you.'

'Me? Why?'

'Just to see that you're all right.'

'Why shouldn't I be?'

'Oh, I don't know. I thought you might be lonely. Chris said you'd left the office. Can I come in?'

I let him in and went mechanically into the kitchen and put the kettle on. I made some tea. Jimbo stood and watched.

'Do you want anything to eat? There's beans and bread and butter. And some chocolate wholemeal biscuits, only they're rather old.'

'Thanks. I'll have some biscuits.'

We sat down. I had never had a conversation with Jimbo. He sat sipping his tea and looking at me with big rather brilliant brown eyes. His hair was a matching brown and fairly short, presumably so as to keep it out of the way when dancing. He sat with rubbery grace, like an eastern god, one knee up, one foot upon his chair. I sat and let him look at me. Did he think I was going mad or what?

'You heard Mick is back inside.'

'Is he? Good.'

'He got picked up for another job.'

'How are the Waterbirds?'

'Fine. Chris and Len have taken on Phil instead.'

'Phil?'

'Oh you haven't met Phil. They've moved into his house. He's got a house.'

'Lucky Phil.'

'Chris felt bad about you.'

'I felt bad about him.'

'Is it true Tommy's getting married?'

'Yes.'

'What will you do?'

'Continue the daily round and the common task.'

'Have you got another job?'

'No.'

'Do you believe in astrology?'

'No.'

'I'm not sure if I do. But it seems to me there must be something in it. I mean it stands to reason, everything's caused. Otherwise they wouldn't be able to send space probes to Jupiter. Think of it. They send up this thing and it goes all the way to Jupiter and takes photographs. They couldn't do that if everything wasn't fixed, it would all get lost, wouldn't it. And they can predict eclipses centuries ahead. Do you believe in flying saucers?'

'No.'

'I think I do. Think of it, all those millions of planets just like ours, somebody must be there, but such a long way away they'd have to be terribly clever to reach us. I'd like to think we were being looked at by sort of superior beings, wouldn't you?'

'I hope whoever's looking has a sense of humour.'

'Do you believe in God?'

'No.'

'I'm not sure if I do. My father was a preacher in Wales, well he still is. We lived up this valley. He used to preach to the sheep. He was a bit odd. They seemed to like it though. They let him stroke them.'

'Who?'

'The sheep. They had such lovely eyes. We used to have home prayers and kneel at the sofa, and my father would hide his head in a cushion and groan.'

'I must try that sometime.'

'Hilary, don't be sad, life is good.'

'Jimbo, just go away, will you, dear kind boy?'

'Hilary, you will be all right, won't you? Shall I come in tomorrow?'

'No, just go away. But thank you for coming.'

'I wanted to give you something.' He brought a little package wrapped in tissue paper out of his pocket and laid it on the table. Then in a second he was gone upon his light noiseless feet.

I stayed in the kitchen and opened the package. It contained a cheap metal cross on a chain, the sort of thing which hucksters sell in Oxford Street for fifty pence. I swept it into the kitchen drawer. As I did so I saw a black shrivelled object on the window ledge: it was the potted plant which Jimbo had given me and which of course I had forgotten to water. I hoped that he had not noticed it. I could see that Jimbo's silly visit and Jimbo's silly cross were a little piece of the purest kindness; but it could not touch me. Christ himself, I felt, could not have touched me then, not because I was so wicked, but because I was so mortally sad. I sat for a while. I recalled that it was Tuesday and Arthur would be expecting me. I left the house at about half past four.

Kitty came out at ten minutes to six. I was frozen and all jumbled up with misery and a black awful joyless excitement at the thought of seeing her. I had gone out almost to the end of the jetty. The night was extremely dark, a little foggy, but more as if the fog itself were black, thickening and coagulating the air, as in Pliny's description of the eruption of Vesuvius. At the end of the jetty all was dark. The lamp half way down gave a little enclosed baffled blurry glow. The river was obscure, the lights all veiled which might have touched it, the tide half down and running out fast, the emergent mud banks invisible. I could hear the very faint sibilant murmur of the snow-fed Thames and a faint tap now and then as some piece of driftwood struck against the wooden supports of the jetty.

Kitty came quickly and in a second I had my arms about the mink coat. Her head was bare, I could feel her hair soft and cold upon my cheek.

'Oh my darling, my sweet, my dear love.' My body worshipped her, seared with love and tenderness and desire, my mind shuddered, tottered. The sense of rightness and properness, her belongingness just here and now, the perfection of the present moment, the cosmic achievement of our meeting and our love and my arms being about her, overwhelmed me. Could I commit, against that, the crime, as it seemed, which I had coldly meditated?

'Hilary, my dear, I'm so glad to see you! You're so cold. Won't you come inside?'

'No. Where's Gunnar?'

'At a cocktail party at number ten.'

'Oughtn't you to be with him?'

'I made an excuse, I don't always go to these things. Then he's going on to a city dinner. Oh Hilary, I'm so terribly glad to see you, let me touch your face, you're icy, I must warm you. Oh I do love you, I just do, it's so simple, it must *be* simple. I looked up *Hassan*.'

'*Hassan?*' I had forgotten about *Hassan*, I was miles beyond that, *Hassan* was child's play.

'About the poor lovers who have to choose, I do see. But I think that we—'

'Listen, my darling,' I said.

The tone of my voice silenced her. I could feel her anxiety, her intaken breath, her heart.

'Kitty, I've got to leave you.'

She was silent, trembling in my arms.

'Kitty, we can't continue this any more, you know it and I know it. You can't belong to me. This seems, perhaps it is, a great thing between us, it's certainly a great thing for me, but all human emotions are full of illusion and the years and the time we would need for trying this, for making it real, don't exist. We are in a false place and our love is all shot up with falsity. You say you love me but what does it mean, what can it mean, reality rejects it, you know it does. It's not your fault, it's not even in a way mine. We've run into this so fast. The world is full of causes, otherwise they wouldn't be able to send rockets to Jupiter. But from here another step and we are destroyed. We mustn't let irresistible forces make us destroy and be destroyed. We must resist the irresistible and we can. We shall survive. You have had a mad generous fancy, but it will pass as fancies pass. You know, you must have known, that your second plan was absolutely impossible. And the first plan is impossible too. How could we, after we have held each other like this, meet in Gunnar's presence and deceive him with ordinary smiles? We can't do

369

it, Kitty, we're done for. I can't deceive Gunnar a second time. If I've helped him, and if this is a service to you, I'm glad and joyful and this is a kind of blessing I never thought I'd have in my life any more. I must be content with that. And I've held you and kissed you and that is a gift from the universe which will bless and gladden me forever. And you will realize that you've just had a dream, and for you it will all pass quickly away. I've got to go, Kitty, absolutely and forever, and I've got to go now. You must have expected that I'd say this.'

'Yes.' The word, almost inaudible, came with a weak shudder and she lay against me as if she might have fallen. 'But, oh Hilary,' she went on after a moment, 'could we not somehow later on be friends? He may want to see you again—'

'I won't see him. Kitty, he doesn't know, does he, he doesn't dream that we've ever met, except those two times with him?'

'No, of course, he doesn't know.'

'So we can get clean out of it. And we must.'

'Couldn't we find each other somehow later on—I can't bear it that you should go away into a desolation of loneliness and not be loved and looked after when there is so much love for you in my heart—'

My eyes were closed with anguish and I held her violently. 'We can't find each other later, that's a lie and an illusion. There is no place and no time where we can ever meet. You pitied a worthless man, and that is all there is. We mustn't meddle with each other any more. Kitty, we aren't strong enough not to make some awful mistake. It's all wrong, it's all impossibly wrong. Better to part now. Let me go quickly, make it easy, make it like you said simple, oh for Christ's sake, my dear, let me go now.'

'Hilary, my darling—'

'Make it easy, make it easy—'

The jetty trembled faintly beneath my feet and I opened my eyes. Over Kitty's shoulder I saw Gunnar. The faint fuzzed light of the lamp showed him to me unmistakably, though all I could see was the big silhouette and a hint of the faded Viking hair.

I said 'Gunnar', not to him but to Kitty, and thrust her quickly away. I had some words for him in my throat but they were never uttered.

Gunnar did not exactly hit me but he launched himself

370

upon me. It was like the charge of a bison. I was unprepared and off my balance, one hand still touching Kitty's shoulder and her coat, where I had put her aside. Gunnar blundered against me chest to chest with a crash which took my breath away and sent me back on my heels. I stumbled and trying to recover myself slipped and fell sideways resoundingly onto the wood. I got up quickly. Gunnar must have been winded by our collision, as he did not immediately pursue his advantage. As I became upright I received a violent painful jolt on the side of the head. Gunnar must have hit me very hard with his open hand, only nothing could now be seen, we were too close together and his bulk was between me and the lamp. I could not fight him, but I was not going to stand there and be punched. I grasped his overcoat and drew him up against me. It was like a violent embrace, almost as I had just now held Kitty. 'Gunnar, please, stop, stop.'

He was uttering a continuous panting growling sound and trying now to thrust me away from him by forcing his knee violently into my stomach, the fingers of one hand gripping my collar and the skin of my neck. Hampered by my own bulky coat I held onto the stuff of his and we reeled about, swaying against each other like two rounded dolls. At the same time I had twisted my foot behind his and was trying to overbalance him by forcing him back against my rigid leg. If he would only fall I could get past him and run before he could get in another blow.

Kitty, during the minute occupied by the grapple, had not exclaimed or cried out. She said now in a low intense penetrating voice, 'Stop this, stop it at once. You are not to fight. I am coming between you.'

I felt, though I could not see, the mink sleeve in front of my face. I stepped back, releasing my hold on Gunnar's coat, leaving him still between me and the embankment.

Gunnar then spoke. 'Get out of the way. I am going to kill him.'

'Darling, stop—' said Kitty.

I realized I had gone as far as I could. Behind me now was the drop into the water.

Gunnar had thrust Kitty aside. He now had the advantage which he had wanted. I had to move forward, and I moved quickly, trying to keep my head safe. Gunnar's fist crashed into my shoulder. I nearly fell, grasped at his sleeve and tried to swing him round in order to get past him Then there was a wild cry.

Gunnar and I drew apart, looking around us like two drunken men. We were alone. Kitty had gone. She had fallen over the edge, over the side of the jetty into the darkness below.

Gunnar gave an animal wail. He threw himself down, looking over the edge. I knelt. The darkness was almost impenetrable.

Then in a moment of exquisite relief, we heard Kitty's voice from below. 'I'm all right, you two, don't panic, I'm perfectly all right.'

Her voice, shaken but clear, was the very voice of courage, and that 'you two' was suddenly piercingly reassuring.

I said to Gunnar, 'You stay here, find a rope. I'm going down.'

'It's awfully muddy,' said Kitty below.

I leaned over the edge, peering down into the darkness. There was a crisscross structure of wooden supports. I threw off my overcoat and let myself down, my feet questing for the slanting wooden beams. I got a firm foothold, moved my hands, began to descend further. I said to Kitty in as ordinary a voice as I could, 'I'm coming, I'm coming.'

There was no reply. I grasped the slimy cold slippery beams and lowered one foot, dabbing for a foothold. It was not difficult. In another moment or two I felt the yielding surface of the mud, and, still holding onto the jetty, turned myself about, spread-eagled against its base.

The space below had seemed to be entirely black, but now that I was in it the distant shut-in lamp above was giving a little, a very little light. I could see the vague colour of Kitty's coat, and beyond the scarcely perceptible movement of the swift running water.

'Kitty—'

'I'm afraid I'm stuck in the mud.'

'Are you all right, nothing broken?'

'I'm perfectly all right, it's too silly—'

'Are you in the water?'

'No, no—I just fell straight into the mud, it's like jelly. My coat's all messed up.'

I thought if she can worry about her coat she is probably all right.

'I'm coming.'

'Be careful,' said Kitty, 'you'll just get stuck yourself. Better get a rope or something. I can't move.'

Now I could hear the panic in her voice. Holding onto the

base of the jetty I began to move towards her. Where I had climbed down the mud was fairly firm, but after a step or two it began to be soft and gluey. My next step plunged me over ankle-deep. I stopped again. My eyes had now become more accustomed to the darkness and I could now see Kitty and immediately beyond her the water. She was almost upright in the mud, knee-deep, leaning over a little to one side in an unnatural attitude, perfectly still.

I took another step. The mud was suddenly softer, more unstable, bottomless. I put my weight on my hands, holding onto the wooden structure behind me.

'Don't come out here or we'll both be stuck. Just reach out to me.'

I was trying to do that. I was now as near to her as I could get without letting go of my support and plunging out into the jelly. I braced one foot against the wood and reached out with one hand. I touched something. Her fingers. This sort of pulling would be no good. I should simply fall myself.

'Can you not move at all?'

'No. That's what's so silly. When I started to slip I jumped and both legs just went straight in. Just as well, otherwise I would have been hurt.' The brave voice, but the panic.

Something loomed up above. For the moment I had forgotten Gunnar. I called up, 'Don't come down, get a rope or a plank or anything. I can't reach her.' There were sounds, hollow echoes from the boards. The whole scene was strangely shut in, almost silent. The traffic passing on the embankment made a background murmur, but here even the sound of the river seemed louder. We were alone in a small cold cavern of dim light and thick air.

'I think I'll take off my coat,' said Kitty. 'I'll throw it to you.'

'Better keep the coat. Just don't plunge around. We'll have a rope in a minute.'

The mink coat arrived in a bundle, soft and warm and smelling of Kitty's perfume. Only the hem was muddy. It was a strange thing now to handle. I thrust it up above me, hanging it over one of the wooden supports. And as I reached up I felt how much my shoulder was hurting and how much the side of my face was hurting from the blows I had received from Gunnar.

'Your coat's all right. I'm going to have another try at reaching you.'

'I'm falling over,' said Kitty. 'Oh it's so stupid—'

I could see her more clearly now. The effort of pulling off

the coat had thrown her off her balance and she had descended
a little further into the mud, as if she were kneeling on one
knee. She seemed also to have fallen away from the jetty and
the distance between us was greater. I tried to keep very
steady and to calculate. I prayed that she would not start
struggling and crying out.

I held onto the slimy wood with one hand, taking one step
out into the mud and extending my arm to its utmost. I
touched nothing, not even her finger tips.

'I can't—,' said Kitty, 'my arm's caught on that side—
I can't—I'm sort of sitting down now—' Her courage was
giving, her voice, high, not quite breaking.

I shouted up to Gunnar. 'Get help, get help, find somebody,
ring the police—'

There was silence above, probably he had already gone for
help.

The step which I had taken away from the jetty had
plunged one leg into the mud up to the thigh. I struggled to
extricate it, clamping myself onto the sloping wooden support now with both hands. It was becoming very hard to
hold on because of the cold, the soft sliminess of the wood,
the pain in my shoulder. My leg came out of the heavy grip
of the mud with a sucking sound and I drew myself up to
the jetty in a kneeling position, suspended by my arms which
were now trembling with weakness. I called out 'Help! Help!'
The cries slipped like small birds into the thick dark. Behind
me Kitty was groaning.

'Kitty, don't panic. Someone will come in a minute. Just
don't move. Look, I'm going to take off my jacket and throw
it. Grab one sleeve if you can.' I took off my jacket, hanging
on batlike. Holding one sleeve and with my other hand
clawing the wood, I threw the coat across the gap between
me and Kitty. I could see her hand take the sleeve, felt the
material tighten between us. But it was at once clear that it
was hopeless, she was too tightly wedged. All that happened
was that the moment of tension dislodged my now practically
frozen hand from the slimy wood and I plunged back over
my knees in the mud, letting the jacket drop.

'It's no good,' said Kitty. 'I'm falling over more and more.'
She was trying hard to speak steadily.

'I can't reach you. If I get in the mud too I can't lift you.
They'll bring a rope—'

'I couldn't hold a rope, my hands are too cold, I wish I'd
kept my coat—'

'Someone will come in a minute—'

'I think I'm dying of cold.'

'Shall I throw your coat back?'

'I couldn't get it on.'

'Courage, Kitty, darling, courage.'

'It's all my own fault—'

'What the hell can have happened to Gunnar— Oh God, if I could only think of something else to *do*—'

'The water's just here,' she said.

I was shifting my position, edging along a little. I could see her now sitting, almost reclining in the mud, so close to me, a matter of feet, and yet inaccessibly lost and, I could see, sinking. The tenacious bottomless mud held one leg to the knee, one to the hip, and one arm which she had stretched out when she lost her balance. Another bout of struggling and she would keel over onto her back. I could see her dress, it was the mousy brown dress, an ornament glinting at the neck. I could see, for a second, her face. She was crying. I grimaced and gasped at the idiotic terrible helplessness of it all. I had decided that if Kitty lost her head and started to struggle or sink, I would launch myself out towards her. But for the moment I was more use watching, talking even.

'If I could only get into the river I could swim.'

'Kitty, the river would kill you.'

'I'm a good swimmer.'

'It's too cold. Just wait. You're OK. Wait. And for God's sake *keep still.*'

'I can't wait,' said Kitty, her voice breaking. 'I'm gradually falling back. It's coming onto my shoulder. I think I'll just try and flounder into the river.'

'Don't, don't, you'll only make things worse!' I lunged towards her again, in a desperate attempt to cover somehow that fatal gap between her hand and mine. Again the mud simply took my footstep, burying my leg to the knee, to the thigh, and I had to draw back, my arms cracking, one knee braced against the wood, the captive leg rising slowly.

At that moment to my immense relief I heard the rumble of footsteps up above. There was a trembling in the wood and I saw that somebody was beginning to climb down just beyond me almost at the end of the jetty. I could see the bulky form and feel its weight. It was Gunnar. 'Kitty,' said Gunnar's voice, 'Hang on, they're just coming.'

I was about to call out to Gunnar when there was a

slithering scrabbling sound and then a loud sticky watery report. Gunnar had fallen.

He had fallen between me and the water and I could see that like Kitty, he had immersed himself almost thigh-deep and had at once keeled over sideways away from the jetty. I could hear the plopping thrashing sound of his struggle to right himself.

'Gunnar, don't do that, wait, wait.' I moved monkey-like along the edge. I could not see him clearly, but I could almost at once reach him, touch him, fumble at the stuff of his coat. I felt his shoulder, his arm, then his hand gripping mine. 'Don't struggle. Pull on me.' For a moment my arm and shoulder took his weight. I gasped with pain. I heard footsteps and shouts up above. Then I was clamping his hand onto the lowest of the wooden beams and he lay below me, holding on now with both hands, like a stranded whale, while over him I suddenly saw, dim yet somehow clear, Kitty floundering madly upon the very edge of the dark racing river. For a second it seemed that she was up to her neck in the mud, only her head emerging from the muddy agitation. I cried out, and leaving Gunnar I let go of the jetty and plunged towards her. I saw her turn over, her whole body now encrusted with mud, as if she were about to sink at last into the hole which her own struggles had created. Then and I heard her scream as she did it, with a last wild panic-stricken flurry she was beating the water; and then in a second she was gone. She had got herself into the river and the river had taken her away.

I was now myself unsupported in the mud, already falling forward onto my front. One leg lagged, held below as if some fiend had actually got hold of it and were tugging it down. I kicked the fiend in the face. I hurled my body towards the water, attempting to slide upon the muddy surface. One arm was caught by another fiend. Mud slapped one side of my face, touched my mouth. Then I felt upon my outstretched arm a new grip of coldness such as I had never felt or conceived of, a coldness beyond coldness. I screamed. I was in the river.

After that there were no more purposes, or rather only one purpose, the intent to survive as, in an awful jumbled darkness, the Thames rushed me onward, squeezing me with its icy coldness, squeezing the remaining warmth out of my body, whirling me about and hurrying me onward and trying to kill me, to crush me to death in its cold embrace.

IT WAS later, later, later. There were no more days. I was pressing my key into the door of Clifford Larr's flat in Lexham Gardens.

Kitty did not drown. There was no water in her lungs. She was even alive when she was taken from the river. She died of exposure. The poor body had become too cold, the blood froze and never recovered its pathways. She died in hospital.

I was not in the water for very long. During that time I forgot Kitty, I forgot everything except the absorbing task of not dying, of getting out of that cold hell before it killed me. The current was swift and powerful, the banks steepish and slippery. A huge dark chain appeared and I hung onto it. A moored barge, a trailing cable, led me from mud to stones. I crawled on hands and knees up some steps and sat on the pavement with my back against the embankment wall. The hue and cry after Kitty actually passed me by. Shouts, a police launch with a floodlight, people running to and fro. 'They've taken a woman from the river.' 'Is she alive?' 'Yes.' On that I went home. I walked. No one, on that dark night, marked me. I heard the news the next day from Mr Pellow, who saw the name of my department mentioned in the newspaper report. There was a picture of Kitty, also of Gunnar. *Whitehall Chief in Wife Rescue Bid.* There was nothing about me. Once again I had dropped out of the story as if I had never existed.

I pushed open the door of Clifford's flat. It was an evening, not Monday. I had telephoned him both at home and at the office and had had no reply. I wanted to see him. He was, at that time, the only person whom I wanted to see. I had come to Lexham Gardens on a sudden needful impulse and had seen with a pang of relief that a light was on in his sitting-room.

There was a faint clattering in the kitchen. The flat felt slightly odd. I was about to call out to him when I saw, looking into the drawing-room, that the Indian miniatures had been taken from the walls. Unfaded rectangles of Morris wallpaper stood in their stead. Then my gaze found upon the hall table a large Chinese bowl, now filled with an unusual

377

collection of oddments. I saw among these something which stopped my breath even before I fully took in its significance. Lying there among the miscellany of things, matchboxes, letters, keys, was the chain with the signet ring upon it which Clifford had been used to wear about his neck.

I must then have made some sound. A bald round-faced man whom I did not recognize emerged from the kitchen and stared at me with hostile surprise.

'Excuse me,' I said. 'I was looking for Clifford.'

'Oh. You didn't know?'

But by then I did. 'Is—?'

'I'm sorry to have to tell you that Clifford is dead, he committed suicide.'

'I see. He—often said he would—' I stood for a moment looking through the drawing-room door at the miniatures lined up, leaning against the wall: the princess on the terrace watching the thunderstorm, the prince leaving his mistress by moonlight, two girls of transcendent beauty striding through a garden, a girl rather like Biscuit braiding her hair. Presumably they were on their way to the sale room.

I turned to go.

'I say, one moment, would you mind giving me those keys? I am the heir and—'

I handed over the flat and the front door key, which I was still holding in my hand, to the piggish cousin, and made my way downstairs.

Milder weather had come and it was raining slightly as I made my way back through Cornwall Gardens to Gloucester Road Station.

Just before I reached Gloucester Road I noticed the church, St Stephen's, at which, Clifford had once told me, T. S. Eliot served for many years as a churchwarden. Obeying an imperative need to sit down I went into the church and sat in one of the pews in the darkness. As I did so I suddenly began to wish that I had asked the cousin if I could have the signet ring and the chain as a memento. It was impossible to go back now; and anyway, who was I to wear that now forever mysterious token? Clifford had been carried away by the cold river and I had not stretched out my hand to him, not even touched his fingers.

I sat in the obscurity of the church and stared at the high golden wall of the reredos and watched the little baffled lights flickering in the dark, like the light upon the jetty at Cheyne Walk, and tears of vain tenderness and self-pity

378

came into my eyes. I needed Clifford, needed his mockery which was cold and yet not cold, needed him to hear that which now could be told only to him. Only he was gone, and it felt to me as if I had killed him in a fit of anger, as I had, in a fit of anger, killed Anne. And where there might have been the relief of reconciliation or even the relief of retribution, there was blankness and solitude, a greater blankness and a quieter solitude than ever before. I had been turned silently out into the desert, there was no one now to whom I could speak at all of the things which were hourly and minutely devouring my heart.

It only dawned on me gradually, as I suffered the shock of Kitty's death, that no one knew that I had been there at all. At least, Gunnar knew and conceivably Biscuit; but no one else knew and I had told no one. I had not revealed to Crystal when it was that I was going to see Kitty to say good-bye. Kitty's accidental fall from the jetty and her husband's heroic effort to save her burst in upon the story from the outside, and when I saw Crystal afterwards I did not conceal my shock, but let her assume (and she did) that death had forestalled my final scene with Gunnar's wife. And no one else, except Arthur, even knew that Kitty and I had ever met except as mere shadowy acquaintances. In deciding not to tell Crystal what really happened I made an important and in some ways terrible decision. I had let the full weight of Anne's death fall upon my sister, I had let her share everything. This, I decided, I would deal with alone. I would not inject into that innocent life this further and perhaps at last fatally crippling nightmare. But my silence divided me from Crystal in a new way, and obscurely she felt that some deep severance had taken place and we looked at each other across a gap with puzzled sorrowful eyes.

I wondered in the days afterwards whether I should write a letter to Gunnar explaining—and yet what explanation would serve my turn? I could not write the truth without seeming in some way to cast blame, or at least responsibility, upon Kitty; and my own conduct in any case was inexcusable. I wondered too whether Gunnar would write to me, and for a while I watched the post like a lover, hoping to see, whatever horrors it might contain, an envelope with his tiny handwriting. But none came. (He resigned from the department almost immediately after the catastrophe and went back into politics. A timely by-election took him into parliament where he shortly became a junior minister. But this was at an even later time.) I wanted him to know that I was saying good-bye to Kitty forever when he found us together. But as time passed it seemed a pointless attempt at extenuation. And was it even true? I would also like to have known who had sold me. Who had told Gunnar, who had prompted that apt arrival? Biscuit? Clifford? Was it even conceivable that it was a plot prearranged between Gunnar and Kitty to set a scene for murder, was I to *that* extent exonerated? It was an exoneration for which I could not wish, and of course I did not really believe Kitty to have been, even half willingly, her husband's instrument.

I sat in St Stephen's Church crying for Clifford as I had not cried for Kitty, and just then his death seemed even more awful than hers. Crystal had seen Kitty as a *femme fatale* luring me to my doom. In fact I had lured Kitty to her doom as I had lured Anne. But the world's will had mingled in our loves and the purest of chances had been present at those deaths. I could at least see that much now. Clifford had died differently, he had died of being unloved and uncared for, as if the door had been shut upon him on a cold night. I did not know, and would never know, how much he had really cared for me. Perhaps he had died as a part of some quite other drama, for someone of whom I had never even heard. And I wept, and gradually in the vagueness of misery, wept for Kitty, for Gunnar, for Anne and in some quieter way for myself. And after a while I began thinking about Mr Osmand, and how he had died alone, and how he had once taught me out of Kennedy's Latin Primer to conjugate the verb of love, his shabby coat sleeve pressing gently against my arm.

In the few days after the river scene I had expected to go mad. I passed the time alone in my bedroom, sitting on the side of the bed. The resolution not to tell Crystal came early, without its reasoning, just as an imperative. This albatross, I could not hang around her neck. But could I bear it alone? It did not then occur to me to talk to Clifford, I had as yet no grain of desire to expose this delicate horror to his mockery, to his, as it seemed, bottomless coldness. At first the thing itself, wrapped up in this awful sentence of silence, simply confronted me and I felt that no rational or even conceptual judgment could be made upon it. It and I were alone together and my mind was frozen by grief and fear, and the possibility of madness seemed like a refuge. Later, as I became able to talk to myself and to reflect and turn the matter round and, in however chilled a way, to see facets, the desire to speak to Clifford, the memory of, in spite of everything, his wisdom, and of, however self-mocked, his affection, made him appear providentially as a last resource. Now there was no resource and that too seemed like the work of a mercilessly just providence.

It was indeed crucial that, this time, I had not told Crystal. *Then* I had someone, a passive spectator who was also a fellow sufferer, to enact it all to. I suffered before Crystal as believers suffer before God; only doubtless the latter derive more benefit from their suffering than I did. And she, innocent loving darling, connived, out of her sheer goodness and her identification with me, at an establishment of pure desolation. I was determined that our lives should be wrecked and she, poor sparrow, had so readily made her little nest in the wreckage. How profitless it had all been I could now very clearly see. Repentance, penance, redemptive suffering? Nothing of the sort. I had destroyed my chances in life and destroyed Crystal's happiness out of sheer pique, out of the spiteful envious violence which was still in me. It was burning the orphanage down all over again, only now there was no one to stop the work of destruction. I had spoilt my talents and made myself a slave, not because I sincerely regretted what I had done, but because I ferociously resented the ill-luck which had prevented me from 'getting away with it'. What had impressed me really was not the crime itself but the instant and automatic nature of the first retribution, the loss of Oxford, my 'position' and the fruits of my labour. If I had indeed got away with it I could perhaps have recovered. As so often, as in my own childhood, guilt sprang from the punishment rather than from the crime. And I perpetuated my suffering out of resentment. If I had been the only recipient of this violence the incident might have been, in some recording angel's book, regarded as closed. But I deliberately made Crystal suffer with me. Could her pure suffering have redeemed me? In some ideal theory, yes, in reality, no.

Of course I regretted what I had done. I regretted all those wrong choices with their catastrophic results, and not just as pieces of ill luck. I saw where I had behaved badly, the selfishness, the destructiveness, the rapacity. But I could now see too how hopelessly this 'penitence' was mixed in with the grosser elements which composed almost all of me. There are religious rituals for separating out the tiny grain of penitence. There are rituals for this, even when, as anything experienced, the penitence does not exist at all. But I could not use these machines. It all remained, for me, grossly muddled up, penitence, remorse, resentment, violence and hate. And it was not a tragedy. I had not even the consolation of that way of picturing the matter. Tragedy belongs in art. Life has no tragedies.

I wondered about the future. Was another cycle of misery, intensified, more dense, beginning for me? If so, it would last out my lifetime. Did not the same crime twice committed merit more than double retribution? Or was it now quite a different scene? I was older, I lacked the recklessness of youth and its generosity. When I was in the cold Thames I soon forgot about Kitty. The deepest me who knew of no one else was desperate to survive. The middle-aged are more careful of themselves. Would such a desperation, or such a mean carefulness, now at last and in this more awful need, guard me from the self-destruction to which I had earlier doomed myself? Would it help me now that I could more coolly see the ingredients of chance? Was it cynicism to hope this? Would even cynicism help me? Or was I perhaps actually wiser? How Clifford would have loved to discuss these questions. Certainly I could better measure now, what had been invisible to me then except as a provocation to rage, the amount of sheer accident which these things, perhaps all things, contained. Then I had raged at the accidental but had not let it in any way save me from my insistence upon being the author of everything. Now I saw my authorship more modestly and could perhaps move in time towards forgiving myself, forgiving them all. Or was this the most subtle cynicism of the lot? There is a religious teaching which says that God is the author of all actions. What I wonder is its secular equivalent?

My grief for Kitty and my memory of her love for me, whatever it had meant, remained and would remain clear. Perhaps such griefs are the most unalloyed and enduring things in the fickle muddled selfish human heart: grief existing not as guilt or calculation or rational regret, but as pains and pictures. These would go with me secretly until the end. I wished, with a surly bitter sadness, that I could communicate even once more with Gunnar, but that was impossible, and even to imagine that he would one day return to kill me was a romanticism which the more awful reality of life forbade. There was simply a loose end which guilt would twist and the only salve, indeed the only duty, was to recognize the impossible, standing as it were at attention before some end-point of human endeavour.

There was, however, one glint of light and I was blessed to have, amid these fruitless burdens and these blank obstacles, a place of decent labour after all. I could still, before it was too late, try to make Crystal happy. Before I had had the force to envisage that future, some right instinct had led me to keep the catastrophe concealed. I would look after Crystal now, as I ought always to have done, as if she were my child, not darkening her soul with my private atrocities, but working practically to give her happiness and ease and the kind of simple joy which was so native to her but of which I had so consistently deprived her. Everything could please Crystal, provided only I were well, every simple little thing could please her. So it was a monstrous scandal that she had not had a happy life. I could not work for her now as I had meant to do when I was young, as I had thought it and envisaged it at that moment in Oxford when she had said, 'This is the happiest day of my life.' I could not give her *that* happiness. But I could work myself weary to give her another smaller shorter more modest happiness wherein her native joy could frisk about at last. This would be now my only task. Crystal was the only being whom I loved and I was fortunate to be able to express this love in innocence and fullness of heart and to devote to it what remained of my life. I would take her far away from London and find in some country place the very best-paid job which my talents could command. And I would live with her in a cottage and she should have her garden and her animals and all her little heart's desires, and I would simulate with her a kind of peace, perhaps even a kind of joy, into which some of the reality of these things might merge at last. We two alone shall sing like birds in the cage.

I got up to leave the church. I felt exhausted by grieving and the thought that Clifford was now dead came freshly again to my heart. I walked into the south aisle to make my way out. At one end of the aisle under a tasselled canopy the Christ child was leaning from his mother's arms to bless the world. At the other end he hung dead, cut off in his young manhood for me and for my sins. There was also, I saw, a memorial tablet which asked me to pray for the repose of the soul of Thomas Stearns Eliot. How is it now with you, old friend, the intolerable wrestle with words and meanings being over? Alas, I could not pray for your soul any more than I could for Clifford's. You had both vanished from the catalogue of being. But I could feel a lively gratitude for words, even for words whose sense I could scarcely understand. If all time is eternally present all time is unredeemable. What might have been is an abstraction, remaining a perpetual possibility only in a world of speculation.

CHRISTMAS EVE

'WHO giveth this woman to be married to this man?'
'I do.'

'I, Arthur Mervyn Fisch, take thee, Crystal Mary Burde, to my wedded wife, to have and to hold from this day forward, for better for worse, for richer for poorer, in sickness and in health, to love and to cherish till death do us part, in accordance with God's holy ordinance; and thereto I plight thee my troth.'

Arthur mumbled his part. His eyes were glowing with joy, his face was blazing with triumph, but he was shuddering as if at any moment he might fall to the ground. Crystal, who was crying as if her heart would break, whispered her part. When I touched her to perform my act of giving her to Arthur she was rigid. Arthur fumbled the ring onto her finger and she stared at it through her tears with a sort of amazement, then turned round to me with the look of a frightened child. 'With this ring I thee wed, with my body I thee worship, with all my worldly goods I thee endow . . .'

It was over. The parson led us to the vestry to sign the register. Crystal wrote her maiden name for the last time: Crystal Burde. Arthur dropped the pen and made a blot. I signed my name as a witness. Tommy signed hers, taking up a great deal of space with various Scottish flourishes: Thomasina Uhlmeister.

The rites had been blessedly short. Crystal had wanted us to sing *He who would valiant be*, but with my last act of authority in her life I had vetoed that. Ours was the last ceremony of the day and the parson, who was probably anxious to scurry along to some seasonable celebration, shook our hands and smiled his way out. It was Christmas Eve.

Tommy and I were left alone with Mr and Mrs Arthur Fisch. Tommy had also been in tears throughout. 'Well, congratulations, Arthur,' I said and shook his hand. He had resumed his moustache but happiness had in other ways improved his appearance.

'Don't greet so, my poor bairn,' said Tommy to Crystal.

'Must you use these affected Scotticisms?' I said to Tommy. 'Stop crying, Crystal, my duck, there's my darling. You're a married woman now.'

'That's what's fashing her,' said Tommy. 'Oh dear, oh dear—' Tommy's own tears overwhelmed her.

I tried to exchange glances with Arthur, any cliché would have helped, only he was hovering over Crystal and seemed about to start howling himself. Someone at the back of the church coughed meaningfully. No doubt they wanted to flossy the place up for midnight mass. Arthur had now endowed Crystal with the Empire State Building firescreen and the aeroplane armchair and was licensed to worship her with his body. Tommy had made for the fifth time the joke about Crystal having changed from being a crystal bird into being a crystal fish. I had given my sister away. It was time to go.

All sorts of matters had been moving fast. This was in fact the second wedding to which I had been invited since the events of Chelsea. I was asked, but of course did not go, to celebrate the (registry office) union of Alexandra Marilyn Bisset (spinster) and Christopher Jameson Cather (bachelor). At the time when I received my invitation I had not as yet realized they were acquainted. However it appeared that Biscuit, visiting the flat on various occasions in search of me, had seen and coveted Christopher. Why not? The marriage was generally considered to be her idea (I was not so sure), and had attracted, according to Arthur who was my informant, some cynical comments. I could only bow my head before another impenetrable mystery. Biscuit had found her prince, Christopher, one hoped, the 'true lover' desiderated in his song. Both could be lucky. Biscuit was now, it was rumoured, a rich woman as the result of Kitty's will. The couple were honeymooning in Benares. Christopher was proposing to use Kitty's money to launch Biscuit as a model. Nothing more had been heard of the Waterbirds.

In so far as this could touch me I felt rather sad about Biscuit. I had somehow got used to her, there had been a sort of servants' hall complicity, and I could not help wondering how much better things might have turned out if only I could, as befitted my station, have loved the maid and not the mistress. I would have liked to see again that sallow waif-like face raised in naive anxious questioning to my own. I had felt akin to Biscuit because we were both wanderers in society, both disinherited, both lost and both unclaimed.

I would have liked to kiss Biscuit again, not passionately but with a kind of exhausted sadness. Now she was Christopher's, she belonged to a man in whose eyes I must figure poorly, even without the information about me which Biscuit must by now have imparted. I felt sad about Christopher too. He had liked me once. We might have been friends. I had almost systematically destroyed his respect and affection and finally driven him away. I had indeed busied myself thus with most of the people whom I had known. It was the more remarkable that Clifford had hung onto me for so long. Yes, I would have liked a talk with Biscuit. I would have liked to ask her, out of the compassion of total shipwreck, whether it was she who had betrayed me. Or whether perhaps she did not even know that I had taken part in Kitty's death. But for these questions, as for so much else, it was now too late.

Crystal's decision, suddenly so firm, to marry Arthur, came like a bombshell. I had completely forgotten Arthur. I thought about him, oddly enough, on that awful Tuesday night, thought how he would be waiting for me with the tongue and the potatoes and the peas and the cheese and the bananas. Would that I had been with Arthur on that night, that he had had the power to compel me. After that Tuesday he vanished completely from my consciousness until the moment when Crystal told me, with a new voice and a new face, that she had decided to get married. Why? I could not help feeling that in some blind secret way my decision not to tell her about what had happened to me had brought about her resolution to leave me. The perfect communion between us had been broken by a silence on my part which she must have felt, though she could not interpret it, and a deep fear, a sense of losing me, may have driven her into Arthur's arms. So by my heroism perhaps I had lost her, and if I had weakly told her everything she would have pitied me and stayed with me. Or it might all have been simply the fruition of a long intent, Crystal's desire for a child, which she knew so much annoyed me, or indeed a genuine love for Arthur, which she had not mentioned because she knew that it would annoy me even more. This was another question which would have to remain eternally unanswered.

So now I would never live with Crystal, we two would never sing like birds in a cage. Arthur, not I, would look after her and love her and fulfil all her little heart's desires. She and Arthur were going to move out of London, Arthur had asked for a transfer to Harrogate, they were already searching for a country cottage. They would live up there far away in the Yorkshire dales and I would visit them occasionally, more and more infrequently, and hear them call me 'Uncle Hilary' and see their children stare at me with hostility and incomprehension. That this would be so I of course concealed from her loving tear-filled eyes. In this time I had pretended and pretended, and the sheer rigour of the play-acting had been itself to some extent a distraction from the agony which occasioned it. I feigned pleasure at the marriage, enthusiasm for Arthur, happy anticipation of my nephews and nieces (who would certainly arrive, adopted if necessary). I even spoke blithely of perhaps moving up to Yorkshire too. (I had by then left the office, and had found a job in an insurance company, duller but better paid.) Whom did these lies convince? Crystal needed to at least half believe them and perhaps she did. She clung to me till the last moment, with a face of terrified guilt and a torrent of exclamations of love. I play-acted heroically. The last thing I could do for her was to send her to her fate with some peace of mind. Callousness would doubtless have its feast day later on.

We came out of the church (not St Stephen's) into the extremely cold night air. There was an illuminated Christmas tree in the churchyard. I remembered that I had never taken Crystal to see the decorations in Regent Street. We walked to the car which Arthur had hired and in which tomorrow he would drive Crystal to Christmas celebrations with his cousins in Lincolnshire. Tommy and I crawled into the back. Arthur and Crystal sat in the front. Crystal turned round and gave me her hand and I heroically held it and squeezed it and smiled though I wanted to howl like a dog. Arthur drove with careful efficiency towards the wedding supper at Blythe Road. We climbed the stairs, Arthur first, Crystal still holding my hand, Tommy. The table was laid, the chicken and the plum pudding were warm in the oven. The room was decorated with paper chains. In festive mood Arthur had put little paper hats on the two ladies representing Dawn and Dusk. There was laughter and tears. We took off our coats. Arthur and I were in our best suits. Tommy was wearing a most unsuitable dress with sequins, Crystal an orange satin robe which fought with her hair. I kissed Crystal and told her to stop crying. Tommy kissed her. The women went on weeping and trying to laugh. Arthur and I began to open the champagne.

CHRISTMAS DAY

I WAS walking home. Tommy, whose path lay in the other direction, was still walking with me. A few snow flakes were appearing here and there under the street lamps and floating idly about before descending and vanishing upon the frosty pavements. Tommy was wearing her blue knitted night-cap and had pushed her ringlets inside it for extra warmth. We had walked for some time in silence.

I was picturing, as I was now condemned to do for the rest of my life, Kitty floundering in the mud on the edge of the river. What had happened to the mink coat? Human beings might perish but valuable properties like mink coats had to be looked after. Perhaps Biscuit had it now.

'Hilary, are you crying?'

'No.'

'I thought you were.'

'No.'

'Hilary, I've got something to tell you.'

'Mr Spranger has made you pregnant. OK. It's nothing to do with me.'

'No, no. I did something awful and I feel I must tell you.'

'Does it really matter?'

'Yes. I've got to tell you. I wonder if you'll ever forgive me?'

'Time will show no doubt.'

'I wrote a letter about you to Gunnar Jopling.'

'You what?' I went on walking.

'I wrote him a letter about you, about you and Lady Kitty.'

I went steadily on, not looking at her. The snow flakes were more frequent. 'What did you write to him about me and Lady Kitty?'

'I told him you were in love with her.'

'What made you imagine that? Perhaps you invented it?'

'I saw you kissing her in Kensington Gardens, that day when I came to tell you about Kim.'

'How did you know it was her?'

'I'd seen her picture, and I saw her in your office. I recognized the coat.'

'It was clever of you to find us.'

'I came to the flat looking for you and you weren't there, so I went out in the park. I knew that garden at the end of the lake was one of your special places.'

'How did you know that?'

'You took me there once. You told me you called it the Leningrad garden. You've probably forgotten.'

I had. 'What exactly did you say in the letter?'

'Just that you were in love with his wife. Nothing about her.'

'When did you post it?'

'Oh—after that—'

'Which day?'

'I wrote it and posted it on the next day—that would have been the Monday. I did it out of—sheer jealousy and spite— it was a wicked action—I thought, you see, that there was another woman and that it was because of her you wouldn't— I thought it was Laura Impiatt—then when I saw you with Lady Kitty I realized it was her and I couldn't bear it—she was so lucky and rich and now she had you as well—it was too awful, I felt I'd go mad—and I thought if only she'd leave you alone I'd have some chance—at least I don't know what I thought—because I'd sort of left you then, only of course I hadn't—I was sort of insane with misery—it was a dreadful thing to do—and then the next day the poor lady was dead—'

'So you needn't have sent the letter anyway.'

'So I needn't have sent the letter anyway. Well, that's a terrible way to talk—it was so awfully unkind to him, to Mr Jopling, and so unkind to you—but I expect he didn't believe it—I typed the letter, I didn't sign it—and I only said about you not about her—I expect lots of people think they're in love with his wife just because she was a famous beauty, they fall in love with her photo—perhaps he thought it was that, or else that it was a letter from a mad person—and then she was dead anyway. He never said anything to you?'

'No.'

'Then I expect he thought that it was a mad letter, people like him must get lots of them.'

'I expect so.'

'It's been so on my conscience, I simply had to tell you, it's been eating me up. Can you forgive me?'

So it was little innocent thoughtless Tommy who had brought it all about. Out of her childish resentment and woman's spite Tommy had shopped me to fate. She must never know. Another lifelong secret. Gunnar must have got her letter on the Tuesday morning. Then when Kitty made the excuse so as not to go to the party at Downing Street he decided to test his suspicions. He came back and—what? Shook Biscuit until she told him where we were? The details did not matter. Unknowing Tommy had brought about the encounter which killed Kitty and married Crystal and brought double-intensified eternal damnation into my life and Gunnar's. Not Clifford, not Biscuit, not, thank God, a dreadful plot of spouses to punish a detested criminal. I felt a kind of crazy relief combined with a renewed agony at the accidentalness of it all. If only I had had the sense to take Kitty somewhere else on that Sunday morning, almost any other place would have saved us.

'Can you forgive me?' Tommy repeated.

'I expect so. As I said, time will show.'

'You sound very cold about it. Perhaps you don't care much what I do.'

'Perhaps not. That's your way home, this is mine.'

'I'm coming with you.'

'I hope you'll invite me to your wedding with Mr Spranger. I'm getting used to weddings, I rather enjoy them.'

'I'm not going to marry him, I'm going to marry you.'

We were standing at the corner of Kensington Church Street. It was beginning to snow quite fast now. The bells of St Mary Abbots were ringing Christmas in with wild cascades of joy. Other churches nearby had taken up the chime. The Christ child, at any rate, had managed to get himself born.

'Happy Christmas, Tommy.'

'I'm going to marry you, Hilary.'

'Are you, Thomas?'

'Yes, I'm going to marry you.'

'Are you, Thomasina?'

Bestselling European Fiction in Panther Books

QUERELLE OF BREST	Jean Genet	60p	☐
OUR LADY OF THE FLOWERS	Jean Genet	50p	☐
FUNERAL RITES	Jean Genet	50p	☐
DEMIAN	Hermann Hesse	40p	☐
THE JOURNEY TO THE EAST	Hermann Hesse	40p	☐
LA BATARDE	Violette Leduc	60p	☐
RAVAGES	Violette Leduc	50p	☐
MAD IN PURSUIT	Violette Leduc	40p	☐
IN THE PRISON OF HER SKIN	Violette Leduc	35p	☐
THE TWO OF US	Alberto Moravia	50p	☐
THE LIE	Alberto Moravia	50p	☐
PARADISE	Alberto Moravia	35p	☐
COMMAND AND I WILL OBEY YOU	Alberto Moravia	30p	☐
LASSO ROUND THE MOON	Agnar Mykle	50p	☐
THE SONG OF THE RED RUBY	Agnar Mykle	40p	☐
THE HOTEL ROOM	Agnar Mykle	40p	☐
RUBICON	Agnar Mykle	50p	☐
THE DEFENCE	Vladimir Nabokov	40p	☐
THE GIFT	Vladimir Nabokov	50p	☐
THE EYE	Vladimir Nabokov	30p	☐
DESPAIR	Vladimir Nabokov	30p	☐
NABOKOV'S QUARTET	Vladimir Nabokov	30p	☐
A VIOLENT LIFE	Pier Paolo Pasolini	40p	☐
INTIMACY	Jean-Paul Sartre	40p	☐
THE AIR CAGE	Per Wästberg	60p	☐

Bestselling Transatlantic Fiction in Panther Books

THE SOT-WEED FACTOR	John Barth	75p ☐
BEAUTIFUL LOSERS	Leonard Cohen	40p ☐
THE FAVOURITE GAME	Leonard Cohen	40p ☐
TARANTULA	Bob Dylan	50p ☐
MIDNIGHT COWBOY	James Leo Herlihy	35p ☐
LONESOME TRAVELLER	Jack Kerouac	35p ☐
DESOLATION ANGELS	Jack Kerouac	50p ☐
THE DHARMA BUMS	Jack Kerouac	40p ☐
BARBARY SHORE	Norman Mailer	40p ☐
AN AMERICAN DREAM	Norman Mailer	40p ☐
THE NAKED AND THE DEAD	Norman Mailer	60p ☐
THE BRAMBLE BUSH	Charles Mergendahl	40p ☐
TEN NORTH FREDERICK	John O'Hara	50p ☐
FROM THE TERRACE	John O'Hara	75p ☐
OURSELVES TO KNOW	John O'Hara	60p ☐
THE DICE MAN	Luke Rhinehart	60p ☐
COCKSURE	Mordecai Richler	40p ☐
ST URBAIN'S HORSEMAN	Mordecai Richler	50p ☐
MYRA BRECKINRIDGE	Gore Vidal	40p ☐
MESSIAH	Gore Vidal	40p ☐
THE CITY AND THE PILLAR	Gore Vidal	40p ☐
TWO SISTERS	Gore Vidal	35p ☐
THE JUDGEMENT OF PARIS	Gore Vidal	50p ☐
WASHINGTON D.C.	Gore Vidal	37p ☐
JULIAN	Gore Vidal	50p ☐
SLAUGHTERHOUSE 5	Kurt Vonnegut Jr	40p ☐
BLUE MOVIE	Terry Southern	60p ☐
MOTHER NIGHT	Kurt Vonnegut Jr	40p ☐
PLAYER PIANO	Kurt Vonnegut Jr	50p ☐
GOD BLESS YOU, MR ROSEWATER		
	Kurt Vonnegut Jr	50p ☐
WELCOME TO THE MONKEY HOUSE		
	Kurt Vonnegut Jr	40p ☐

Bestselling British Fiction in Panther Books

Bestselling British Fiction in Panther Books